Legends

Awakening

Miles Allen

Other books by this author

The Walkers of Legend (Book One)

For more information visit

www.thewalkersoflegend.co.uk

About this Author

If you would like to know more about
Miles, you can visit his website at

www.milesallen.net

Legends Awakening

First Edition (paperback)

A REDBAK Publishing Book: ISBN 978-0-9928041-7-6

First published in Great Britain by REDBAK Publishing.

Copyright © Miles Allen 2015

REDBAK Publishing
United Kingdom

Cover Design by
Think Tank inc Design
thinktankincdesign.com

This second book is dedicated to the memory of Joanna Good, who passed away in 2014 after fighting a long battle with cancer.

To those who knew her – she was a Legend.

With sincere thanks to:

Richard and Claire for their time
checking the story.

My editor, Benjamin, for his usual insight and
being on the same page.

All my fans who have kept me going throughout this
ten-year project to date and the pain they have
suffered waiting to see what happens next.

Chapter 1 – Downgrade

The softest jolt stirred Tristaric from troubled dreams into unpleasant heat and humidity. Clamminess under his arms disgusted him and he touched the plates of his staff changing the environment within the cabin. It was two days since leaving the capital and the four magii should have propelled his carriage halfway across the Empire to his destination by now.

Snapping his fingers and pointing to the window, one of the six servants pulled back the curtain. Searing sunlight poured in. Recoiling, a flick of his staff propelled the servant away, rocking the carriage as it slammed into the side to fall crumpled to the floor.

The curtain fell back into place.

He pointed again.

Without hesitation, another servant moved to open the curtain. This time Tristaric was prepared and a film of semi-darkness fell over the window reducing the sunlight to a pleasant level.

He was going to miss much about his home, the environmental mana dome over the city being one, filtering the sunlight and maintaining the temperature at pleasant levels. Even the colour of the dome was changed to meet the Emperor's desire of the day.

Peering out, he saw the carriage passing through the golden gateway to his destination in the dreary north-western edge of the Empire – the city of Straslin. He made a bitter face, the entrance was no bigger than the one to his estate, and contemptible to the main gateway of the capital.

He cursed the Emperor again for sending him from his side to handle this mess created by the former head of Straslin's magii shodatt. The man died casting the Rite to Rakasti – a spell taking three months to complete. The magic was imperative to begin the invasion of another land to supply new souls needed for the chambers and extract their blood under torture. It was the only way to create the yellow liquid, *Yan*, and stocks of the life-extending elixir were running low.

The Emperor had been irate at the delay and decreed the invasion was to restart in one month, and Tristaric was to ensure this happened. Recasting Rakasti in less than three months was impossible, so he knew he had to do something unorthodox. High-energy magic was inherently dangerous, and he would have to push the limits beyond anything he'd done before with no time for caution. It was a recipe magii's didn't normally survive. But the reward would be worth the risk. Once the supply of Yan from the torture of a million conquered heathens started to flow, he would win back his place.

The mountains loomed in the distance, the natural barrier to the Empire's normal tactic of overwhelming an enemy using sheer force of numbers. Beyond them was so-called Mlendria, the last remaining population of heathens in the land, soon to be absorbed into the Empire and all history of it and its culture erased. Once gone, the Empire would be one.

The city's central palace came into view. Every city had one, housing one family of the Elite. He counted twelve storeys, topped with glittering golden domes. It was a pathetic sight compared to the Emperor's palace reaching through the clouds, mana swirling around it shaped like huge sea serpents and other exotic creatures disguising its impenetrable magical barrier.

Dismissing the servant, the curtain dropped back.

Out here on the edge, everything was feeble by comparison to home, and staying a moment longer than necessary, away from his city and the Emperor and Xrearna, was insufferable. The carriage ran over another of the minutest of stones, making it judder almost undetectably. He closed his eyes in irritation. Such imperfections were not tolerated in Ashnor.

Chapter 2 – Returning Home

Ducking under the branches of the final treeline, his family's farm came into view. As he picked his way down the furrows between the seed lines of this season's crop, a hired hand appeared carrying planks of wood to repair the frost damage each winter brought to the farmhouse. Garamon didn't recognise him. The hand called out a warning to the house, no doubt mistaking him for a mercenary in his grubby leather armour.

Moments later, Garamon's father came out of the house carrying a club. His sister followed, supporting their mother. Garamon was horrified, his mother's eyes were sunken, and her skin sagging and pale. She'd lost a lot of weight, and aged twenty years in the days he'd been away. Suddenly, nothing of the impending invasion and horror he endured mattered in comparison to the silent misery he'd enforced upon her. The need to rush over and hold her and say he was sorry was overwhelming. Instead, she inflicted the worst pain possible upon him and turned and walked back in. His sister gave an accusing glare before following.

As he approached, his father showed no expression. 'Did you find him?' The words were spoken flat as if the response, whatever it was, didn't matter.

'Yes, Father.'

His father registered a little surprise. 'So the Arch-Mage was wrong, he wasn't over the border.'

Garamon didn't know how to answer, considering what had transpired over recent days.

'I met Falakar.'

His father's eyes narrowed as if everything his son now said was to be treated with suspicion. 'The Ranger?'

'He was pursuing Jontal the bandit, who was...' Garamon faltered at the horror of the encounter. 'He killed a man before I could get to him. Falakar found me with the dead man.'

'Falakar didn't instruct you to return?'

Garamon could hear the doubt in his father's voice. His actions of late had undermined the man's unquestioning trust of his son until then.

'At first I didn't tell him who I was.'

His father's eyes closed, displaying a deeper level of disillusionment with his son.

'Where is Falakar now? Off into the mountains, I suppose, unable to uphold your story.'

'We separated on the mountain road at the outskirts of the farm. He was heading into town.'

'Was he mounted?'

'No, we had to travel on foot.'

'Get out of that armour and clean yourself up, the stench of death lingers on you. I will go speak with Falakar. If I cannot find him, or you are not here when I return, I promise I will track you down and return you here at all cost. You will then remain on this farm for as long as I deem necessary, even if I have to chain you to it.'

'Yes, sir. Can I see Mother?'

'No. When you're cleaned up, wait in the study.'

Garamon felt crushed at the thought of not making it up to his mother. Watching his father disappearing into the stables, he turned and entered his home. The place felt empty, lifeless. There was dust on the surfaces, as if nobody had lived here since he left. His mother was always so house proud, cleaning and polishing daily.

He climbed the stairs to his room. It had been searched. Once his deception about his whereabouts had been uncovered, his father and the Rangers would have hunted for clues as to his true location. He then realised his family may have thought him kidnapped too. After all, it had been the kidnapping of his friend, Chayne, that had started the whole thing. His mother would have believed the worst, and knowing the other victims were never found, it would have crushed her.

He cleaned himself up before moving to the study. The sound of his father's horse on the stone path to the house made him stand from the soft chair, warm from the deep red flame of the fire.

He waited.

The door opened and his father walked straight to his desk, retrieving a decanter of golden liquid and pouring two glasses. Garamon had never been exposed to alcohol in any form and knew little about it. Some of his friends reported drinking the yellow liquor, saying it burned like fire in the mouth and back of the throat.

His father walked over to him and offered one of the drinks.

'I was going to reserve this for your twenty-fifth birthday as a sign of your full manhood, but from what Falakar has told me you proved yourself a couple of years early.'

'Father, I am sorry-'

His words were cut short with his father's raised hand.

'Drink.'

Garamon looked at the liquid with some trepidation, unsure what his father was doing, and sipped it. His lips began to tingle. As he took his next breath, strong vapours made him cough.

'No, take it all back – like this,' his father said, raising his glass to his mouth.

'To the start of manhood,' he said, and took back the whole measure in one go.

Garamon looked at his glass then did the same. The acrid taste and burning in his throat took over all else. He choked as the liquid went down. His father smiled, showing no signs of such suffering.

'You drink this stuff for enjoyment?' Garamon rasped.

'In time you will come to treasure it,' replied his father, sitting down in the soft chair opposite, and gesturing for his son to do the same.

Garamon sat.

His father became serious. 'I can never forgive what you have done to your mother. And be assured – neither will she. By your choices you have changed your relationship with her forever, and I know there is no greater penance I can inflict upon you, so the matter of punishment is done.'

Tears welled up in Garamon's eyes adding to those created from the harsh drink.

'But such are the destinies of some men. It was with increasing disbelief I listened to Falakar as he relayed your exploits, courage and strength-of-will in your part in providing warning of the coming invasion. You have helped create a valuable delay for us to prepare.'

Garamon went to speak, but his father raised his hand again and continued.

'What you did was beyond bravery, and although it's clear you have been lucky, I should have given you more credit in the beginning. You have come of age before your time and are a man after your grandfather.

Garamon saw a serene look pass over his father's face as he looked into the fire, as if recalling some pleasant memory.

'Your grandfather said something to me when your brother was born. As he stood over his first grandson in your mother's arms, he told me his axe would choose one of my boys, and I must promise to support them in their decisions when it does. I took it as mere wistfulness created by the moment, nevertheless I smiled and promised I would.'

'I had forgotten about it until I heard Falakar talking of what the thing had done in your hands.' He then faltered for a moment, as if finding the right words. 'I am…a conservative man by nature. You, on the other hand, have a courage I never possessed.'

'Father, you are the most courageous man I have ever known!'

His father dismissed the comment with a wave of his hand.

'I keep my promises, son. I'll not hold you back again. I'm going to honour your grandfather's wish, and the request of Falakar, and release you into the Ranger's charge for his personal mentoring.'

Garamon's jaw dropped.

'You interrupt me three times in a few moments, then when it comes for you to speak, you are silent.'

Garamon closed his mouth and gathered his wits. 'I'm confused, Father. I was expecting your anger.'

'It's there, and well justified. Your method of gaining what you wanted was thoughtless in the extreme, causing great pain to those closest to you.'

Garamon dipped his head.

'However, while I was doing what I believed to be right, I was not. As such, I must share the blame for what happened.'

He rested back against the soft red leather of his chair, thumbing his empty glass and staring into it.

He looked up again and smiled. It held great sadness.

'Now I shall tell your mother of this.'

'Do you think it possible she will understand?'

'No, son. Women like your mother have no capacity or need for conflict or war, and the world would be a better place for that. But it is not the case, and so I shall be guarded with the truth and the full peril you placed yourself, and what you're about to do.'

He got to his feet.

Garamon stood on reflex. 'Thank you, Father.'

'At dawn, the day after tomorrow, take your axe, armour and provisions for three days and head for Highpoint. Falakar said he would meet you there.'

He held out his hand for Garamon's glass. 'Let's hope future consumption of this is for celebration.'

'I shall do everything I can to make you and Grandfather proud.'

His father smiled again. 'I know you will, but all I want is for you to come back safe.'

And so it was done. His father left him alone.

He sat down again, the fire adding to his overheated body from the effects of the drink. He tried to take it all in, expecting permanent grounding and loss of the axe. Instead, his actions were supported and his father was helping in extending them.

He slumped back. Things were moving too fast. All he wanted was to come home and do jobs for his father until the invasion began. At least a short period of normality. But those days were over. Once in the training of the Ranger's, his life would be dedicated to their cause and he would leave his future life of a farmer and woodsman behind. He thought back to the days of running and fooling around in the woods with his brother. They were wonderful times. The short warm months between harsh winters were carefree and the happiest times of his life. Now all was about to change with the Ashnorian Empire coming to rule them. The Rangers could put together a strong force, but in truth, everybody knew the stories of the Ashnorians. Their armies were huge and their magiis more powerful than any within Mlendria.

He rose from his chair feeling unsteady on his feet. He heard this to be an effect of the fiery drink, but was surprised how quickly it happened. He walked with added concentration out of the study and considered which way to go. Should he disobey his father and try to apologise to his mother, or go to his room and wait? In the end, he decided to walk the farm for a while. After all, he didn't know what Falakar had planned for him, nor when he would return.

Chapter 3 – New Strategies

Chayne sat in the finest lab in the city, the envy of every resident master magii. He inherited it from his deceased mentor and master, Lathashal, but the others deserved it far more, and he knew there would be manoeuvring, both political and treacherous, to take it from him. He didn't want to lose it; the place was his home almost since his arrival after being abducted by the Empire. More than that, it contained a treasure of magical study and experimentation stored in Lathashal's personal bookcase. Somewhere in there had to be the man's private notes. All master magiis had such caches representing their life's work. They were covetous of each other's discoveries and went to great pains to hide them, and he'd yet to find Lathashal's. The man had been a genius, a colossus of power and manipulation of mana. His secrets would be invaluable for advancement in magic and survival.

A replacement magii was said to be on the way, arriving in a few days from the capital itself from the Emperor's very side, someone of great power. The thought of a magii at least as powerful as Lathashal didn't do anything to calm his nerves. There would be no chance to stop the Rite to Rakasti this time, no chance of *heathen* interruption. In three months, the invasion would begin again. He hoped the current delay and alerting of Mlendria would give them a chance to mobilise a defence. Although he knew it would be too little, for what could stop the Empire.

Reaching out to a bubbling jar, he poured a clear yellow-tinged liquid into a delicate ornamental glass. He smelt the brew before sipping it carefully. It was new to him and something the Elite were drinking. Fruity and bitter, like biting on a lemon, it nevertheless had an agreeable taste with the after effect of lifting his spirits. He sat back, letting the vapours diffuse throughout his air passages, the warmth of the drink settling into his stomach creating a calming effect.

Why was everything so quiet? The leader of the city's magii shodatt was, after all, a most senior post, and whose sudden death must have far reaching implications for the tidy bureaucratic structure binding the Empire. Why weren't doors being broken down and suspects dragged off to the torture chambers for questioning? After all, even minor transgressions would receive *corrective punishment* – the Empire's euphemism for torture.

He took another sip.

There was a knock on the door of the entrance chamber and his hand clenched, cracking the glass, spilling the hot tisane. He gave a yelp and placed a hand over his manasphere. Immediately the burning pain diminished. Before being taking into the Empire as an apprentice magii, he would have plunged his hand into cold water. Now, using magic was second nature. He knew he was becoming dependent upon his manasphere, something he'd seen of all magiis. They were never without them. It wasn't because of the convenience they provided, there was something more. A pull, a desire.

Addiction?

He went to click his fingers at a servant to open the door and stopped himself. There was a growing compulsion to order the servants with such contempt. It was commonplace for all other citizens of the Empire to do so, and he despised the practice. Somehow the habit was transferring to him. Servants were not allowed to speak, or even be spoken to. Both would cause the servant to be punished by torture.

He gave a hand-sign instead.

So was this it, an armed guard to take him away? Had they discovered something incriminating he'd missed, and he was to spend the remainder of his short life in agony?

The servant returned with a parchment stamped with the Empire's official seal. It was a summons from the city's Lead Councillor to attend an irregular meeting of the council. Without his dead master, as his *Zintar*, he now represented the magii shodatt in the city until a replacement master was appointed. Well it wasn't a death sentence at least. He got his things together and headed off.

Turning down the final corridor leading to the meeting room, he was struck by how everything had settled down into a normal routine after the aborted start to the invasion. The Empire was an amazing machine, built on unwavering repetitive routine, and, of course, the human cogs of the servant class lining the walls within alcoves every few paces.

A broad-shouldered military man stepped out from a corridor ahead. Sharp salutes and nervous looks came from the guards as he passed. His long stride soon caught up with two lumbering councillors heading in the same direction and blocking his path, each nodding at the other's overloud comments.

'The only good news from the debacle was the idiot died in the process. Spell failure at that level creates a horrific death, or you turn into a gibbering imbecile or something.'

The other man nodded slowly, stroking his chin. Chayne didn't know either man. They were two of the unlimited cogs creating the gears of control within the bloated bureaucracy.

'I must admit my surprise at the news though,' continued the first. 'My few meetings with the man marked him as ferociously self-controlled, brutal in his determination to succeed, and sadistic to those who didn't meet the highest standards. He was perfect for the role.'

'Well, now the war will have to wait for the Emperor's replacement to settle in and recast the Rite,' said the second councillor.

As the first councillor moved his head in agreement, the military man caught up, his powerful deep tones cutting in, causing both men to jump aside. 'I have a million men poised to strike out across the mountains to annex the North. I don't need to wait weeks for the Emperor's new spell crony to get comfortable in his surroundings so I can know where a few scouts are located.'

The two councillors attempted to recover their composure and exert some measure of authority over the man with looks of distaste. He was six inches taller than both of them and larger in build – although not across the stomach – but his mental presence was enough to reduce them to the size of rodents.

'You will offend the Emperor, General Zanthak,' squeaked the second councillor. 'He has sent his personal magii to assist you.'

Zanthak snorted without looking at either of them and pushed through.

Chayne darted through the opening to keep up with the man. So this was the Empire's famous General Zanthak. The man was littered throughout the military section of the Main Library as the leading role in conquering much of the land in the name of the Empire. His strategic and tactical skills were celebrated as the finest in the Empire's history. Although, frustrated with no battles to fight for fifty years, the man was said to be open to the occasional unguarded remarks at the expense of the Empire and its non-military officials. Younger generals were sensing an opportunity, and jostling for his esteemed position.

They entered the council chamber, Chayne feeling uncomfortable in such surroundings standing in for his dead master. The long room contained the majority of the forty members and their aides, one per councillor, milling around the table the length of the room. Along the centre were rare wines, juices and expensive sweetmeats. Chairs were placed at the standard spacing to prevent writing being overlooked by the attendees on either side. Aids would stand behind them, their job to record the thousands of words spoken in the meeting. Chayne now knew this was all such nonsense, as the minutes never reflected what was said or motioned. They were altered to support the secret agreements, brokered and broken before and after the meetings, as each councillor plied his skills to gain the right political position to match the Emperor's fickles and fancies. It was another of the cracks he'd discovered threaded throughout the seemingly perfect officialdom of the Empire.

An usher spoke to each arrival, giving instructions for where they were to sit. Chayne separated from Zanthak as the man headed for his seat on the opposite side of the table. He watched him search for his name tag, weaving his way through the groups of attendees, huddled in last-minute discussions confirming agreements were still intact. The distance you sat from the head of the table was a statement of influence. He saw the General go straight to a chair opposite his own, check the name tag, and sit down one seat closer to the head.

A young voice chirped up from behind him. 'Excuse me, General. That position is reserved for Councillor Gruldi.'

Zanthak made an exaggerated movement with his head, looking between the two nametags before picking up Gruldi's and exchanging its position with his own.

'That's – you cannot – I must...!'

Zanthak turned to the head of the room. 'Lead Councillor Leorrt, I would like to begin immediately, there is important business I must attend to this morning.'

The room went silent.

While the General was of the highest ranking members of the military, and Leorrt a middle man in the vast structure of the Empire's hierarchy, the military were always the tool of the politic.

This didn't seem to bother Zanthak.

Leorrt, unhurried, paused his conversation and turned. 'General Zanthak, I believe everybody in this room has important business waiting on them. This meeting is planned to start on the hour, still three minutes away.'

Leorrt re-engaged his conversation.

There was a flurry of disapproving whispers, which appeared to provide the General with a moment of amusement. The man began strumming his fingers loudly on the table.

Chayne scanned the room, watching the usual false smiles and practised laughter between individuals, supposed to engender trust and friendship between the players. It reminded him of a pack of hyenas. He then caught the stare of Zanthak looking at him. His eyes betrayed intelligence and perception. In that brief moment Chayne felt the man was reading his thoughts.

He looked away.

The three minutes were up, and Leorrt gave a final nod to the lower councillor he'd been in conversation, and called the meeting to order.

Chayne sensed someone sat next to him one position further from the head of the table than his own. The man's full head of dark curled locks contrasted with his own straight white hair. He was dressed in an immaculate robe of garish light-greys, red and gold. Although not out of place in the Empire, the cut and materials made even the ostentatious councillors look dull and unimaginative by comparison. The man's face though, was unpleasant; white and pasty, almost to the point of dead-looking. His features were sharp, his eyes small with tiny pupils. It made him difficult to read. The name tag was hand-written, as if last minute. This was unusual, as change didn't happen without due planning, and Chayne would have been notified.

A small bell chimed and aids were dispatched to the head of the room, each given an agenda and notes for the meeting. Not having an aid, Chayne got his and returned to his seat, noticing the newcomer hadn't bothered to get one. He sat down and noted the General also didn't have an aid and remained seated. As Gruldi's aid returned with a pack, Zanthak snapped his fingers twice at him. 'Get me one of those, boy.'

'It is customary to bring your own aid, General,' said Gruldi.

'Oh, I would, but an accident at the barracks had one of the men lose several fingers in a practice dual. Terrible mess. Blood, bone, sinew everywhere. I offered my aid's assistance to help scoop it up and clean the floor and walls. I think it's good for them to get as broad an experience of life within the Empire as possible. Don't you?'

Gruldi's face expressed revulsion.

'Perhaps we can arrange an exchange for a week or two?' offered Zanthak, indicating Gruldi's aid. 'It might be good for both of them?'

Chayne watched as blood drained from the aid, followed a muffled *whump* as he hit the deep carpet.

Zanthak's gaze didn't leave Gruldi. 'Perhaps not.'

He then shifted his eyes to the next aid in line, who, acting on reflex, gave the General the pack still to be given to his own councillor. Then, realising what he'd done, moved quickly to retrieve another.

Zanthak faced inwards. Councillors were pushing their plates of food away, some of their faces looking almost as pale as the unfortunate aid.

Chayne couldn't help but warm a little to the man. Clearly, he wasn't the usual empyrean lackey.

The General looked to his acquired meeting pack and the agenda. 'I need to discuss the forthcoming attack on Mlendria as the first item.'

More looks and sounds of disapproval.

'That's agenda item four, General,' replied Leorrt.

'The attack into Mlendria should already have begun, there is no issue more important to discuss,' pushed Zanthak.

'*Our Cultural Modernisation Programme* for the Northern Lands has been delayed due to failure of casting of the Rite of Rakasti,' replied Leorrt, in complete control of his own tone. 'This is reflected in its order on the agenda.'

'I don't need spells to defeat the Mlendrian Rangers,' Zanthak retorted. 'I have superior numbers to overwhelm any resistance.'

'It has been our way to cast the Rite of Rakasti before any major engagements since the massacre at Diolonche, General.'

'I am aware of military history and regulations, Lead Councillor. I have been the instigator of many of the existing protocols. Diolonche was a special case, when the Empire was smaller and the General in question, incompetent.'

'Nevertheless,' replied Leorrt, 'it would take the Emperor himself to approve such a departure from procedure.'

'A technicality,' scoffed Zanthak.

There were gasps from the room.

Leorrt allowed the moment to settle.

'Referring to the Emperor's approval in such a casual way is not to be repeated in one of my meetings,' Leorrt said, evenly.

Zanthak closed his eyes and took a long breath.

'Perhaps...'

The voice came from the newcomer sitting next to Chayne. The man was in an obvious false pose of contemplation for dramatic effect.

A clerk next to Leorrt chirped up after receiving a nod from the Lead Councillor. 'The council meeting recognises new member, Master Tristaric.'

'You wish to add something, Master Tristaric?' Leorrt prompted.

Tristaric took a moment before answering, attempting further to add importance to his next statement. 'I have been sent by the Emperor to deliver his command; he will not tolerate a three-month delay for the attack on the heathens. He has decreed the attack will commence within a month.'

Noise erupted from the assembled councillors. Frantic re-planning and repositioning would now be required to realign with the Emperor's new order.

Chayne was alarmed. If this was the case then the Rangers would be caught unprepared. He began to wonder who this new person was. A courier of information? He seemed too important.

'I have always been told the Rite to Rakasti takes a minimum of three months to prepare,' Leorrt said.

'Perhaps there is a way to mitigate the debacle my predecessor left behind,' Tristaric replied with an air of superiority.

'We are not here to listen to impromptu ideas, Master Tristaric.'

'My apologies, Lead Councillor,' Tristaric replied, with a respectful tilt of his head. 'As I've just arrived, there hasn't been opportunity to prepare fully. However, I believe I have a solution to satisfy both the General and the Emperor, for, having come from his Excellency's side as his personal magii, I have an understanding of how the Emperor is currently thinking.'

Chayne looked at the newcomer. Could this be Lathashal's replacement?

'Very well, Master Tristaric.' The first signs of irritation were in Leorrt's voice, perhaps because the magii was attempting to leverage weight by emphasising his former relationship with the Emperor in such a way. 'We shall, on this occasion, elevate this topic and deal with it now. I believe it's in the interest of all present not to detain the General any longer than necessary from his…important business. You may continue with the details of your proposal.'

'My apologies again if I have misled you, Lead Councillor,' Tristaric replied. 'I can provide no details at this time, for the alternative I am suggesting involves magic too complex to be understood within the timeframe of this meeting.'

'Are we to assume you wish us to sanction an action without any idea of what it entails?' said Leorrt, now pushed to the edge of sarcasm. There was stifled laughter throughout the assembly as they attempted to show favour for the Lead Councillor who appeared to be winning the contest of authority.

Tristaric pulled a false smile and continued unaffected. 'As the Emperor's *personal* magii, for five years I have become familiar with the processes and protocols of central government.' He widened his smile to the point of smugness, showing an array of brilliant white teeth, as again he attempted to put Leorrt in his place.

Leorrt looked on for a few seconds without speaking, as though the man was counting to ten in his head. 'Then what *can* you provide us, Master Tristaric?'

Tristaric looked to be contemplating, as if it was going to take some great feat to bring the discussion into words the councillors could comprehend. 'Well, as you are aware, the *cultural modernisation* of the heathens is hampered by the need to first cross a vast mountain range. As we wish for the maximum element of surprise to support the lessons learned at Diolonche, we cast the Rite of Rakasti. This spell provides the casting master magii with a vision of the entire incursion point for the attacking General, allowing all enemy defences and scout locations to be pinpointed and neutralised without raising alarm within the enemy for the maximum time.'

'We are knowledgeable of the Rite, Master Tristaric,' Leorrt said. 'Are you saying there is an alternative in this case?'

Tristaric nodded. 'It might be possible to cross the mountains, avoiding detection without the use of the Rite of Rakasti.'

'You cannot be suggesting some form of mass invisibility? We have been told the energies involved would exceed that of all the magiis of the Empire. It's only approved for use in small, tactical manoeuvres.'

'I see the Master Lathashal has kept the council well informed,' Tristaric replied. 'But I am not speaking of existing magic.'

'You are suggesting something…unconventional?'

Such action, Chayne knew, would never be sanctioned by the council without full approval from the head of the central board of magii in Ashnor. But he was now concerned in what Tristaric had to say.

Zanthak spoke up at the remark. 'Are you telling me there is something new you can do to allow my forces to move now?'

'Sadly, not immediately, General. The delay could be reduced to a few weeks to meet the Emperor's timing, instead of the months for my re-casting of Rakasti. While I can provide a magical solution though, it may also need some unusual tactics from yourself and your men to tie up some lose ends. I'll need you, General, to work with me to resolve these.'

The room exploded in a verbal blur of simultaneous objections from the assembled councillors. The recent hard labours of hurried negotiated deals caused by the unexpected three month invasion delay would be thrown into disarray again.

Although doing his best to hide it, Chayne knew his eyes were showing alarm. Again he felt the gaze of the General, boring into him.

He had to do something.

'Lead Councillor Leorrt, I must raise an objection to Master Tristaric's proposal.'

The room went silent.

'You wish to raise an objection against a proposal made by your own shodatt, Zintar Chayne?' Leorrt replied, sounding surprised.

'As the Master Lathashal's chosen Zintar, in the event of his death, all his authority over the city of Straslin, for matters relating to the magii shodatt, fall to me. Master Tristaric has not passed this proposal by me for approval; therefore I cannot allow this council to be so informed of its contents until I have given such endorsement.'

'I am aware of the transfer of authority,' Leorrt replied, 'but Master Tristaric is a very senior magii. You, on the other hand, have been within the Empire a short time. Do you expect us to consider your position as more than honorary?'

Chayne felt beads of sweat break out on his forehead.

'The master Lathashal was the ruling magii in Straslin. He saw reason enough to grant me such an influential position.'

'The master Lathashal is also dead by his own error,' Leorrt countered. 'Do you not think it wise we cast some doubt upon all his recent unusual decisions?'

'I quite agree,' answered Tristaric, beating Chayne to a response. 'The Rite of Rakasti was not beyond Master Lathashal's abilities. To be so consumed by his manasphere during its casting indicated the man wasn't himself.'

Chayne was flustered.

Leorrt waited, and seeing no reply, continued. 'Master Tristaric, how long do you require to prepare a more informed proposal to the council?'

'I can have something for you in a few days,' Tristaric replied.

Leorrt turned to Zanthak. 'General. It seems to me we have an opportunity here.'

'How so,' Zanthak replied.

'The reports of a recent incursion into the city around the time of Master Lathashal's death, mentioned there were a number of barbarians involved?'

'Yes, three and a Heslarian. I fail to see what bearing it could have on any military opportunity.'

'I am sure your men are impatient to begin their task,' continued Leorrt.

'Of course. What's your point?'

'Well, as we have an army held up for some weeks, positioned on the edge of the northern mountain range, one that hasn't fought for decades, perhaps a practice exercise would be sensible?'

'Lead Councillor, my men could not be better trained, nor more ready than they are now,' Zanthak replied, hotly.

Leorrt turned to a small round-faced councillor close by. 'What is the current state of slaves in the mine?'

'We are at eight of ten capacity, Lead Councillor,' replied the clerk without needing to check any documents.

'Councillor Leorrt!' Zanthak burst out. 'If you're suggesting my men should be used in the mines!'

Leorrt waved his hand dismissively. 'I'm proposing you engage some of your men in an early strike against the barbarians, returning with a few hundred of their strongest to relieve the shortfall in the mines.'

'You have authority to do this?'

'While it is the Emperor's exclusive right to initiate war on another race, I can, with a majority vote, sanction retaliation for the attack on Master Lathashal.' Leorrt turned to the round-faced clerk and gave him a nod.

The clerk stood and straightened his official regalia before pushing out his chin. 'Lead Councillor Leorrt Monticilly, upon this day...'

Chayne zoned out as the charge voiced the proposal, and envelopes for the secret vote were distributed. Containing three circular pieces of starched parchment: one with a raised cross, another with a circle, and the third with nothing, he kept his hands inside the envelope and snapped two, leaving the crossed one intact indicating his rejection of the proposal, and sealed his envelope. The envelopes were shuffled before being emptied in front of the small clerk who counted the tokens. When finished he stood.

'Proposal four-six-two-six-five-seven has been carried with a majority of five votes. Nine councillors were undecided.' He sat back down.

'Very well,' Zanthak said, surprised at the opportunity. 'I shall make preparations for immediate action.'

'Thank you, General,' Leorrt said. 'There will be an emergency security council meeting in three days to discuss Master Tristaric's proposal.'

'Will the meeting include the Zintar, Lead Councillor?' Tristaric asked.

'That is an internal matter for the magii shodatt,' Leorrt answered in a tone stamping an end to the matter.

'We shall resume with the original item one on the agenda.'

Chayne's mind disengaged. He was stupid to make such an impromptu objection, and now he'd also exposed his position against the new proposal. He'd panicked, and that wouldn't do if he was to survive without the protective umbrella of his old master.

He looked up to see the stare of Zanthak bearing down on him again. What did the man see?

The General rose from his seat to leave. Tristaric got up and intercepted him and they spoke briefly before leaving together.

Chayne didn't know how far his Zintar authority would carry him, but he had to buy time for his people to prepare. 'Councillor Leorrt, I must excuse myself from the remainder of the session. In light of the Master Tristaric's unexpected announcement, there are things I need to do with some urgency.'

Leorrt contained his anger at yet another interruption. 'I think that is best, Zintar Chayne.'

Chayne stood and bowed. Leaving, he could see Zanthak and Tristaric in the distance turning a corner. He wanted to run after them and insist he be privy to the discussions, but his shaky authority had been pushed far enough for one day. If he created too many waves, his status could be revoked.

He wished Illestrael was here. The spy would have found out all Tristaric was planning without the man knowing, and fed it back. He missed her and didn't realise how much he depended on her in his operations and her friendship in this cold and conspiracy-ridden land.

What he needed in her place was to seek out Stalizar for his counsel on the matter, but it could cast suspicion on them both. He was isolated and couldn't do this alone. He headed to his lab to contemplate a plan.

Chapter 4 – Calling Home

Tristaric left his meeting with Zanthak. He hadn't let the General know his idea didn't yet exist. His decision to declare there was an alternative was a gamble, but then he hadn't become the youngest ever Emperor's personal magii without being bold, and stamping his authority within the outlying city had to be done.

Right now, though, inventing a solution would have to wait, for tonight there was something pushing even that goal into second place.

He crossed the city to one of the Towers of Communiqué, the highest points in the city other than the principal spire of the palace itself. Standing on the lifting plate he glided to the top of the tower and stepped onto the transmission platform. Turning a polished metal handle, a cover exposed the focussing crystals in the direction of Dirante, where there would be another tower. The lens there would be opened in two directions, one to receive the mana beam from Straslin, and the other to allow it to pass through and onto its next destination lens. This would occur many times until the beam reached its end – in this case the Empire's capital, Ashnor. The communication streams were set on a rotation, giving a brief time before the lenses would be reconfigured for the next predefined connections across the Empire.

While Straslin had a half-dozen lenses to cope with the traffic flow to and from the city – Ashnor had hundreds. After tonight the next window to Ashnor was another two days, so the towers were restricted to the most imperative information only, such as updating the Emperor with progress on his plans.

However, maintaining the tower was the responsibility of the magii shodatt, and Tristaric had temporarily gained authority. It wasn't difficult creating a phantom problem with one of the mechanisms to give him time for his own purposes.

He waited for the head-sized viewing ring to fill with a sickly green translucence the colour of rotting meat, indicating the connection was made. The background of Straslin behind the ring faded out as the system began to work. A face appeared, shifting in the magic's flow. It looked ugly as the image distorted. Over such distances there was no way to overcome the fidelity of mana transfer through so many ring hops. Even so, it was a face Tristaric recognised and knew well. He reached out his hand to touch it, withdrawing it realising the absurdity of the action.

'Tris, is that you?

The voice was similarly distorted. Even so, it sounded tender to the man who had heard the real thing so many times. His heart felt like a hand was squeezing it.

'Xrearna, yes it is! It's so long since I touched your sweet face, I almost tried when I saw you.'

The image of her face appeared to screw up into a contorted ball, making him feel he'd said something wrong, before it resumed and showing her laughing. Relieved, he laughed with her. Nothing he did for himself or even the Emperor made him feel such happiness.

'You are so sweet, beloved. I hope the journey wasn't too bad?' she replied.

'I swear servants have suffered less in the chambers.'

Another peel of laughter from the other end, twisting from deep to high tones with the occasional sound of normality. Tristaric couldn't help smiling to the point where his mouth hurt.

'Are you going to get into trouble for using the imager like this?'

'The imagers are maintained and controlled by the magii shodatts for each city, my love. Here, there is a young Zintar in charge of the shodatt who is of no consequence, and if he came between you and me I'd turn him into a frog in an instant.'

Another peel of laughter. 'Can you do that?'

Tristaric loved the way she laughed. It made him swell with pride. 'No, not really, it's all about relative mass. The two objects have to be of roughly equal size and density to be transposed.'

'Oh stop, you know I don't understand such talk.'

He felt for a moment he'd displeased her and his heart sank. 'I can't squeeze all his innards into such a tiny thing,' he offered by simple explanation.

She stayed serious as if he'd upset her.

'Do we have long?'

He sighed in relief, she was melancholy at their separation.

'Straslin is a long way from Ashnor, we only get moments every few days, my sweet.'

Tristaric heard a faint sound from the imager, like somebody was speaking, only her lips didn't move. It was deep, like a man's voice.

'Who is with you, Xrearna?'

'No one, my love. I'm alone, always so alone without you.'

'I heard a man's voice,' Tristaric reproached, not managing to disguise his jealously.

'I would never share these precious moments with anyone else. Could it be the mana stream thingy you try to tell me about?'

Tristaric's anxiety began to abate, he nodded into the imager. 'I guess so.'

'You have nothing to fear, my love, I'm yours and would never betray what we have.'

Tristaric calmed some more and even managed a shaky smile. 'I just worry, that's all.'

'Of course. You have no need, I miss you. Must it be a whole month before you return?' Tears began to roll down the image of the face. She began to sob.

He couldn't stand to hear the sound and clutched his chest where the pain stabbed him like a knife.

'I shall complete this faster than even the Grand Arch-magii would believe possible,' he proclaimed, but the image flickered and disappeared as the transmission window closed leaving the spire in the distance visible again, not making it clear whether his last message had gotten through.

He smashed his fist down onto the mechanism. The thrinium made no indication of the impact, and only served to hurt his hand.

He still wasn't sure why the Emperor sent him away or who dealt the blow, but he was going to find them on his return and make them suffer for his separation and the hurting of his beloved.

Impatient to wait the time the lifting ring would take to return him to the ground, he leapt out and dropped the several seconds to the ground before slowing his fall to land as if no more than a hop. He turned and looked in the direction of Ashnor, obscured as it was by Straslin's many buildings and hundreds of miles of distance. Turning to the nearest servant he threw his power into it, smashing it against one of the thick beams holding up the tower. He pushed with his anger and magic until the servant's back snapped and skull fractured. He let go and the thing fell like a doll to the ground.

'I will return and have my vengeance.'

He looked up at the tower and the focussing ring, annoyed he couldn't even get a true image of his loved one. Thinking of the way it concentrated mana over long distances, a thought came to him. He then realised how he was going to complete his task, rid himself of this loathsome place and get back to his love's side and the Emperor's. It was the riskiest plan he'd ever considered, with everything to play for – including his life.

The imager disconnected and Xrearna dropped her pretence.

'You see, he's a good choice,' she said, trying to suppress the fear she felt whenever in the presence of her benefactor, sitting out of sight of the imager. 'When he completes this task he will be placed in high regard by the Emperor, and again provide us with privileged information to keep us in the Emperor's favour.'

There was a pause.

'And if he fails?' The voice was deep, filled with distain.

'Then we will not be exposed. There is no risk to us.'

Another, longer pause.

'For your sake, you had better be right.'

Chapter 5 – Highpoint

Garamon pulled himself up onto the small plateau forming what was locally known as Highpoint. It was no more than fifty paces across with a few species of hardy grass and shrubs that could survive such exposed conditions. It was a geological anomaly for the area and stood up from the thick woods and rolling hills making up the terrain around Tiburn. A troublesome climb, it served an excellent view of the valley in which sat the town. Garamon expected the meeting to be at the bottom of the landmark, but a symbol of the Rangers was scratched into the stone at its base with an arrow pointing up. He'd no idea why Falakar would choose to meet him at such an obscure place.

He glanced around, and seeing the Ranger hadn't yet arrived, sat down at the edge to look down upon the people of his town going about their business. They were no more than ants from this distance. A knife was slipped under his throat and a restraining hand was placed around his head. A body pressed in from behind trapping him in a tight embrace. He fought the rising panic. Any move could cause the knife to cut him.

'Good,' said a voice from behind. The knife withdrew and the grip released.

Garamon span around and took a step back. Soil crumbled under his heal to fall far below.

It was Falakar.

'I didn't hear you approach.'

'Clearly.'

'You could have scared me off the edge.'

'A fitting first lesson, then.'

'What do you mean?'

'We have no time for formal training. I must teach you at dangerously fast rate. It may break you. You may even die.'

'That doesn't seem fair.'

Falakar sheathed his knife and stepped up to the edge. 'Look down over your town again.' The Ranger pointed to a rise far below on the outskirts of Tiburn. 'Imagine the Ashnorian army pouring over that hill. It's the most likely place they will approach, and from what we have seen, there will be hundreds of thousands of them.'

Garamon did imagine it. The town wouldn't stand a chance.

'We cannot match them in numbers,' Falakar continued. 'So we'll be looking to defend a pass where their numbers would count for less.'

Garamon nodded, remembering such things from the many battles he'd read about in history books.

'Look around and tell me where it would be.'

The morning mist was light and he could see for miles. 'I can see no such place.'

Falakar said nothing.

Understanding struck Garamon. 'You're not going to defend the town!'

'It would be a futile exercise. The purpose of Tiburn's barracks is to provide patrols to warn of the enemy coming through the mountains. Then to delay them long enough for the town to escape north through Thunder Pass. It's where we hope to defend and hold them while our main army is assembled. It's our only hope of stopping them from taking all Mlendria.'

Garamon was horrified at the pragmatic strategy.

'There will be times in the coming weeks you will want to give up the training. Your body will be at the point of collapse. Your spirit will be all but broken, and yet I will continue to push. When it occurs, delirium and exhaustion will make you want to cry out for me to stop. During those moments, recall this vision of your town being overrun, of Mlendria and its people and your family in chains. Enslaved and forced to level every building to rebuild them to Ashnorian designs. The stronger men will then be sent to the mines until they die. The finest women will be enslaved. Everyone else will be tortured to make their elixir.'

'How do you know all this?' Garamon said, looking at the pained expression of the Ranger.

Falakar closed his eyes briefly, as if detaching from an unpleasant memory. He changed the subject. 'Have you heard on the Unyari?'

'No, sir.'

'They are highly cultured scholar-warriors to the East. I trained years with them, and they taught me many things. How to survive alone when I should die; how to know without thinking; to see when there was no light; to hear in the silence, and how to fight without fear. Some of what I learned, and what the Rangers taught me, I shall pass on to you. If you learn quickly, and have the stomach for it, you may become a capable Ranger – maybe more than that.'

'Like you?'

'No. I am no Unyari Master, and could not hope to teach you much of their ways in such a short time. I will do what I can though. Hopefully enough to keep you alive.'

'When do we start?'

'From the moment I slid the knife under your throat,' the Ranger replied, drawing his sword. 'Now let's see if you've remembered your lessons during our recent visit to the enemy.' He jumped with a slicing attack aimed at the Garamon's middle.

Garamon's reflexes took over and he sucked in his stomach, rounding his back as the Ranger's blade sliced within an inch of his armour. He released his axe and deflected the return stroke. Falakar's blade slid around the hasty defence and nicked his hand.

'Ouch,' Garamon yelped. 'That wasn't fair, I wasn't ready.'

'You think the enemy will give invitations!' shouted Falakar, this time sweeping his sword in from the right, aimed at Garamon's shoulder. Garamon took a step back to give his axe time to block the strike. Again his foot stepped close to the edge of the drop. He knew Falakar could defeat him in a moment and was testing him, but the Ranger seemed to be playing by different rules than before.

'From now on you will always be on your guard. Assassins do not play fair, and neither will I.' His sword glanced off the clumsy parry and turned back in for a stab into Garamon's side.

Garamon sidestepped with only a moment to spare. He was still off-balance from the original attack and Falakar wasn't allowing him to recover. He remembered what he'd been told. Large axes required two hands, and it meant in a melee they acted as both shield and weapon. He pushed the axe out in front of him, watching each thrust and swing of his opponent. He managed to extract himself from the edge, creating more of the plateau behind him.

'Good, but don't follow my sword – read my body!' The instructions continued over the clang on the weapons. 'See how my weight is distributed, and what each move means I'll do next. It will give you more time to react.'

It was too much to think under the pressure, and one desperate parry followed another. A new edge of the plateau was approaching and Garamon glanced behind to get a firm fix. As he looked forward again, Falakar's sword point was an inch from his throat.

He stopped and swallowed loudly.

'What can you hear?'

Garamon was confused.

'Don't stand there like a dolt. What can you hear?'

'I – I can hear only you.'

Falakar sheathed his sword and sat down. 'Sit.'

The command went straight to Garamon's legs, much like a puppy under training.

'Not like that. Copy me.'

He pulled his legs in under him and crossed them as shown.

'Tell me what you hear – every sound.'

Garamon watched a hawk fly close overhead and it cried out. The sound seemed muffled.

'The hawk.'

'Yes, although your sight is distracting you. Close your eyes.'

Garamon did. Moments passed. 'There is nothing else.'

'Can you hear the waterfall?' asked the Ranger.

'But there is no waterfall in this region.'

'Listen.'

Garamon listened hard. It was true, sounds up here could carry long distances on the wind, but there wasn't even the slightest breeze this morning.

'I hear nothing.'

'It's there, and it's loud.'

Garamon tried again, and was startled. 'The rushing sound?'

'It's the blood coursing through your veins close to your inner ear. It's blocking out other sounds. Keep your eyes closed and relax. Your heart will still be pumping faster than normal due to the fear of the sparing session. Continue.'

Slowly the interfering sound reduced, allowing other sounds to become apparent. He heard his breathing, and the sound of a dog barking in the town far below. Eventually he heard nothing new and went to stop.

'Continue until I say otherwise.' Somehow the Ranger sensed he was about give up.

'I can hear nothing more,' Garamon said, feeling restless. He wanted more fighting practice. If he was to face the enemy, he wouldn't be sitting down with his eyes closed.

'Continue...'

Garamon continued, and time passed.

His patience gave in. His legs were cramping and his back was starting to ache. He opened his eyes. Falakar was having no such trouble, still in the same position. The man's face looked serene and content.

'What's the point in continuing? I hear nothing new.'

Falakar raised a finger to his lips, indicating silence. Without opening his eyes he moved his finger to the ground. It stopped next to a small brown beetle. The little creature was scurrying between the blades of grass, oblivious to the Ranger's intruding digit. Garamon watched as the finger moved along with the tiny animal.

He couldn't believe what he was seeing. He placed his hand up to block any chance of Falakar cheating from under his eyelids. Still the creature was tracked perfectly.

He put his head right down close to the creature and listened. He could make out the tiniest occasional rustle in the grass.

'How can you do that?'

Again the Ranger placed a finger to his lips, followed by tapping his ear.

Garamon sighed and responded to the mimed order, closing his eyes and listening hard.

Nothing.

'Oh this is hopeless,' he said exasperated by the whole experience. You have exceptional hearing.'

Falakar took a long, deep breath and opened his eyes. 'It's not the difference in our hearing separating us. You are younger and have the better hearing. There was a time when I also could not hear the beetle.'

'Then how is such a thing possible?'

'Our senses are assaulted by distractions. They are filtered out by our mind to prevent us from going insane.'

Garamon was doubtful.

'Can you feel the touch of your clothes and armour against your skin?' asked the Ranger.

'Well, yes of course,' Garamon replied.

'Did you notice them before I asked?'

'No,' Garamon admitted.

'As with the rushing in your ears, constant detection of such things in our conscious thoughts would overwhelm us.'

'What use is there in knowing it?'

Falakar pulled a cloth from his jerkin. 'Ready your axe.'

Garamon did and watched as the Ranger tie the cloth tight around his eyes, blocking all view.

'Attack me.'

'Sir?'

'Come at me with your axe. Don't hold back. I absolve you of all responsibility for the consequences.'

Garamon hesitated before taking a tentative step forward. He swung his axe at the Ranger, ensuring the swipe, while close, would miss him.

Before his axe got close, Falakar's sword intercepted the blade, forcing it to the ground and stinging Garamon's fingers.

'Try harder,' said the Ranger.

Garamon took the next swipe more seriously, this time sweeping up from under the Ranger's guard. Although still not wholly committing to the strike, it could injure if making contact. The Ranger's blade went to block and Garamon changed the angle of the strike, but the sword moved in sympathy with the deception. The blade went under the axe and forced the weapon up and over Garamon's head. With a well-timed boot in the chest, he went over to land on his back with an undignified thump.

Falakar stood back ready once more. 'Fully commit this time or I'll send you home to be a farmer.'

Garamon got to his feet, annoyed with the Ranger. He crouched into a fighting pose and approached as if attacking the man without a blindfold. He was unnerved to see the Ranger crouch into a similar position and move always to face him. Garamon then attempted to move without sound.

'Better,' Falakar said in response, but still facing his every change in direction.

The dance continued until Garamon realised he wasn't gaining an advantage. He chose his moment and made the first serious lunge. It was met with a block. He leapt away from the counterstrike. The circling continued. This time he feigned a lunge to the left and switched to the right. Falakar seemed to be moving to the real attack line before Garamon changed the weapon's direction, and parried the strike.

The exchanges continued and the frustration grew as thrusts, swings and feigns all came to nothing. Eventually, he lost his patience and made a powerful overhead swing at the Ranger, using his strength and weight of the axe to overpower any block from the lighter sword.

The next moment, he lifted his face out of the snow-muddied dirt, blowing more of the stuff from his mouth. He rolled over to see the predictable view. Falakar was standing over him, his sword resting a few inches from Garamon's throat, still blindfolded.

'I know the difference in the sound of the leather between your left and right boots when you move,' Falakar answered Garamon's unspoken question. 'With this I build a picture in my head of what you're doing. Also, I have taught you only a few attacks with your axe, and so you use simple pre-determined moves. These I can *see* in the sounds I hear, and therefore know what you're going to do next.'

'But when I did something you hadn't trained me to do, it was still countered.'

'Your last move was driven from temper. I could feel your frustration growing and knew you would do something rash. Such lack of finesse in your final attack created obvious signals.'

'But that's because you know me. You would have no such prior knowledge when fighting somebody new.'

'And so you must build up an understanding of your opponent. The closer you're matched, the longer you must take to expose a weakness.'

'But Kinfular killed every man he fought with one or two strokes.'

'The barbarian is a freak. The most gifted fighter I have ever seen,' Falakar replied, simply.

'Why is it so easy for him?'

'I wondered too, and at times watched him. Most men think of one thing at a time in a fight. Countering the current move of their opponent, or their own next strike. Some Unyari masters predict five moves ahead. I can work with three.'

'And Kinfular works with more?'

'No. As I said, he's a freak. He is so natural a fighter he doesn't need prediction. As I watched, it became clear to me the man *controls his opponent*. He makes them do what *he* wants. I doubt he even knows he's doing it, and wonder if even a Unyari master could defeat him.'

Falakar removed his blindfold. 'Enough for now. Let's hunt for lunch in the woods. I have requested an emergency meeting with the council in two days to warn them of the Ashnorian's plans.'

Garamon liked the sound of breakfast. The Ranger's cooking was exemplary, and his extensive knowledge of roots and herbs gave the meat he cooked such wonderful flavour. Attending at a council meeting didn't sound so good. It was made up of the most powerful men in Tiburn. He hoped not to let Falakar down if asked to speak.

He retrieved his axe to find the Ranger staring towards the snowy peaks of the Hammerheads, gazing at something glinting. It continued for a while then stopped.

'What was it?'

Falakar's brow furrowed. 'A coded Ranger message aimed at Tiburn's barracks.'

'Is it important?'

'I couldn't decipher it, and I know all the codes.'

'What do we do?'

'Let's do some hunting and eat. Then I'll pay a visit to an old friend I've been away from too long.'

Garamon followed the Ranger as he climbed down.

Chapter 6 – Unwelcome Help

Jewell stood outside the command tent, the subject of the raging row from within, heard by all around. The impromptu assembly of three-thousand soldiers ready to attack the barbarians were in formation waiting to depart, and many were looking at him. None wanted him along, or any magii, or indeed any member of another shodatt other than the military. No, it was simply protocol to have a magii along with any soldier contingent. The reason was to provide information on the enemy ahead, and to attack at range as the Empire didn't use archers. Magii were far more potent.

The Commander was venting his objection at being bestowed a gradia eight magii, who were significantly less powerful than the master level he should be have been allocated, but all masters had been commandeered by Tristaric for some other purpose.

There was a final peak of yelling before the tent flap burst aside and the military man stormed out.

'With me, Magii!'

Jewell fell in behind. They stopped at the head of the column and he peeled off to take his place within the command section, receiving disapproving looks and shaking of heads. He wanted to be here as much as they wanted him, and he kept his gaze low, shifting uncomfortably from one foot to another, waiting for the command to march.

It didn't take long, and with the order given, the group head in the direction of the barbarian plains.

Chapter 7 – Faust

Faust dropped into a state of meditation before opening his eyes to inspect the ground where the two yhordi operatives killed each other. He absorbed every detail in the gloom until the minutiae of the fight emerged. Neither the angle of the blood splashes, nor the tiny scuffs made from the soft-soled boots in the fine covering of dust, matched the positions marked where the bodies were found. He repeated the procedure from different angles.

When finished, he began the task of retracing the steps of each operative up to the point of the fight, starting with the controller's. The footprints led two levels below to the controller's room. Nothing complicated there, the man had left the room and headed without deviation to the point of contact with the female yhordi, Illestrael. Faust entered the room, sitting down in Maric's chair. He closed his eyes again to achieve a state of complete awareness. Opening them, his centuries of honed skill scanned every item on the desk.

In his experience it was the tiniest details that made the difference between the truth and an untrue obvious explanation. He scrutinised the blotting parchment on the table where Maric had written his orders. Some ink would have soaked through the written parchments here and be absorbed by the blotting parchment below. It was by no means a complete message, nothing more than a series of broken patterns. To anybody else they were an incomprehensible set of dots and short lines mingled with one another. But Faust was the definitive spy, although no other in his profession aspired to be him. In part, because no one could ever get close to his skills, but also because he was no more than a shadow in the Empire. A myth, unknown to definitely exist other than by each Emperor. So for all but the current Emperor, the *Unnamed Assassin* had passed into legend.

His eyes pulled out the freshest ink stains. He slewed his point of focus across the blotter, piecing together the words and reading the written parchments over the last days as if they were the originals.

When completed, he turned his attention to the two draws of the desk. Convinced there had been no tampering of the locks, he used the key taken from the controller's body and unlocked each. He found what he was looking for and opened the log book and inspected not only the words, but every aspect of each of the last six pages representing the recent entries. It was three pages back he found what he wanted. He scanned every facet of the entry, picking up the underlying meaning of the words and how they were written. He became convinced Maric carried out his duty properly. The man held suspicions the female operative had somehow become emotionally compromised with the young Zintar. Faust agreed after reading Maric's interview with the woman and her subsequent actions earlier in the day of the fight. He closed the log and returned it to the draw. Scanning the room for anything out of place, he found all to be as it should have been.

He left the room and returned to the scene of the attack, this time retracing the steps in the direction the female had approached. There were three sets of prints. Two additional people came and returned. One was attempting to step into her foot placements to mask their presence. Faust looked more closely. His eyes narrowed in displeasure. The two other sets of prints were not made by yhordi. The female had led, either willingly or under duress, two people through the tunnels to the secret door of Lathashal's lab and opened it. For a yhordi, for any reason, it was treason and punishable by death.

He tracked the prints back to their source, already guessing where they had come. It was the small banquet hall on the administration level in the North wing. It was where the group of Mlendrians had taken final refuge during an implausibly deep raid into the palace a few days earlier. Illestrael had opened the secret door to the Ancillary Banquet Hall and led two of the enemy to the entrance of Lathashal's lab. The very place where the magii was found dead during the casting of the Rite of Rakasti, and which would have been the start of the invasion into Mlendria. And now the Mlendrians had disappeared, apparently set free by the Lan-Chi.

He returned to the scene of the fight and removed the false brickwork revealing the spy lens into the room beyond. All was clear and he opened the secret door. He knelt down at the entrance and checked out the floor from the corridor. The polished surface held few remaining clues. There was a patch a few paces in, not shining so much. It was what he'd been looking for. Despite the expertise of the servants in the palace, not even they could remove all traces of blood to an eye trained as highly as his. It was still another twelve feet from where Lathashal was killed, too far for so much blood to pool in one place from the attack on the master magii. Faust removed a pack of slim coloured circles of glass from his pocket. He inspected the faded blood patch through each.

The first four showed a dull stain, while the fifth revealed streaks of blue-green running throughout. The shade of colour indicated a poison, probably Tratixlia, a crude but affective substance taken from the plants of old Calencia to the East. The way it was loosely mixed told him the blood had run over a blade, smeared with the poison.

It was the last piece in his jigsaw. The reports said Lathashal lost control of his manasphere and was consumed by the magical energies. Such a thing was inconceivable for a master magii of his standing, and Faust's first clue to foul play. Now there was no doubt, Lathashal was murdered. Illestrael had somehow been in contact with the Mlendrians, aiding a small strike team to enter the palace. She used the yhordi secret passageways, threaded throughout the palace to bring them to Lathashal's lab to strike at the magii. Maric had discovered this and attempted to stop them. He killed the traitor in the passageways and then attempted to take on the attackers inside the magii's lab, but they fought back and killed him, and then Lathashal. He didn't think it likely Lathashal could be defeated by two foreign assassins, but then spellcasting was a dangerous business and could make you vulnerable during the final moments of the major spells, and Rakasti was one of the greatest.

He returned to the scene of the fight in the tunnel to fill in some final details. Somebody attempted to lay the bodies to suggest a mutual killing, but it wasn't what happened. He placed himself in the position of Maric and allowed his combat training to take over. Combining the details he'd seen earlier, he re-enacted the movements of the controller. The attack had been short, and at one point the two had displaced positions. It was odd, placing Maric with his back to the Mlendrians. Unless they'd already entered the room?

Faust then understood, the light from the doorway would have created a silhouette of Maric's body, hiding his strike. A basic ploy. Yhordi carried small blades, and only a strike near the well-defended chest area would have allowed their poison to act fast enough to give him a chance to engage the Mlendrians quickly. Also, Maric had been stabbed in the back, and the position of the woman's wound meant the speed of the poison would not have given her time to strike at the retreating yhordi controller.

It left the question of what part the Zintar played in all this. Providing the timing of the spell? Faust could remember little of the archaic role of Zintar. It was a position of unusual trust though, a scarce commodity in Ashnoria. Lathashal was no fool. If he'd chosen to appoint the young Mlendrian to such a position, a despised outsider at that, it must have been important to the powerful magii. It marked the Zintar as important to Faust, at least until he eliminated him from his investigation. He decided to track him down.

Later that day he sat disguised as one of the general clerks, a few tables from the young man in the tertiary dining hall in the southern wing of the palace. He now knew his name as Chayne and a Mlendrian recently captured by the Empire before the invasion. People able to wield magic were rare and the Empire didn't want such a valuable commodity being lost in the attack. But why had one of the most formidable and ambitious magii's in the Empire taken special interest in him to the point of providing him a rare and powerful position of influence? Did this Mlendrian have power he deemed important enough to imbue Zintar status, then to somehow allow it to defeat him? It seemed unlikely. Faust had travelled into Mlendria many times in his long life, and never once uncovered even a rumour of such potent magic existing there. Certainly, this young man had the motivation to kill the magii after being kidnapped, and no doubt learned of the coming invasion. Being so close to Lathashal, he would know of the Rite to Rakasti, and how stopping it would delay his people being invaded. But how could a non-Ashnorian orchestrate in a few months the defeat of such a powerful master magii? And how could he have organised a team of Mlendrians and barbarians to attack at the right moment, so deep within the defences of a major city? It required unthinkable amounts of infiltration into the Empire without the yhordi uncovering it.

And how did he coerce the female yhordi into breaking ranks, and how many others were involved? It bordered on delusional to think these Mlendrians could taint the yhordi itself, the very organisation set up to foil such subversions, and one not even known to exist other than rumours within the Empire, let alone to outsiders. And if they managed it here, was it possible the Emperor was at risk? It seemed fantastic.

He waited until Chayne finished his meal and followed him from the hall. At the heart of the palace it was an easy job to become one with the throng and not be noticed. He stayed a few paces back and shadowed him to his lab, slipping unnoticed into a servant recess to disappear through a secret doorway into the tunnels behind. It was a short walk to the spy hole seeing into the lab. The Mlendrian settled onto a soft couch, unusual in itself in a lab, and pulled a manasphere box onto his lap. His lips moved and he lifted the lid.

Faust prepared for a lengthy wait, the young magii was about to embark on some spell training, no doubt. He dropped into a semi-sleep state, a regular practice allowing him to remain awake almost indefinitely, avoiding the need for full unconsciousness. His mind was closing down as the Mlendrian lifted his manasphere to its raised position wrapped both hands around the orb.

Faust snapped awake. Magii's only placed their fingertips upon the orbs to restrict a potential fatal flow of mana. It was the number one rule of using manaspheres, and all but the most powerful of magii's could risk full contact, even then for a few seconds. If he could achieve such a task, it could mean he was more directly involved in the overcoming of Lathashal.

This one had more to tell, and with the protection of Lathashal gone, he was going to be targeted by other magii for his position, and Faust needed him alive.

Chapter 8 – Open Threat

Chayne heard the door to his lab open and his spell of detection release as a bell-sound. It was one of the few sustaining spells he'd mastered so far, although it only triggered a sound rather than something more sinister a master magii would have created.

He looked up to see Tristaric, minor sparks dying on his magical shield where it discharged the spell. The magii stopped the shield and walked in.

'Is that supposed to be a deterrent?'

'There is little more I can do at this time,' Chayne replied. 'I'm hoping to improve.'

Scattered around the lab were notes on his investigation into Tristaric. If the magii read them…

Tristaric idly thumbed through a parchment as if preparing for what he was about to say. It contained vague references to Chayne's delving into the magii. Fortunately, he held the more incriminating notes in his hand. He slid them into a drawer.

Tristaric didn't seem to take in the material, or didn't care. He pushed it away, untidily.

'I wasn't impressed with your defiance within our ranks in front of the council. Such a thing will be talked about.'

'It matters little to me,' Chayne said.

Tristaric walked further up the bench and sniffed at a bubbling mixture, withdrawing his nose quickly. 'And what *does* matter to you?'

'The safety of my people.'

'Including killing your former master?'

The intimidating presence of Lathashal was missing from this magii. He seemed genuinely younger than other masters. A fact that was troubling. If such a young man could become the Emperor's personal magii, he must be extraordinarily intelligent and scheming.

'I couldn't have achieved such a thing, even if I wanted.'

'And yet he's dead.'

'Not by my hand.'

'No, so you say. And I agree the idea of you defeating the man, quite farcical.'

'What do you want?'

Tristaric continued walking around the lab. His hand brushed over a smooth black plate of material unknown to Chayne. It was harder than anything he had encountered, and even though it was only the area of a small desk and an inch thick, it weighed more than he could move. Although dry, it was slippery as if covered in oil. Tristaric also seemed at a loss for the curiosity.

'I'm not happy with your meddling.'

'It's my right as Zintar to question decisions to do with the shodatt for the city.'

'I didn't become the Emperor's personal magii without dealing with my share of troublemakers, all of whom were far more of a challenge than you, *Zintar*.'

'Is that a threat?'

Tristaric seemed amused by the comment. 'Of course it is. Do you think you have some protection due to your archaic title? I can assure you, I could deal with you without lasting repercussions.'

'Is it why you are here then, to kill me?'

Tristaric raised his staff with a menacing glare.

Chayne stood his ground, not giving the man the satisfaction of showing his fear. If the man was going to kill him now, there was nothing he could do to stop him.

Tristaric stabbed his staff forward.

Chayne flinched.

Nothing happened.

Tristaric laughed. 'I'm not going to kill a Zintar in straight confrontation. The *Formalities of Justification* are too time-consuming.'

'Then why are you here?'

'I'm taking this lab.'

'You can't have it.'

Tristaric ignored the rejection, something had caught his attention on the far wall. It was the illusion wall designed by Lathashal, used to provide spectacular imaginary sceneries. The magii walked over to it and placed his fingertips upon a small manasphere held in a sconce in the wall. Chayne had no idea what the manasphere was for, or had the desire to touch the thing in fear of what power of demon was contained.

The plain wall faded and was replaced with a stunning view of a huge city sprawling out to the horizon. It seemed greater than anything Chayne believed possible to construct by man. Thousands of shining spinnerets, some touching the clouds, rose up from dome-shaped buildings of identical architecture to those in Straslin. Polished gold and thrinium cladding adorned every surface that should have created bright reflections, and yet the sun was subdued through some filtering dome stretching over the city.

Chayne knew it was an illusion, but the realism was breathtaking. Tristaric then made a movement with his free hand and the image zoomed in, racing across the rooftops. It left the main city and settled on a set of buildings in their own grounds on the outskirts of the city. Tristaric twisted his hand and the image dove through an archway equal in size to Straslin's main gateway.

The image sped along a winding smooth pure-white road to finish at the main building in the grounds. It continued into the building and flew its way across floors and ornate stairways before coming to a stop at a closed set of gold and thrinium-laden double doors, inset with scenes of battle magiis fighting monsters Chayne didn't know.

The door opened and the image went through to reveal a magii's lab many times the size of the one they currently stood.'

'I don't *want* this lab, Heathen. I *want* to return to my own.'

'That is your lab?' Chayne said, astounded.

Tristaric touch the illusionary wall, brushing over its surface like he was trying in some way to connect with it. A door opened on the far side of the illusionary lab and a woman walked in. Although in the distance, Chayne could see she was beautiful, her translucent dress showing her naked body beneath, flowing in the breeze as she walked. She smiled in their direction. Tristaric's hand moved over her image. His fingers closed as if trying to hold her tiny impression in his hand.

Suddenly, becoming aware of what he was doing, he withdrew his fingers from the manasphere, irritated by what he'd done. The image blinked out.

'I don't know why the Emperor sent me away, for some amusement of his own perhaps, but when my plans here are completed, I will be a hero across the Empire and he will be begging me back.'

Chayne couldn't believe the relationship between the Emperor and any of his cronies worked like that, but it was interesting to hear one of his closest so demean the ruler.

'It's why I'll not allow you to interfere with my work, heathen.'

'What if I did?' It was stupid to so openly defy the man, but somehow this Ashnorian's arrogance wound him up like no other he'd met. Continually referring to him and other Mlendrians as heathens, didn't help.

Tristaric picked up his staff and levelled it at a delicate set of glass tubes and bottles Chayne had connected in some experiment.

The largest of the bulbs containing the most liquid began to tip.

Chayne went forward to stop it.

Tristaric stabbed his staff forward an inch, sending the bulb over. It rolled into smaller, connected objects, pulling them apart and smashing some. Various liquids were spilled and mixed across the bench, some combinations reacting to produce smoke of different colours.

Chayne placed his fingers upon his manasphere and created a bubble field trapping the gas. The act seemed to surprise the master magii for moment.

'I'm taking charge of the magii shodatt from you, immediately.'

'I will oppose it,' replied Chayne, who had no idea if he could do it.

Tristaric seemed amused at the response. 'A single communication with the Ashnor magii assembly and your preposterous title will be revoked. Is that what you want?'

Chayne didn't. He needed the title, for it provided him with many privileges within the city making his movements and access easier. He shook his head.

'Then have your things and these experiments removed by first thing tomorrow. I want these benches cleared.'

'I have nowhere else to go.'

Tristaric shrugged.

'What about my studying and experimentation, some of these experiments are months old?'

Tristaric levelled his staff at the long row of delicate equipment. 'Easily solved.'

'Wait!'

Tristaric pulled his staff back to an upright position and headed for the door where he stopped and looked back. 'My task set by the Emperor will be completed, one way or another, on time. If your death is required to achieve that, it will be of no concern to me.'

He walked from the room.

Chayne sat down, contemplating his position. The magii could be bluffing, but if he wasn't the consequences were too dire. He dropped the fingers of one hand on his manasphere and raised the other hand in the direction of the tipped experiment. The bubble field capturing the gas drifted to a copper hood. A servant began pumping a lever that spun fan blades within the hood. Chayne released the field under the hood and the smoke was sucked away.

Other servants approached to clean up the mess and he gave the hand-signs for *danger* and *leave alone*.

He let go his manasphere and closed the box.

Tristaric didn't hold the menace of other masters, perhaps it was because he was younger. He did seem less predictable, though. With Lathashal you knew where you stood. Cross him, even on the slightest detail, and disproportionate punishment was assured. Tristaric on the other hand radiated a certain emotional volatility that was unsettling.

He needed an advantage, something unexpected to help him against this powerful magii. Lathashal somehow survived the attack after his shield collapsed. There was some kind of secondary shielding Chayne never discovered in the Great Library or from other magiis. He wondered if the master had uncovered something unique to him, something giving him the edge over his peers allowing his rise to power. If it could be found, it may be the advantage he needed, but there wasn't so much as a parchment on the man's work in his private quarters.

He looked to Lathashal's magically secured cabinet. He'd been in there several times since the magii's death, using the man's special key, and while some of the books were rare and couldn't be found in the great library, they held nothing unique giving the man any distinct advantage. Was it possible the man kept the knowledge in his head alone? Chayne dismissed the idea. The mathematica to manage the powerful spells was too long and intricate for even a master to risk to memory alone.

He took the key from his pocket and opened the cabinet. The key disengaged the shield magic long enough to remove or replace a book. Lathashal had taken no chances.

The mana shield disappeared and he dragged a block of books from the top shelf. They tumbled to the floor. The shield returned. He used the key again and repeated the procedure enough times to empty the cabinet before peering in through the glass. There was no sign of any hidden compartments or false sides.

Disappointed, he went about the task of reloading the books when a colour caught his peripheral vision. It seemed to come from below the lowest shelf, and yet there was nothing below but the base of the cupboard. Moving his head from side to side, something appeared and disappeared below it. He knew what it meant; an avoidance field was in place and running out of mana. Such a spell only worked if attention wasn't drawn to the subject matter. With concentration, suddenly, rows of worn notebooks appeared, filling the width of the cabinet and three layers deep on a shelf unseen until now. Some looked old and delicate, and he didn't want to risk handling them roughly. Opening the cabinet again, he used his manasphere to levitate the complete nearest row of books to the nearby bench.

Standing over them, his heart pounded. They were of the same style; thick with a ruby red cover and gold lettering. The ones on the left looked older, whereas the right-hand ones looked almost new. Whatever was in these books, Lathashal went to a great deal of trouble to ensure they wouldn't be found.

He took the newest rightmost book and opened it at the first page. What he saw made his eyes go wide. He flicked forward. It was half-full and he read the last entry. He closed the book and scanned across the others, counting them. Thirty-two in all. He took another out of the middle of the row and opened it at any page. He couldn't believe what he was seeing. He put it down too, as his eyes were drawn to the first book at the far back, still in the cabinet. He took up the key again, noticing his hand was trembling. He used the key and concentrated on the tome. It resisted for a moment before coming free. Dust and cracked leather fell away. He floated the thing out and brought it to his free hand. His fingers closed upon the fragile cover, not sure if the thing would fall apart in his hands.

Placing it on the bench, he sat down. Damp finger-marks darkening the cover from the sweat of anticipation. He opened the cover. It cracked and came free, being held by a few horse hairs used in the binding. Without risking damage to the first written page, he looked down upon the initial entry, swallowing hard at what he saw.

11th Agunii 961 – I have been accepted into the magii shodatt. There is such rivalry, I hope I can survive.

With great care, he opened the book in the centre.

23rd Jaii 962 – I was given two days leave. It was wonderful to see mother and father again. They were very excited about my advancement. Sadly, students are not allowed to take home manaspheres, so I was unable to demonstrate what I learned. They seemed to think I was harder, but that's parents for you – always needing something to worry about.

He thumbed through some more to an entry many pages on.

12th Juii 964 – Returned from my visit with mother and father. They were becoming irritating, asking questions about what I have been doing and why I am so cold now. They are so stupid. I've changed for the better, toughening up in readiness for the life of a magii. I've never noticed how trivial they are in their meaningless lives.

A page at the end stood out from the rest, due to its crinkled edges. He turned the page. It was affected by splashes of water.

17th Febrii 969
They are dead. I hadn't intended to do it. They became so boorish of my views and work. I stood over their ripped and blooded bodies with the knife. How could I have felt anything for them before?
I feel nothing now

The final words were underlined and etched hard into the parchment, as if written in anger. There were signs of drops of water just after. Was the last phrase a showing of inner conflict of his feelings? Was the watery punctuation tears?

He closed the tome. The rows of books represented the missing research notes. Lathashal's diaries from the very first day of his inauguration into the discipline of magic. Over four-hundred years of insight into the man's life, his thoughts, his experiments and his political manipulations since becoming a student magii.

Such a find was of immeasurable value. If it was discovered by the others, they would fight for it. It was going to take years to read, understand and practice the many lifetimes of gathered and researched knowledge.

A thought then struck him. He placed the first diary in a draw and began taking others, trying to locate a particular moment. It became hours of painstaking work, but finally he came across the entry he was looking for. It represented around a century ago:

16th Juii 1251 – Prellious has informed me manaspheres contain demons!!! Such things I believed to be myth, but I have seen one with my own eyes. It is terrifying to think I challenge one of these evil things each time I use a manasphere. Why would they risk such a thing?

What changed the man's views? At the end of his life he was comfortable using the manaspheres knowing they contained demons, and even dealing directly with them.

He began removing the remaining books. He had to get them hidden from Tristaric.

Chapter 9 – Separation

Kinfular lay low behind scrub with what was left of his decimated party. His scout had been one of the casualties, and without him to guide them, and in their eagerness to return home, they'd run into of one of the nomadic tribes on the plains. Generations of conflict had reduced the plain's barbarians to a few large groups, each with a few hundred families. The one before them looked to be one of the largest, which meant a strong warrior force. Their only chance to avoid detection was the darkness, and they were four, providing less chance to be noticed.

He looked back at his three companions. ThreeSwords, so named for the triple scabbard on his back, his skin as black as the night sky itself, wielded two swords. The hilt of the centre sword was wrapped in cloth and no one had seen him draw it, ignoring questions about it. His enigmatic character causing him to speak rarely. Then came Sholster, a near-seven foot aberration who carried a weapon and shield to match. His unique brand of rallying cries in battle did as much to bolster the courage of the men around him as the destruction he caused. Fiercely loyal to Kinfular, it was like having his own personal army. Lastly his eyes fell upon Shinlay. Beautiful and unmatched with the bow, and his concubine for many years. She'd followed them, defying the decree of her father, their tribal chieftain.

Now all four of them were returning home. Kinfular to face the disgrace of losing his men, and Shinlay to face her father's wrath and judgement for disobeying him. Utal was growing old, and there was a pretender to the leadership, Baltrac, who would make much of the opportunity to seize the clan from a chieftain who cannot even control his own daughter.

Over recent days, Kinfular's pride had made him act rashly to lose his men in an ambush. Only the four of them escaped due to this headstrong woman. It was the tribe's way for the men to dominate their women, but events had weakened his position and strengthened hers in a way he would never have thought possible.

Without a brother, she was the only blood Utal had to carry on the leadership of the tribe, and a woman had never ruled them. It was possible she could soon be the first, but she would now have to prove herself and establish her right to lead.

She caught him staring at her and looked up, her large brown eyes reflecting the starlight. She smiled and he felt a wave travel through him from foot to head. He took a deep breath to help cleanse the feelings. Warriors did not love.

She was having to be their replacement scout, a task for which she lacked adequate experienced.

'Your judgment?' he said.

'We should back out and find our way around.' She looked unsure, her response almost questioning for approval.

Kinfular's impatience showed through. 'It will mean heading back towards the Yellowskins. If they are coming after us, we may run into them. If we go around, there is no guarantee we won't meet another tribe, anyway. Can we not continue through?'

Shinlay wanted to please her mate, but they had to face the truth. 'The plainsmen's scouts will be far better at seeing us than I will them. This is their homeland.'

'The Yellowskin called Stalizar said his spell would protect us from detection.'

'We cannot trust to magic, Hlenshar!' said Sholster, voicing the usual fear of magic he shared with all barbarians.

'He also said it would last a short time,' ThreeSwords reminded.

'Then we rely upon Shinlay's skills.'

'She is no Rainen, Hlenshar,' said ThreeSwords in his usual matter-of-fact way, ignoring Shinlay's feelings. The Heslarian spoke rarely, making his occasional words have all the more effect.

'Your suggestion?' Kinfular said.

'I offer no other suggestion, Hlenshar. I shall, as always, follow your lead.'

Kinfular knew his men would follow him without question, but until the events of a few days ago he'd never made a serious error. Now most of his men were dead, and his impatience was to blame. He'd then attempted to exorcise the demons of his guilt with a vengeful encounter against those not even responsible for his loss. Many died by his hand, including a young man who stood no chance against him. It was an act bringing him to his senses. Even so, he felt both the men now before him retained at least a little doubt over his current choices.

'I see no alternative. Also, any Yellowskin pursuit would be forced to give up against the idea of moving through the plainsman. We would be free of having them follow us back to the tribe.'

As if supporting the decision, fast moving clouds began to sweep across from behind them obscuring the starshine. Kinfular instructed Shinlay forward.

She led the group off at a jog, deeper into the camp. Her task was all the more difficult considering the seven-foot Sholster, who stuck out in any setting. He had at least bound his huge metal club in cloth to prevent it from reflecting light from the various camp fires.

As they deepened their incursion she led them between the broadest gaps amid individual family campfires. A patrol appeared on the edge of sight and she slowed to a walk and relaxed into a saunter as if native to the camp. Their leather clothing wasn't an exact match for the plainsmen, but it might prove good enough to disguise them if they kept enough distance. She adjusted her direction to create the best advantage. The patrol walked on without seeing them.

For half-an-hour, the tactic had working flawlessly, but now they were entering a more populated area she had been trying to avoid. Instead of scouting around the outskirts of the camp, it now looked as though they were passing near to the centre.

The tents became tighter spaced and the population thickened. She could sense the staring eyes of several plainsmen. She fought to keep her calm as the denser campfires raised the level of light.

A young plainswoman then crossed their path with her head down and struggling with a heavy double pail of water upon her shoulders. At the last moment she looked up and was caught by surprise at Sholster's size. She jumped and the pails slid from her grasp to the ground. Shinlay kept walking, trying to lead them from the point of attention, but Sholster stopped and lifted the heavy wooden pails up for tribe girl. Wary of the man, she allowed him to replace the largely-spilt pails back into position. She thanked him. The words were accented with the plainsmen's dialect, but understandable. Sholster, not realising his mistake, replied politely.

The plainswoman recognised the strange mountain accent and her eyes opened wide darting around, alarmed. Sholster backed away, trying to indicate he was no threat.

'Run!' said Kinfular.

They sped off as the girl entered the nearest tent. A group of men came out with bows and swords, and gave chase, collecting more men as they ran.

Then a single scream split the night to the left. A woman was standing, her face in horror. She stopped screaming long enough for two words to ring out as she pointed at ThreeSwords.

'Black Devil!'

'We're going to be caught at this pace,' Kinfular said referring to the slower Sholster. 'Split up. ThreeSwords and I shall draw them away. Get clear and wait for us at Ironclaws. If we're not there by sunrise then head home.'

Shinlay shot a glance at her mate, worried for him, but the seasoned warrior was already away, making for the better lit areas where they would be seen.

Jungar was first out of the tent and caught a glimpse of the woman. She was a rare beauty and he wanted her. He was the youngest son and yet to have earned his mate. Watching his father and brothers head in the direction of the devil, he headed off after her alone. His young legs soon brought her into view. She had the huge one with her, but while she had a bow, her quiver was empty. Jungar was good with his bow and the giant was an easy target from this distance. If he could bring him down it would be an easy task to subdue a woman and claim her. He would be the envy of his brothers, and make his father proud.

Once in the outer parts of the camp, the sub-tribes thinned and he followed his quarry into a wide open area. The woman kept changing direction and almost lost him at one point, but his god was with him as the clouds parted, providing starlight to keep them in view. He got within bow range and set his arrow. Sprinting hard to give him time to stop and fire, he slid to a sudden halt and took aim. The arrow sped off looking true. He hadn't quite taken into account the distance his target would move away while running and the arrow dropped below its intended point. It flew into the lower leg of the giant, who went down. Now he would be alerted and at a difficult angle, but Jungar would not be deprived his prize. He took another arrow and aimed. He watched in amazement, as in one fluid motion, the woman stopped, pulled her bow from her back, yanked the arrow from the giant's leg and fired almost without aiming as his own arrow left his bow.

Shinlay knew the plainsmen's arrow was on target and her attempt to duck was too slow. Then there was a thud as the arrow plunge into the top edge of Sholster's shield.

'You move fast for a big man.'

'Given time to think, I may have not bothered after you ripped that arrow out of my leg.'

'How is it?'

Sholster stood with difficulty. 'Deep into the muscle. It'll get me back home.'

Shinlay cut a strip from the barbarian's ample soft leather jerkin and tied it over the wound to quell the bleeding. 'You think they'll follow us into the mountains?'

'Well I doubt his death will be put down to suicide,' Sholster replied, looking back to the arrow sticking in the young man's chest.

'Then we'll hide within Ironclaws and wait for Kin to find us.'

The two moved off at little more than walking pace, Sholster limping.

Kinfular and ThreeSwords ran south trying to keep ahead of the wave of shouts following them, but it overtook them and now they were trapped, ringed by plainsmen warriors with many more arriving. A large plainsman carrying a torch pushed his way through the ring to break into the centre. The plainsmen in general looked old before their time due to the amount of sun they received on the plains, drying out their brown skin, but this one looked older than most. He walked right up to them, unarmed and looking unconcerned by the weapons they carried. Neither of them made a threatening move.

The torch carrier peered at Kinfular, looking into his eyes and then up and down at his clothing, weapon and shield. 'Grun taug,' he said, and a murmur went up from the circle of plainsmen. It meant nothing to Kinfular. The plainsman pointed to Kinfular's sword, knife and shield indicating he throw them away. Kinfular, seeing no choice, did so. ThreeSwords copied.

The man then waved his hand again, and some men broke from the circle and collected the weapons. He then walked away. As he left the circle so the plainsmen rushed in. Kinfular was held by several men and pulled away while ThreeSwords was pulled to the ground. The plainsmen began punching and kicking him. Kinfular shouted out, and fought against his holders. He pulled an arm free and landed a powerful blow to the jaw of the nearest plainsmen knocking him to the ground. The others holding him responded and clamped him tight. The struck warrior got to his feet and directed several blows to Kinfular's face and stomach, making him buckle under the attack, before being dragged away. He craned his neck around in an attempt to catch a glimpse of his friend, but the black warrior was surrounded by a sea of the plainsmen, continuing their brutal attack.

Lesh returned with his two eldest sons from the devil hunt. His three wives were inside with knives drawn protecting their youngest.

'Worry not, we have the devil and the Peaksman. Where is Jungar?'

'He went after the girl and the giant,' said his eldest wife. She was in her fifties and as handsome a woman now as when he won her in his teens. 'He wanted the woman and set out alone to take her. He is not with you?'

Lesh cursed. 'That boy couldn't find his way to the bottom of a river. We'll go get him.'

His missing son left an easy path to follow, ending at the foot of his body. Roan checked for a heartbeat and wasn't surprised to find none. He checked the arrow and found Jungar's mark on it. 'They used his own arrow to kill him,' he spat, bitterly.

Lesh checked his dead son's quiver. 'He fired two arrows. Find the other.'

The two brothers spread out with torches aloft to cover the area. Brank soon called back, 'Here!'

They converged and Lesh took the arrow. Wooden splinters clinging to the head.'

'Do you think they plucked the arrow from a shield and fired it back?' questioned Brank.

Lesh looked down and spotted the glint of wet in the sand. He dabbed his finger into it and smelt it. 'Blood,' he informed.

'So he hit one of them, they are wounded?' Brank said. 'We could catch them and return them to the Chieftain.'

Lesh looked in the direction of the parting tracks towards the mountains, hatred in his eyes. 'No, my son. We'll track them, then take our time enacting our revenge for Jungar.

Chapter 10 – Orders

Tristaric pulsed the magic code and passed through the new defences surrounding his commandeered lab. With the Mlendrian evicted he'd some space to work on the initial experiments for his intended solution.

His earlier visit to the heathen was incautious. He'd shown too much of his own world, his use of the scene projector in Lathashal's lab opening him up to his longing to return home. The appearance of Xrearna in the scene was unexpected, his own subconscious creating the image. The heathen saw her in a way only Tristaric had. The thought riled him. The Zintar had to die.

He rested his staff against one of the room's experiment benches. Snapping his fingers at a chair, a servant brought it to him and he sat down. He was still tired from his long journey and the need to maintain constant vigilance from possible attack. If the heathens could get to someone as adept as Lathashal and kill him, then as his replacement, his own life would be targeted next.

His eyes glanced across at the rows of gradia ten manaspheres the dead magii charged for the invasion. It was useful to have such a supply and would save him time with his experiments into his alternative solution. He knew what he was proposing had never been achieved before. All had tried and died.

He closed his eyes to relax for a moment. Such negative thoughts would not do.

'A touching moment with the projection wall.'

Tristaric open his eyes and grabbed his staff. Something sticky on it caused pain making him let go. His hand became paralysed and it spread throughout his body.

'She has you like a love-struck Yamin. She's playing you for the influence you provide her.'

Tristaric felt a prick in the side of his mouth and his jaw became free. 'Release my body,' he yelled. 'I come from the Emperor's side.'

'As do I.'

Tristaric couldn't turn his head to see the face of the voice. 'I have spent years with the Emperor, and never heard your voice before.'

'Yet I know you,' the voice replied.

'The Emperor would not keep such a person from my knowledge,' Tristaric rasped, straining with everything he had against the paralysis, making no progress.

'You can't kill him, you know.'

Tristaric kept fighting the drug preventing him from moving. Not a muscle would respond. 'There isn't a living soul in this backwater I couldn't snuff out. Who are you talking about?'

'The Mlendrian.'

'The heathen! He's getting in the way of my orders. I'll do as I please, and I want him dead.'

'I have orders from the Emperor too. Until my work is done here, the Mlendrian will remain unharmed. You will do as I say or there will be unpleasant consequences.'

'Consequences,' Tristaric sneered. 'I'm going to find you, reduce you to ash and have you swept away. Only the Emperor can order me.'

Another tiny dart stuck in the back of his hand.

Movement returned to his body and he pulled his utility staff from his robe and spun around.

The room was empty again. He scanned the walls for human thoughts, finding no readings.

So the Emperor had sent a yhordi assassin to ensure he didn't fail. But what was the significance to the Emperor of a heathen? Or was it just another typical move by the monarch to keep those close to him off-balance by giving full autonomy to two people to act as required in his name with conflicting goals?

He didn't like threats over his own head, and insults from a yhordi about Xrearna's true love for him, even less, but it was part of the games the Emperor liked to play. No, he would have to dispose of the Zintar without even an Emperor-dispatched assassin knowing he was the agent. It would remove both threats in one move; the Zintar would be dead, and the yhordi would have failed the Emperor and be put to death.

Chapter 11 – Call to Arms

Stimm took the gift of Kaliden Granderier cigars from Brinley. Sitting down, he slit the seal on the guilt-edged display box and removed one of the fine smokes. He then went about the ritual of removing the end with a silver cutter. All the while the trader on the other side of the desk negotiated the precarious operation of landing his bulk into the guest chair. Stimm lit the cigar and drew on it creating little flares of flame igniting the tightly rolled leaves. It was one of the many luxuries coming his way since joining up with the wealthy trader. The man was quite repellent to look at and to smell. Not that he smelled of sweat, although it could be detected in the mix. No, it was the cloying pervasion of oils and spices the man overused to obscure his lack of general hygiene. It filled the room requiring Stimm to endure an hour of chill with windows and doors open to clear it after each of the man's visits.

He took his first long drag on the cigar and settled back into his chair, placing his feet up on the corner of the desk. He watched as Brinley gave a grunt, squeezing into position the last roll of fat resisting moving past the arm of the chair. It dropped into place, releasing a sigh from the man.

'Invest in some luxury furniture,' Brinley admonished.

Stimm blew out a long plume of smoke that travelled to the top of the cabin and flattened out amongst the rafters. 'It wouldn't be so good for the discipline of the men. They don't come in here to be pampered.'

'Well, I'm not one of your men. I'll have a chair delivered. Make sure it's in place each time I call.'

Stimm dropped his eyes down to the trader. He didn't like being spoken to in such a manner by a civilian. Beads of sweat permanently inhabited the folds of the man's red, bloated face, giving his thinning fair hair a constant greasy look. But the man was a scheming businessman of no equal, who came to own much of the trade flowing into and out of Tiburn. Stimm didn't like him, but he was rich, and being in his pocket in such an influential position as Barracks Commander meant Brinley paid highly for his co-operation. He also wasn't a man to upset, so it was best to give up some of the normal authority he portrayed when dealing with civilians.

He nodded his head just enough to be noticed, attempting to mask any weakness. 'I'm sure it can be arranged.'

Brinley snapped his fingers. Strack, the trader's right-hand man, left the window he was peering from. Strack was a veteran of the wrong kind, in every way, working with the trader for many years. He wasn't the normal brainless hired thug, he was chosen by Brinley for his intellect, which was more of the cunning sort than educated. He also controlled his own network of muscle and informants proving invaluable to the trader.

He walked over to his benefactor and handed some parchments before returning to his lookout position.

Brinley lifted the first one and digested the information.

'You have reduced the guard on route twelve.'

Stimm took a moment to recollect which route the number represented. Brinley insisted on using a simple coding to obscure the meaning of his documents should they fall into the hands of the authorities he hadn't yet bribed. It was the secondary trade route running north down to Coots Bay, once a vibrant community acting as a port for luxury goods before the Empire captured its points outside of Mlendria. 'The thaw is here, bandits are venturing from the mountains again. I need to keep the southern outposts well-manned.'

'I don't trade south. I need my northern caravans protected. The value they contain is far beyond anything masquerading as trade through the mountains.'

'More valuable to you perhaps,' Stimm said. 'The mining communities rely on us, and we are increasing trade with the barbarians every year.'

'Those mines are almost dry,' Brinley rebuked. 'They should be shut down. And we should not be increasing our ties with the barbarians, their goods are of poor quality.'

Stimm couldn't help a smile. 'I have heard their leatherworking is exceptional, and people prefer them to your offerings. I think you're more concerned the barbarians transport their own goods to us, and you aren't getting a cut.'

Brinley took on a dangerous calm. 'My good fortune is your good fortune, Stimm. If I find you're unable to provide the service I need, you may find yourself falling back down the ranks as fast as you have risen.'

Stimm knew Brinley had a hand in his rapid promotions, and didn't doubt the man could reverse his luck. He gave up his smile. 'I'll see to it.'

'We have a guest,' Strack said, looking out the window.

'They can wait,' Brinley said.

Stimm gave the man a glare for giving the instruction in his own cabin. Brinley returned the gaze, eyes steady. It was Stimm who broke off first.

'It's Falakar,' Strack said.

Stimm withdrew his legs from the desk, not resisting the urge to sit up straight.

Brinley laughed at him. 'The man's not even a formal Ranger anymore, and yet even a barracks commander jumps to the sound of the man's name.'

'Hide those papers,' Stimm said.

'Calm yourself. The Ghost Ranger is a spent force. His leverage was through Lindeg, and he's no longer here. Tell your men not to let him in.'

Stimm faltered for a moment before flicking a hand at one his two internal guards. The guard left the hut to join the two on the porch, closing the door behind him.

There was some discussion heard from outside. Falakar's voice became louder as the conversation continued.

Stimm reacted nervously.

'Just stand your ground,' Brinley said. 'He'll be rendered useless.'

The hut shook and shouting came from outside the door, alarming even Brinley. 'By the gods, what in all hells is going on out there?'

Stimm rose from his chair as the door to the hut opened revealing the outline of the Ranger. Stimm's remaining guard pulled his sword halfway from its scabbard, hesitant.

'Don't be ridiculous, man,' Falakar said in even tones. It wasn't a threat, more a statement of absurdity.

Stimm gestured him to stand down. The sword was slid back. Out beyond Falakar at the bottom of the stairs the three men were brushing the dirt from their leathers. One of them, Denin, didn't stand for the humiliation and rushed up the steps.

Without looking back, Falakar stepped into the room, pushing the door with his heal to have it click shut just as Denin reached it. It shook, almost popping the hinges.

With the silhouette gone, the light revealed the Ranger's face.

'Falakar,' Stimm said, evenly.

The door burst open. The weakened upper hinge gave up and splintered off. Denin faltered as the leading edge of the door dug in causing the man following to stumble into him. Both went sprawling onto the floor. Stimm's look conveyed something unpleasant was going to happen to them in their near future.

'Idiots.'

The men got to their feet. Denin gave Falakar a look of wanting his revenge.

'I wouldn't consider doing what you're thinking, Denin.'

'He made a fool of me!'

'You are a fool,' Stimm replied. 'Now get out and send the carpenter over here to fix the door.'

Denin gave another dangerous look to Falakar before storming out of the hut.

Falakar waited for the men to leave before turning on Stimm. 'What are you doing in charge?'

Stimm waved the remaining guard and Strack from the room. Strack didn't move. Stimm didn't push it.

'I think the code of behaviour is to address him as *Major* Stimm,' Brinley said, after the door was pulled shut as best it could.

Falakar ignored the trader.

'Where's Lindeg?'

Stimm tightened a little at seeing the Ranger giving no response to the trader's remarks. 'You think he's untouched by ageing? You have been gone six months this time.'

Falakar's expression changed. 'Is he…?'

'No, he's alive, but his lungs couldn't take another damp winter. They retired him from the plateau to the North. The Bay of Waves, I think. He asked me to pass on his farewell. He waited for you until the last moment, hoping to see you.'

Falakar felt pained to have let the old man down so.

'You were close, I understand,' Brinley said.

'He was my mentor in the early days. Between us we were responsible for the reinvention of the Rangers into the modern form.'

'I had no idea,' Brinley lied. 'I thought your statues were earned through murder in the field?'

Stimm watched as Falakar resisted the taunt. He'd gone rogue years ago as his obsession to hunt down the bandit Jontal took over everything. Now, with Lindeg gone and

Brinley sitting in the room, it wouldn't be hard for the veteran Ranger to put together why Stimm was smoking cigars way out of his pay range. He needed to assert his authority. He sat back down, drawing on his cigar and puffing another grey cloud of smoke into the air above him.

Brinley stirred in his chair in an unsuccessful effort to face Falakar. 'I'm in an important debriefing on security of the trade routes. Perhaps you could come back later.'

Falakar looked at the man for the first time. Brinley was a big fish in the medium pond that was the far southern edge of Mlendria. He was well known to all in the district as a ruthless merchant who accrued his wealth through the creation of an extensive trading network.

The Ranger turned back to Stimm without answering the trader. 'I need to issue a Code Twelve.'

Stimm stopped puffing at his cigar. 'None of my men have reported anything unusual in the area. The bandits couldn't amass such a frontal attack, and last I heard the barbarians were on our side. Why should I call in the main army?'

'Ashnorians.'

'The Empire?' Stimm said, incredulous. 'They haven't attacked for fifty years. I have over a hundred men in the mountains, none have reported tens of thousands of armoured soldiers pouring through the passes.'

'The attack will take place in three months.'

'How do you know this?'

Falakar pulled out a parchment and dropped it onto Stimm's desk.

Stimm reached out and unrolled it. 'A map of the Hammerheads with strange symbols. So what?'

'It's part of an Ashnorian invasion plan.'

Brinley gestured to Stimm who flicked the parchment to the trader. He gave it a cursory glance. 'These could be anything. Educational drawings perhaps.' He threw it back to the desk.

'I was given it by one of their senior healers. He is responsible for setting up the field hospitals along the front line,' Falakar replied.

'You've been into Ashnoria?' Stimm said, dangerously.

'To the first city.'

'On whose authority?'

'I need no authority, technically I'm a civilian.'

'You of all people are well aware of the standing orders. All incursions into Ashnoria require authorisation from G11.'

'Then I made a field decision.'

'And risked incurring a response,' Brinley reproached. 'If these plans show an attack, how do we know it isn't in retaliation for your incursion?'

Falakar began to show his patience was wearing thin with the trader. 'I believe such discussions should be within the military, and civilians not be present.'

Brinley scoffed. 'You choose to call yourself a civilian when it suits you, and soldier at other times. I doubt you're useful as either now.'

Falakar tipped Brinley's chair back to balance on two legs making the trader feel he was going to fall, giving out a yelp. Strack leapt forward and Falakar stopped the man with a glare. Brinley's fat wobbled as he unnecessarily tried to get his balance, being perfectly maintained by Falakar. The Ranger pushed his face close to the trader's, whose sweat had doubled already.

'The meticulous planning of Ashnorian invasions is a lengthy process. They use a spell which alone takes months to prepare. If we hadn't stopped it they would be here already. It will take another three months to recast it, at least.'

Falakar lowered the trader's chair back down onto four legs.

Brinley mopped his face with a handkerchief, recovering some composure. 'Inconclusive scaremongering. No barracks commander would dare risk making himself look such a fool, calling in the army on such evidence. If you're wrong, Stimm would be demoted in an instant. Or is that your plan, perhaps? Getting too old, Ghost Ranger? Time to find an easy position to keep some of your former glory? Perhaps you were going to offer Lindeg the chance to retire?'

Stimm intervened. 'None of our best operatives have made it as far as their nearest city.'

'Yet,' Brinley continued, supporting his crony, 'you claim to have reached it and made a senior healer provide detailed information. Do you even speak Ashnorian?'

'They can turn their magic to translate what we say,' Falakar answered.

'Oh, very convenient,' Brinley snorted. 'If they're so powerful, why don't they turn us all into frogs and be done with it.'

Falakar retrieved the battle plan, rolling it up. He looked to Stimm. 'I don't know how far you're in his pocket, but I hope for all our sakes it doesn't go far beyond expensive cigars.'

Stimm couldn't respond to the accusation.

This seemed to be enough for Falakar, who turned and made for the door. 'I'm calling a meeting with the council.'

'I will oppose any call on the army without further investigation,' Stimm called to the Ranger's back. 'Without my support it will not be sanctioned for action.'

Falakar pulled open the door which gave up and came free in his hand and clattered to the floor. He turned back to Stimm. 'One last thing? I noticed a coded flash-signal earlier from the mountains. It wasn't one I recognised. I'd like the cypher.'

'Cyphers are for Rangers only,' Stimm said.

'Lindeg allowed me access to new cyphers.'

Stimm just stared back and took another draw on his cigar.

Falakar pursed his lips to curb his response and left.

Stimm sat back, relived the man was gone. 'They didn't look like educational drawings to me. And he's not a man to raise an alarm without good reason.'

'Send out patrols, if you must,' Brinley protested. 'But I want any news straight to me first.'

'What about the Code Twelve?'

Brinley shrugged. 'If the stories are to be believed then nothing will stop the Empire. If you want to feel safe, I've a boat moored, kept ready in a small fishing village on the northern peninsula. From there I can head out across the North Sea to some remote islands even the Empire wouldn't bother with. We could stay there for the remainder of our lives, without detection.'

'You would doom Tiburn and its people?'

'They would be doomed the moment the Empire looked this way. There would be nothing either of us could do.' Brinley pulled himself free of the tight-fitting chair, adjusting his robe to get the creases out. 'Just make sure my southern trade routes are looked after. And get that chair replaced.'

As the trader left the cabin, Strack gave a departing smirk. Stimm knew what the look meant. The man considered him nothing more than a lackey, a bought soul. Maybe it was true, but Stimm was still a military man at heart, and if he could save the town, he would.

He dragged on his cigar and it returned a sour taste. He looked to see it had gone out. For a moment it reminded him of himself. He flicked his wrist, throwing the thing against the far wall.

Chapter 12 – Meeting of Demons

Chantel's cat tail swished from side to side. She didn't like Chaynie's new room. It was smaller and smelt musty. It was also very different from their old home in the woods from where she'd followed him after his capture months ago by the Empire.

She'd been with him years since one of his spells misfired and sucked her from her world into his. It wasn't supposed to be possible. She'd arrived disorientated and saw him unconscious on the floor. There was smoke rising from every surface in the small wooden-walled room as if some great energy had been released. He was like her, only without scales, and his legs were straight and his skin pale. She decided he must be some kind of *smooth demon*.

She didn't know what to do and left the place.

Months of surviving off the creatures in the surrounding woods, she then became hunted by the *smooth-demons* who were afraid of her. Then she learned of a curious new ability she had in this world; she could change her shape. She studied the smooth demons in their settlements from a distance and found they liked small furry creatures they called cats. She returned to the cabin in which she was summoned. With only the initial smooth demon there, the risk would be small. She changed into cat form and wandered up. He took her in and they were together ever since, although she dared not show her true form.

The other smooth demons would call him Chayne, but one of the female smooth demons used to call him Chaynie. She liked it and so that was her name for him.

She looked down from her new perch behind the bulbous glass jars on a high shelf. They made the room warp into an even tinier space allowing her to see everywhere at once. Chaynie would chuckle at seeing her behind one. It was a sound she enjoyed hearing.

Right now she looked down at him with curiosity. It was a feeling becoming more compelling the longer she stayed in cat form. His hand was on the shiny ball again. He would sit like it for hours. Soon though, he would leave to eat, that meant he would be gone for some time.

His eyes opened and he lifted his hand free, stretching out his arms and looking very happy with himself. He hummed a little noise, and left the room.

It was time to sate her curiosity about the ball.

She jumped down before shaped-changing into her new smooth-skinned female form. It was something she worked hard to create. Her long golden curls flowed down over her shoulders in the way of the females who attracted the most mates.

Speaking the word Chayne used to open the box with the ball, it gave a tiny click and the lock sprung open. She raised the golden ball out of the box until the mechanism locked in place with a soft click. Closing her eyes she spread her hands over it, feeling it pull at her mind. She let it happen and opened her eyes to find the room was gone and everywhere was dark, tinged with a misty pale-blue colour. The feeling of being pulled was stronger here and she felt herself falling. It wasn't pleasant and she resisted it, immediately slowing to a stop. On the edge of her hearing was a sound. It was a voice all too familiar.

'Silly mage, now you are mine. You will come with me to my home, die horrible death and give Zystal power.'

In the distance she began to see an aura. It was blood red, and getting larger. In this place it was difficult to judge distance, and she couldn't be sure of its size. One thing was clear – it was another demon.

It came close enough for them to see each other through the mist and it stopped its advance.

'*Nonononoonoooooo!*' It spun on its heels and went to run. Chantel wanted it to stop and somehow the creature began to run on the spot. She pulled with her mind and it slid backwards against the running motion. It screamed and its legs burst into a sprint of speed making them rotate into a blur of movement. It kept coming until it was just in front of her. She grabbed it by its sinewy neck and rotated it until it was facing her, its eyes inches from her.

'*Please don't eat me, mistress,*' it squirmed.

'Why are you in here, little one?'

'*The masters trapped me, as they have you.*' Its arms and legs grappled and pushed at her arm.

'I am not trapped. I am here because I want to be.'

'*Why would Mistress want to come here?*' it said, still interested in escape.

'I was curious, what is this place?'

'*It is a demon-prison, mistress. The masters trap us and make us store mana for them.*'

It dug its claws in her arm. She shook it once by its throat to calm it, and it stopped fighting.

'You store mana willingly?'

'*Yes, mistress. If we collect enough, we can open the portal that brought us here, and go home.*'

'Why do you not control the masters when pulling mana through them?'

'*I have tried. They are too powerful and wicked to me.*'

Chantel knew the little demon had to be talking about Chaynie. 'Your current master is wicked to you?' If he was cruel to his demon, he would be the same with her when he found out the truth.

'*No, mistress. The nice master is kind to Zystal. He helped Zystal, and even healed him after terrible fight with Glzatcherous.*'

'Such demons exist in this place!' She looked around, alarmed.

'*No, mistress. It came to punish me for helping the nice master. A different, terrible master, helped it get to me from another prison, but the nice master stopped it and healed me.*'

'Your current master is the *nice master*?'

'*Yes, mistress.*'

So the metal balls were prisons for demons of different power. It seemed she got lucky by connecting to one with a minor demon far below her caste. She released her grip on him. 'You can scurry off now.'

It turned and fled.

'Oh, little one,' she called after it.

'*Yes, mistress,*' came the response from the distant mist.

'If you ever tell any master about me, I shall return here when nice master is away, like now, and be very wicked to you.'

'*Yes, mistress,*' came the dejected reply.

She thought about the outside again and it felt like she was rising. At some point the mistiness gave way to Chaynie's room. She saw herself holding the ball again, and removed her hand.

So Chaynie would be good to her if he found out she was a demon.

It was time to take their relationship to the next level.

Chapter 13 – The Council

Garamon sat against the back wall of the council room, several paces behind Falakar who was seated at the foot of the long council table. The council room was dreary after three days with the Ranger in the forest being taught fighting and tracking techniques. Opposite Falakar at the head of the table sat Dering, the Commissioner Prime for Tiburn and the surrounding areas. Down either side of the table sat the other council members, most of whom had bothered to turn up because Dering was attending, which gave the meeting importance. It brought the council to its maximum presence of twenty-four.

Two Rangers at each of the two doors ensured the meeting would not be disturbed.

Garamon was waiting for his moment to give his testimony. He'd never spoken to such an intimidating group before. Dering was currently talking. The man's brown and grey hair provided for a distinguished look suiting his position. His reputation also preceded him. A good man by all accounts, firm and fair. He looked calm and in control. To his left sat Major Stimm, the man responsible with maintaining peace in the area, and the man in charge of the local barracks. Garamon had been warned of him by Falakar, who considered the man weak.

The other side of Dering sat Archmage Thrane, who by Mlendrian standards was a most capable manipulator of magic. His clothes were bright compared to the councillors, with silver sequins sown into his dark blue robe. Garamon now knew the man's magic, and clothing for that matter, was a pale comparison to an Ashnorian magii's.

The rest were other important people in the town, representing the various trades and utilities Tiburn required to function.

All accept one – *Trader Brinley*.

His reputation also preceded him, but for the opposite reasons to Dering. Falakar explained he carried influence over decisions in the area, as his business skills brought the town a higher profile across Mlendria than would otherwise exist. This, in turn, brought jobs to the people, and knock-on wealth to the other business owners. He would, however, oppose any call-to-arms, as this would put more Rangers in the area and Tiburn coming under military rule. Brinley ran a network of unofficial lines of trade undercutting his competitors. Such a network would be exposed to greater scrutiny to operate by the rules with a high military presence. His profits would diminish.

The meeting was in progress for an hour and things were coming to a head. Brinley branded his silk handkerchief around with flourish like a sword as he raged at Falakar.

'This is absurd! The Empire gave up conquering over fifty years ago, they knew the challenge of taking Mlendria wouldn't be worth their time.'

Even from behind, Garamon could tell Falakar was struggling to maintain his patience.

'As I stated before,' Falakar replied, 'we now know the old Emperor died some months ago. His replacement does not share the need for caution and has already assembled an army large enough to swamp our current defences.'

'Then where are they man!' Brinley exploded. 'If they have such overwhelming numbers, why are we not seeing the glint of a thousand swords streaming down out of the mountains?'

'I already told you,' Falakar said in a voice betraying he was holding his temper by a thread. 'Due to our intervention, we prevented the casting of a powerful detection spell, delaying the attack.'

'A detection spell,' Brinley scoffed. 'With the overpowering troops you claim, why would they bother with such things?'

'I do not pretend to know the details of Ashnorian tactics. They are a secretive people, as you are well aware.'

Garamon could just see Archmage Thrane raise a forefinger. Such was the presence of the reserved man, it quietened even Brinley.

'You must admit, Falakar, all this does seem quite difficult for us to believe. If it were not you standing before us making such a claim, the council would have not taken up this special session. Even so, it stretches even your reputation to call upon the council to raise the army based upon the dubious claims you're making. We all know the Empire rebuffs outsiders, taking great efforts to keep their way of life hidden from us. None of our best scouts have returned from such a deep incursion, and yet you tell us you led three barbarians, a captured thief and this young woodcutter into their very midst, infiltrating a large city and killing a powerful magii, then escaping.'

There was a loud snort from Brinley. Murmurs from the rest of the councillors seemed to indicate agreement.

The Councillor Prime raised his hand to bring quiet to the room. 'Let us hear from the woodsman. His father has often spoken with us and is respected within the council. Perhaps he shares some of his father's wisdom in these matters.'

Falakar beckoned Garamon to the table.

Garamon swallowed hard and got to his feet. He watched the sea of faces staring at him as he approached. Some were looking back to their notes, shaking their heads at the waste of time. Brinley was grinning.

Dering indicated he should sit down.

'I would rather stand, sir,' he said. His voice sounded timid. He cleared his throat.

'As you wish. Please tell Archmage Thrane what happened when you attacked the Ashnorian magii.'

'Yes, sir. It all happened rather fast, so there isn't much to tell. I was helped by an Ashnorian woman who showed me a secret door to the magii's room. When I opened the door I could see the magii holding my friend against the far wall using magic. He was crushing him to death. I shouted out and the magii turned. He flicked his head toward me and I flew backwards to hit the wall behind, dazing me for several seconds. When my senses returned, I saw my friend floating in front of the magii. I rushed forward to hit the magii in the back with my axe. There was some kind of invisible barrier I hit and bounced back, but I saw my axe flare with a blue light as it went through to sink into the magii's back.'

Thrane held up his hand and whispered something to the Councillor Prime, who nodded in reply.

'What happened next,' Thrane prompted.

'There were a few moments were I saw the magii remain standing, as if struggling, before collapsing. My friend then fell to the floor also.'

Thrane and the Councillor Prime entered into a private conversation, too quiet for the others to hear. When finished they looked up and Thrane spoke again. 'There was no other Ashnorian in the room?'

'There was another, he came up behind me after the magii was dead. He attempted to kill me, but Jontal stopped him.'

'The bandit?' asked the Councillor Prime.

'Yes, sir.'

'Why would he do such a thing? By helping the Ashnorians he stood a chance of getting away from his capture by Falakar.'

Garamon knew Falakar had gone to great lengths over the years to keep the secret about him and Jontal being brothers. He looked to Falakar to see if the Ranger was ready to divulge the fact, but nothing came back.

'I do not know, sir.'

The Councillor Prime pursed his lips.

Thrane took over again. 'So you are saying this single magii maintained a powerful shield around him, while holding your friend hard enough against a wall to crush him, and at the same time throw you against the opposite wall with nothing more than a nod of his head?'

Garamon knew where this was going. The power of the Ashnorian magiis was far beyond anything the Mlendrian mages could muster. Thrane wasn't going to believe his magic was small by comparison. But Garamon could think of no alternative, as it was the truth. 'Yes, sir. It seemed that way to me.'

Thrane shook his head. 'And yet you claim your axe passed through the barrier with ease.'

'I saw a flash of blue light on the blade's edge as it passed through.'

Thrane sat back for a moment, thinking. He took a deep breath before giving his verdict. 'I'm sorry, Falakar. This does nothing but weaken your case. Magic works on a substance known as mana, which exists all around us. As it's used, so it is drained. Even if one of these magiis could control such power, which I might add is far beyond even me, the local mana would have depleted. It would be impossible to carry out all the functions in one place. I think you have been deceived by the fanciful imaginings of a young man trying to impress, and taken in by the exaggerated stories of this axe.'

Falakar stood with his face filled with barely contained fury.

Brinley reinforced his stance. 'You expected us to initiate war on the testimony of this delusional young man who, a week ago, was a woodcutter. You have fallen a long way from the man you used to be, Falakar.'

'If it hadn't been for this woodcutter,' Falakar replied, his voice rising, 'this council, this hall and the entire town would be levelled to the ground and all of you enslaved by now.'

'Pish,' Brinley dismissed with a wave of his hand.

Falakar slammed his fist down onto the table in frustration. The nearest glasses jumped and two came down on a tilt and tipped their contents over the table.

'You're too hot-headed, Falakar,' Brinley admonished. 'Violence is so obviously how you live now, trying to reclaim old glories. You look for any opportunity to engage in its vulgarities. Now we have a wine-stained table to clean.'

Garamon had never seen Falakar so enraged. He thought he might draw his sword.

Dering broke the moment. 'Councillor Brinley. Ranger Falakar has a reputation far beyond anybody in this room. That reputation is of excellence in warfare, but also of maintaining the peace as his first priority. He has proven this many times and we owe him much. Nobody in this room is going to accept such an accusation.

'Then where is his proof!' Brinley exploded.

Garamon boiled with fury at the slur the repugnant councillor made to a man a hundred his worth, and the mental picture of his hometown being overrun due to this wealth-hungry profit monger. He raised his axe, and before anyone could move, brought it down with all the force he could into the table.

There was a flash. The sound alone could have knocked the first dozen councillors from their seats. But it wasn't the sound that did it. The table split down the middle into a long wedge shape. At Garamon's end the gap was two feet wide. It ended at the Councillor Prime's a few inches across. Most of the councillors were on their backs, their chairs pushed over by the movement of the table. Brinley was screaming out his distress as he rolled around on the floor, his huge bulk requiring assistance to rise.

Dering, his facing betraying his shock at the display of power, stood.

Garamon looked through the dissipating black smoke to each councillor, ending with Archmage Thrane.

'The magic in this axe is real, as is the power of the Ashnorian magiis. Their army *is* coming, and if you don't listen to Falakar, our town, our people, our homes, our land and your profits will be worthless.' He turned on Brinley. 'And those who are too *fat* to work the mines will be tortured to death to produce their elixir of life for the Emperor and his Elite.'

He turned his back and headed for the rear exit.

'Disarm and arrest him,' Brinley ordered. The two nearest door guards drew swords and approached without confirmation of the order from Stimm.

Garamon turned to Falakar for direction.

The Ranger beckoned Garamon to him and drew his sword.

'Stand away,' he said to the two guards.

'Outrageous behaviour,' Brinley announced. 'Do something, Stimm!'

Stimm waved to the two guards on the other door. 'Arrest them.'

Falakar squared off and pulled Garamon with him into a defensive position as all four guards approached, cutting off the route to the doors.

'Rescind the order, Stimm. I don't want to harm these men, but we are both walking from here. The whole of Mlendria is at stake. I will do what I must.'

Stimm faltered and his men stopped.

Brinley burst out. 'Arrest those men this instant!' He then turned to one of the younger councillors.' Get a patrol here, immediately.'

It wasn't Brinley's place to order other councillors, but for whatever reason the man obeyed and ran from the room.

Bolstered by Brinley's apparent command of the situation, the four men closed in.

'Please back off,' appealed Falakar to the four guards. 'I do not want to injure you.'

'Drop your sword, sir,' said one of the guards. 'We don't want to harm you either.'

Garamon held his axe ready. He trusted in Falakar's decision completely, but didn't know if he could swing his axe at one of these Rangers who were forced to obey orders. And despite his claim, he wasn't convinced Falakar could either.

As they backed up, Garamon bumped into the wood of the council cabin, giving them no more room to manoeuvre. Remembering what happened to the table, he swung his axe around, back-first, and hit one of the support stays holding the wooden wall planks. The thing blasted outwards taking many splintered planks with it. He put a leg through and squeezed his head under the sharp edges to drop out the other side to the ground.

Falakar faced off the four guards for a moment longer before jumping headlong through the narrow opening. He landed to complete a summersault.

'I must warn Father!' Garamon pleaded.

'They will be waiting for you,' Falakar replied, looking to his escape route. 'I'll get word to them somehow. Now we must run.'

They set off for the nearest buildings and the call went up.

Brinley caught up with Stimm outside, who had been organising the pursuit.

'Ensure the men who witnessed the axe are sent far away from contact.'

Stimm nodded.

'And I want the boy killed. Without him and his axe, Falakar will have nothing to confirm his claims.'

'That's not part of our arrangement. I agreed to help manipulate the guards' routes in your favour. Nothing about killing.'

'I warn you, Major. If that man ruins my set up, you won't just lose your generous percentage, you'll lose your head with it.'

Stimm's eyes narrowed. You're walking a dangerous line, Trader. I took your offer for mutual financial gain, not to turn the barracks into your personal murder squad.'

Brinley held the gaze for a moment as if weighing something up before breaking out in a broad smile. 'Of course, Major, what was I thinking?'

Stimm calmed a little. 'We won't catch them without Ajoah, anyway. He's the only one skilled enough to track him, and he's out on patrol.'

'Then perhaps you should have him returned immediately.'

Stimm nodded.

As Stimm walked off, Brinley beckoned with a finger. Out of the shadows, Strack approached.

'Things have changed. Ours fears the Major would be unable to step up to the next phase are confirmed. Get a message to our friends to delay no longer.

Chapter 14 – The Next Level

Chayne woke and felt a presence. He rolled over to see a brown-haired woman sitting on a chair pulled up to his bed. Her looks were as uninspiring as her plain clothes. Her nose was slightly bent to one side and one eyebrow was marginally higher than the other. One cheek was redder than the other giving the impression she was lazy with her makeup.

Her eyes however, seemed out of place with the rest. Perfect, and a brown so deep they were bordering on black. Strangely, they reminded him of his cat who, unusually, wasn't around.

She smiled an ever-so-slightly crooked smile.

She'd gained entry to his quarters without setting off his magical alarms and yet didn't look like a yhordi. He then realised he'd no idea what a yhordi should or shouldn't look like. She was no Illestrael, though.

'Good morning.' Her voice was clear, almost musical. It was accompanied with a smile only her eyes got right, as if the rest of her face was new to it.

'How did you get in here?'

She paused for a moment, thinking. 'I can be quite catlike when I want.'

Her face moved into a new position. It was unlike any expression he'd had ever seen before, giving him no idea what it was trying to express. Again, though, her eyes gave the best clue and projected a little sparkle. Mischief?

He sat up and his covers fell away to his waist. Her eyes flicked to his bare chest and betrayed desire to see lower below the cover line. The rest of her face moved into yet another random unfathomable expression.

She'd licked her lips.

He pulled his bed shirt to him and slipped it over his head.

She seemed disappointed.

'Do you want a lemon tea? I know how you like it.'

Chayne nodded and waited until she turned away before getting out of bed and letting the bed shirt drop down to its full length.

Following her into an area he'd set up as the kitchen, he watched her take the particular glass alchemy bulb he used for brewing his tea, and went about putting in the exact ingredients and correct quantities for his breakfast drink.

Utensils were collected from the drawers first time without the need to search. Her movements were precise, a combination of angelic and athletic. However incongruent her facial movements, the discord didn't extend to the rest of her body.

In record time the drink was placed before him. Her eyes extending the offer to try it.

'It's too hot when it's first made. I always let it cool.'

She gave her head a few quick shakes. 'I've made it the perfect temperature.'

'But I saw you just boil it. It will burn me.'

She pushed a finger into it and held it there for a few moments showing no discomfort. 'See, just right.'

No steam was rising from the liquid, which should have been the case. Picking up the glass, it was hot, but not uncomfortably so. He took a sip. It was the perfect temperature, something that couldn't have happened naturally in the time since boiling moments before. The flavour was also excellent.

She smiled again with the same facial effect as before, or was it slightly better this time?

'You're Magii then?'

She gazed around in thought for a moment again before answering. 'In a way, I suppose, yes.'

'I didn't know there were female magiis. There are none on the palace's roster.'

'Am I special then?' The words spoken as if inviting an encouraging reply.

He shook his head as if dislodging the final remnants of sleep.

'Who are you and why are you here?'

'To make you tea and be your friend.'

'But we've never met. Why would you do this?'

'Don't you want to be friends?' Her eyes showed a little distress.

Chayne took another sip of the morning brew, helping him wake up to the strange situation. 'If you've come from another city in the hope to curry favour, you're going about it in an unusual way.'

This appeared to make her happy, as if he'd indicated a good thing. She then left the kitchen with a spring in her step and went about arranging his undergarments and a fresh robe from various drawers in his bedroom and laying them on the bed. She then poured water from metal jug into the bowl he used each morning to wash and shave and placed a hand over it for a few moments.

'There, the perfect temperature.'

He walked over to the bowl and dipped a finger in. It was indeed just right.

It was possible to do Ashnorian magic without a manasphere, by pulling the mana straight from the air, but places like the palace, where manaspheres were regularly charged, the mana density was low and only weak spells could be cast and took longer. He knew it would have taken him many minutes to warm the water in the bowl to that temperature direct from the air. It's why magiis always carry manaspheres and use them without thinking when casting.

'You did it without a manasphere.'

Another moment of panic had flickered across her face.

'I lost mine.' She looked on expectantly.

'Manaspheres are more precious than life to a magii. They would never lose one, nor speak of it so lightly.'

There was no reply as the look of panic was turning to something else he couldn't make out on the incongruent face.

'So you're not a trained magii and yet you use magic. You're not a servant and yet you do things as well as them, and your entry to my room would indicate yhordi and yet you don't behave like the ones I've met.'

'Oooooooo, this is so difficult!' She stamped her way to the door, setting of the magic alarms. A servant opened the door and closed it behind her as she left.

The alarms settled down and all was quiet.

He shook his head. 'This Empire is the weirdest place imaginable.'

Pulling off his bed shirt he began washing.

Chapter 15 – Rite to Live

Keeping his eyelids all but closed, Kinfular watched a young plainsman approach flanked by two warriors. From his cocksure swagger and the look on the faces of his two guardians, Kinfular guessed he held his station through bloodline and not achievements.

The three reached his position and the young one forced a foot hard into Kinfular's stomach. 'Wake up,' he said in a dialect similar to Kinfular's people. The accent was rougher, which seemed to suit the nature of the plainsmen. Kinfular remained still.

The young man responded with a more powerful kick, aimed lower down.

'I said, wake–'

Kinfular intercepted the attack, catching the foot and rolling to bring the youngster down over him, sprawling face down in the dust. Kinfular followed the fall to bring his face up close to the plainsman's to see his fear. The gaze lasted but moments before the two escorts grabbed him and pulled him to his feet.

'Hold him,' said the young man as he got to his feet. He aimed a punch into Kinfular's stomach. Kinfular responded by tensing his battled hardened muscles. As the blow landed he made no indication of being struck; while the young man winced at the contact, trying to hide it behind a faltering smile.

Kinfular smiled back.

'Take him to my father!' he snapped.

As they walked away, Kinfular let out the word, 'Bunter,' for greenhorn warrior.

One of the escort warriors chuckled at the comment.

'You would show such solidarity with the enemy?' Kinfular said.

'You are no enemy,' said the man, not bothering to turn his head. 'You are Kinfular, an Esscantian of the Riaan tribe; Hinsha to the mountain tribes. I spy on your tribal *Contachca* each year.

'It may have been wise to inform your younger friend,' Kinfular replied. 'And it's pronounced, Hlenshar.'

'He is no friend of mine, and we have no time for such games as Contachca, nor words for them.'

The three continued in silence.

Tents of all sizes were erected as far as the eye could see. Few people seemed interested in a prisoner being walked through their midst. He guessed it wasn't as rare an occurrence as it would be in his own tribe.

'What have you done with my friend?'

'The Chieftain will talk with you,' replied the second warrior. 'Although ware naming the devil a friend.'

A guarded tent came into view towering over the rest. He was taken inside where sat a heavy set man. His long, mostly grey hair and matching beard were well-trimmed for a barbarian. He was eating fruit which was a luxury for a people roaming the plains with no fixed area to grow plants. The man's eyes fell upon him. In them Kinfular recognised the casual self-assurance of one who answered to no one, mixed with the weight of troubles of a man who was responsible for many.

Next to him stood his second in command or bodyguard.

'Why do the Riaan spy on us?' said the one standing.

It confirmed the man as more than a bodyguard.

'Why did you attack my friend?' Kinfular replied with a steady stare. Within the tribes, the two men were of equal standing.

'We deal with intruders how we see fit, devil-friend.'

'He is no devil, he's a Heslarian from the southern lands.'

'The devil has bewitched you. Only Yellowskins live in the southern lands.'

'He is descended from a family who escaped the Yellowskins invasion. I wish to see him.'

'Your devil has been given the welcome he deserves.'

'I tell you he is a man!'

'I and say you are bewitched!'

The seated one raised his hand, then stepped down and approached. His body was no stranger to combat with many long-healed scars visible on his arms and legs. A heavy gash ran under his hairline on the right side of his head, cut through the ear. He circled Kinfular, looking him up and down before stopping and facing him, his ageing grey eyes trying to penetrate Kinfular's deepest thoughts.

'Why do you enter my territory?' The words were spoken quietly, the voice rough and gravelly.

'I am returning to my people to warn of an attack from the Yellowskins before the summer ends.'

There was a general murmur from the men within the tent. The Chieftain raised his hand again and they quietened.

'They have not attacked the North since I was a boy. What makes you think they'll do so now?'

'I have come from their nearest city.'

Stifled laughter erupted around him.

The Chieftain appeared to join in with a smirk of his own. 'How is it you have returned from the Yellowskins where no one else has? Perhaps your devil helped?' There was a stronger murmur of approval at the reasoning.

Kinfular doubted the truth would seem credible. He could barely believe it himself. Also, the fact he was helped by the

Ashnorian's magic would not go down well with the barbarians.

He decided to keep quiet.

The Chieftain turned away then swung back with a powerful blow from the back of his hand. 'I am Grostro, Chieftain of the Kundi, the greatest tribe on the plains. Yet here you stand before me, a captured spy, with the impudence to travel across my territory with a devil, and dare not answer me!'

Kinfular regained his position, taking time to spit out some blood. 'I will answer your questions, but first I would know the fate of my friend. And understand this, Grostro of the Kundi, greatest tribe of the plains. I have seen the armies of the Yellowskins first-hand. When they come, and they will, they will sweep away you and your people along with all the plains tribes and all and every mountain tribe too, unless we unite with the Mlendrians.'

'The scholars?' mocked Grostro. 'So it is true the mountain gods have bred weakness into your tribes. Now you must ally with the weaker races.'

'Let me remove this fool from your presence, sire. I'll get the truth from him.' It was the second in command again.

'You will not get what you seek that way from this one, Gallern. He will be no stranger to pain and will no doubt have a good story to tell if he was caught. No, take him away and shackle him well, I have other things to attend to this morn. Arrange the Circle of Truth for noon. I know how to get the answers to our questions.'

Grostro turned and walked out of the tent.

Gallern snapped his fingers at two warriors and they grabbed Kinfular and hauled him out again.

The sun burned overhead as Kinfular stood in a wide circle of plainsmen. To one side was a raised gallery, on top of which sat Grostro. In front of him at ground level were his guards. To his left stood Gallern.

The circle parted behind Kinfular and a warrior brought a sword and threw it to the ground by Kinfular's feet. The plainspeople closed up again.

'You have been brought here for judgement under Huewn. By his will you shall fight to prove your truth or expose your lies. If you live then under the law of Huewn you shall be considered truthful. Death shall be the worthy outcome if you have lied. Therefore, under the eyes of our god Huewn, do you swear you are not a spy?'

Kinfular looked around the circle. There must be more than two hundred souls assembled and yet there wasn't the slightest sound to give them away. They were waiting to hear his answer.

'I am no spy.'

A cheer went up from all around as the excitement built at the prospect of the afternoon's entertainment.

'Then you shall be judged under Huewn, as is our custom.'

Kinfular picked up the weapon. The edge was dull and the quality poor overall. He understood its purpose well enough. It was meant to prolong suffering, taking time to kill the opponent. He walked to the middle of the arena and put it through a series of swings to get a feel and weight of the thing. The circle parted again and Kinfular turned to face his opponent. What he saw made him sick to his stomach and incensed. ThreeSwords was pushed forward to stumble to the ground. The circle erupted in laughter and cheers. A sword was thrown in after him.

Kinfular shot Grostro a stare, but there was no give in the Chieftain's expression. Gallern however, stood with a wide grin.

'I fight with two swords,' ThreeSwords said, looking down at the single weapon offered. The crowd erupted again at the demon's words. His lips were swollen and split, slurring his speech.

A plainsman replied with a glare of hatred and spat on the ground near the sword. ThreeSwords picked it up getting to his feet, and moved to the centre of the ring.

Kinfular looked his friend up and down. His normally pure black skin showed huge bruising over his body. His left leg made him limp and his left arm he held to his middle.

'If the black devil kills the warrior-champion of the mountain barbarians, he must be a devil and will be put to death,' Gallern announced. 'If he is killed, it's a sign from Huewn the barbarian is to be set free. If the sands run out and there is no victor, then both are guilty and shall be put to death, one as a demon, the other as a spy.'

Kinfular began making a number of impressive warm-up moves making the crowd noise rise in anticipation of the fight to come. He'd taken part in enough tribal Contachca to know how to manipulate a crowd, and he was forming a plan.

ThreeSwords stood still. 'I will not fight you as amusement for these animals. I will die quickly by your sword so you may go free.' The words were barely intelligible as before, as if spoken by a simpleton. This brought greater laughter from the gathering.

Kinfular responded with a fast and intricate move requiring him to leap high in the air and turning over in flight to land several feet away in perfect balance. It had the desired effect on the assembled plains people and diverted attention away from his friend. They responded with whooping and cheering.

'Kill me Hlenshar, so I may be free of this!' The crowd cheered again, mimicking his attempt to speak.

Kinfular then embarked on the most spectacular and outrageous sequence of all. He twisted and twirled, cutting, stabbing and slashing the air as he leapt and span, all the while watching ThreeSwords' eyes.

'Why do you behave like this in front of these savages? You act like a love sick Podo. You shame us and the Riaan.'

Kinfular responded with a high forward summersault to land in a crouching position facing the black warrior and resting the tip of his sword against his chest. The gathering roared with support for the move. Kinfular, sweat glistening on his face, spoke a single word swallowed in the din to all but ThreeSwords and masked by his body from the chieftain and his personal guards, '*Yolan*'.

ThreeSwords looked down upon Kinfular whose eyes were locked onto his and burning with the confidence and passion ThreeSwords knew meant one thing; the Hlenshar was about to unleash one of his reckless plans. He was referring to a sizeable village where they'd escaped through a daring manoeuvre by the sword-master.

The moment was interrupted by Gallern's announcement as he rotated a timer. 'The sands are turned! May Huewn bless the righteous who face death before Grostro.'

ThreeSwords moved first, striking Kinfular's sword away and stepping back into a battle pose. The first clash of steel brought a roar of approval from the plains people.

Kinfular came at him with a rapid lunge ThreeSwords deflected away to his right side. He returned with a slash across Kinfular's face missing as Kinfular pulled back just enough and reversed his deflected sword down into ThreeSwords' hip. The black warrior was already moving and brought his own sword down in a defensive swipe across his body clashing just in time with the incoming blade to stop the hit. The two men faced off one another again.

This time it was Kinfular's turn to attack. He ran around ThreeSwords, leaping and turning. It was all such nonsense in a fight but the crowd was building into frenzy at the display. On one of his spins he landed and darted in, catching ThreeSwords by surprise who stumbled to fall onto his back. Kinfular leapt forward and brought down a heavy strike aimed at ThreeSwords chest. It was a clumsy stoke by the Hlenshar's standard but the crowd thought he was about to win. ThreeSwords rolled to one side avoiding the killing blow. Kinfular's sword struck the stone ground with enough force to create an array of sparks.

ThreeSwords rolled up onto his feet and jabbed back. Kinfular batted the sword away and rushed headfirst into ThreeSwords' stomach, hoisting the black warrior from his feet and running him towards Grostro's stand. The crowd went mad as ThreeSwords was thrown to land heavily on his back at the feet of Grostro's guards. Kinfular then rushed at ThreeSwords who scrabbled to his feet as if ready to take the charge, but at the last moment he dropped his hands, linking them together. Kinfular leapt at him as if to make the killing strike, and put his foot into the hands of ThreeSwords who lifted with all his strength.

Intent on the killing stroke and masked by ThreeSwords body, none of the guards reacted in time as Kinfular summersaulted over their heads to land a solid kick in Gallern's chest who went flying out back of the makeshift stand. The kick slowed Kinfular to a halt and he dropped down next to Grostro, sliding his sword under the Chieftains throat, his other hand wrapped around the man's head to hold him firm.

The guards turned to protect their Chieftain and were halted by the threat from Kinfular as he applied more pressure from the dull blade.

'You think my men will let you go in exchange for my life?' Grostro said.

'They will.'

'So now I must decree you go free and unharmed – even the demon?'

'No.'

'Then what?'

'We have no quarrel with you. We are not spies and my friend is no devil. I have spoken the truth about a coming army and our need to work together if we are to stand against them.'

'Is this always to be with a sword at my throat?'

'No, in this I must trust to my judgment of you,' Kinfular replied. He then flipped his sword and presented the hilt to the leader.'

Gallern leapt up onto the stand and pulled Kinfular away from Grostro and placed his own sword across Kinfular's throat.

'Just give me the word, sire. I shall remove his head.'

A disturbance broke the moment when a young warrior burst into the ring.

'My Chieftain, warriors approach from the South!'

'South? How many?' called Gallern, knowing they were already at the southern limit of the plains.

'I have never seen the like before,' replied the warrior, wide-eyed and fearful.

Grostro stepped down from his stand. 'Are these your Yellowskins, Esscantian?'

Gallern tightened his grip on Kinfular. 'You said the Yellowskins would not attack until the end of summer.'

'So spies they are,' decided Grostro. 'This was all a deception to divert our attention.' He turned to Gallern. 'Kill the dogs and gather the warriors.'

'Wait, Grostro,' called out Kinfular. 'I tell you we are no spies. Let us help you. I don't know why they attack now, something has changed. But no tribe can stand against them alone.'

Grostro ignored the request.

'They will have Yellow Demons!' shouted Kinfular.

Grostro stopped and looked unsettled at the mention of the magiis.

'You are spies, nothing else,' yelled Gallern. The timing is too great to dismiss. You think us fools if you believe we would not see through such an obvious ploy. If we let you go you will head for the Yellowskins and tell them of our numbers.'

The reasoning of Gallern seemed to dislodge the doubts of Grostro, who nodded his agreement with the assessment.

'At least keep us alive for now,' Kinfular said. 'If things go badly, what will you have to lose?'

'You are pleading for your life, Peaksman. You will say whatever you need to live,' Gallern countered.

Grostro held up his hand to Gallern's caution. 'There is some truth in his words. Secure them well and have them guarded until I return.'

Gallern consented with a reluctant nod and waved a hand at the nearest guards to take over.

Grostro turned his back to leave.

'You're making a mistake, Chieftain of the Kundi,' called out Kinfular. 'We have seen the Yellowskins' army in the desert. Take your people north while you have time.'

Grostro continued on his way.

'They are foolish not to listen,' ThreeSwords said, quietly.

'As were your people and many others,' Kinfular replied. 'We must hope Grostro realises his error before his people too are lost.'

Their hands were bound and they were taken away.

Grostro returned to his tent and began putting on his battle leathers.

'I believe it was a mistake to let the spies live,' Gallern said, lifting the chieftain's heavy chest piece into place.

'Did you see the fear in the scout's eyes when he told us of the Yellowskin warriors,' Grostro replied, fumbling with a difficult tie.

Gallern reached around and took over the task. 'He is young and prone to exaggeration in front of you.'

'Perhaps he could do so with his words, but his eyes held dread. Even in our presence he feared for his life.'

The two men completed dressing and Grostro took up his gleaming four-foot, two-handed broadsword. They left the tent and Grostro's personal guard gathered around.

'Keep alert,' ordered Gallern to the men. 'There may be more spies.'

They headed off. As they approached the southern edge of the settlement, tents were being abandoned. Even in the presence of their Chieftain in full battle armour, surrounded by his best warriors, these tundra-hardened people were fleeing.

They continued further until reaching a natural rise at the southern end of camp. His warriors were assembled along the rise, looking south. Three hundred toughened fighters backed up by another two hundred younger, less experienced tribesmen.

As he approached he became irritated they were so unsettled. He crested the rise to gain his first view of the approaching enemy. The sight before him made him stop and almost step back.

'Huewn be with us,' Gallern whispered, echoing Grostro's thoughts. 'They make us look like a raiding party.'

Grostro scanned the army before him. They stretched out wide and deep, their rear ranks disappearing in the heat haze of the afternoon sun. They were aligned in perfect rows. He'd fought for decades on the plains, and through conquest of other tribes, assembled what he believed to be the largest and most formidable force to be found. But Gallern was right, compared to the force before them they represented little more than fleas attempting to stop the dog they were riding on.

'Move the camp as the Peaksman said,' Grostro ordered. 'Lead our people north with all haste. Take our best hundred warriors, and half of the younger ones.'

'My place is by your side my Chieftain,' Gallern protested.

'Your place is to do as I command,' Grostro corrected. 'You are my closest advisor and good friend, but there is nothing you can do here to resist such a force. We will die on this battlefield in the hope it provides you time to get our people to safety.'

'Then I should be the one to stay. You are our Chieftain, and must remain with the people. They will need you more than ever now,' Gallern pleaded.

Grostro smiled and placed a heavy hand upon Gallern's shoulder. 'Take our people north,' he said, and held out the leadership rod.

Gallern looked to the rod as if the thing would burn him.

'You will make a good leader, Gallern. I have confidence our people will live on under you.'

The air seemed to come alive making the hairs over Grostro's body stand out. All his men were suffering the same discomfort. A ghostly apparition a hundred feet tall appeared floating in front of his warriors. It was a man, dressed in flowing coloured robes. Grostro tried not to look unnerved.

'Heathens,' boomed the apparition.

Some of the younger warriors dropped their weapons to place their hands over their ears.

'I am Jewell, twenty-third magii of the Shodatt-tey-Straslin. For your crimes against the Emperor you have been sentenced to retribution.' The volume of the voice was overwhelming, driving some of the youngest warriors to their knees. 'Send forth an emissary to declare your surrender as slaves, or be destroyed.'

'How can we fight that?' Gallern gasped. Magic was frightening to them on any level, but this seemed impossibly powerful.

'Hide your concerns, Gallern, the men are watching. If these yellow demons are so powerful, why do they bring an army, or bother with the cowardice of keeping such a distance from us.'

Grostro took a step toward the apparition and held his axe high in the air. 'We understand little of your words, demon.' His normal powerful voice sounding thin and weak compared to the magic of the demon mage, but the words were not spoken for the enemy. 'Speak through the spilling of your blood, or be gone. You disgrace us dressed in the colours and cheap trinkets of a whore. You delay the deeds of true men on the battlefield.' He then began the tribe's battle song to Huewn. His men took up the song, emboldened by the sound of their leader showing such defiance. Soon the air was filled with the deep chanting call to their god for glorious death in battle. The apparition disappeared and a cheer went up.

Grostro turned to Gallern in the clamour and had to shout into the plainsmen's ear. 'We'll hold them as long as we can.'

'It has been my greatest honour serving under you,' Gallern said. His voice wasn't raised enough to be heard by Grostro, but the meaning was obvious between the two.'

Grostro took another look to the south as if in contemplation for a few moments. He then turned back to Gallern, pulling him in close. 'Release the Peaksman and have them brought to me.'

Gallern went to object, but Grostro gripped the man's arm. 'This is my last order to you, Gallern. Do as I bid. Be quick.'

Gallern held his chieftain's gaze for a moment before nodding his consent.

'Do not let them see you are heading north.'

Gallern nodded again and reluctantly took the tribal Rod of Leadership.

He headed off to choose the men who were to become the tribe's new army if they could escape.

Chapter 16 – First Contact

Chayne was sitting once again in his old lab. Tristaric had left for the afternoon leaving him alone for the first time for any length of time. The magii was keeping him under close scrutiny, and at the same time not allowing him near the work he was doing. It was frustrating to be so close to the man and yet have no idea of his intended solution. A continuous flow of trivial tasks were supplied to keep him occupied.

The light in the room shifted as the illusionary wall altered scenes. It was on a rotation that changed every few hours. Mana flowed from the wall manasphere connected to the tendrils of thrinium running out across the wall in a fine lattice. How much longer it would work until the sphere ran out was unknown. The new scene depicted a glass window overlooking an elaborate panorama of forest stretching out to the horizon above which hung twin crescent moons. It was beautiful and a testimony to his merciless previous master's deeper soul who created it. How such an evil and brutal man could create such a vision was beyond Chayne's understanding. Would, one day, he have to create such an elaborate scene of the woods around Tiburn backed by the Hammerhead Mountains? Would the Empire destroy Mlendria, and only visions through such magic exist to remember his old home?

He pulled out a square of cloth from a deep pocket within his robe and stared at the dried blood stain. It was from the night Illestrael died. A morbid token and the only thing he had of her. Rubbing his thumb back and forth across it, it helped to maintain some connection. In the short time of knowing her, a bond developed he'd not known before. Love?

Placing the other hand on his manasphere he practised his new skill at creating his own illusions. Mana swirled ahead of him for a moment before coalescing into the shape of a human head. He narrowed his concentration and began to fill in the detail of the face. The features were less than clear, although the eyes and lips were better represented than the rest. A tear welled in his eye and the image blurred. He turned his attention to her voice and attempted to have her say "hello". The word came out misshapen and sounded like one of Tiburn's town drunks. It was a repellent imitation of Illestrael's beautiful voice. He snapped the illusion away. Creating illusions was a useful but delicate skill he still had to master. Few could do it well. He wanted to see and hear Illestrael again, in any form, but until he mastered the ability he needed to find a different subject to test rather than create deformed versions of her.

'So, how did you do it?'

Chayne span around on his stool, creating a shield ahead of him. The intruder looked no older than thirty-five, but had the manner of somebody much older – someone who was gifted with plenty of Yan. It made him important within the Empire.

'She was an experienced operative,' continued the intruder. 'Not the best, but even so, not someone to succumb to the magic of a magii, or the charms of barely more than a boy. Our training is as much of the mind as body.'

'You're Yhordi.'

'Something tells me I should dispense with the usual evasions reserved for normal empyrean citizens.' He walked across to the soft armchair and dropped into a slouching position. 'I consider myself talented at my job, but I must admit in this case I'm at a loss how you pulled off the whole Lathashal thing.'

Chayne tried to mask his surprise.

The man smiled to himself. 'So you were involved.'

'I want you to leave.'

'What I don't understand is how you managed to coordinate with your people. I could do it, but then I've had centuries to create the contacts necessary. For you to have the knowledge and ability to execute such an undertaking leaves me puzzled and somewhat surprised, which is not something that happens to me.'

'I have no idea what you're talking about.'

'You and your friends have been too demonstrative in your work, something which I feel you were forced into because of the invasion. It raised your profile to the attention the Emperor. Worse still, you have delayed his plan to invade – something of a pet project he has been working on for some time, and he's not a man to disappoint.'

'I care little for the Emperor or his plans. If he leaves my people alone then nothing will come of it.'

'Bravo, I admire your conviction. It counts for nothing of course. I'm already uncovering how you stopped Lathashal, and I'm ordered to round up everyone involved for the Emperor's pleasure. It's what I do and I've been doing it for a long time. I don't fail.'

Chayne stared at the man, his sureness unsettled him. He wanted to use his manasphere to throw a glass beaker at him, just to make him react and break his karma.

'She was an attractive woman.'

Chayne looked puzzled at the off-topic question.

'You're attempt at an illusion,' the yhordi explained. 'I knew her as a child, you know. It was me who rescued her from the leisure slaves. Without my intervention she would have become a woman of use to the rich. I saw her potential as an operative and enrolled her. You should be grateful.'

The yhordi flicked a coin from his thumb far into the air. It span, almost touching the ceiling before returning. He held out his hand a few inches in front of him to catch the thing. At no time did he take his eyes from Chayne.

'You should consider joining us you know. Your talents would be a great asset. It would be a waste for you to perish with your people in some futile attempt to prevent us taking them.'

'You will not find Mlendria so easy to subdue as the others you have taken. We are a people unlike any other, and will hurt you. If you knew of us, you would think twice about invasion.'

'It's quite the opposite,' the yhordi replied, moving the coin, almost on a blur, through a number of intricate small hops across his fingers. His dexterity was extraordinary. 'You know, I'd be happy to put in a good word with him to save your soul. The Emperor, that is. I'm not a vindictive or churlish man, I have lived far too long to bother with such fruitless endeavours.'

Chayne stayed quiet. All the time the man was talking he was giving away information.

'Did you know the body shows signals when under pressure to conceal something – such as when lying. Or, for instance, if I say *murderer*,' he paused for just a moment. 'Your pupils changed size and your body moved minutely as it squirmed under the allegation.'

Chayne attempted to relax.

'Oh, you're no born killer. That's evident. But it tells me you were involved in Lathashal's death. I've known the man for over a hundred years, you know. In my opinion he would have been Emperor one day. He was even the assassin who killed the old Emperor elevating Estatoulie to current monarch. He's survived countless assassination attempts and challenges to his position. So it's quite the mystery to me how *outsiders* achieved where so many others have failed.'

He got to his feet. 'So I'll be watching you, Mlendrian, until I find out how you did it and who were involved, and assemble you all before the Emperor. I have a feeling it won't be such a pleasure for you as for him.'

Chayne wanted to stand and confront the man, but his legs weren't feeling so defiant and he remained seated. 'If you don't want to end up as Lathashal did, I suggest you head back to your Emperor and make up some suitable story to satisfy him.'

'Death holds no fear for me, young magii. Threats even less. My reputation is something else, though.' The yhordi headed for the door. 'I look forward to your exploits. They will serve to give away what I need to achieve my task.'

Chayne watched the man leave the room before sagging onto his stool. He dropped the shield and released his manasphere. The encounter reminded him of the first time he'd met Illestrael. She appeared without warning into the lab too. Though this time there wasn't the feeling this new yhordi was going to be sympathetic to his plans.

He needed to get to Stalizar, but if this character was indeed a yhordi of some standing, Stalizar could be exposed as a traitor. That, he wouldn't risk.

Chapter 17 – My Enemy is My Friend

Jontal sat on the stone floor, his back feeling the cold of the cell wall seeping through his leather jerkin. Cool air poured in through the bars above his head, bringing the welcome sensation of being outside. The smell of the mountain pines was beginning to permeate the air as the temperature rose and melted their long imprisonment in the winter snow. He closed his eyes and imagined running through the trees and across the rocks of his home for so many years. He'd volunteered to give it all up for his brother, and was already having second thoughts. Falakar convinced him, because of his efforts to avert the invasion of Mlendria, his sentence would be minimal.

Jontal wasn't convinced. Years of thieving and killing wasn't going to be forgiven with a few days of good deeds, no matter how many people it could save from slavery and death.

The man in the next cell stirred in his bunk. 'Godsdamned bed,' he mumbled. He lifted himself onto one arm and punched his mattress a few times. In anger or to flatten some lumps, Jontal wasn't sure. It made him laugh.

The man turned over to face the sound. 'What in the hells are you finding funny?'

He had the appearance of somebody who washed regularly and walked around in clean well-cut clothes. Smoothed-faced, without the crags and creases of the malnourished and weather-exposed, he looked his middle age. His voice also carried the unmistakable enunciation of the educated.

He was covered over in an ankle-length fur coat Jontal would have considered a significant steal.

'You're not a man used to sleeping in such accommodation.'

'No, I'm damned-well not! I like my comforts.'

'Such as?'

'Hot and cold running water. Carpets your toes disappear into, and a soft downy bed large enough to swallow a cow.'

'There aren't many who could boast of such trappings in Tiburn.'

'Damned right. Now I have to put up with living like a common criminal.'

'You should have thought of that before you committed your crime.'

'I didn't commit any damned crime.'

Jontal laughed again. 'Of course not.'

This agitated the man more than Jontal would have expected.

'Gods man, I don't need to break the law. I own half of Tiburn!'

'I think Dulmurn may have something to say about that.'

Jontal saw the man stare back.

'You're Dulmurn?'

The man nodded, miserably.

'Then why are you here?'

'Because that thieving bastard has always wanted my trading clients and my mansion.'

'And that would be?'

'Councillor damned Brinley.'

Jontal's eyes narrowed. The man had fenced much of the goods Jontal had 'acquired' over the years. He wasn't to be trusted beyond an unfair deal in his favour, but to displace a prominent member of the Tiburn community in such an open way meant his influence and ambition had grown far beyond just his trading routes.

'How did he convince the Rangers?'

'I don't know. They raided my mansion in the middle of the night and brought me here. I've not been told the charges and they've kept me cooped up in here for two weeks. Damned thing of it all was, I would have been gone in a couple of days to my cabin in the mountains. Not even the Rangers know of it.'

'Was anybody else taken?'

'No, and there's nobody else in here.'

The open plan arrangement allowed all the cells to be seen. It was empty.

Jontal jumped up and grabbed the small window ledge. Pulling himself up he looked out into the barracks courtyard beyond. The place looked normal enough. Rangers were being drilled and put through their fighting practice. He glanced across to the bronze statue of his brother. Each barracks had one on prominent display as a reminder of the excellence they were expected to strive for. Falakar hated them of course, he would always say it was just his job. Jontal noticed something unusual with this one. His brother would often grumble about the rivalry between barracks in having the best polished statue. This one was tarnishing.

He lowered himself back down. Something was definitely wrong.

Chapter 18 – The Iicators

Chayne entered the Iicators room. He hadn't expected to live through the ordeal of stopping Lathashal, and now he'd been summoned and was about to be questioned as part of an investigation into the magii's death.

The first room was plain with no adornments, unusual for the palace, which was unnerving. A man stood from behind a small desk and approached. He was dressed in a white, well-tailored two-piece garment.

'I am the steward to the Iicators. Surrender your manasphere and weapons.' He held out his hands.

Chayne handed over his orb box. 'I carry no weapons.'

The steward placed it on the desk and then checked Chayne's clothing for anything hidden underneath. Satisfied, he gestured towards a door at the back of the room.

'When you enter, sit in the chair.

'Do not adjust its position.'

'Do not turn your head.'

'Do not delay or refuse to answer a question of an Iicator.'

'Do not provide false, misleading or missing information in your replies.'

'Do not speak unless asked a question.'

'Magic of any kind is forbidden within the room.'

'Failure to comply with these instructions will result in level ten punishment and execution. The interrogation is over when you are told you may leave.'

The steward returned to his desk and sat down, leaving Chayne wondering what to do next.

The steward looked up from his paperwork. 'Not promptly entering the judgment room is taken as an admission of guilt and punishable by level ten correction and execution.'

Chayne entered. The room was lit to the point of dazzling, and the stark white and light greys of the room added to the intimidating setting.

It was circular in shape and domed. In the middle was a raised semi-circular dais over ten feet high with six white high-backed chairs, on which sat six people in full-length white robes. Each one had a white hood over their heads, with white gloves and shoes. No part of their bodies could be seen.

In front of the dais was arranged six plain chairs. They were in a smaller semi-circle, and on each sat a bald man in identical light grey robes wearing white masks cut with a long slit to expose their eyes. The semi-circle faced inwards to a single red chair. It was the only unoccupied seat. The scene was intimidating, but with no indication of blood splatter or implements of torture, it didn't seem so bad.

Remembering the steward's instructions he sat down with his back to the dais, facing the bald grey-robed figures. They were watching him intently. Not just staring, but turning their heads this way and that as if trying to drill into his every facial movement. He guessed in the absence of magic, these passed as finders of untruths. With the six high-seated mystery men behind him and the close scrutiny of the *face-inspectors* in front, it wasn't a place for easy deception.

There was a shuffle from behind and Chayne decided it was the Iicators removing their hoods.

'Why were you present at the casting of the Rite of Rakasti?' The voice came from behind and happened without any warning. It was stern and accusing.

Chayne was caught off-guard by the sudden start. After a slight hesitation he answered. 'I wanted to witness the casting of the powerful spell as part of my training.' As he answered so the intensity of the scrutiny from the face-inspectors increased. They twisted their heads and scanned their eyes across his face, looking for something, before relaxing. Simultaneously they nodded to the men behind.

'How was Master Lathashal killed?' It was a different voice from behind and equally intense.

'An assassin.'

The heads bobbed and nodded.

'Why did you not warn your master or stop the assassin?' It was a third, strict voice.

This was the tricky part. He didn't know how good the men in front of him were at detecting lies compared to magic of a magii, but he wasn't going to take any chances. He had to tell a truth. He decided to let out some new information. 'The master was angry with me for interrupting him and was enacting my punishment.'

The six heads bobbed feverishly, and again nodded.

'How was it you, a student, survived?' This voice was higher pitched than of those previous and carried with it an especially accusing bite.

'I was unconscious at that point and could not witness.'

Six nods.

'You are Mlendrian?'

'Yes,' replied Chayne, relieved by the change in questioning.

'Those who killed the assassin and spared your life were Mlendrian. Were you in collusion with them?' At this point the face-inspectors sat forward as far as their reach could manage without leaving their seats, their eyes darting in their sockets.

'The arrival of the Mlendrians was a complete surprise to me and I played no part in their infiltration of the Empire or the palace.'

The face-inspectors fell back into their normal positions and nodded again.

There was a pause in the Iicators questioning. It was followed by a new voice. It was calm in contrast to the fierceness in the previous questioners. Strangely, it held greater gravity and consequence.

'Are you loyal to the Emperor?'

He'd not prepared himself for such a question and knew his continued life was held within his next words. He looked to the face-inspectors, their faces void of accusation. They stopped their gyrations and held his gaze in a steady focus of singular concentration.

'I believe the Emperor rules over a land of great knowledge and a disciplined people.'

There was a pause from behind and he knew he hadn't answered the question directly.

'That is so,' came the eventual response from the same voice. 'But you are Mlendrian and could have confused loyalties to your previous people. You are either loyal to the Emperor, or to your old people. You will answer which it is.'

Chayne paused again. Answering or not, he would be executed either way. He then jumped at the high-pitched voice of the third Iicator. 'Are you loyal to the Emperor!'

'Yes.'

The face-inspectors took no time to return their verdict, and each shook their heads once.

There was the sound of clothing moving behind. 'You may leave,' said the initial voice.

Chayne got to his feet and faced the Iicators. They were once again hooded. He walked from the room where the steward picked up his manasphere and passed it back to him.

'Communication of any kind describing anything from the moment you entered here shall be punished at level ten and execution. You may leave.'

Chayne took the manasphere. He was being let go? And being warned of anything said, to be punished with nothing less than the very punishment he was surely going to be dealt anyway?

He left the room expecting to be greeted with a pair of guards to escort him to the dungeons, but no such thing happened.

Returning to his lab he slumped into his soft couch. It was the nearest thing to the one he loved so much from his cabin back home. He closed his eyes and went over the questions and answers during his cross-examination, trying to understand what happened and how he was allowed to leave. Fireball jumped up on the couch and laid down resting against his leg. His hand went down and began stroking the cat. It began purring, energetically.

---//---

Ducilly removed his white hood and dismissed the Truth Seers.

'It's fortunate you were chosen to head this investigation,' said the eldest-looking of them.

'He did well answering the questions.' It was Erran, Ducilly's most trusted operative within the Lan-Chi. 'He faltered on the loyalty question, which is understandable, but nevertheless is all we need to justify execution.'

'So the question is,' said another of the Iicators, 'do we want him dead?' It was Lucor. Unlike Erran he was more impartial, always needing to hear out the arguments before committing to a decision.

Although in law it was Ducilly's final decision, the others were there to advise and argue the case, but this was no normal group. All the Iicators had been chosen by Ducilly, and all were senior Lan-Chi in the city. He still was the most senior in Straslin, but nevertheless it wasn't a good idea to push any of these men too far, for he needed their support.

'What say you, Kennet?' Kennet was the third Iicator. Nervous and cautious in his decision. He usually went with the majority.

'I would like to hear what everyone has to say.'

'As always,' Linarati replied. 'I fail to see why we bother including you in our sessions.'

'Yes, you would like that,' Kennet snapped. 'So you could suggest one of your extremist friends in my place. You are too ready to incite change at the expense of caution. If you had your way we would all be dead by now.'

'Better to light a fire and burn like a beacon for others,' Linarati retorted. 'More would then know of us and rise up.'

Ducilly raised his hand to put a stop to the argument before it grew into another row between the two. 'Joshwer, I would have your say in this.'

The youngest of the Iicators did not immediately reply, choosing his words as always before he spoke. He was the replacement for Ganpow who was injured in a recent Lan-Chi operation. Although a quarter of the age of the others, the young man's input was often insightful, and Ducilly saw him as a candidate for his post in the decades to come.

'It seems to me the young Mlendrian has managed to orchestrate an attack by his people to help defeat the most powerful magii in the city. How he managed to contact them and arrange for their incursion into Ashnoria and the palace, we have yet to discover. This must make him a gifted operative sent in by the Mlendrian army. A match for any in the Empire. He will prove useful if we can control him.'

'He is too dangerous,' Jannet said. 'He doesn't know how the Empire works and will slip and we'll all be exposed.'

Linarati got to his feet and paced to the edge of the dais. 'He has proven himself beyond our greatest expectations. Who of us believed he would succeed in stopping Lathashal, let alone survive it? We should not be hasty in wasting such a resource.'

Jannet went to reply and Ducilly again held up his hand. 'Assign someone to monitor and report back. If he looks like exposing us we can take action before it happens.'

'Most of our operatives have gone to ground to avoid being called to Iication,' Lucor said.

'Then choose one of the more promising runners,' Ducilly ordered.'

Chapter 19 – Enforced Trust

The tent flaps were thrown aside and Gallern entered with two warriors. He withdrew a slender knife and approached Kinfular. Kneeling down he sliced through Kinfular's ankle bonds, and then ThreeSwords'.

'I have seen the sea of Yellowskins you described. Spies, demons or not, you will make little difference either way now. Grostro has commanded me to release you both and send you south to him. These men will ensure you do. Grostro will order you from there.'

'And what are you to do?'

'None of your concern, Peaksman,' snapped Gallern. 'I do not agree with letting you go, and keep in mind, should you betray Grostro or my people and I learn of it, I will find you and kill you.' He sheathed his knife and hurried from the tent.

They were hauled to their feet and pushed out into the hot sun. Kinfular blinked the dust from his eyes being kicked up by the plains people frantic in their actions to uproot their camp.

The further south they went, the more desperate the scene, even items were being left behind and the presence of a black devil scarcely distracted them.

They arrived at the assembly of warriors, lined on top of a ridge looking out over the southern desert.

'They cannot hope to win with so few,' ThreeSwords said.

'Grostro isn't planning on defeating them.'

They saw the war chief surrounded by his guards. Runners came and went as he gave his orders.

In the distance, strange wooden contraptions, three times the height of the tallest men, were being assembled. Ropes and pulleys were being attached. Kinfular had no idea of their function. Other men were digging in another area, laying wide boxes to which ropes were being attached and buried in a long line back to Grostro.

As they arrived, the Chieftain was patting a young warrior on the back and sending him off on some task. He then turned to them and beckoned. 'Untie their hands and return their armour and weapons.' Grostro faced them off. 'I take great risk in this, but what I have seen in the last hour has given me little choice. Come with me.'

They crested the brow of the rise to see the Ashnorian army set against them.

ThreeSwords stared on impassive.

'You do not fear them, Demon?'

'I am no demon,' ThreeSwords replied. 'But I feel my ancestors wanting vengeance. The more I kill, the more I put those they slaughtered to rest.'

Grostro felt the black warrior's conviction, and for the first time began to believe the warrior may be just a man. He broke his contemplation and spoke to Kinfular. 'We must divert them from my people. Normal battle on the plains is head to head. We'll not last long against such a force.'

'Then we take them into the mountains,' Kinfular said.

'We're not mountain warriors, Peaksman.'

'You are more so than the Yellowskins, and their metal armour will work against them in the cold the higher we climb.'

Grostro saw a gleam in the Peaksman's eyes as he spoke of his mountain home. 'You appear as a warrior who believes he can win.'

Kinfular's gaze raked across the wall of snowbound peaks to the West, as if recalling something. 'I have been forced to survive in their land under their rules. Now they will fight to survive in mine. But first we must ensure they follow us into the mountains.'

A broad grin spread across Grostro's rugged features. 'When I've finished with them, they will hunt us into the hells themselves.'

A yell went up from one of the Plainsmen. Kinfular looked to see the Ashnorians had started moving. Grostro had chosen to camp on a high ridge running to the mountains. The only way for the Ashnorians was via the east side where Grostro had his men digging. He shouted his orders and his men scattered to their positions and tasks. Those covering the long ropes sped up to finish off the remaining exposed sections. The tall wooden devices were aligned in a row to face where the enemy would approach.

They watched as the Ashnorian column of soldiers bent around the end of the ridge, keeping in perfect formation. Grostro's men lined up to face them, the wooden contraptions behind. Six of the strongest Plainsmen apiece were holding the ends of the eight buried ropes. Large woollen bags were bundled into wooden bowls on top of the wooden contraptions, Kinfular still no better understanding their purpose.

The Ashnorians formed up, fifty abreast, their red and silver armour and polished weapons glinting from the bright sun. There was the sound of a horn, and as a man they moved forward. The layer of sand over the baked earth muffled the sound of their sandaled feet as they hit the ground in unison, almost as if the army were whispering.

Grostro's men set themselves ready. The thin line of leather-armoured warriors looked a fragile barrier to those advancing. As the Ashnorians reached a hundred paces, Kinfular began to question whether Grostro was going to do anything. The leader turned his head and called out to his men behind the line. His men took up the slack and heaved on the long ropes. The line of Plainsmen parted in eight places as the ropes rose from the sand, tightening all the way into the front rows of the Ashnorian ranks. A few soldiers tripped. It didn't seem a very effective attack.

Then cries went up from the behind the front line. More erupted. Soon the ranks behind the front were in chaos. Men were screaming and moving in all directions, weapons being used in desperation hitting each other. Grostro held up his hand and let it fall. The strange wooden machines were hit with axes cutting through taught ropes causing the large bowls to throw the woollen bags forward at great speed.

Kinfular had seen nothing like it before as he watched the bags unravel as they flew over the heads of the Plainsmen towards the Ashnorians. Squirming creatures scattered into the air and landed on top of the soldiers. More screams joined the first and now there was total panic in the front dozen ranks of the Ashnorians. Half were jumping around to avoid attacks from the floor, spreading out from trap boxes with the covers now released, while the other half were attacking their shoulder guards and helmets as more of the creatures landed on them from the aerial attack. They were running and knocking each other to the ground, frantically getting up again from the creatures there.

Kinfular turned to the Plainsmen's leader with a look of dismay at his use of such creative and insidious tactics.

Grostro grinned at the spectacle, and caught Kinfular's curious gaze. 'Plain's Red Vipers and Spear-backed Scorpions. All we had, taking years to collect. A very painful death. I hope you have something as entertaining in the mountains for us?' He then turned and called to his men. The front line broke and the Plainsmen headed west.

Kinfular had one last look at the Ashnorians in disarray before also turning back to face his mountains, his feelings mixed. He would at last be returning to his home territory, but be bringing an army of warrior's right to the edge of his people, bent on seeking them out and destroying them.

'We cannot defeat them with snakes and scorpions, Hlenshar,' ThreeSwords said. 'How are we to stop them?'

'Lead them to our home. You must delay them until the Ritual of Giving.'

'Sunrise tomorrow? The Plainsman are not mountain warriors, we are too few to hold them for so long, Hlenshar.'

'Use the narrow passes to engage them, then retreat and run to the next.'

Kinfular could see the doubt in the black warrior. It wasn't fear for himself, merely the worry he would fail the command. Kinfular placed a hand on his friend's shoulder. 'We are fighting for the survival of our people against a great enemy. I do not believe Rolk would set us this task without a chance of victory. What I have planned carries great risk, and you must have them follow you into our home at the exact time of the Ritual of Given, or all will be lost.'

ThreeSwords, uncomfortable with the contact even from his closest friend, pulled away. 'What are you planning?'

'Only a god could stop such an army. I have done much and risked my life many times in the name of Rolk. It's time to see if he repays his debts.'

Chapter 20 – On the Run

Jontal woke to the sound of a key entering the lock of his cell. It was still night. Was he to be murdered in his bed, is this what happened to the other occupants of the prison? He readied himself to catch them by surprise.

'Jontal?'

He recognised the voice as well as his own and jumped to his feet. 'Fal!'

His brother approached, face blackened so only his eyes were visible. He handed over a small jar. 'Blacken up, we need to move fast.'

Jontal opened the pot and recognised the black soot inside. He began applying it to his face and hands. 'Do I come to the implausible conclusion you're breaking me out?'

'We must get some distance before they wake and raise the alarm,' Falakar said.

'Get my things from the locker.'

Falakar prised open the lock, not wasting time looking for the key on the jailor's keyring. Inside he found the unmistakable tools of his younger brother's trade; bottles of coloured liquids and packets of powder. Next to them were his weapons and an assortment of strange intricate devices.

Jontal finished covering his face and hands and joined him. Guards were sprawled around the jail. There was no blood.

'You spend years getting me in here, to break me out a few days later?'

'Something's wrong with the barracks. Lindeg has been retired from the plateau and Stimm's now in charge. Brinley's got some power over him and they're refusing to accept the coming threat from the Empire.'

'And this is helped by making you a fugitive, how?'

'I'll explain when we're clear of the town. I need you to hide us while we plan what to do.'

'You're not serious. Word will have no doubt spread of me giving myself up, there's not a thief in the whole of the Hammerheads that would trust me walking around with you. Don't you have places yourself?'

'Ajoah is aware of them all.'

'One of your students, I presume?'

'My last protégée. I showed them to him as I was planning to retire.'

'Your students are pretty sycophantic about you, as far as I remember. You cannot trust him to keep silent?'

'I've trained him to follow to code. Stimm knows how close Ajoah was to me. He will order him to hunt me down. Ajoah has no reason to doubt Stimm's motives as anything but honourable. He'll follow his orders.'

'Then let me introduce a guest to our party.' Jontal took the keys from his brother and unlocked Dulmurn's cell. The man was snoring through the whole breakout. Jontal shook him and placed a hand over the man's mouth as he began to object.

'I'm getting out of here. You want to come? I need the safety of that cabin of yours.' He took his hand away as Dulmurn sat up.

'Damned right I am,' Dulmurn whispered.

Jontal blackened him up too and Falakar led them out of the prison building over guards scattered around the floor and at desks, unconscious. Waiting until it was clear, he made for a hole cut in the fence and they were out, heading for the woods.

As they entered the treeline, Falakar stopped. A figure appeared from the near pitch-black. Jontal strained to see before recognising him. 'So you're an accomplice to this treachery.'

Garamon's teeth showed up as a wide smile. His face blackened like Falakar's. 'Good to see you again, Jontal.'

'Not the bandit I hope,' Dulmurn said, attempting a joke.'

'The same,' said Jontal.

Dulmurn's eyes went wide. 'What lunacy is this? I'm now a collaborator in breaking out one of the most notorious villains in the mountains!'

'He is required to complete our task,' Falakar said.

'Oh great. And who are you, *the diamond thief of Impseria*!'

'He's Falakar, the Ghost Ranger,' Garamon answered, proudly.

Dulmurn squinted at the man before him. The combination of darkness and blackened face making him impossible to recognise. He'd met him of course, Falakar was a prominent figure amongst the law keepers and heads of power in the town. He was the right height and build at least.

He pointed a finger at Jontal. 'He's a damned murderer and thief, stealing a fortune in goods from me over the years. Are you telling me I must keep company with this vermin while being hunted by Rangers?'

'There is reason,' Falakar replied.

'What could justify it!'

'In three months the Empire is going to invade.'

Dulmurn went silent, mouth open.

'You may walk away now, we'll not stop you. You can sneak back into the cell.'

'And be caught like a rat in a cage while those torturing zealots knock on the door,' Dulmurn said.

'Or you could run,' Garamon offered.

Dulmurn shook his head. 'I would be penniless. Brinley will already have my assets seized and my trade contracts under his name.'

'I cannot help the situation. Each of us is sacrificing everything we have,' Falakar said.

Dulmurn had no reply. The world he knew was gone.

'Grandfather used to say there are times you must choose if you are a lamb or a wolf,' Garamon said.

'Dulmurn puffed out indignantly. 'That's an irritating way of making a man judge himself, lad.'

'It's your choice,' Falakar repeated.

'I don't trust *him*,' Dulmurn replied, pointing at Jontal.

'We are entering difficult times. Allegiances will change and who we can trust will also. Jontal has shown himself to be useful in combating the Ashnorians, and we are going to need his special kind of resourcefulness in the mountains. If we fail, little of our previous allegiances will count for anything anyway. Besides, I would prefer to succeed and spend my remaining years in jail, than fail and be subjected to torture and death in the mines working for the enemy.'

A horn blew from the direction of the town.

'Time's up. Stay or come, I do not care,' Falakar said. He led off in the direction of the deeper wood. The other two went after him, disappearing in the dark.

Dulmurn stood, his head changing in direction between the two fates of his lives. Of all the things said, it was the young woodsman's words that rang in his head: lamb or a wolf? Dulmurn never considered himself much of a wolf, more a fox, cunning in negotiation. But even a fox couldn't outwit what was coming. Well he was damned sure he wasn't finishing his life as a tortured lamb.

He heard the sound of shouting from the barracks.

He looked back into the woods.

'Wait for me!'

Chapter 21 – Protecting the Asset

Makarec opened the door to Lathashal's old lab. It was the best in the city and a prize worth far beyond the difficulty of the deed to earn it.

He clutched his stave's thrinium plates to detect any magical traps. There was a simple alarm trap expected of the novice and he disarmed it with ease.

He walked in and saw his target sitting on a soft sofa, eyes shut in some kind of meditation, no doubt trying to comprehend a simple spell. This was going to be easier than he expected. He admitted it was disappointing. He wanted the outsider to at least use some pitiful spell he could knock away before smashing the life from him.

He then noticed the raised manasphere on his lap. Perhaps he would be able to put up a fight after all. Then he noticed both palms lying flat on the orb. Such an action should be fatal and yet there were no signs of the Mlendrian being in trouble.

He checked the young man's aura to find it indicating total calm and relaxation. There was also a translucent nature to the aura, as if the Mlendrian's consciousness wasn't completely present.

He moved closer and inspected the scene. He clicked his fingers a couple of times in front of the outsider's face with no response. Thoughts of waking him to interrogate about the mystery crossed his mind.

Something pushed at his leg and made him jump. He looked down to see a large multi-hued orange cat with unreasonably bright-coloured fur. It sat back on its haunches looking at him as if reading his thoughts, as he felt all cats seemed to do. He hated cats, and kicked out at it. He missed, having no idea how such a heavyweight was able to avoid it. It sat back down just a little further away looking at him again with the probing stare.

He became suspicious and checked its aura making sure it had only animal intelligence.

'My apologies!' he blurted and jumping back. It was far more than an animal. 'I've been sent here on the orders of Master Tristaric to kill the outsider. I did not mean to interfere in such high dealings of the Emperor.' He bowed his head low and waited for a response. He'd never heard of a magii being able to shape-change to such a degree. Whoever they were, they were amongst the most powerful in the Empire and had to be here on the Emperor's bidding.

The cat jumped and landed on his head and began raking with its paws. He pulsed a repulsion field outward in all directions at once, painfully tearing it from him and leaving deep rakes across his scalp. It flew across the room, scattering metal containers to clang to the floor. He raised his shield with full force and sought to escape. The cat shimmered and changed into a creature of myth: a red-scaled demon. What was this magii doing? He would know I'm too weak to challenge him, why was he bothering to play such tricks?

He moved for the door, the magii-in-demon-form moved to cut him off.

'What do you want from me? I've already told you my intervention was in error. I'm happy to leave and report back to Master Tristaric.'

The demon magii crouched and long talons extended from its hands.

Makarec then knew he'd stumbled upon something he wasn't allowed to live with. He dashed for the door. The demon-magii leapt. Knowing a shield would be futile against such a powerful magii, he flicked his staff at the edge of a research bench powering it across between them, spilling the array of apparatus upon it.

The demon-magii hit it hard and fell to the floor, dazed. Without pondering his good fortune, Makarec fired everything he had into a shockwave. It slammed into the bench causing it to tumble over, taking his foe with it to crash into the corner of the room against the wall. Everything settled and nothing moved.

Makarec scanned again. The aura indicated the magii was alive, but unconscious. So why hadn't he turned back to his true form? It wasn't an illusion and no sustaining spell was present. He readied his staff to launch another attack if needed, and moved in. He knelt down and felt the thing. It was solid and *real*. He'd no idea what experimentation could have produced such a weird manifestation, but then the greatest magiis were involved in all kind of research far beyond his insight. He could only dream of a day when he could create something so magnificent. He guessed it belonged to Lathashal and now the Zintar, so would pass to him when he killed the outsider. He was thrilled at his additional acquisition. If the outsider, as a novice, had mastered control of it, then he could also.

Without wasting any more time, energy swirled into a thickening flurry of red and blue colour around his staff. The strike would not kill his target, merely immerse him in a field of pain to distract him so his manasphere would get control and turn him to ash.

Feeling the growing power at his command he looked across to confirm the demon-creature was still unconscious. He held out his hand to release the spell and steadied his mind. Spreading his fingers to their widest and pushed his hand to release the energy.

His throat went tight in an instant, choking off his air supply and cutting the blood to his head. Something clicked at the back of his neck and he fell to the floor unable to take even the slightest breath. His vision was going dark and he clutched at his throat finding a thin wire wrapped there. He tried to get his fingers under the line, tearing with his nails to the point they were ripping off. He had seconds of life. He stretched out his hands in desperation to find his staff. His fingers touched the wood. It was nudged away as he lost consciousness.

Faust checked the magii was dead before walking over to the strange demon-like creature. He was no stranger to the secrets of the Empire. What he hadn't been taught, or been privy to as the personal assassin to centuries of Emperors, he'd learned in the field. He knew the manaspheres contained demons, but never heard of one getting out.

He left it alone and returned to Makarec, releasing the magii-killing garrotte of his own design. Thrown from a distance, it encircled the throat of the victim, connecting up at the back of the neck. Wrapping around itself, it then created a metal thread, snapping off and leaving the weapon in place with no way for the victim to remove it. Once on, even a magii would blackout within seconds and death would follow shortly after.

Taking a specialised tool from his belt, he removed the thing. Then opening a small flat case, he revealed a line of sealed corked metal vials and a syringe. He drew liquid from one vial into the syringe and injected it into the dead magii's heart. A few seconds later the body spasmed and the magii opened his eyes, taking a deep gasp and coughing violently.

Faust filled the syringe with a different liquid and administered it.

Makarec pulled away from the jab of the injection noticing Faust for the first time. 'Who are you?'

Faust sucked the content of a third vile into the syringe and held it. 'I have just injected you with serum dissolving your body from the inside. The pain you are feeling in your lower back is where it begins in your kidneys as they process the blood to remove urine. In forty-seconds they stop functioning.'

Makarec placed a hand on his lower back as he felt the pain increasing.

'Help me, please.' Pain began to sweep through his torso.

'Now it will start to affect your liver and other internal organs, all of which are being similarly destroyed,' Faust continued conversationally.

'Why, what do you want from me. Help me.' The pain was increasing and he started to yelp as it stabbed in places.

'I hold in my hand, instant relief,' Faust said, holding up the third syringe full of liquid. 'Tell me who sent you.'

Makarec shook his head. 'You don't understand, he's too powerful, I would be tortured for an eternity.' It felt like his intestine was being filled with burning coals.

'No, it's you who don't understand. The serum I have given you will not kill you for hours. It's designed to cause pain beyond endurance, and it has been perfected over hundreds of years. It's as thorough as I am at what it does.' Faust smiled a smile devoid of compassion. 'Now tell me who sent you and why, and I'll relieve you of your torment.'

Makarec curled up and then reversed, arching his back. The look on his face told Faust the time was near and he brought the syringe close. The man started screaming as the pain wracked through him. At one point he flung a hand out so hard it hit a bench causing the wrist to break. He didn't notice it.

'Who sent you? I give assurance he will not punish you, and that comes from the Emperor himself.'

The body in front of him stopping thrashing around and began to vibrate. Both eyes were balls of blood red and almost out of their sockets. The mouth was moving and trying to say something through the pain now filling the body with a single raw fire.

Faust leant forward and placed his ear up against the tortured lips. A name was spoken. It was no deception, the need to escape the level of pain was absolute. He administered the final syringe of liquid and the body remained vibrating for a few moments longer before going still. Cracks then appeared on all exposed areas of flesh as the moisture was being removed. The skin across the nose split and curled up and the eyes shrivelled and fell back into their sockets.

Faust began checking through the robe of the man as he further dehydrated as a result of the powerful desiccant reducing his body to nothing more than human leather, bones and powder. He tugged at the robe at one point, unable to get to the pockets underneath the body. The spine cracked in two as he pulled it through. The pockets revealed nothing of interest. He snapped his fingers and two servants began the task of clearing up the remains and placing them by a section of wall.

The Mlendrian was still within the orb, and oblivious to his assassination attempt. 'You were lucky this time. I can't be around always to watch you.'

Faust got to his feet and took a last look around. Satisfied nothing remained to indicate he was here, he picked up the magii's staff, avoiding its thrinium plates, and took it and the remains of the body through the room's secret door.

Chapter 22 – Dead or Alive

Ajoah paced up and down in front of Stimm's desk. 'This is wrong. His teachings, strength and moral code are the backbone of everything we stand for. That we are now using Rangers to hunt him down like a criminal must be a mistake.'

Stimm sighed at the prolonged objection and continued signing the pile of papers he'd been given by the clerk who had long-since departed.

'Such decisions are for Command, not field soldiers.'

Ajoah didn't like the connotation he was nothing more than an unthinking soldier. He was Falakar's last personal trainee and it was well known Falakar thought highly of him. It was an intended insult and he knew Stimm was trying to put him in his place.

'I joined the Rangers because of him, as did many others.'

'You talk of him as some kind of god. He's just a man, Captain, and one that left us years ago to hunt down one bandit, only to set him free again within days. He's lost his mind, and more a danger to the public than protector.'

'I can't believe it, the man has sacrificed his whole life for the liberty of others.'

Stimm stopped writing and calmed his irritation. 'I have given you a direct order, Captain. Follow it, or I'll find somebody who will. There are plenty of men in line for your position. Some almost as good as you.'

'You would demote me over this?'

'Gods man, my orders are to be obeyed, by you or another! Now make your choice, go with my order or give me a name to replace you, who will.'

Ajoah's eyes flared at the command. If anybody was going after Falakar it was going to be him, and Stimm knew it. He stood to attention, saluting sharply and left the cabin, leaving the door open contrary to protocol.

Something moved in the shadows and the door closed with a click. Strack walked into the light.

At the same time, the door to Stimm's bunk room opened and Brinley walked in.

'He cannot be trusted. You should send someone else.'

Stimm threw his pen across his desk and sat back. 'There is no one else capable of tracking Falakar. The two are close. Ajoah trained under him for years.'

'And if he's persuaded to join him?'

'Ajoah believes in the code to his core. He will follow out my instructions, or die trying.'

'Are you sure, Stimm? It's not just *his* life in his hands.'

Stimm didn't like the reminder of the threat on his life by the trader. 'Well send your hound to check on him.' he said, flicking a glance to Strack. It would also get rid of the man for a while. His presence made him uncomfortable.

'Oh, I intend to,' Brinley said. 'You may be willing to risk your career, Major, but I need a little more assurance. If Ajoah decides against carrying out his orders…'

'If you think your hound can take Ajoah then good luck with that,' Stimm said. 'And Ajoah knows him as one of yours. He'll come for you.'

Brinley chuckled. 'Oh Strack isn't a match for your man in face to face combat. But then he fights with no moral code to restrict him. Your Captain will wake up living the final seconds of his life drowning in his own blood, with evidence it was Falakar.'

'I want nothing to do with this, Brinley,' Stimm warned.

'Of no consequence, Stimm. You are mine until I'm done with you. I've enough records in our partnership to have you court-martialled and hanged – unless you also want to join Falakar on the run?'

Strack sniggered. The thug made the motion of a rope yanking upwards around his throat.

Chapter 23 – Revenge Trail

It was three days with no sign of Kinfular or ThreeSwords, and Shinlay and Sholster had moved on from the meeting place as agreed. Three men had been tracking them, but once in the mountains the advantage was Shinlay's and she was convinced they had turned back. Sholster's injury was getting worse through infection and she had nothing to stop it. He was struggling to walk, and progress was slow.

They had stopped for the night, sheltering in a shallow cave out of the chill breeze falling down the trail from the mountain.

Shinlay told Sholster to rest while she collected wood and started a fire. When it caught, she sat at the mouth of the cave and stared back down the trail.

Sensing her anxiety, Sholster moved up and placed his arm around her shoulders.

'He'll be alright, lass, I've fought alongside those two for a long time. It'll take more than being captured deep within a hostile camp filled with a few hundred enraged plainsmen to keep those two away for long. He saw her give a resigned nod.

'How do you feel?' she asked.

A big smile spread out across features as rugged as the rocks around them. 'Never felt better.'

She gently nudged his wound with her knee, his face showed pain. His smile forced its way back through the grimace.

'Just a bit of cramp, is all.'

She knew he was attempting to stop her worrying.

'Can you keep the fire alight while I hunt for dinner?' She'd amassed a good stock of dried wood to take them through until morning. With the smell of blood and infection from Sholster's leg, it would draw all manner of night scavengers.

The idea of a hot meal perked the big man up better than any tonic. 'It'll remain a fire fit for the lord of all demons,' he beamed.

Shinlay picked up her bow and set off. She found a suitable tree and went to work fletching a couple of arrows from a branch. She held up her handy work to the fire and was happy enough. They were for penetrating a small meal and only needed to stay true over a short distance. She placed them in her quiver and left the cave.

Returning to Sholster a while later didn't need her tracking skills. The light from the fire lit up a column of smoke rising high into the sky. As she turned the last corner so she looked upon Sholster's construction. Fit for a demon it was. The flames roared higher than his head, crackling and spitting as they devoured the various sizes of dead branches.

'I don't usually make the fire,' he called out above the noise. 'I've put on too much wood.'

Not a twig remained of the wood collected.

Shinlay accepted the apology and skinned their meal. She then sat a suitable distance from the inferno while Sholster's appetite made him brave the fire, almost cooking himself as much as the meat. With constant turning and finding the cooler areas he soon created charcoaled meat. Shinlay cracked through the blackened exterior to discover raw meat inside, and resigned to a grumbling stomach by preference. Sholster, of course, ate everything but cleaned bones, grease dripping down his chin in a frenzied feast of delight. He discarded the last one with a little regret and sat back, the look of a man who had been through the night with forty whores.

Shinlay took another look up at the smoke ascending far enough to be seen from halfway across the Sinserti Plain. 'We will need leave at sunrise. Your beacon will leave them no doubt where we are.'

Sholster looked up. 'Sorry lass. I didn't think.'

The next morning, Shinlay woke him. It wasn't an easy task at the best of times, but this time seemed harder than usual. He was warmer to the touch than was normal too. His wound was red and puffy around the edges. She didn't believe the arrow had been poisoned, but neither had it been clean. She tried again to wake the big barbarian, shaking him as roughly as she could, barely moving his bulk. In the end she thumped him in the head. His eyes opened and he went to grab her. She withdrew her arm out of reach, knowing what the huge warrior could inflict upon someone of her size without thinking.

With some effort he lifted his head to look at her. He relaxed. His eyes were a pale red and his face lighter than usual. 'Morning, lass.'

They travelled until noon, and although she was still far from familiar territory, at least she was in her mountains. They felt welcoming which she knew would not be the case when she returned to the Riaan. She looked forward to seeing her father, but not so the penance she would receive after disobeying and going after Kinfular. She hoped the knowledge of her defiant action saving the lives of three of the tribe's most beloved warriors, including the Hlenshar, would appease the Chieftain a little.

Sholster was breathing deeper than normal. For a moment she caught his anguished look which betrayed the extent of his injury before the big smile burst out on his face.

'I think I ate too much, lass. I'm carrying extra weight.'

She needed to give him a rest without dishonouring him and looked back down the trail. 'Wait here while I check if we are being followed.'

'Aye, good idea, I'll rest for a bit to let the meat settle in.' He slumped down to the ground, relief showing as the weight was taken from his legs.

Even from her position she could see his wound looked bad.

'I won't be long,' she said. 'Guard our things.'

He merely nodded his head.

She returned a while later to find him asleep on the bare rocks where she'd left him. She threw a rock close by. He woke up and she stepped back into view as if for the first time.

He spied her and quickly sat up. 'Any luck,' he said, all trace of problems erased from his face.

'I couldn't see anyone, but the view wasn't ideal. They could have been in many folds in the rocks behind us.'

'Perhaps they didn't see the fire, lass.'

'We should get moving, all the same,' she said.

He pushed himself to his feet using his club.

'I need to move slower through this section. I'm not familiar in this area and I don't want us to have to double back into anyone following,' she said, kindly.

If Sholster caught the lie for his benefit he didn't show it.

They travelled for the rest of the day. He stopped several times, making various excuses and using his club as a walking stick. By the end of the day his strength was gone. Shinlay called camp and he lay down, immediately falling unconscious. His wound revealed a good deal of puss. Removing the makeshift leather bandage she took out a dagger and pried the wound open. After probing she found what she was looking for. At the bottom of the wound was a fragment of metal from the tip of the Plainsman's arrow. It was surrounded by mud. She cursed the coward for dipping his arrow into the ground before firing as it almost guaranteed infection. She cleaned the wound as best she could, but what she needed was Locan leaves.

Neither of their pouches contained any, all of it was used during their encounter with the Ashnorians over the past few days.

The elusive plant grew on the shaded parts of exposed isolated rocks within the cracks. They grew elsewhere in the shade, but any accessible places were cleared out by the wildlife.

Some likely foliage in the fading gloom turned out to be plain shrub. She set out further afield. Night fell, and using the weak light of her glowstone she found one in its first season, not yet full size. She reached out to grab it, and heedless of its desperate attempt at existence, gave it a hearty yank to tear it free from the crack in which was growing.

Heading back, taking the shortest route across the rocks, brought her down from above as opposed to the obvious path. She heard muffled talking and dropped to her stomach. Pocketing her glowstone she eased herself forward to peer over the rock. Her hereditary night vision of her people soaked up the details hidden to others in darkness. There were two men with Sholster and he was tied up. The big man was weakened badly to allow such a thing to happen without at least a few bodies scattered around.

Scouting the area, one other male could be seen up the trail where she'd departed. She pulled free her bow. The two simple arrows she crafted for hunting would not have the penetration to breach the leather armour of the men, nor be accurate enough to find the gaps to clean flesh. She sat back and thought for a moment before deciding her course of action.

Roan stood up the trail from his father and brother. Their father tossed a coin deciding which brother would have the privilege of meeting the woman first, while the other two would push their boots into the big man's wound to make him cry out and bring her back to them. Unfortunately the brute had passed out, so they waited. Roan was to stun her and drag her back. She would no doubt be carrying one of those peculiar glowing rocks to give away her position long before she saw him. He was looking forward very much to what his father had described as a fitting punishment for killing their brother. It wasn't going to be a quick death, and the first time Roan was to take a woman. At eighteen he relished the thought of it after what Brank told him it was like. He became aroused at the thought and his vision began to darken as his anticipation increased his heart rate. He closed his eyes and took a deep breath, calming himself. He didn't want to make any mistakes when she came back.

A sharp pain across his throat snapped his eyes open. Heat spilled down his chest and he went to call out. The only sound was bubbling as he choked on his own blood. His legs went limp, but he never felt himself hit the rocky ground.

Lesh heard the thump up the trail towards his youngest son. He turned to Brank and smiled. 'Your brother has been granted his wish.'

Minutes passed and the youngest brother didn't appear.

'Come now, son,' called out Lesh. 'Don't have all the spoils for yourself. Let's see what your brother died for.'

No response came.

Exchanging glances they pulled free their swords and advanced. Twenty paces up the trail something glistened on the ground.

'He's cut off her damned head.'

Brand swore. He expected more from his younger brother. It was hours of pleasure ruined. The disappointment at the lost revelry vanished when his father lifted the head and gave a strangled cry. He faced it towards Brand. Even in the dark, Brand could make out the hatred in his father's eyes as they shed tears. Brand then knew who the head belonged to. Fury boiled in his brains. He was about to run up the trail, all thoughts of using the woman replaced with a need to hack her to pieces, when a holler went up from back down the trail.

'By Geraminan's rotting manhood, woman; are you trying to rip my shin out?'

Father and son ran back to see the large barbarian leaning on the Peakswoman, struggling to get to his feet. The woman was doing something to his wound. Upon hearing the approaching men she stood. The wounded male picked up his club, leaving his shield on the floor and hopping on one leg.

'Great gods, wench,' Sholster said. 'You cut off his head?'

'Would you have preferred it something else?'

Sholster grimaced at the thought.

'You killed my two youngest sons,' Lesh said, his voice on the edge of control.

'For me to live, he had to die,' she replied.

'Then that's something we're about to change.'

Sholster took a painful step using his club for support as he made room from Shinlay for combat. 'I feel for your loss, Plainsmen, but we did not start this. We only sought safe passage across your tribe as we had no time to go around. There is an army approaching.'

'We care nothing for your excuses, nor fear any army. We came here to find and make you suffer for taking the life of my brother. Now we have twice the reason, and you will suffer twice as much.'

Sholster limped around to get an angle for a single swipe. It was doubtful he would get a second. 'Then come try to take your revenge. You'll have one chance to stop me, for when I hit you, you will fall and not rise again.'

'If I cannot take down a crippled ox and a mountain hoar, I deserve it,' Lesh replied.

The men advanced. When they got within five paces, they rushed in.

Shinlay waited for the final move and reacted fast, pulling her bow from behind her and snatching a shot at the face of the older one attacking Sholster. It wasn't going to be a threat to the man, the arrows were too flimsy and the shot too hasty. Its purpose was to distract him, giving Sholster his one chance. Without time to see if the action had the desired result, she threw her bow towards the other man and jumped away, drawing her sword.

The younger plainsman batted the bow away. He pulled his sword down in a predictable high slash driven by his fury and the desire to cleave her in two with a single strike.

She raised her sword, crying out as the deflection jarred her arm, forcing her to fall on her back. There was a moment where her head bounced back from the rock floor and she lost her senses. Instinctively, she rolled to the side, saving her life as the plainsman's sword struck the rock. She jumped to her feet as he rushed in making a reckless backhanded swipe. It tore across her chest slicing through her leather armour and creating a shallow cut across her breasts. Both were now off balance and stepped back from each other, ready for the next attack.

The plainsmen dropped his shield and held his sword in two hands. 'The next one will cut you in two, you bitch.'

There was a flash of golden-silver from the left and the plainsmen was lifted him from his feet to land face up, unable to move.

Sholster's club settled to stop nearby.

Shinlay walked over. The plainsman's sword arm was broken and twisted. By the way he couldn't move, it looked like his back was broken too. She pushed down with one foot on the arm break, making the plainsmen scream out. Looking into his eyes she pulled her sword out to one side and held it there for a moment. 'I think you were trying to do this,' she said, and swung her sword across him, cutting a line from one side of his stomach to the other. Innards unfurled and spilt out.

'The wolves will find you easier this way. Long before you die.'

Picking up Sholster's club, she returned to him. The other plainsmen's head was all but gone, smashed to pulp into the rock.

'A thousand defecating slugs, lass; I hope I'm never on the wrong side of you in a fight.'

'Good aim in the dark,' she complimented.

'It could as easily hit you,' he admitted.

'Are you okay?'

'The bastard got a hit in, just above the knee.'

'Let me see it.'

Sholster struggled to get up and Shinlay placed a hand on his shoulder to make him stay. His new wound was pumping blood freely and she tore strips from her leather jerkin to stem to bleeding.

'I'd rather you keep it to yourself I cried out like a puppy when you stuffed those leaves into my wound. Any further and I swear you could have dragged out my last meal.'

'Nothing that goes in your mouth would so easily be given up,' Shinlay replied, pulling the bandage tight.

Sholster grunted.

'Any more of them out there, you think?'

Shinlay shook her head. 'A father and three sons we have destroyed this night.'

'Well, they deserved it.'

'Your wound is deep, it has cut some muscle.'

'You look concerned, lass.'

'It's going to slow you down more, and you're losing more blood.'

'Not to worry, I have enough to fill an ox.'

'I hope so. Do you think you can walk the rest of the night?'

Sholster got to his feet, testing his doubly injured leg. 'I won't catch a snow cat, but the pain is less,' he answered.

Shinlay could see blood already seeping through the bandage.

'The Locan will only kill your pain until noon tomorrow.'

'Any good news?' Sholster said, taking his club from her.

'We do make a good team, Mountain Man.'

'Of course I do,' blustered the giant. 'I'm an army.' He used the club as support and began limping up the slope.

Shinlay was worried. If they didn't get back home quickly, the huge barbarian would blackout from lack of blood. He also needed the more powerful medicine of their shaman, otherwise the infection would spread. Sholster would soon either lose his leg, or his life.

She took a cleansing breath of mountain air, spoiled by the smell of blood and spilt bowels, and looked out into the darkness. 'Feed well this night, scavengers, and remember our gift when it comes to our turn, and be swift to clean our bodies, afore they rot.'

Chapter 24 – Seeking Advice

Chantel followed the couple to a room. After the debacle with Chayne and her first attempts to have him like her, and then the attack on his life by the other smooth demon, she decided she had to do something else, and quickly. She'd been observing couples in one of the large areas where groups of the smooth demons met, carrying out the strange ritual of marking thin material and then passing it around one another. It occupied a great deal of time for many of them each day.

They lived in such peace. So pointless. Never did one male attempt to dominate another, neither did the males attempt to mate with the females. She'd been following couples leaving the room together for days and none of them mated.

This time, however, she noticed a couple whose auras changed to pink whenever they came close to one another. Following them in her cat form into a room, she barely needed to use her deception field, they were so intent on one another.

She settled down to observe. Already they'd removed their outer coverings and were lying together in an embrace on a wide, soft surface. Their auras were deepening and movement became desperate. At last the male would dominate the female and force himself upon her! This happened, although the female didn't seem in any distress. It certainly wasn't a very spirited resistance, and her aura was still a deep pink.

This carried on for some time, and at one point the female even managed to overpower the male and pin him down. She forced down with her body weight over and over. This appeared to be causing them both some distress. Eventually the male reclaimed his supremacy and threw her over again, becoming frantic. The female's suffering increased until it became a scream which Chantel could at last appreciate.

Moments later the male briefly joined in with cries of his own and the yelling died away. They then lay together, both panting with exhaustion. The auras of deep pink began to lighten and be replaced with a flowing green, indicating relaxation.

Was that it? And now they are stroking each other and talking softly!

She watched for some time, but their auras gently changed to the white of sleep as they lay in each other's arms.

Shaking her cat head she jumped down and changed shape. Stealing some of the female's discarded coverings she wrapped her naked form, at a loss for what just happened, and left them.

As strange as the ritual of mating was, she went back to Chaynie's room, forming her plan to get him to mate with her.

Chapter 25 – Escape

'Rest here,' Falakar ordered, coming to a halt in a small clearing amidst the dense trees.

'Thank the gods,' Dulmurn blurted, barely managing to get the words out and collapsing to the ground. 'We must have run all night and day.'

Garamon showed no signs of tiring, his eyes alert looking back in the direction from which they came.

Falakar again looked to his protégée. The boy turned man, turned Ranger. He knew he was in safe hands with the woodsman watching, for what he lacked in experience he made up for with the eagerness of youth and passion for his task.

Jontal caught up from being rear guard. 'You're showing your age, my brother,' noticing how Falakar was taking deeper breathes than either himself or the young woodsman.

Falakar didn't rise to the comment.

'Want me to make a fire?' Garamon offered.

Falakar nodded.

'I'll look for wood,' Jontal said.

Falakar gave a distrusting look.

'I'll stay in sight if it makes you happy.'

Falakar shrugged. 'If you want to run and live the rest of your days hiding in the mountains away from civilisation, I'll not stop you, or expect any less.'

Jontal looked hurt and trudged off, snatching up dead wood from around the area.

Falakar turned away. 'We'll split the watch between the three of us. You look the freshest, so you go first, then Jontal.'

Snoring came from the direction of Dulmurn.

'What about him?'

'He has neither the ability to detect approaching Rangers, nor means to stay awake.'

'I don't mean to be rude about him, but he seems to provide no value. And if anything, he's a burden.'

'No less for me when I first met you.'

'But he's...'

'Old?'

Garamon reddened. 'Well, yes.'

'Age brings knowledge. And in his case a place to hide even I didn't know.'

Garamon went to continue but Falakar held up his hand. 'I'll take my sleep now. Make sure the wood is dry. We don't want any patrols picking up the smoke.'

Falakar woke from a shake of his arm. Jontal's other hand held up in front of his face. 'Everything's fine. We decided to split the shift between the two of us and let you sleep, snoring like a docker.'

'There was no need,' Falakar said getting to his feet.

'You're welcome,' replied Jontal.

The Ranger walked away to the dying fire.

Rummaging in the hot embers with a stick, he pulled out a capped jug and poured steaming water into a mug, throwing in some leaves from his belt pouch. Sitting as close as he could to the heat, he pulled his blanket around him and wrapped his gloved hands around the hot mug.

Jontal sat next to him. 'You still drink that stuff?'

Falakar blew on the brew, cooling it while the leaves infused, not answering.

'Not very chatty this morning?'

Still Falakar didn't engage.

'Spare any hot water?'

Falakar gestured to the pot.

Jontal emptied what remained into his own mug before adding a powder and mixing it with a stick until the powder dissolved.

The smell from the drink wafted over Falakar, who wrinkled his nose and showed a look of disapproval.

'I only drink it in the mornings,' said the bandit. 'It wakes me up.'

'It's a narcotic and addictive,' Falakar said.

'Only to the weak-minded.'

'Plenty dead in the ground who said the same.'

Jontal shrugged. 'I doubt it will be the thing that kills me. It's saved my life a few times, too. It improves your reflexes and heightens the senses.'

Falakar let it go. It was an old argument. He finished his tisane and got to his feet, shaking the drops from the mug before reattaching it to his belt.

'And I don't snore.'

'Distant thunder it was then.'

Dulmurn was on the edge of the camp, skinning several small animals.

'Where did they come from?'

'He's quite the trapper in his spare time. Between you and me, I don't think lording over his manor is a natural calling. At least we get a good meal with him around.'

'The lad?'

'Still on patrol. He should be back soon. You know, he reminds me a lot of you at that age.'

'I don't see it, myself,' Falakar replied, shivering while walking back to the bed and rolling up his blankets.

'There's a thick mist hovering over the tree canopy. It would mask a new fire if you wanted warming up. We could get a hot meal to carry us through the day.'

'Cooking will attract a nose for miles. We'll eat cold breakfast and move out.'

'Yes, sir,' Jontal replied with a mocking salute.

Falakar stopped for a moment. 'I'm glad you're still here this morning.'

Jontal went to reply when Garamon returned, grabbed half a loaf and some cheese and sat down by the fire.

'I take it you found nothing,' Dulmurn said, wondering over.

Garamon had a full mouthful of bread and cheese not to be swallowed anytime soon. He nodded up and down, alarming the trapper.

Falakar filled in the unspoken words. 'Two squads will have been dispatched at dawn, quartering the area. His return means he found both of them, and from their position and movements knows when they'll reach us. As he's not in a rush, we're safe for now.'

Garamon finished the first sortie on his food. 'We have about forty minutes,' he confirmed, before ramming in another mouthful.

'We'll head due south and be within the mountains by nightfall, leaving them far behind,' Falakar reassured.

They completed their meal and were packing when Falakar stopped moving, his head turning from side to side. Jontal picked up on his brother's stance and grabbed Dulmurn, indicating to the trapper for silence. Dulmurn froze.

Falakar pushed a finger to his lips then waved his hand rapidly south.

Dulmurn went to grab the spoils of his hunting.

'Too late, they're on us,' Jontal said, lifting one of the traps from Dulmurn's belt as he pushed him towards the other two leaving the camp.

Garamon settled in behind Falakar whose silent footfalls were negated by the trappers closing in behind.

'I'm sorry, Falakar. I don't know how I missed them.'

'It's Ajoah. He knows how to track me.'

'Can he catch us?'

'Yes, with present company they will overrun us.'

As if to support the statement, Dulmurn took a near tumble, only just keeping upright.'

'What do we do?'

'We may have to leave him behind.'

Garamon saw the Ranger was serious.

They kept up the pace, making abrupt changes in direction to throw off pursuit. Dulmurn was beginning to slow, and his footing showing more signs of faltering. At this speed it was only a matter of time before the man tripped and fell.

Falakar veered right and Dulmurn glanced into a tree causing his feet to catch one behind the other. He pitched forward and landed with a grunt. Garamon dived down next to him.

'We cannot stop.'

Dulmurn shook his head, panting and went to sit. 'I just need a second.'

Garamon pulled him up. The trapper was shaking his head, but Garamon dragged him on. Just then a shout went up from behind. All looked back to see the Rangers darting between the trees behind them. Dulmurn began to run.

'Follow Falakar,' but the trapper ran in his own direction. Garamon caught him up. 'We must go this way and follow Falakar.' He gently tugged at the man's arm while dodging and jumping over various natural obstacles in his path. The trapper began to respond and changed direction when another shout was heard from behind. Dulmurn whimpered and put on another wild sprint, continuing as before.

Then Falakar was next to them, making no sound at his approach. 'Dulmurn, if we continue in this direction for much longer I won't be able to avoid them. You must follow me, *now*.'

Dulmurn managed no more than a brief glance at Falakar, his eyes wide with fright and showing no hint of comprehension. Then there was a cry far from their left of someone calling for help. Falakar flicked a foot out to catch

Dulmurn's ankle and at the same time pushed the trapper sideways to land in a large bush. 'Keep him quiet, I'll be back.'

Garamon dropped, concealing Dulmurn deeper into the bush and placing a hand over the trapper's mouth. 'Quiet now,' he whispered into his ear. 'Falakar is going to draw them away. They are very close, make no sound.'

Dulmurn nodded.

The yelling continued as if someone was in serious distress.

Soon the bush opened and Falakar's face appeared. 'Come quickly, Jontal used one of your traps on a Ranger and secured it shut.'

'What of the others?'

'They are tending to him and should buy us some time. Jontal thinks he has an escape route, we must hurry.'

It was no more than a moment of running before a shout went up again. Falakar looked back, frowning.

'What's wrong?' Dulmurn said.

'They've left the injured Ranger.'

'What does that mean?'

'It means Ajoah's picked up more from me than just his training. We must get to Jontal before they get to us.'

Garamon looked over his shoulder and could see a number of Rangers breaking through again not far back. One of them saw him and put out the call. Falakar angled his run away from them.

'They're gaining!' Garamon said.

'We have to make it to the end of the trees. Keep pace with me,' Falakar shouted back.

'I don't think Dulmurn can keep up with us.'

Just then the edge of the trees came into view ahead, giving Dulmurn hope. They broke out onto a thin mud shoreline around a mist-filled lake. Falakar had turned right and was already some way along the shore, increasing his pace on the open terrain. Garamon followed, pulling the trapper with him.

A large bush stuck out ahead on the water's edge but there was no sign of Jontal. Falakar reached the bush and disappeared behind as Jontal stepped out and fired his bow at the chasing Rangers. It was a slow shot to arc over the trapper and woodsman the Rangers could easily dodge, but it slowed them a little as they scattered each time. Jontal fired more until the gap was too close to risk hitting the wrong targets. One Ranger was ahead of the rest and was almost on Dulmurn. Jontal fired another shot at full strength which almost hit the trapper. Masked by his body, the Ranger behind was surprised and it struck him in the thigh, sending him sprawling.

Garamon reached the bush and saw Falakar floating in a concealed rowboat a few feet out, oars dipped in the water, ready to go. Not stopping, he ran into the shallows first, wading briefly to his knees before jumping up and pulling himself into the boat.

Dulmurn reached the beach. With Jontal's aim now clear, the Rangers dived for the treeline and began removing their own bows. Dulmurn hit the water without the strength to remain upright and fell in creating a bow wave that pushed the boat even further out. Falakar hauled on the oars, trying to hold the boat's position. The cold shock seemed to bring some life back to Dulmurn and he began to half-swim, half-drift towards the boat. As he reached it, Garamon grabbed his collar. 'Jontal!' The bandit threw his bow out over Dulmurn to be caught by Garamon. He sprinted to the water's edge making a leap up onto a sturdy branch of the bush growing out into the lake. With two agile steps he then jumped and cleared the gap, landing in the boat.

Falakar rowed and the Ranger patrol emerged around the bush. Jontal had already gathered up his bow and fired another shot to keep them back, almost catching one who then fired back, the arrow skipping over Garamon's head as he ducked and narrowly missing Jontal and Falakar. Another of the other Rangers stood forward, holding out his hands.

'Down weapons!'

The patrol lowered their bows.

The Ranger called out. 'What are you doing, Falakar? Tell me so I can understand.'

Falakar pulled another long stroke taking them further into the mist. 'I will not stand by and watch Tiburn razed to the ground while the council stand by doing nothing.'

'But the Council have ruled against action. They say there is another way.'

'Then it's time to choose your orders or your instincts. You know me well enough, my friend.'

The mist wrapped around as the boat moved out. One moment the shore could be seen, then it was gone.

'What can you do?' came Ajoah's voice fading in the mist.

'What I always have to.'

Garamon tried to pull Dulmurn into the boat. Falakar stopped rowing while he was hauled aboard. The trapper flopped in like a pile of wet clothing. Jontal opened a flat locker at the bow of the small boat and removed two thick blankets throwing them to him. 'Lie down, and keep yourself below the side of the boat. A chill breeze from the mountains will pick up the further we move out.'

Dulmurn took the blankets and wrapped himself up, shivering.

'Where are we going?' Garamon said.

'Bandits use this during the summer for night crossings after raids on the trade route west. There is a hideout on the other side,' Jontal answered.

'I didn't realise you were so organised?'

'We are neither poorly resourced, nor stupid. It's a way of life for many outlaws they would gladly give up if they could.'

'What about you? Falakar is a Ranger and yet you are a thief.'

'We never had the same choices,' Jontal replied, with some bitterness, taking another blanket from the box and wrapping it around him to sit with his back to his brother, looking out ahead into the mist. Falakar showed pain at Jontal's reaction, but made no further comment. The lapping of the water as the oars entered the misty surface grew louder to Garamon in the awkward silence.

The moments passed until Jontal spoke again, still facing out from the boat. 'You still haven't told me why you rescued me and made yourself a fugitive of the very law you have upheld for so long?'

'I cannot stand by and watch a self-interested Council destroy both itself and the people they represent. Your recent behaviour indicated you could be willing to help save the town, rather than die in a cell.'

'And there was me thinking it was for brotherly love.'

'I do everything for the people of Tiburn and all of Mlendria.'

Garamon saw Jontal's shoulders slump. He then laid down with the blanket over him. 'Let me know when we're at the other side of the lake.'

Falakar didn't reply and continued to pull with a gentle rhythm on the oars, his stare lost far out into the enveloping mist.

Strack watched from the cover of the trees, hearing the exchange between Ajoah and Falakar. Stimm's man hadn't taken the chance to finish the job. He expected as much. Now he would have to deal with both of the Rangers. He would keep tracking and bide his time. Neither would be an easy kill.

Legends Awakening

Chapter 26 – Heroic Endeavours

Chayne sat in one of the gardens. His position as Zintar afforded him some privileges, such as wandering the magnificent grounds surrounding the palace. A mix of petite bright-blossoming trees, and ones with trunks as wide as he was tall, broke up the sweeping lawns, marble paving and water features. All around were the ubiquitous twenty-foot statues of the Emperor.

Slowly turning the pages of a beginners magic mathematica tome he was feigning to read, he pondered his next move. Garamon and the Rangers were preparing for an attack from the Empire in three months that was now going to start in less than one. He needed to know what Tristaric had in mind to achieve it, and find a way to delay him.

To complicate matters, there was the new yhordi spy under direct orders from the Emperor. He could be anywhere, listening in on any room at any time.

The openness of the gardens seemed as safe a place as any.

Everything he now did had to be misdirection. Even his choice of library book had to give the impression he was a lowly student. He doubted it would fool the new yhordi for long, but the isolation of information between competing shodatts worked to keep as few people as possible knowing the truth, and that was good. He especially wanted to keep any spies working for Tristaric in the dark.

A servant approached indicating there was someone to see him. Chayne was delighted, it could only be Stalizar. They'd created a cover story that Chayne was to be trained in the arts of magical healing. As a Zintar he'd the right to be taught directly by the powerful master mage-surgeon, and so Stalizar could visit from time to time without raising suspicion.

Chayne signalled the servant and it stood away to reveal a young man of no more than nineteen. His honest face, plain clothing and simple bowl haircut, made him stand out from the garish appearance of the members of the higher palace levels. He had a number of pale freckles that, combined with his ginger hair, gave him a childlike appearance.

Standing a few paces away, hesitant to approach, he looked an unlikely candidate for assassin, especially in so-open an area. Even so, Chayne reached for his manasphere box. 'I don't know you, and I am very busy.'

The newcomer looked to the box. 'I'm no threat.'

Chayne attempted his best look of the nonchalance, such as a powerful magii would conjure up. 'I assure you of it.'

The newcomer rocked from one foot to the other, now looking less sure of himself.

'What do you want?'

The young man checked if it was safe to continue. 'My name is Pelenno. I am with the Lan-Chi.' The last word, he whispered.

Chayne had learned from Illestrael of the spy holes in every room, accessible via the thread-work of secret corridors the yhordi used. Did it extend to the gardens? Were there secret tunnels beneath with spy holes near all the seats? Was the new yhordi standing under him right now, listening? It was unsafe to take chances with a stranger.

'I'm not familiar with that word. Is it a shodatt?'

'I understand,' the young man smiled. 'I am little more than a runner for them at this time. I pass messages back and forth between the palace and the advanced guard post. It was me who delivered the message to your friends so they could find you on the night Lathashal was killed.'

Chayne considered the resistance a mixed blessing. It used him as much as he it. But at what risk this time? He decided he couldn't take the chance, especially with someone as inexperienced and loose-tongued as this one. 'I'm sorry, I have no knowledge of this. Please leave.'

The young man looked crestfallen. Then his face brightened up. 'If I could find out what-' he made the letter T with his hands, 'is planning with a certain General, would that be of help? Uncovering such information would be quite expected of you in your position. It wouldn't implicate you with us, merely be considered normal intelligence-gathering between magiis.' The young man was positively beaming. Clearly he was well versed in Ashnorian politics.

'I have no knowledge of this Lan-Chi you speak of, but that information would be useful.'

'Leave it with me,' replied the young man, spinning around on his heels.

'You will not risk coming to harm in this?' asked Chayne to the retreating back.

The young man stopped and looked back, his face suddenly serious to the point of melodramatic. 'We play a dangerous game. I live with risk every moment.'

He turned away again and left the gardens.

Chayne sat. There were so many factions to be balanced within the Empire. Without Illestrael he was struggling to gain traction. He knew he was juggling fire enlisting this Pelenno, but with so little time before the invasion, as long as he wasn't implicated as a collaborator with the Lan-Chi, this eager recruit was all he had.

Chapter 27 – Twisted Bodies

Angry from the latest failure, Tristaric swiped the depleted manasphere from its pedestal sending it across the room to crash into the stacked chairs of the eighty-foot meeting hall. It was converted into a makeshift laboratory for experimentation of his new solution. While portal tunnelling magic in itself wasn't new, hundreds had tried to realise a solution for mining uses, none had achieved a safe stable tunnel longer than a dozen paces. For even those required huge amounts of mana to sustain for only minutes.

He wasn't about to give up though. With so much at stake, including his own death by torture, he was going to make this work, or die in the attempt. He was one of the brightest minds in the Empire, rising to become the Emperor's personal magii at half the age of any predecessor. So far he'd managed to get the portal to reach halfway down the room, a feat already noteworthy in magii history. But it wasn't enough. The current mathematica for magic wasn't adequate. He needed something radical, something truly ground-breaking.

He walked up to the crumpled form of a servant, the subject of the test, its body barely recognisable from its kind, and more resembling a bag of pulped organs and broken bones. He gave a flick of his utility staff and the body unstuck itself from the floor and slapped into the wall to land atop the pile of previous failed transportees. He stood at the end of a line of twenty-four greasy pools of bodily residue down the middle of the room. Each represented a stage of his adjustments to refine the magic and form the tunnel a little further. This was the furthest transport so far.

He wrinkled his nose. The smell from each subject as it released its bowls before dying was becoming unpleasant. He hadn't expected it and it was starting to encroach on his concentration. He returned to the starting point where other master magiis stood aiding his experiment, and placed the next manasphere on the pedestal. He was draining the mana of a gradia ten sphere with each attempt. Only twelve remained. He had a team of magii recharging more.

The solution to his promised alternative to the Rite to Rakasti had escaped him for over a week now. His rate of progress was too slow. He needed a breakthrough soon for it was too late starting afresh with another idea.

He looked up at the dwindling line of waiting servants, considering them only as components of his experimentation.

Placing the new manasphere into the tripod he aligned the converging rings into the next configuration. They acted as mana-lenses, shaping the mana to create a tunnel of portal magic for materials and people to walk through. He'd got the idea from the Towers of Communiqué focussing rings, converting for people instead of signals.

With each test he learned a little more about the dynamics of the mana as if fluxed through the combination of lenses to converge better. It took a master magii per lens to hold the mana field in place at the beginning, but each ring doubled the portal distance from the last, requiring additional magiis to handle the stability of the field for the later rings. The rings were made of thrinium and worth an Emperor's fortune in total. He was consuming the Empire's entire output and reserves of the metal by order of the Emperor. Only three rings were made at this time, the rest were being manufactured across Ashnoria. If he failed to get even the first three to work then the rest were useless and the remainder of his short life would be subject to providing Estatoulie with compensation for failing him. Tristaric had witnessed that many times, sometimes being the one causing the victim's torment.

He indicated to the magiis to initiate the stabilising mana flow for the next test. The blue-green energy began to condense around the thrinium rings.

The next servant stood in the portal.

Tristaric placed his fingertips upon the fresh manasphere and stretched out his other hand. A complex mix of purple, blue and scarlet mana left his fingers in a continuous stream to the first ring. It spread out as a cone creating a tunnel on the other side to meet the second, larger ring five feet further along. Again, the tunnel appeared on the other side and extended to the third, final ring. Tristaric let the flow of mana increase and watched as the portal grew in length passing the third ring until it reached the position at which it previously failed. He smiled. The new lens configuration had improved the field stability. He was on the right track.

As pre-instructed, the servant walked down the tunnel as Tristaric let out a greater flow of mana. He controlled his excitement as the tunnel continued to lengthen. It was almost at the end of the hall when the mana began to flicker.

'No,' he cried.

He increased the flow of mana. The tunnel still flickered and began losing integrity.

'Increase flow!' he yelled at the other magiis.

The tunnel increasingly wandered from straight until the edges began to cross over the servant making it buckle to the floor, each time causing its body to change shape a little more. The end of the tunnel began flailing about like a snake, smashing chairs and tables on the edge of the hall to the ceiling as if made of parchment.

With effort, Tristaric pulled his blackened fingertips from the manasphere. 'You idiots!' he shouted, thudding the newly-drained manasphere away.

He desperately needed readings from inside the tunnel by a magii. None in the room would do it after seeing the consequences. He needed someone ignorant of the dangers. Someone expendable, who he didn't need for the final solution.

A smile spread across his face.

He signed to a servant and it left the room.

'Take fresh manaspheres,' he ordered. 'It's time to solve this problem and take care of another.'

He didn't have to wait long before the door opened. A servant entered and rejoined the queue of other servants.

Chayne walked into the long room. At his end stood Tristaric before a line of three heavy thrinium rings, each larger than the previous and spaced ten paces apart. The first was no bigger than a serving plate while the last halfway down the room was large enough for someone to walk through. Whatever this was it demanded a king's treasure of the rare metal. At each of the two larger rings stood a magii on either side, four in all. From their apparel they looked to be masters. The power such a group could create was substantial.

'Good morning, Zintar. I hope this day finds you well?'

Chayne noted the too-casual tone. There was danger here.

'Please, come in. I thought I'd make amends for our difficult introduction. I have a fascinating experiment here involving circular shielding. It's completely new to the Empire and will help the safety of miners. If I succeed in stabilising the field then whoever is involved in the project will be recognised by the Emperor himself. Perhaps you can help.'

Chayne knew neither Tristaric nor the Emperor cared for miners or their wellbeing, and even less so about sharing recognition for discoveries. This had to be something to do with restarting the invasion early, which meant it was worth staying.

'What do you want me to do?'

'I'm having difficulty keeping the sustaining field threaded throughout the shield. I need somebody to stand inside the shield tube and use a mana probe to isolate the breakdown.'

Chayne remembered his first encounter probing a sustaining shield, when trying to break into Lathashal's cabinet. It almost cost him his life.

'What if I cannot control the pull?'

Tristaric stalled for a moment as if not expecting the question. 'I won't let it get that far. When you find the destabilising mechanism I will stop the shield energy. It's perfectly safe.'

Chayne looked at the man's disarming smile. He couldn't be trusted, but how far would he go in harming him. He had little choice if he wanted to know what the magii was planning. He nodded his consent.

'Excellent! Stand just before the large focusing ring at the end, then as the shield grows around you measure the leading rim.'

Chayne positioned himself. His nose wrinkled at an unpleasant smell and he searched for the source, recoiling at the pile of bloodied flesh and bone. 'What's that?' he said, pointing.

'I use servants to test for any fatal mana leakage.'

Chayne looked horrified at the man. 'How many have you killed?'

'I've no idea.'

Chayne caught the bile rising in his throat at the grotesque act.

'What?' Tristaric said, genuinely mystified.

Chayne now had to help, if only to stop more servants being sacrificed. He raised his manasphere and placed his fingertips upon the surface.

Tristaric placed his hand upon the first manasphere and multicoloured mana poured out of his hand into the first ring. The colours swirled around until they consolidated into a regular pattern. The magic leapt from ring to ring and spread forward. Chayne closed his eyes to better see the mana flow and noted the threading of the sustaining field as it created a web of control throughout the shielding, holding it together. The complexity of Tristaric's creation was astounding, and rivalled Lathashal's. Incredible for such a young magii.

He began measuring the relative values of the different types of mana attempting to understand how it worked, but the intricacy was beyond him. It was truly an awe inspiring sight to see such a piece of magical engineering. As the tunnel grew towards the end wall the first fluctuation in the beautiful symmetry occurred. The moment was fleeting and there was no chance to locate the cause. He was watching the spot for recurrence when another appeared on the other side. Again he reacted too slowly. The fluctuations increased in rate and he began to see the beginnings of a pattern; timing and positioning the moments of breakdown. He sent a mana probe to intercept a point when he estimated one would occur. On cue the sustaining field snatched at the probe as with Lathashal's cabinet, but this time he was ready and placed a weak point in the probe to break the connection if the drain became too much. The probe spun out into the shield and circled around him. He watched it weave in the shield magic as he took readings. The energy flying around him was enormous.

The probe then snapped and he watched as the magic began to weave sideways. It increased in movement where the sustaining spell was losing resonance and breaking down fast. If he was still inside when it did, the energy of the walls would cross over him and disperse through his body with fatal effect as it had with the servants.

He tried to head out of the tunnel. The end whipped across to the right and blocked his exit, the right side passing close enough for the hairs on his body to rise from a huge static build up. The return swipe would definitely pass over him.

Instinctively he dropped to a crouch, masking his manasphere from Tristaric and the other magiis before placing hands fully on the surface. In desperation he threw everything he had into a beam of crude polarised shielding straight at the weakest point of the collapsing tunnel field before creating a shield around himself. It had little chance of doing more than prolonging the inevitable.

The walls of the tunnel magic stabilised for a moment before continuing to thrash around and hit his shield. Suddenly, a hole appeared in the tunnel and his body was brutally pulled back to the start of the experiment where Tristaric was standing over him. The tunnel self-destructed, scattering unformed mana in all directions to dissipate into the walls, floor and ceiling. All the magii's in the room were in mana shields, and Chayne now noticed one over Tristaric and himself too, created by the master magii. He stood, his face burning with accusation at the man.

Tristaric ignored it. 'What did you do to the field to make it reform?'

'It could have killed me.'

'All experimentation has risk.'

Chayne stared the man down, although such actions were pointless, the man cared only for his work. 'The sustaining field is too weak to hold the shield together.'

'That's obvious,' Tristaric rejected. 'I sent you in to determine why.'

Chayne knew he would have to say something credible and yet somehow not give away his full findings.

'Do you have the answer or must I continue with the rest of the servants?'

'When the shield almost touched me, I felt static. The further you push the shield, the greater the static mana attraction multiplies. I thought it could be causing the shield lines to pull together shorting out and pinching off the sustaining field lines. I injected a polarised shield matrix to keep the shield lines apart.'

Tristaric pondered the answer. Mana attraction played so little part in mana manipulation it was normally ignored in calculations. Then again, he was creating exceptionally high energies.

'I have no knowledge of this polarised shielding you speak.'

'It was something Lathashal was teaching me. I believe I can adapt a solution based upon his work, but I will need a month to perfect it.' In truth he knew had no such solution, but creating a delay was key.

'You have three days,' Tristaric replied.

'I need longer.'

'The next three rings will arrive in two days and will have to be installed in a new larger area and these ones relocated there too. You have until midday in three days' time. If you are not ready I will continue my experiments using the servants. If you have no solution, they will die.'

'It's murder.'

'They're servants.'

'They are still people.'

At this point Tristaric almost laughed. 'You may have advanced at a remarkable rate with your magic training, but it's equalled by the strangeness of your heathen ways.'

Chayne's hatred of the young master deepened. There would be no negotiation with this fanatic. Killing him was losing its usual repulsion for him taking a life.

He left the room and returned to his lab, sitting on his sofa and placing a hand on his manasphere. The moment he materialised within it he halted, the sphere was no longer blackness. A swirling ethereal blue mist threaded its way all about him. His concern turned to Zystal. He raced deeper into the orb to the normal position he found the demon and called out. He was relieved to hear Zystal's voice in the distance. It was slurry and not quite making sense.

It got closer until the demon appeared out of the mist. After it was horribly mutilated during the attack on Lathashal, it didn't seem possible it could have survived, but the demon possessed remarkable recuperative powers and already its broken bones were knitted and skin disfigurements were all but gone. It did, however, look decidedly drunk.

'*Maaaasteeerrr.*'

Its eyes were having difficulty staying locked onto where it as going and its legs weren't exactly in control.

'Zystal, what's happened?'

It tripped and fell on its side. It seemed perfectly happy with this and smiled up at him.

'*Sooooo muuuuuch maaaammmnaaaaaa.*'

The mist was the same colour as the mana pulled into the sphere's holes when recharging. He waved his hand through it and watched it swirl round in the wake of his movements.

He didn't like the idea of being in here with the demon in his current state, and returned.

Back in his body he looked for something suitable to safely discharge the excess mana. He spotted a four-foot diameter metal ball, for which he held no idea its purpose. Placing his fingertips on the manasphere he let a beam of heat leave his other hand to warm the ball. Instead of a controlled ejection of mana, it shot out more concentrated, hitting the ball and heating the thing at an alarming rate. Within seconds the point of contact was red hot and growing as it spread out across the ball.

The rate at which the power was being released was beyond his bearable limit and he throttled back until he could release his fingers. They snapped away leaving the familiar greasy blue-black smoke. A third of the huge mass of metal was now red and the centre where the spell entered was white hot.

He entered the manasphere again to see if there was any effect. The mist had diluted a little. There was a lot more work to do.

Chapter 28 – Hiding Out

The shore on the other side of the lake came into view. The mist was gone, thinned to eerie wisps of white, swirling as if having a will of its own. The water stirred from the surfacing of its tenants seeking the sun's meagre spring warmth.

'Wake them,' Falakar said.

Garamon pushed on the arm of Jontal.

The bandit woke and from instinct, stayed low. 'Trouble?'

'Not yet,' Garamon replied.

Jontal sat and stretched, seeing the shore. 'You took your time crossing, Brother. 'The mist is lifting, your Rangers may see where we land.'

Dulmurn stirred and wrapped himself up more in his blanket.

Jontal kicked out a boot into the man's side. 'Wake up, Trapper, time to move.'

Dulmurn yelped from the kick and turned over angry to reply. As he rolled he discovered he was tighter bound than expected and his arm didn't come out. He rolled off the narrow bench, landing in an inch of ice-cold lake water in the bottom of the boat. It ran inside his covering and against his neck and back. He managed to throw the blanket off and stood up, furious with the bandit. As he did so the boat rocked and he sat down quickly almost pitching overboard.

'Kick me again and I'll make sure you regret it.'

Jontal rocked the boat, making Dulmurn respond instinctively throwing out his hands to either side of the boat, his eyes wide with alarm. Jontal stood up in perfect balance

177

and scanned the approaching shoreline. 'There's the bush to hide the boat,' he said, pointing.

Falakar angled the boat.

It wasn't long before the gravel and rock bed of the lake appeared through the water, soon followed by scraping as the boat came to a stop. Falakar and Jontal jumped out up to their knees and Garamon followed. The trapper was last, and all four of them pulled the boat ashore and hid it within a large bush on the edge of the lake. They shouldered their packs.

'Dulmurn looked anxiously out across the lake, catching glimpses of the far shore through the evaporating mist. Will they still find us?'

'Ajoah will have organised the search into two groups,' Falakar replied. 'One around each side of the lake. They will not be far away.

A horn blew and for a few seconds a gap in the mist opened to show a group of rangers in the distance heading their way. The mist closed again.

'He's good,' Jontal said.

He was my best,' Falakar replied.

A responding horn blew from further away in the other direction along the lake.

'They will be tired from the run around the lake, we can get a lead,' said the Ranger.

Dulmurn didn't look happy. 'I've barely rested. I don't think I will last long.'

Falakar unexpectedly grabbed the trapper by the jerkin and pulled him close. 'We cannot be caught. We need a place to hide, and that means your cabin. So you will run, and run hard until we're safe.'

Dulmurn stepped back speechless at the outburst from the normally controlled Ranger.

Garamon looked to Jontal who seemed less surprised at the outburst. There was a sadness in the bandit's eyes.

Another horn blast came from the first group.

'Where's this hideout you speak of?'

'Aldor's Ridge,' Jontal replied.

'Lindeg and I long suspected it to be a place for a hideout, but never found anything.'

'It's well concealed. Don't expect a warm welcome.'

'I thought you said it was only used in the summer,' said Dulmurn.

'There's always a holding contingent. Five or less.'

Let's go,' Falakar ordered, and led off again.

Garamon went second and Dulmurn looked wary as Jontal fell in.

'Right behind you,' smirked the bandit.

Dulmurn tightened his money belt as he ran.

They entered the new treeline. The trees were denser than the other side of the lake making for a slower run but easier to lose those following by changing direction often.

They ran for an hour before Falakar stopped in a rocky area, the first indication the mountains were ahead.

Dulmurn took the opportunity and collapsed to the ground again. 'Will they be far behind?'

'Ajoah correctly guessed I'd do the opposite to what I've taught him,' Falakar replied. 'For the last hour I've gone back to his training. It will trick him for a while.'

'I'll lead from here,' Jontal said. 'You need to know the right way in.'

Falakar pulled Dulmurn to his feet and pushed him towards the retreating Jontal.

It was evening before the ridge appeared through the trees, a hundred feet of moss and ivy-covered sheer rock face.

'We need to climb?' Falakar asked.

'No way, Ranger,' Dulmurn said. 'I could no more climb than fly up it.'

'We could pull him up on ropes?' Garamon suggested.

'We're not doing that,' Jontal replied.

'Don't leave me here,' Dulmurn begged. 'I don't want to go back to that jail.'

A horn sounded from high above. Rangers were spreading out on top of the ridge.

Another horn returned the call from the forest behind them. It wasn't far away.

'I know a trap when I see one,' Jontal said. 'Looks like your man thinks more out-of-the-box than you give him credit. This way.' The bandit stepped through some prickly bushes and down a dip of rotting pine cones and needles. It led to the foot of the rock face out of sight of those above. Parting some ivy he pushed at a sliver of rock roughly his height. It moved inwards to reveal a slender passage and he followed it in beckoning the others. One by one the group slipped into the tight opening. Dulmurn needed to be pulled and pushed from both sides to scrape through. When the last of them was in, Jontal pulled the ivy back across the gap and pushed the rock back into place. It clicked into position and he swung a heavy iron bar down across the back of it to lock it. 'It will take them days to break through without specialist mining equipment.'

The blackness pushed back as Jontal lit a torch from one of the wall sconces. He drew his sword and led them deeper into the rock until it opened out into a cave the size of a barn. As he lit more torches around the edge so more openings were exposed. Upon closer inspection they revealed smaller rooms chiselled from the rock, each with an array of boxes of different sizes. To one side of the main room stood a cooking range with a chimney disappearing into the ceiling.

Jontal looked puzzled, checking each of the small rooms. 'I've never known this place be empty.'

Falakar checked the ashes in the range. 'Cold.'

'Well, that's a damned blessing,' Dulmurn said, relaxing at last onto a wooden bench. 'Any chance we can get that thing alight. I could do with drying out.'

'The smoke is trapped in special filters. It doesn't escape,' Jontal said, belaying his brother's concerns.

'You've been busy,' Falakar said, not able to contain begrudging approval in his voice.

'Nothing to do with me,' Jontal admitted. 'This has been here since before I chose my life in the mountains.'

'Who built it?'

'We have no idea. It was run down when discovered by one of the bandit groups, suggesting the owner had long since departed or died.'

'This is no job for one man,' Dulmurn stated.

The bandit shrugged his shoulders indicating he didn't care. 'We are perfectly safe here for the night. There are a number of tunnels we can use to escape if we go before light tomorrow.

Falakar tapped Garamon's back. 'Let's go explore the tunnels. I don't like the idea of being trapped in here.'

'You've never discovered them before,' Jontal said.

Falakar pointed to one anyway.

'Yes, sir,' Garamon replied automatically, and took the lead.

Dulmurn watched them go. 'You kick pretty hard, Bandit,' he said, rubbing his side.

Jontal continued with what he was doing. 'I don't care for dead weight, you almost got us caught back there.'

'The Ranger doesn't seem to share your opinion.'

'We need your cabin, not you. And we won't make it if he or that idealistic woodsman attempt some foolish rescue of your hide if we get chased again. There are no more lakes to save you.'

'Your words are sharper than your kick.'

'If it were me, I'd get you to tell us the location of your cabin and then kick you out.'

'I'd never tell you where my cabin is unless you took me with you.'

Jontal pulled a small pouch from his jerkin, and poked it at the trapper. 'This is pollen from Distralay Ipakular. More commonly known as Head Banger. It's a nasty little powder, which, when correctly administered, causes an immediate short-lived headache beyond your wildest imagining. A few rounds of this and you would tell me every little secret.'

Dulmurn withdrew. 'You're a vile man.'

'Best to remember it,' Jontal replied, tucking the pouch away again.

The heavy mood hung in the air as Jontal went about starting the fire. 'Get out of those clothes. If we're heading to the mountains you won't want your clothing freezing on you. There are some dry ones in the room to your left.'

'Are they clean?'

'Of course, we have servants on call too.'

Dulmurn grumbled and began removing his clothing.

'So what's it like being an outlaw?'

Jontal poured a little oil on the fire and pushed one of the torches into it immediately flaring the fire into life. The smoke rose and disappeared into a wide funnel drawing it away.

'Hard and dangerous. If I were you, the first chance I get, collect as much wealth as you can on the back of wagons and head for the ocean. Then trade for a boat and head off to the ice lands. It's just godforsaken enough you might get away with the rest of your life without the Ashnorians bothering you.'

'Leaving you to plunder what's left behind.'

'Money and possessions aren't going to be worth a damn.'

'Then why aren't you following your own advice?'

'I've got my own plans, and they don't involve saving your wretched arse from capture and torture by the Empire.'

'You really think we have no chance?'

'There are millions of them. Even if the entire population of Mlendria picked up a weapon, they still wouldn't stand against such an army. And that's not to mention their magii.'

'Are they as powerful as they say?'

'They have some great secret that reduces our best to little more than party magicians.'

'If Mlendria is lost, why does Falakar continue?'

'He doesn't know when to give in,' Jontal spat. 'He'll continue if there's a single Mlendrian remaining to save.'

Dulmurn removed the last of his clothes and hung them near the fire. He disappeared into the small room Jontal indicated and returned wearing a tight-fitting green jerkin and long pants. 'Don't they have bigger?'

'Bandits are lean and fast. The slow ones are dead or in prison.'

Dulmurn sat down to the sound of loud rip from his backside. He cast his eyes upwards in resignation, picked up a blanket and used it as a cushion to avoid his bare cheeks connecting with the cool stone of the seat.

By the time the fire was roaring, Falakar and Garamon returned from their scouting. Garamon walked to the fire and slid a dead fawn from his shoulder.

Dulmurn perked up at the sight. 'A hot meal?'

'One of the tunnels came out behind the search party. This fawn was almost on top of it.'

'Skin it, I'll cook it,' Falakar said.

'It's a deal,' Dulmurn replied, removing his skinning knifes.

Ajoah called up to the men on the ridge above him for sign of their quarry.

Hands were raised indicating the men had no idea.

'Where did he go, Ranger?'

Ajoah jumped upon hearing Strack's voice from behind. The thug managed to elude his detection, which was worrying. Clearly he'd received significant training at some time. Three of Ajoah's men drew swords.

'He's the *Ghost Ranger*,' grinned Ajoah. 'How do think he got his name?'

Strack moved in close enough for the spit as he spoke to land on Ajoah's face. 'You think this funny?'

The Rangers took a step forward, and were stayed by their Captain's raised hand.

Strack held his stare. 'You're a brave man with your boys around.'

'Happy for a one-to-one anytime,' Jontal replied, resting a hand on his sword hilt.

Strack hawked and spat on the ground. He then backed off a few steps. 'What do you intend to do?'

Ajoah removed a hand from his sword and waved his men away to continue searching. 'They know we're here, so no point hiding our location. We'll have a fire and cook a decent meal. I think tomorrow we'll be heading into the mountains.'

Strack didn't move.

'You're not welcome to stay and eat with us,' Ajoah said, cheerfully.

The henchman returned another threatening stare.

Ajoah didn't flinch.

Strack walked back into the trees.

Chapter 29 – Too Cold

Jewell stood shivering in the shade of a rock face, recalling the first task given to him by the Commander, which was to kill the tiny creatures thrown into their ranks at the first encounter with the barbarians. It was a chaotic mess of men thrashing around wildly to escape the stinging things, and he could think of nothing else to do than send out a shock wave along the ground. It certainly destroyed most of the creatures, but also took the legs away from those caught up, bringing them down hard onto their backs. This didn't engender much goodwill with the soldiers, most of whom were left limping for some time, and it delayed the pursuit of the fleeing barbarians.

The final toll was over three-hundred men dead or unable to continue. The Commander had been irate.

Now the barbarians were lined across a narrow pass, just seen in the first glimpses of light in the sky. Jewell was no military man, but it was clear even to him how the vast numbers of empyrean soldiers couldn't wear down the heathens in the usual way. Perhaps only fifty at a time could engage at once. He could see the Commander looking around in the gloom for another route to get around behind them. There were none.

Jewell cared nothing for that, only that the sun was rising somewhere behind those mountains ahead of him, promising to raise the freezing overnight temperatures. He'd lived all of his twenty-eight years within the confines of the Empire where it was dry and hot. He never conceived of such a forsaken place as this. In the permanent shadows lay a form of solidified water. It had a cold and uninviting appearance, but to touch it was to know cold. It was fragile though. Just a moment on a warm hand would change it back to water at a fraction of its volume. He made note to look it up in the library upon his return.

A light breeze moved the morning air finding a gap in his robe spreading shivers throughout his body. He'd occasionally suffered the cold of a desert night, but nothing prepared him for this damp, icy chill. He hated it. Looking around he could see the soldiers were suffering the same discomfort. None of whom came prepared for fighting in the cold mountains. Well, maybe they had to suffer, but he couldn't bare it. He placed his fingertips upon his manasphere and a waft of warm air encircled him. It would gradually empty his manasphere, but after his first attempt to aid them he didn't think it likely he would be called upon anytime soon. After all, they were fighting a simple race, few in numbers and devoid of magic. He wasn't likely to be needed again.

With such reasoning he convinced himself to increase the temperature, and smiled at the warmth returning to his bones making him involuntary shudder. He noticed soldiers looking at his feet. There was water pooling where he stood. He ignored their looks of disapproval and moved to a position nearer the centre of the army where magiis where expected.

He watched as the independent sections of men each followed the same procedure as they packed their tents, maintaining a perfect synchrony of timing. Soon after, a command was given and the army set off. Jewell kept pace, bored at the thought of another day not at his experiments.

Shortly after, the characteristic cries came from ahead signifying the start of the day's fighting in the name of the Emperor.

Chapter 30 – Seduction

Chantel finished off the final touches. She was pleased with her latest incarnation of a smooth-skinned demon female. Her skin was soft and blemish-free. Her nose, small with a tiny round ending. Her eyes surrounded with large, black eyelashes. Her fingernails were bright red, as were her lips. Getting them to glisten and sparkle had been difficult, but she at last got it. Her breasts were doubled in size as the males particularly liked this feature. Her waist was narrow and her rump, plump and firm. She wasn't completely happy with the legs though. In her own form she'd a second joint above the ankle reversing the line of the leg. These smooth demons didn't have such a feature and she still found it difficult to balance. She tried to introduce the second joint into her smooth form, but the response from the males was very negative, so she just had to put up without it.

Finally, she checked the flimsy upper garment exposed the upper part of her breasts, and adjusted the hem to reveal as much of her legs as possible without quite showing the lower part of her bottom. If all this failed, there had to be something wrong with him. She headed to his room.

Along the way the males were looking at her as she passed. She checked their auras and they were all changing to the crimson of mating. All was set.

She arrived and knocked. A servant opened the door and she invoked her avoidance. The thing just stood there as she walked passed it.

There he was, sitting on the soft chair with the demon prison held in one hand. She knew his habits well now, and he would be coming out of it soon. She sat down next to him and adjusted everything to her satisfaction. The chair was lower than most and it caused her leg covering to ride up. Everything was now on display. She pulled at it and wriggled, but could only get it some of the way back. It would have to do.

She waited.

Chayne opened his eyes and let go of the sphere.

She opened her mouth and pulled her lips back over her teeth to expose their whiteness. 'Hello,' she said.

Chayne leapt from the chair, his manasphere tumbling out of his grasp to land on the floor, ejecting the orb from its fixings to roll to the other side of the lab.

The reaction wasn't quite what she expected. Were the teeth too white?

'It's okay, I'm not here to harm you. You won't need your demon prison.'

Chayne was alarmed at the open declaration of the true nature of manaspheres. She looked like one of the palace's concubines used by the Elite to satisfy their needs. But if she knew the secret of manaspheres then she was something far more. A master magii under an illusion? Though to call it a *demon prison* was odd for a master magii. Had she provided services to one who'd been lose-tongued? It seemed impossible to believe.'

'Why did you call it that?'

'What?' she replied, disappointed his aura had not a wisp of crimson.

'A demon prison.'

'The ball thing, it holds your low-caste.'

'How do you know of such a thing?'

'Should I not?' she replied, innocently. His aura was changing to one of stress. This was going wrong again.

'How did you get in? My servants are instructed not to let anyone in without my permission.'

She was getting annoyed with questions, they should be touching by now and removing their garments. 'I'm able to go wherever I choose.'

So she was yhordi, and one who knew of manaspheres, making her high ranking. 'What do you want with me, I've already been visited by one of your people?'

With no idea what to do next, she fell back on her original plan in the hope the questions would stop. She gave a bright smile. 'Can we mate now?'

Illestrael had been forward, but nothing like this. 'What do you want?'

'To mate. Is it the wrong word?' She cocked her head to one side.

'I mean, what do you *really* want?'

She was confused and stood up causing Chayne to back away a little. 'Do you not want to mate with me? I've done everything I can to make myself desirable for you. Are you not attracted to me?'

Surely her displayed naivety was far too obvious to be genuine, even to the point of being imbecilic.

She stepped closer and jiggled her upper body from side to side giggling, flicking her eyelashes.

Chayne stepped back further. 'Get out of my lab.'

'Is it the breasts, are they too big?'

Then she remembered one last thing the smooth-skinned demon female did to set off the mating. She walked over to the bed and lay back, outstretching a hand and beckoned him over with a single finger.

Chayne pointed to the door. 'Get out of here!'

Chantel was distraught. It had all gone horribly wrong, again. She stood up. 'What is wrong that you don't want to mate?' She stamped a foot creating a little flare of fire on the floor and headed out. A servant closed the door in the usual calm and exact manner they do all things, unaffected by the conflict.

The ring of fire died out leaving Chayne open-mouthed. The stamping of the foot and the storming out reminded him of the other woman who had appeared and wanted to 'be his friend.' Was it the same one in another illusion or was this to be expected of woman in the Empire and such things would continue to happen?

Chantel went back to the room she knew was empty and ripped way the clothing she took so long to find. She looked at her reflection in the shiny surface on the wall. Cross at losing her chance to mate with Chayne, she lashed out at her image. It smashed into pieces, which surprised her as she thought it was some kind of magic. She stamped her foot down again at the whole weirdness of this world and pain shot up through her foot making her hop. There were fresh cuts bleeding from pieces of the broken thing stuck in her foot. Plucking at one it created another sharp pain as she removed it. She shape-changed into cat-form, limping back to Chayne's lab. Scratching at the door, a servant opened it and she walked in.

Chayne was nowhere to be seen.

Limping towards her usual shelf, one of the low-castes lifted her, inspecting her foot. It began to remove the painful objects.

'I've had enough of him,' she said to the servant, who didn't seem bothered a cat was speaking to him. 'If he won't mate with me, he can fend for himself and get killed for all I care. I'll find somebody else to live with who'll be my mate.'

Chapter 31 – Lluuelliun

Two of the three days had elapsed. Tomorrow, Tristaric would resume his experiments using servants. Chayne was exhausted from scouring Lathashal's notebooks. They contained a dizzying array of magical experimentation and spellcasting. The work Lathashal put into his profession was astounding. Even with his Yan-enhanced lifespan, it was beyond imagining the amount the man had discovered, formulated and brought under his control. So much was there he felt sure he could find something to stabilise Tristaric's shielding. What he needed was a lot more time.

His head was spinning from the effort and he decided to see how the little demon was now that much of the excess mana had been poured into the iron ball.

Inside the manasphere the presence of the demon grew stronger from out of the gloom. '*Stupid mage, fooooolish mage. Zystal's now, Zystal's forever.*' The words were spoken with increasing manic pitch followed by hysterical laughter and getting closer. Chayne concentrated for a moment and a bright ball of light appeared in front of him. The little creature came to an abrupt halt inches from Chayne's chest, its feet and hands extended forward with vicious claws protruding.

'*Master!*' it said with glee. It glanced down at its claws, withdrawing them and cowering. '*Forgive Zystal. Zystal not know it was Master. Forgive, forgive, no hurt Zystal.*'

'Calm yourself, Zystal. I will not harm you.'

The creature smiled to the point its mouth stretched halfway around its head. '*Why Master come visit poor Zystal?*'

Chayne looked at the creature and was amazed to find no hint of injury anywhere upon its body. It healed injuries in days that would take a human months, even if they could have survived at all.

'Have your injuries fully healed Zystal?'

The creature looked perplexed. *'Which injuries Master, poor Zystal has suffered so many?'*

Chayne found within the manasphere the demon had trouble placing events in order. Often, he would have to remind the demon like this.

'In the fight against the Master Lathashal and the great demon.'

Zystal looked puzzled a moment longer. *'Oh yes, YES Master! All pain gone and Zystal can now perform fully for the Master – see!'* It carried out a number of rapid summersaults and other complex twists and turns half in a blur. He stopped abruptly, facing Chayne exactly as he started and smiling with joy at his ability to prove his full health to his Master.

'Yes, I can see that now, Zystal. The Master is very pleased.' Chayne learned this kind of modest reward allowed for an easier session with the creature.

Zystal seemed ready to burst at the acknowledgement and went into a laughing frenzy for several seconds with more gyrations, ending abruptly.

Chayne smiled, it was like a puppy yapping after bringing back a ball, wanting it to be thrown again. He watched the little entity, marvelling at its capricious nature. One minute wanting to unleash horrific pain and the next ecstatic to please.

'Master?'

Chayne jerked out of his thoughts. The demon had asked a question. It had never done such a thing before.

'Yes, Zystal?'

'I have a question for you.'

If Chayne could have put a word to the limited expression the demon was capable, he would call it compassion, something which the creature must surely be devoid.

'Yes, Zystal, what is it?'

The thing paused for a moment as if getting the courage to say it.'

'You look troubled, Master.'

Chayne understood. The thing was always looking for a weakness in his captor. It was checking his assertiveness. Any weakness would be exploited.

'Master is fine and completely in control. You shall not attack him or he will cause you great pain.'

The little demon's face fell. Sadness?

It slowly shook its head. *'Zystal never harm Master. Master good to Zystal and take care of him.'*

Chayne had to believe it was some kind of ruse, but he didn't feel the creature was smart enough for such a deception, and the thing looked so damned hurt.

'Master is sorry, Zystal. Demons are so dangerous, he forgot you were different.'

'Zystal is different, Master. He is different because of you, and what you have done and shown him.'

'Thank you, Zystal. I enjoy are meetings.'

The creature's face relit with apparent joy.

'In answer to your question, yes, Master is troubled. He has something to do that's very important and Master doesn't have enough time. Other...good masters...are going to suffer and die.'

The little demon's head hunkered down and turned to look behind it, as if ensuring it wasn't to be overheard, even though it had always claimed nothing else occupied the sphere. *'Lluuelliun, Master.'*

'That isn't a word the Master knows.'

'No, Master. It is forbidden for any demon to speak of it to the masters.'

'But you will tell me?'

'*Yes, Master. Master good to Zystal.*'

'What is it?'

'*Lluuelliun here, Master.*'

'I'm sorry, Master not understand.'

'*Lluuelliun is...here, Master.*' The creature seemed at pains to explain any better. Realising this wasn't enough it strained for a better answer. Its face sprang into action once again. '*It fast. Heals Zystal! Like Master moves slow, and Zystal moves fast. Here...*' it said, waving its arms indicating all around it, '*...is slow. Lluuelliun is fast.*' It repeated the animation a few more times.'

'Is Lluuelliun another place?'

The little creature's face dropped as if this was its personal failure. '*No, Master. Here is here. Lluuelliun is here. Master make this hard for poor Zystal.*'

'So Lluuelliun isn't here, but is here?'

Zystal screwed up his face for a moment. From the extent of the distortion it was clear the demon possessed the ability to distort its features beyond its apparent bone structure.

'*May...be,*' it replied.

Chayne sighed. It was often the way with the diminutive entity. Its limited knowledge of the human language, combined with a half-animalistic level of intelligence, made for troublesome communication of anything other than simple concepts.

'*Zystal take Master there to see!*' said the demon, excited.

'Take me there?'

'*Yes, Master. Zystal think of no other way.*'

'You can go to other places?'

'*No Master, only here. Lluuelliun is here and not here, and easy to travel. Zystal strong, Zystal powerful, Zystal–*'

'Yes, Zystal is powerful,' interrupted Chayne, knowing these self-gratifications could go on for some time. 'Show me.'

'*Zystal take Master now?*'

'Yes, Zystal, if it causes no harm to Master,' Chayne added quickly, knowing the creature would execute instructions literally without question.

'*No, not harm Master. See Zystal knows much,*' it replied, beaming again.

'Very well, when you are ready, Zystal.'

'*Master?*'

'Take me to Lluuelliun.'

'*Master?*' The creature looked unsure. '*We are here.*'

It looked the same. 'But we are still within the manasphere?'

'*Yes, Master.*'

'And we are in Lluuelliun?'

'*Yes, Master.*'

Chayne ran his fingers through his long white hair. 'How can I tell?'

Zystal looked around and waved a hand as if that was enough. It seemed the demon had some perception a human did not.

Chayne gave up on the idea and decided to question the demon regarding the shielding. This continued for some time as he attempted to put something so complex into words the demon would understand. An hour later he was getting nowhere. It was time to leave the orb before he became too exhausted. On his first encounter with the demon there was a battle of wills that he only just survived. If it had succeeded, Chayne's soul would have been taken back to the demon's world to give it power and jump up the demonic caste system. Chayne had no idea how this worked, there was no comparable biology in the human world. Despite its later declaration of friendship with him, it didn't seem to be able to stop a small subconscious drain on its Master's mind.

Curiously though, he wasn't feeling the normal tiredness. He felt better than he'd done in weeks. The demon had mentioned Lluuelliun was fast, but also healed him. Perhaps this was how the thing mended so quickly.

He dismissed Zystal and returned his consciousness. Opening his eyes, the laboratory was no longer a mass of bubbling glass tubes, convoluted metalwork and assorted jars of various compounds. Apart from his body, all around was a shifting mix of grey hues.

Had he left the manasphere incorrectly?

Looking down, the golden orb was no longer to be seen. He fought back his panic and noticed his outstretched arm was slightly translucent and returning to solid. He looked at his body and found the lower half of it was translucent also. He thought about his body and it returned to solid again.

Doing the same with the manasphere, it started as a round grey patch in front of him and coalesced until it looked complete. He expanded his scope of concentration. The mechanism holding the orb became visible, then the box. Finally the bench surrounding the orb started to appear.

He began sifting through every detail of what happened as he left the manasphere for clues of what might have gone wrong, but nothing came to mind. He went further back, through the discussion with Zystal, and then further still to the start of his meeting with the demon until he remembered the demon *took* him to *Lluuelliun*. Was this Lluuelliun in the human world? He hadn't thought to instruct the demon to return him, and so perhaps this had some effect on exiting the manasphere. He returned to the manasphere. To his relief he heard the creature's threatening greeting.

'It's Master, Zystal,' interrupted Chayne, creating a bright ball of light stopping the demon in his advance.'

'*Master! Zystal so sorry, didn't reali–*'

'Zystal, are we still in Lluuelliun?'

'*Yes, Master.*'

'Master needs to return now.'

The demon stared back.

'Zystal?'

'*Yes, Master?*'

'Please take me back.'

'*We are back, Master.*'

Again, no discernible change.

Returning to his body, he opened his eyes tentatively. The laboratory was back to normal.

He wanted to follow up on this discovery, but was out of time. He collected up his notes and locked them away in readiness for later.

Checking the laboratory's timepiece, he frowned. He was in the orb for well over an hour and yet the time only advanced minutes. It wasn't likely he misread the hour, exact observation and precision of memory and thought where critical for the survival of a magii when handling Ashnorian magic. And the timepiece itself was intrinsically accurate.

As he'd visited the demon inside the manasphere many times and suffered no change in time, he could only explain the time difference as having some connection with his time spent in Lluuelliun. He remembered what the demon said. *Here, but not here, and fast.* He still wasn't grasping the first part, but the second now made sense. Time in Lluuelliun somehow passed slower. This allowed the demon to heal quickly, not only from the strange well-being effect of the place, but also by accelerating him compared to normal time. If this was the case then there was still a chance to read Lathashal's diaries in time and create the solution Tristaric was looking for and save the servants. He laid out the diary and his notes across the desk and dove back into the manasphere.

Chapter 32 – Into the Mountains

Long shadows from the morning sun, cast by the Hammerheads, stretched out across the forest from where they'd come. Far below, smoke spiralled from Ajoah's camp of Rangers. Falakar knew the man wouldn't be in the camp now and left the fire burning so as not to give away the time he'd started his pursuit. Ajoah hadn't known of the underground bandit tunnels, and this gave the fleeing group a head start before their tracks would have been picked up.

'We'll be there by nightfall,' Dulmurn said.

They continued their ascent and by midday found an easy path for a while. Having a chance to relax after the previous day's chase, the mood in the warm sun was good. Even Dulmurn and Jontal were exchanging banter as the bandit took a rest from forward scouting because they were away from patrol routes.

They turned a corner to see eight Rangers walking toward them. Jontal flipped his hood over his face and tightened it up to mask most of his features, dropping back behind the others.

'What are they doing here? This isn't a standard patrol this route.'

They at least have come down from the mountains and won't know about us yet,' Falakar said. 'Stay calm and keep walking.'

The patrol walked up and stopped before them.

'Any sign of Perlic activity ahead?' Falakar asked, sounding relaxed, his voice carrying his usual authoritative tone when speaking to Rangers.

One of the men stepped up and looked Falakar up and down, and then the other members of the group. His gaze fixed longer on Jontal, trying to see the man's face. Jontal tilted his head away.

'Lieutenant?' Falakar pressed, not liking the attention his brother was getting.

The lead Ranger returned his gaze to Falakar, not rushing to answer. They stared each other out for a few moments before the Ranger shook his head. 'We don't spend our time on patrol looking for game.'

Falakar smiled. 'Glad to hear it. I'm sure Major Stimm will be pleased to hear he has such diligent men.'

The man looked indifferent to any recommendation and resumed his interest in Jontal. 'Who do you have there?'

'This is Glerrin, a merchant from Tiburn with his son and brother,' Falakar replied. 'I'm taking them on a hunting trip.'

'Perlic, it's a delicacy of mine,' Dulmurn said with a smile of his own, stepping forward for the conversation and further masking Jontal.

'And who's that?' pressed the Ranger, pointing to Jontal.

'His brother, as I said,' Falakar answered, his hand moving to rest naturally on his sword hilt. If the other Ranger noticed, he didn't show it.

'Why does he keep his face covered?'

'A contagious skin disease,' Dulmurn perked up. 'Had it since he was a boy. The cold air of the mountains helps stop the scabs from forming. I'm always brushing them up back home.'

The Rangers took a step back.

'We saw bandits down the trail heading east,' Falakar said. 'If you make pace you should be able to track them.'

'I don't take orders from you,' the Lieutenant replied.

'Do you know who this is,' Dulmurn said, still smiling.

'I know who he is. His statue's been collecting hawk crap in the barracks for months. He's not a formal Ranger anymore and I don't take orders from civilians.'

'Then we won't keep you any longer, Lieutenant,' Falakar said.

The man gave one last look over the group and ordered his men to pass by, giving Jontal a wide birth.

When out of sight, Jontal slipped his hood back. 'They were young. Don't they normally fawn over meeting the Ghost Ranger? That guy knew who you were and was going out of his way to be hostile.'

'I don't know what's happening,' Falakar said. 'Stimm wasn't pleased to see me either. First the new Ranger cypher, then Stimm getting too cosy with Brinley, and now this. I need to know what's going on.'

'I'll go and find out what I can.' Jontal said. 'I'll meet you on the trail above the East Ranger post in four days.'

Falakar nodded to his brother. 'Be safe.'

Jontal flicked his hood up again. 'I've been on the run all my life. It's you who need to look out.' He set off, leaving the others to continue east.

Chapter 33 – The Answer

Chayne's head swirled and he caught himself. The advancement with Lathashal's notebooks was going well and he'd found a whole new branch of shield mathematica that could be applied to Tristaric's problem. Lluuelliun was proving to be everything he'd hoped. Time passed at a much slower rate and he remained alert and energised. However, there was clearly another mechanism at work, for this time exhaustion flooded over him as he left the manasphere, as if all the energy given to him was taken away in one go. He checked the lab's timepiece and saw he still had four hours to Tristaric's noon deadline. Taking a quill he began to write down the formula for a new double-polarised shielding spell. It had to be the method Lathashal used to create a secondary shield.

Several times he jerked out of sleep, his head dropping to the bench. He was almost finished. A short nap. That was all. Surely it would be better? In his slurred thoughts he found his way to the sofa, laying his head on the high-backed cushion.

His eyes opened, his vision cleared and he took in the details of the lab. He'd been dreaming of being in his old cabin back home and the switch was disorienting. Reality kept pushing until a single thought cut in like a dagger and jolted him awake. He checked the time. It was half-an-hour past noon! Jumping up he fell to his knees, his joints stiff and his muscles non-responding. Rubbing both he forced himself back up and grabbed his notes, staggering out of the room. Fighting his way through the bustle that was the Empire during the day he reached the room across the palace. Two guards were standing either side of the doorway and moved to block his entry.

'Stand aside, I have urgent information for Master Tristaric.'

The two guards crossed their polearms. 'No one is to enter.'

Chayne came to a halt, his face red from his run and anger at the delay. 'On whose orders?'

'Master Tristaric,' replied the same guard, confident his authority was intact.

'Well I am Zintar Chayne, I have authority of all things magii in this city until a new shodatt master is appointed, and if you refuse me entry to this room for another five seconds you'll be sent to the dungeons on *my* orders.'

The men looked to each other.

They parted.

Chayne pushed through them and into the room beyond. Tristaric was running up the experiment. Two servant bodies could be seen in a pile to one side. Another was about to take position in the tunnel for the next attempt.

'I have the mathematica,' he shouted. 'I have solved the problem, stop the experiment.'

The smooth flow of mana from Tristaric sputtered creating a flare of mana at the far end of the room. It rebounded and headed back towards him. A pulse of orange magic left the magii's hand. The two opposing spells collided in the middle of the room creating a bright burst of multi-coloured energy bringing the conflict to an abrupt end and knocking over everyone in the room.

Tristaric floated up onto his feet and levelled a small staff from his belt at Chayne.

'I have the solution,' Chayne repeated, holding out his hand with the parchment.

Tristaric was clearly struggling with his desire to enact his anger. Instead the parchment tore away from Chayne's gasp to land in the magii's hand.

'The solution is to keep the shield lines moving so the attraction density building between them is spread over a greater area.'

Tristaric absorbed the text before lowering it.

He stared at Chayne like a predator uncertain of a new prey. Chayne knew it was magic mathematica far beyond his training.

'Who helped you?'

'Stalizar helped me with the mathematica,' he lied. The idea itself came from Lathashal's teachings.'

'It is crude and will take me some days to modify, but I think it might work,' Tristaric said. 'It should be far beyond you. When I have finished my work for the Emperor, I will stay and look into these 'teachings'.

'As you wish,' Chayne replied.

'Two more rings will arrive soon,' Tristaric said to the other magii in the room. 'I want the experiment set up in the final test location.'

He walked passed Chayne to leave. 'Stay away from me and my work. If I see you again, be assured nobody else ever will.'

He left the room.

Chapter 34 – Without Fear

Garamon dragged himself from the thawing mud, losing count of how many times he'd fallen in. With an exhausted slump he lay across the fallen tree trunk on his stomach, legs and hands resting either side on the frozen mud.

They'd successfully lost the Rangers and reached Dulmurn's cabin without further contact. The trapper had chosen the position for his solitude well, far from any trails or Ranger patrols. With three days remaining before the rendezvous with Jontal, Falakar took the opportunity to maintain the rigorous training of his protégé.

'There are stories of voracious mud rats that travel in groups and can devour a man in a matter of minutes.'

Right now I welcome them,' Garamon replied, although moving to lay flat along the trunk.

'Try again.'

'I can barely stand.'

'When we fight our coming enemy we'll be heavily outnumbered, each of us will need to kill many of them. They will die, we will tire.'

'And there'll be a lot of log fighting?' Garamon replied, dryly.

'Our fight will take us into mountains, through forest and across streams and rivers. We'll be using the terrain to prevent their advantage in numbers. You must learn to fight on every footing, and yes on fallen trees if necessary.'

'Won't they have trained in mountain combat to attack us?'

Falakar sighed. 'Your constant negativity drains me at times.'

'I was merely trying to foresee potential outcomes, so we can plan to counter them.'

'And how do we counter it?'

Garamon thought for a moment. 'I guess we can't.'

'So get it in your head *it will not happen*.'

'But that won't make it go away.'

Falakar sat down on the log, crossed his legs and placed his impromptu practice staff across his knees. 'In battle, whether it's one man against another or opposing armies, belief in victory is the most powerful armament you possess.'

'Surely skill and a good weapon are more important.'

Falakar shook his head. 'Do you remember the farmer who fought and killed three rogues who wanted to take his wife and children?'

'Blackston, yes.'

'He was unskilled against three armed men used to combat. He succeeded with a pitch fork and a branding iron. Knowing his failure would result in the unthinkable, the thought created calm, driving away his fear and giving him a heightened sense of awareness. It takes an ordinary man and drives him to extraordinary acts.'

'But you cannot know the man's thoughts, you were not there.'

'I have fought more times than I can remember and have spoken with men before, during and after battle. I know their hearts in such matters and they are remarkably the same.'

'Do you reach this state each time you fight?'

Falakar nodded. 'Through training of my mind I can enter the state at will.'

'Like when you fought me blindfold?'

'Yes.'

'And this has something to do with simple belief?'

'In as much that a lack of belief in succeeding will drive your fear the wrong way to make you weaker. The farmer knew he had to succeed. It made him carefree of his own safety, releasing his fear and allowing his raw reflexes as an animal to come forth.

'How do I achieve it?'

'What is foremost in your mind right now?'

'The tiredness in my arms and legs.'

'Do you think those thoughts are helpful or a distraction when you fight me in a few moments?'

'A distraction, of course. How can I not think about it?'

Falakar pushed up with his legs and stood, seeming a little out of breath. Unusual for the man. He turned and walked back to the bank. 'Come.'

They stopped at the foot of a large tree and Falakar leapt up onto the bark and climbed using small branch stubs for his footings. In little time he was high up on a main limb.

'Climb up.'

Garamon wasn't much of a tree climber and tried to copy the Ranger, throwing himself at the tree and taking a leap, reaching for cracks in the bark and guiding his footing onto branch stubs.

He bounced off and fell onto his back into the leaves which did nothing to soften the blow. He looked up at Falakar for help, but the Ranger had his back against the main trunk, eating an apple. Garamon's stomach rolled. He realised he was starving.

'There isn't much daylight left, you would be best to get up here soon. You don't want to do what's next in the dark.'

Garamon got to his feet. It took him longer but eventually he made it to Falakar's position. He looked around and checked above. The Ranger wasn't to be found. Fear gripped him, some of the Ranger's harsher lessons left painful bruises.

He moved half-a-dozen paces down a solid limb to get a better angle when Falakar appeared from behind the trunk. 'Do you remember my warning I would push you at times to the point of fatal danger?

Garamon swallowed hard, he could see the look in the Ranger's eyes this was no riddle. 'Yes, sir.' He felt like a boy again, facing the legend.

'This is the first one. Now take your guard as I will not suffer pity on a warrior with weak resolve.' The Ranger drew his sword and jumped forward.

Garamon stepped further back along the branch, releasing his axe. Falakar struck out, there was hardly time to intercept and the axe blade caught the sword in time to force it down to strike the trunk. Garamon had never seen the Ranger so serious. The man came at him without pause, swinging his blade out and over to come down on his upheld axe. The crash of steel was powerful enough to knock him back several more steps along the thinning branch which was becoming unstable under the weight.

Falakar pressed the attack, coming from one side then the other. The branch was wobbling. Without his training on the river log, Garamon knew he would have lost his balance and fallen by now. He surged back at the Ranger, angry the man would really endanger him, aiming a sweeping low blow to push him from the branch. Falakar replied by throwing up his arms and using the momentum to jump higher than Garamon thought possible for a man his size, to clear the swipe. The result of the miss was to pull Garamon out wide and overbalance. He reached out a hand to grab a branch but it was too thin to stop him and he fell to one below, landing hard on his stomach. Falakar made an easy jump onto the same branch sending a shockwave, preventing Garamon from getting to his feet. The Ranger attacked with a lunge for Garamon's prone side. Garamon had no other choice and rolled from the branch with no idea what was below. He landed with a painful thud onto his back to a thinner branch that couldn't take his weight. It twisted and he fell from it, facedown. No branch was now below him and rocks were spread over the ground. He was out of luck.

He knew he was going to die and time appeared to slow. Letting go his axe, he pushed out a hand to a slender branch on the edge of his vision. He knew it was too thin to support his weight and his gauntleted hand dug into the soft bark as he gripped. He let the branch bend with his weight and swing him towards the main trunk. The branch bark stripped under his hold and he released it, curling into a ball as he fell towards the bottom of the tree and rode down the skirt of the trunk.

He rolled head over heels several times, coming to a halt with his last rotation perfectly judged to use the momentum to stand. Somehow he'd picked up his axe along the way. He stood there panting, ready for the next attack.

Falakar was still far up the tree. The Ranger sheathed his sword and hopped from branch to branch to drop softly to the ground the way Garamon had seen him do so many times before.

'Is it over?' Garamon asked.

'What's foremost in your mind right now?'

'Whether you're about to pull that sword and attempt to kill me again.'

'Then it's over.'

'The fall could have killed me?'

'Better to die here than in battle where the man next to you is relying on you to cover his flank.'

Garamon continued to stand and stare at the Ranger, getting his breath back.

'Minutes ago you could barely pull yourself up from the log to fight, and yet I just saw your reflexes at the sharpest I've seen. Your balance was fine and you thought with lightning speed as you fell from the branch. Did you feel afraid as you fell?'

'No,' Garamon replied, to his surprise. It was like I was dreaming. Everything was moving slow.'

'Your mind and senses went into a heightened state, thinking and acting fast without distraction.'

'Like Blackstone facing those men?'

Falakar nodded. 'This is the place you must find when you fight. Now you have experienced it, I can teach you to find it again and fight without fear.' He looked up. 'The light is failing, we need to hunt for dinner. For once you've earned it.'

Garamon followed and played his usual game with the Ranger, trying to land in his footsteps as they jogged.

'Falakar?'

'Yes.'

'What would have happened if I hadn't found *that place*?'

'You would have panicked and fallen to your death on the rocks.'

The Ranger picked up the pace, increasing the gap between them, ending the conversion.

Garamon felt something had changed between the Ranger and himself. He wasn't sure what it was, but it scared him more than his near fall.

Chapter 35 – Fever Pitch

The next day's training was on a frozen ridge. Garamon was being put through his moves along a narrow line of rock with long drops either side. The surface was slippery and he struggled to maintain his footing. Falakar was again pushing him beyond safe limits taking risks with his safety.

Garamon lost his footing again from a cross-swing technique, eluding him. Falakar grabbed his arm as he fell, but the grip was weaker than usual and he slipped through. On instinct, Garamon brought his axe down hard into the rock to act as a hook to get grip. The resulting explosion of material sprayed out inflicting tiny cuts to their faces, the sound of the strike shook the area and a multitude of minor snow slides occurred all around.

Garamon was left hanging from his axe buried up to the handle in rock.

Falakar pulled him back up. They both looked down at the axe stuck firm, a blackened section of rock radiating out from its head. Falakar couldn't budge it, but it came free easily at Garamon's touch.

'Why does the axe respond when I need it and not when I'm sparring with you?'

'I believe it responds to moments when you are in great danger, as if it senses your distress.' Falakar wrapped his cloak tighter around him as an icy wind began to pick up. Garamon noticed a layer of sweat on the Ranger's brow he'd never seen before during sparring.

'How can mere metal and wood do such a thing?'

'We have seen how powerful the magic of the Ashnorians magiis can be.'

'But they're people, they can think and understand magic and how to use it.'

'Well let's hope, whatever it is, it continues to respond to you.' Falakar shook off a shiver.

Garamon saw it. 'I'll go collect wood for a fire.'

'No, the wind is gathering fast. There's a storm coming, we must head back to Dulmurn.' The Ranger began to lead the way when he caught himself from falling to one side.

'Are you okay?'

'I'm unsure. I felt it coming on yesterday.'

'You're shivering. A fever?'

'Perhaps.'

'Give me your packs and sword.'

'You've had a hard training session today, I can manage.' Falakar struggled to lift his heavy rucksack.

Garamon grabbed it. 'I'd rather be carrying these than you later.'

Falakar looked anxious. 'It seems to be setting in fast.'

'Then we need to hurry, it took us over an hour to get here.'

'That way.' Falakar indicated.

After half an hour the wind picked up and the storm front was catching them.

'It'll hit us before we reach the cabin,' Falakar said.

The man was mumbling his words and kept his eyes to the ground just ahead of him, attempting to avoid tripping. Garamon continued and heard a grunt from behind. Falakar was down on his knees, barely managing to hold himself against the wind.

'We can rest a while?' Garamon offered.

The Ranger didn't respond and tipped headfirst into the snow.

'Falakar!' Garamon pulled off a glove, the man's wrist was burning and there was a weak pulse. Looking back, the peak where he had trained was now consumed by the storm. It was only minutes away. Leaving both their packs and weapons he lifted the Ranger onto his back, he didn't know if he could make it to Dulmurn's. Even if he did, when the storm struck he could pass the cabin within a few yards and not see it.

He staggered for a short while longer, then the storm struck. There was nothing gradual about it, one moment it was clear, the next the snow was thick and the wind picked up to a gale. Snow and ice was being whipped up around him and it reminded him of the time he first set out from home. There could be no rescue this time.

Falakar was shivering enough to be felt through both their armours. He had to get him out of the storm. Struggling to keep balance, he kept going for some time.

He lost the path and lowered the Ranger to the floor to look for it. Walking a dozen paces on, the Ranger's body was already lost in the dense snow. He fought his way back against the wind, and shielding his eyes could just make out the dark clothing in the snow. It was being buried fast. Exhaustion took over and he stumbled onto all fours and then lay across Falakar to provide what protection he could. As he did, so the wind swirled and he caught sight of a light. Friend or foe, he'd nothing to lose.

'Here!'

Out of the storm came Dulmurn, covered in furs and carrying a lantern. 'What's happened?'

'Fever,' Garamon shouted back, getting to his knees.

Dulmurn took one arm while Garamon took the other and between them they hoisted the Ranger to his feet. Dragging him between them they reached the cabin which wasn't far, but Garamon would have passed right by.

As the door opened, light and heat flooded out from the fire washing over Garamon's face. They carried the limp body into the main room and Dulmurn indicated a bed to lay him. Garamon took over the task alone as Dulmurn shut the door against the gale, dropping two heavy wooden beams across to hold it.

'I've weathered many of these storms. We're safe.'

Garamon covered Falakar with sheets to keep him from shivering.

'No, take those off. We need to bring his temperature down.'

'But he's shivering.'

'It's just the body's reaction to his high fever. Trust me, his body is generating enough heat as it is.'

Garamon reluctantly withdrew the covers.

'How quickly did the fever come on?'

'He said he'd been feeling something yesterday. Then one moment he was teaching me and the next he didn't feel well. We only made it halfway back, before he collapsed.'

'Bloodfire Fever,' Dulmurn said.

'Is it serious?'

'It'll kill a man caught alone in the mountains, but I know how to treat it. He'll be out for two days and as many recovering.'

Garamon sat exhausted on one of the two wooden chairs at the only table in the cabin.

Dulmurn stood by the bubbling cooking pot, skewered a piece of meat and tasted it. 'What part of Tiburn do you come from?' He pulled a face and adding some salt and two pinches of herbs to the pot.

'Oakstead farm.'

'Renous's place?'

'Do you know him, he's my father?'

'I've never spoken with him, but I've heard him speak often enough. His support for higher taxes on trapping doesn't place him high on my list for dinner guests.'

'My father's a great man, he does what's necessary to ensure the poorer families are catered for,' Garamon defended.

'Aye, well, my taxes must have kept a few hundred of those happy over the years.'

Realisation dawned on Garamon. 'Are you Dulmurn of Dulmurn Manor?'

'For all it's worth now,' the trapper replied.

'Why did you build this cabin when you have such a lavish home?'

'The Manor is mine because I inherited it. I like it better up here.'

'So why not sell it and help others?'

The trapper laughed. 'Investment. I didn't have your upbringing. Renous is a principled man, and a father's beliefs tend to rub off onto his offspring.'

'You had a bad father?'

'Let's just say he cared more for his money than his paternal duties.'

'A man makes his own destiny, my father says.'

'Like I said, I didn't have the wisdom of a good man to guide me with such insights.' Using a bowl, he scooped up some snow from a pile created by a tiny gap in the cabin's wooden walls. Here, take a cloth and dip it into the snow. When it's cold and wet through, wring it out and place it on his forehead. It will help with his fever.

Garamon did and it seemed to him Falakar relaxed a little. The man looked terrible, his lips were purple and his face was almost white. Sweat dripped from him soaking his pillow. Garamon lifted the man's head and turned the pillow over.

'They're small ones, but should serve the two of us for breakfast,' Dulmurn said, lifting a pair of perlic from hooks on the wall.

'You said Falakar has Bloodfire Fever?' Garamon said, watching the trapper go about skinning with the proficiency to match any of Tiburn's butchers.

'It's not common. I hear of cases every few years up here. It brings down the sturdiest of men.'

'Are you not afraid you will catch it?'

'It's in the urine of some of the animals. Falakar probably got some unlucky berries around here. When he comes around he'll eat like a horse.'

'With a nosebag,' Garamon said, absently.

The trapper turned, cracking a curious smile.

'One of the few jokes in my father's collection,' Garamon explained. 'It comes from rearing horses, I guess.'

The trapper finished his work and doused the perlic in salt before re-hanging them.

'So why do you get special attention from the legendary Ghost Ranger?'

'He helped me rescue a kidnapped friend. At the end of it he offered to train me to become a Ranger.'

'You must be something special for such personal consideration.'

'I must be ready for when the war comes. They're massing on the other side of the mountains.'

'How do you know?'

'My friend was kidnapped by them. Falakar led a small group of us as far as the nearest city.'

'How long do we have?'

'Months, now. We interrupted some great spell or other that needs to be recast. It locates everybody in the mountains.'

Dulmurn looked alarmed.

'I'm sorry. I think soon your mountain retreat may not be so secret.'

'Do you know where the attack will be?'

'Falakar believes they will cross the mountains on one of the western trails. From there they will make a sudden attack on Tiburn.'

'The Rangers will stop them.'

Garamon looked pained. 'There's a split within the council on what to do. Not everyone shares the belief the Ashnorians will attack. Some even believe we may provoke one if we're seen in force on the borders.'

'Yes, the merchants will be against it. More Rangers will mean tighter control on trade routes and movement of goods.' Dulmurn added some red spices to the cooking mixture, tasting the result with a wooden spoon, this time seeming satisfied. 'Well, for now our jobs are to fill our stomachs and look after your friend, there's nothing else we can do until the storm breaks.' He gathered a number of small jars from the kitchen area and placed pinches of the contents from each into the pot. He then disappeared into the only side room in the cabin, returning with a bundle of vegetables which he placed in the pot. 'I don't see your packs.'

'I had to drop them and our weapons some way back so I could carry Falakar.'

'I'll venture out when the storm has softened.'

Garamon didn't like the idea of the trapper going alone but he didn't want to leave Falakar. 'They're up the trail towards the main peak, southwest. Just after a wide rocky patch with some scattered scrubs.'

The trapper nodded. 'I know the place.'

The meal was excellent and Garamon washed the plates while Dulmurn rested with his boots off and his bare feet on a stool near the fire. He pulled out a long pipe and lovingly packed the bowl with a fine brown smoke weed. 'I'm sorry. I only have one of these.'

'I do not smoke,' Garamon replied.

'Well, it's one of my few extravagances. This is Virgin's Soul. It comes from far to the East.' He lit it from a small device Garamon had never seen the like before. Dulmurn pulled air through the pipe, sucking the flame down into the bowl. Puffs of flame and smoke were expelled until he was happy with his light.

'Does it really taste that good?'

'Aye it does after you get used to it. Mind you it browns the teeth and makes your breath smell worse than a mountain goat's farts in the morning.'

Garamon laughed. 'What will you do when the war comes?'

'Hey, stop trying to spoil a man's after-dinner smoke. Some moments are sacred.'

Garamon apologised.

The trapper laughed back and puffed out a huge smoke ring as he rolled onto his back. 'Just kiddin' lad. I guess I'll head north and get as far away as possible. There are remote places I could build another cabin where I might not be found. It wouldn't be an easy existence, but I like being free. Hey, you could come with me. I could use a good woodsman to source me the wood. We could make it twice as big as this one. Perhaps underground. It'll keep those prying bastards from finding us.'

Garamon shook his head. 'I'm part of the Ranger's now. I'll follow Falakar wherever he leads, and try everything I can to defend Mlendria.'

'Do you think we can win?'

Garamon remembered what Falakar had told him about remaining positive. 'I cannot believe in any other outcome. We're going to stop them, somehow.'

'Well, if you don't mind, I'll have faith in my experience of humanity, and run like hell.'

Garamon felt a pang in the trapper's lack of confidence in a successful outcome. He understood what Falakar meant now. Negative talk did something to the soul. He vowed not to do it again.

Chapter 36 – A Distant Land

Chayne returned from his manasphere after another session in Lluuelliun. As the room came into view he saw one of his servants out of its alcove, waiting for him. The servant signed: *Master - Medicinii - Summon - Urgent*. It was his chance to talk to the man at last, and he hurried to the medicinii. As he entered he saw Stalizar standing over a bed carrying out his healing. He pulled a piece of parchment from his pocket and handed it over without speaking, and resumed his work.

The patient was the young self-proclaimed Lan-Chi, Pelenno, Chayne met in the gardens. There were no outward signs of injury.

The parchment was a single page of magii mathematica. It was beyond his understanding, but clearly a page torn from a longer piece of work. He sat on one of the bedside chairs and waited for Stalizar to complete his ministrations.

When the mage-surgeon finished, he looked grey and drawn with concern. 'His mind has been attacked by a spell designed to confuse and disorientate. Whoever he is, his will is of iron to resist it long enough to get that page and get out before his mind was a mess. I would say he was given mind-training.'

'His name is Pelenno.' Chayne revealed. He made sure no one could see him as he signed *Lan-Chi*. 'He came to me offering his help. He was enthusiastic and I got the impression he wasn't working strictly under his superior's orders.'

'Idealist?'

Chayne nodded.

'He spoke your name and thrust that into my hand before giving in to the spell. It must have caused him unimaginable pain to resist so long.'

Chayne turned the thing over in his hand. 'I cannot understand it.'

'It's part of a much larger calculation, probably the eleventh juncture of a rite, although no rite I have ever seen. I can make out some of the sub-computations, but these crossings out and corrections indicate it's under construction. Whatever it relates to, it's as powerful as the most potent of rites.'

'Who is capable of working on such a spell?'

Such things are not undertaken by even the most powerful of magiis, alone. The only one in the palace able to design something so complex would have been Lathashal.'

Chayne looked up. 'Or his replacement?'

Stalizar sat, looking like he needed to get the weight from his legs. 'This Pelenno was found not too far from Lathashal's experimental lab.'

'Now Tristaric's.'

Stalizar ran a hand over his face. Chayne came to recognise it as a sign for when he was stressed. 'What is he working on?'

'Something allowing him to avoid using the Rite to Rakasti so he can invade my people in two weeks.'

Stalizar looked over the parchment again with greater intensity. He pointed to several parts of the calculation. 'This section uses focusing of some kind in a manner I've never seen before. He's trying to keep something highly unstable under his control. The figures indicate an order of magnitude of power beyond normal high-mana spells. And this sub-computation is for maintaining a curved surface.'

'He's been experimenting with shielding using thrinium rings, creating a kind of tunnel. He made me stand inside one and take measurements. It almost killed me when it went unstable. I was forced to provide some mathematica from Lathashal's notebooks to help maintain it.'

'Any idea what he's going to use it for?'

'No, and he's threatened to kill me if he sees me again.'

'Well, perhaps your friend will tell us something more.'

'He'll live?'

'His body is fine, it's only a matter of whether he'll wake again, and what state his mind will be in. When a victim is rendered unconscious, the spell collapses. He held on against the attack far longer than should have been possible.'

'Why did Tristaric let him get away with the parchment if he attacked him?'

'There were traces of a sustaining spell in the mix.'

'A magical trap?'

'Most likely in the lab,' Stalizar confirmed. 'Whatever this Pelenno was doing he was determined not to fail.'

'He was trying to prove himself to me by finding what Tristaric was up to. He seemed so confident. I guess I was hoping I had another Illestrael.'

Stalizar stood and tucked the piece of parchment in a drawer. 'I have other patients to attend. If you wish to leave the page with me, I'll do my best to understand some more.'

'Thank you. May I stay in case he wakes?'

'It could be a long wait.'

'I owe him that much.'

Stalizar left, leaving Chayne to consider his position. First Illestrael and now this young dreamer. How many more would risk themselves for him?

The hours passed until finally Pelenno stirred. His eyes were distant until he saw Chayne. A broad smile appeared across his face.

He went to speak and only a squeak came out. He pointed to his throat.

'I'm glad you have woken. Stalizar wasn't certain you would. He said you possess an unusual strength of mind to resist the magical attack. It was an incredibly brave thing to do.'

Chayne pulled up his stool to the edge of the bed. 'You're unlike other Ashnorians. More like a friend I've back home.'

Pelenno nodded, having little more he could do to join in the conversation.

'I lived in a log cabin deep in a forest. I hope to return there one day.' He didn't know why he was telling the young Ashnorian, perhaps to provide vindication for what he put him through.

Pelenno pointed to himself, then walked his fingers across his hand and pointed to his eyes.

Chayne understood. 'If somehow it can happen, I promise I'll take you there to see it for yourself.'

Pelenno nodded again.

'I cannot say how much I'm sorry for what happened.'

This time Pelenno shook his head. He pointed at Chayne and then himself and then joined the middle finger and thumb of one hand to make a circle.

Chayne laughed at the *okay* and it's universality across such different cultures.

Pelenno laughed with him.

A quiet moment fell between them as each reflected on how different they wanted life to be.

Chayne went to get up and find Stalizar, but Pelenno pulled him back. He walked his fingers again upon his hand and this time pointed to Chayne's mouth and then to his own ears. 'More,' he squeaked and put a hand to his throat in pain.

Chayne resigned himself for a longer stay and began telling more of his cabin, the forest, Tiburn, its people, the Rangers, and life in general and how it differed from Ashnoria. The young patient absorbed it all, smiling the whole time. It seemed he never wanted it to stop.

Chapter 37 – Slow Advance

Jewell watched the Commander becoming increasingly frustrated with the fleeing barbarians. Their lightweight leather skins and furs meant they could outrun the heavily armoured soldiers. Then, when they did fight, it was with animalistic ferocity, taking down nearly three of his men for each one of them. Jewell couldn't understand why they didn't just run away. They kept stopping at narrow passes where only a fraction of the army could engage at any one time. When the line broke, they turned and run, but only to the next choke point. They had to know the outcome was inevitable; it was only delaying their defeat.

Now they were dividing off a group of twenty-five at a split in the trail while the majority continued straight on. The Commander sent three-hundred men and a Captain in that direction. The majority of his force continued onwards up the main trail.

Jewell stayed with the larger group. Not long after, the trail divided again with the barbarians repeating the procedure drawing another three-hundred men away. Now the barbarians were down to sixty against over a thousand heavily armed warriors.

They carried on until halfway through the afternoon and the next narrow section where they could defend. The Commander only just held his temper, forced to adapt his usual battle tactics of using wide column, and ordered the attack.

The surviving barbarians were naturally the most skilled, taking down the Ashnorian soldiers at a higher ratio than before. The soldiers were suffering from their numbing armour and gauntlets which must be freezing. They looked sluggish and wary of each strike, unlike the barbarians who were clothed in thick furs and moved fluidly without the restriction of heavy armour.

'Magii!'

It was the Commander, some way ahead.

'How many left beyond the gap?'

Jewell wasn't happy about using up his mana supply, he wanted it for his personal heating. He hoped to avoid using any more for the battle so he could be back home in the warm before it run out. He also didn't want the Commander uncovering his misuse. He was given this post ahead of his skill only due to circumstances. If he performed poorly he would be pushed down the rankings, losing many benefits, including his quota of Yan. Rumours were spreading the supply of the elixir was running low. Any excuse to withhold it would be taken.

He dropped his warming field, feeling the chilly air seep in, and conjured up a viewing orb over the barbarians fighting in the gap.

'Forty-five remain, Commander.'

The Commander looked to the sky to see the fading light before returning to his instructions for the front line.

Jewell recreated the warming field. What he hadn't told the Commander, was the barbarians still looked fresh. These heathens were certainly a tough breed. If they could be captured and tamed for the mines they would be a potent addition to the workforce.

With so few engaged at the front, there was no breakthrough and darkness was falling. Jewell heard the Commander calling to him again. He hoped it would be the last time for he was doubtful his mana would now survive the night keeping him warm.

'How do they stand now?' shouted the leader.

Jewell repeated his magic. 'Thirty-four,' he replied, his voice sounding high and weak compared to the Commander's.

The Commander's patience let go. 'Aid us, magii.'

Calling upon a magii to do his bidding when having such an overwhelming force was a humiliation, but that wasn't the problem for Jewell, his manasphere didn't have enough supply to kill even one of the barbarians. He had to do something.

He paused for a moment as if concentrating. The soldiers at the front prepared to rush forward and kill any who survived the magii's magic.

Nothing happened.

'What's the delay, magii?'

Jewell pretended to look beaten. 'Something is preventing my magic, Commander.'

'A spell?' shouted the Commander, shocked an Ashnorian magii could be bested by something a barbarian horde could muster.

'I'm at a loss, Commander. It may be something in these mountains. Such locations are known to us,' Jewell lied.

The Commander cursed. With so many soldiers remaining, his victory had been delayed time and again by the cowardly heathens using the narrow mountain passes to reduce the front line. Now his last resort, the magii, had failed him too. It was humiliating to be held at bay by so few heathens. He came prepared for desert combat, and now he was facing another night in the freezing mountains. They lacked proper clothing and accommodation for such temperatures.

He spun around to face his Captains. 'Withdraw and make camp,' he roared.

He stormed back to his tent, stopping briefly at Jewell. 'I'll be asking questions of a master upon my return why you could spy upon the enemy and yet claim more powerful magic couldn't be made to work. And don't think it hasn't been noticed you stand without a hint of cold.' The Commander pushed passed, forcing the smaller man to the side.

Jewell saw the accusing eyes of the men around. If this information got back to a master within his shodatt, it would mean torture at the least. Somehow the Commander could not be allowed to make his report.

Chapter 38 – Rising Smoke

Two days passed before the storm broke. Garamon built up the fire for breakfast as Dulmurn checked outside for damage to his cabin. He returned with a smile. 'This place was built by some canny woodsmen. Hardly a scratch on the old girl,' he said, patting the solid timbers of the wall. 'Save breakfast for me. I'm going for your weapons and packs. Even under a covering of snow, animals will soon sniff out any rations. Your stuff will be strewn halfway across the Hammerheads in no time.'

The crunch of his footsteps in the crisp snow retreated. 'A fine day on the way, lad!'

It was noon before the door opened and he returned. He kicked the worst of the snow from his boots and stepped in. The packs and weapons were placed against the cabin wall.

'These weigh a prize cow's backside.'

The trapper took off his coat and approached the fire. 'I thought you might at least have a meal ready.'

'I don't know how to cook. But I have prepared the pot with water.'

'Well around here you earn your keep. You said you were a woodcutter, the wood store needs stocking up.'

Garamon gave a broad grin. 'I'll have it filled by tea-time.'

Dulmurn silently chuckled at the prideful optimism of the young. 'Head north for half an hour before felling. Anything nearby would giveaway somebody lives around here.' The man rammed a block of cheese in between two halves of a loaf of bread, tied a twine around it and threw it over.

Garamon caught it and thanked him while pulling on his overcoat, shoving the meal in an outside pocket.

He left the trapper to his work.

The chill mountain air hit his lungs, the air sparkling with ice crystals. The feeling reminded him of an ointment his mother would dissolve in hot water when he had a cold. It stung at first, but then cleared your breathing.

The cabin was in a natural bowl of rock. It was a beautiful setting and good place to be where you didn't want to be found. The thought of it being forgotten to the enforced life of the Ashnorians was not nice. Unless there were resources here for them to plunder, he doubted it would ever be seen by people again.

He wandered over to the wood hut and unhooked the latch. In it were various traps, tools and other supplies for the owner's second life. A pile of logs was a third to the ceiling, enough for a couple of months. Garamon judged how much he would need to fell to fill it as promised.

Taking ropes and clamps he shut the door and left the bowl heading north. Half an hour out, he came across stumps from the trapper's previous visits and chose his first tree. It was refreshing to again submit his thoughts to the simple task he knew so well. Stripping down to his tunic the chill air soon became a pleasant cooling to his muscles as they were brought to bear. Aiming his strikes to chop a V-shape in the trunk, it wasn't long before there was a loud crack as the bark split on the good side. A push and the tree creaked and fell to the ground making almost no sound as it rested into the white powder.

Once the trunk was stripped and the branches chopped into bundles for kindling, he set about slicing up the main trunk into lengths for transport. The ropes and clamps would be used to drag them back to the cabin in a few round trips. Cutting them into fire-sized pieces would be done at the cabin.

He took a rest and pulled out the bread and cheese. Stretching his back and shoulders from the effort of the morning's labour, he wandered to the edge of the clearing. It was a steep drop and afforded a view of the woods and forests far below separating him from Tiburn. The town was too far to see through the mist but Garamon felt warm at the thought of his town and family being there. On the far side he could see the peaks of the Northern Ridge isolating the area from the sea far below. The line of white peaks stuck out of the low-lying spring mist like the jaw and teeth of the world itself. He'd never been much of a mountain man, having spent little time in them. Now he was beginning to understand the lure it had for men like Dulmurn. The calm and reflection it brought to the spirit allowed for a different perspective on life.

He then thought of the mist parting and seeing the landscape below burning in the battle for his hometown, the tiny flashes of swords and shields glinting in the early morning sunshine. He knew he would defend it with his life. Would he be able to take another's life though?

A small pillar of smoke was rising from not far below collecting in a cloud in the still air. It was blue-black, unlike the grey of a cabin's wood fire. He decided to take a look in case somebody needed help.

The climb down wasn't easy, but he finally dropped onto a trail and noted it had been recently trodden. Following, it came out onto a path overlooking a sheltered clearing. He dropped to a crouch. The column of smoke was from a Ranger cabin, its walls blacked with a half-burnt flag fluttering in the heat of the hot smoke.

He considered going back and reporting it to Falakar, but when would the Ranger wake and what could he do for a while anyway? He would also ask for more details.

Raking his eyes over the scene looking for clues of what happened and when, it looked abandoned now. There were tracks leading in and out.

Finding a way to climb down to the back of the clearing, he chose a path to the rear of the cabin to mask his approach. He put his hand on the outside of the cabin wall. Heat penetrated his glove. He readied his axe and made his way around to the front, passing the single shattered window. As he glanced around the last corner he spotted the door was open, and from which the majority of smoke was coming. Keeping flat to the wall he inched his way to the door. Crouching down, he stole a peek under the smoke. The daylight feebly illuminated the interior of blended charred black. The smoke was coming mostly from sections of glowing embers in the walls. Burnt remains covered the floor including strange shapes made from copper pots melted in the inferno. Then he saw what was left of a body. The crisped leather armour was of a Ranger.

Tucking in under the smoke he entered and looked around finding two others. His foot caught something metallic. He was about to disregard it as a piece of kitchen flotsam when he saw it was a blackened metal shoulder guard not of Ranger armour. Dousing it in the snow outside to cool he rubbed away the grime revealing colours that filled him with dread. It was Ashnorian.

Afraid, he looked around. Five Ashnorian soldiers in formation were heading his way. There was only one path out of the clearing and he could get to it before them. He set off. Immediately the soldiers broke into a jog, still in their small two-by-two column with the single at the rear. Their heavy armour, padded with furs, restricted their speed and they were going to be no match for him, but he didn't know his way around and could easily be caught in a dead end. He also couldn't risk heading in the direction of Dulmurn's cabin and give clues as to where he'd came.

Reaching the path with less than half a minute lead, he fell into a steady pace, maintaining his distance. He wanted to sprint, but the ground was too slippery to risk a fall.

A branch in the trail approached, with no clue to the right direction. Looking back, the Ashnorians hadn't yet come into view. He chose the right fork.

It looked good for a while, before narrowing, sides too sheer to climb. If it closed off ahead and the Ashnorians had chosen correctly, he was in trouble. He kept going and to his relief it opened out into a large clearing again with an open view of mountains ahead. He soon stopped abruptly. The clearing was cut short by a sheer drop of hundreds of feet.

Trying to keep his calm, he looked for another way out. The place was enclosed with steep rock and there was no climb down. He turned and ran back.

The soldiers appeared and slowed to a walk, fanning out to stop his escape.

He considered surrendering, but they wouldn't understand his language and they hadn't taken prisoners at the Ranger cabin.

They came on, backing him into a corner of the clearing with the rock face to his left and the sheer drop to his right. It would at least restrict them to two at a time.

He settled the axe into his palms, finding the right balance. His heart was pounding and he could feel prickles on his skin as sweat was being forced out. He'd only used his axe once before against another human. Only the strange power in the axe had saved him then. He hoped it was still there. Falakar had concentrated his training on fighting Ashnorian soldiers, such as these. They all wielded a longsword in the right hand and a large shield on their left arm. It restricted their options for defence and attack. He began recalling the weaknesses in the configuration and the best way to defeat it, though his problem was the training hadn't yet covered dealing with more than one attacker at a time.

As they came close, he took his final calming breath and sank into deep concentration, trying to find the place Falakar had revealed in the fall from the tree. It wasn't coming to him.

One of the Ashnorians moved ahead of the other four, perhaps relishing another easy kill after taken down the Ranger post. The soldier ran in and brought his sword down. Garamon threw up his axe to block the strike. The Ashnorian's sword hit the blade with a loud crack and flash and the sword shattered. Garamon took no time to be surprised this time and committed his counter, swiping from left to right into the man's shield to pull it wide, opening up his defence for a strike into his chest. But there was no need. Such was the force of the blow created by the axe's strange power, the soldier, strapped to his dented shield, flew out over the edge to disappear from sight.

The next two soldiers, shocked at the force of the attack, faltered before closing their shields together intending to push him over the edge to join their companion.

Garamon locked himself into a firm stance. As they came into range he swung into the right soldier's shield, slicing through it, blasting him from his feet into the left soldier. Both men slammed into the rock face and went down.

The last two wasted no time and came in fast, attacking together. Garamon couldn't deflect them both. He remembered the ridge fall with Falakar and brought his axe down hard into the ground before the soldiers. The resulting blast of rock sprayed into all around and shook the ground. It didn't cause any serious harm to the Ashnorians, but it put them off-balance. He brought the axe up under the nearest shield, forcing it high over the man's head exposing his front and then pushed the axe into his chest. The blunt end didn't open a wound, but the power of the axe shattered all ribs, crushed the heart and threw him back dead to the floor. The other soldier had regained his balance and hacked downwards. Garamon, anticipating the only logical strike from the man, was already moving right to the edge of the gorge and pulling his axe to his left. The soldier's sword struck the handle of the axe between Garamon's hands. Nothing special happened to the sword this time, although the move did block the fatal strike.

Garamon's heels cracked the edge of the rock just like on Highpoint. Any backswing momentum from an attempted strike would carry him over the edge. The soldier had him and rushed in.

Garamon instinctively dropped to his stomach and rolled under the soldier's shield. The soldier had no chance to avoid and tripped, flailing wildly to keep his footing. He overbalanced and fell from the edge snatching out at Garamon's chainmail tunic, latching on and pulling him with him. Garamon let go of his axe and scrabbled for a hold through the snow to the rock below. He found none and slid over the edge with the Ashnorian.

There was a jolt and his arm snapped up and he hung there over the edge with the Ashnorian hanging onto his feet. He looked up to see one of Dulmurn's snares locked around the chainmail of his arm. The trapper was holding the securing chain.

'I can't hold you both!' he yelled, as his feet slipped towards the edge.

With no time for compassion, Garamon pulled a foot free and kicked out hard into the head of the soldier. He could feel the chain slipping through Dulmurn's hands, one link at a time. He kicked again, breaking the man's nose, but still he held on. Lifting his knee as high as it would go, he kicked down with everything he had onto the soldier's fingers. The soldier lost grip and fell.

He pulled on the snare chain as the tips of Dulmurn's boots slid to the edge. Letting go of the chain with his free arm he made a grab for the edge. Dulmurn stepped across onto the glove to hold it in place. Yelling out from the pain Garamon pulled himself up with the other onto the ledge as Dulmurn fell back from the slack.

They rolled over, panting heavily.

'Can you get this thing off? It hurts like the hells.'

Dulmurn crawled over and pulled the iron jaws back.

Garamon withdrew his arm and rubbed at the wound through his chainmail. Some blood was seeping through his undershirt.

There was a groan from behind them. One of the first two soldiers he hit looked only dazed.

Dulmurn ran over, pulling out his largest skinning knife.

'No!' Garamon shouted.

Dulmurn plunged it into the man's throat. He then kicked the soldier's weapons away.

'You didn't have to do that, he was defenceless.'

'He tried to kill you.'

'He's a soldier, following orders. The Ranger code is to defeat, not to kill unless necessary.'

'Yeah, well, I'm not a Ranger.' Dulmurn replied, and spat on the dead soldier.

Garamon walked over and checked the other soldiers. They were dead. 'Let's get back and tell Falakar about this.'

'You get no argument from me,' the trapper replied.

Chapter 39 – Reporting In

No further patrols were encountered and Dulmurn and Garamon arrived back by dusk. Garamon pulled out the shoulder guard.

Falakar was sitting up on his bed looking weary with some colour in his face, and saw it. 'They're here already?'

'They attacked the Ranger post to the North and killed all three. They were burned alive.'

A pained looked passed over Falakar. 'How many attacked?'

'A patrol of five chased me. I think they caught the Rangers by surprise and set fire to the cabin. There were no Ashnorian casualties.'

'Where did you lose them?'

'Lose them!' Dulmurn blurted, giving the woodsman a hearty pat on the back. 'Your young Ranger took them apart like they were stuffed toys. He's a damned hero.'

Falakar looked for explanation. Garamon merely lifted his axe.

'Did you see any more?'

'No, sir. Although one of those who attacked had the same markings as one of their Captains.'

'What's the significance of that?' Dulmurn said.

'A Captain wouldn't travel this far with such a small unit,' Falakar explained. 'It was a patrol from a larger camp, not too far away.'

'I'll better get my spare locks from the wood store,' Dulmurn said, going out.

Falakar pulled his covers around him as a flurry of snow settled into the room from the trapper's departure. 'You took down five?'

'I won't deny the axe played the biggest part in it, but without your training I doubt I could have stopped one.'

'Well, don't thank me yet, there's a lot of unpleasant training still to be done.'

Garamon leaned his axe against the cabin and took fresh water to the Ranger. 'Why do you think they're up here?'

Falakar took a sip and laid back, feeling drained from sitting. 'I don't know. We were supposed to have delayed the invasion months.'

'Could they have decided to attack anyway?'

'History would indicate not.'

'But they've a new Emperor, and it's been fifty-years since their last attack.'

Falakar closed his eyes. 'You're right. We don't know enough to make a decision.'

Dulmurn came back into the cabin carrying his chopping axe and a shovel. He kept the axe and pushed the shovel under the handle of the door to secure it. 'What now?'

'As soon as I'm fit, we'll find the Ashnorian camp. We need to know what they're doing.'

Chapter 40 – The Rin-Uri

Chayne returned from the palace library. Having supplied Tristaric with the raw solution to his problem, it was only a matter of time before the man would refine it for his purposes. If it worked, the invasion would begin soon after.

He couldn't conceive a way to stop the man. Two days he'd risked in study to find information on the servant underclass and the strange prophecy of the Zil-Sat-Shra – the deliverer of freedom from their slavery. He didn't believe in prophecies, but there was no denying the power the servant class wielded. The Empire was dependent upon them like the warmth of the sun. Both taken for granted. There were no safeguards in place in the event the servants one day disappeared, any more than if the sun didn't one day rise. *But what if it didn't appear one morning?* Was it really possible to persuade the servants to stop carrying out their labours, to simply not turn up? And how would the Empire respond? They couldn't torture them all – could they? Simply from counting those in alcoves, the servants matched the population one for one, and there had to be at least as many sleeping and working behind the scenes.

But how could he convince them to rebel? The library contained no information on them beyond the codes to be written on them for punishment, and of course, the sign-language. There were no records of institutions to teach them, nor how they were cared for when sick. Not even an indication where they were to sleep or how they were to be fed. It was as if the Empire created them, and now they existed autonomously.

He walked up to the nearest one, waiting ever-patiently and unmoving in its alcove. He stared at its downcast eyes. Any normal human would have reacted to see what the attention was for, but these servants would be tortured for such action.

'Who is in charge of you?'

It blanched, holding out its hand for chastisement marking. Being spoken to, was punishable. Chayne gave the hand sign, *stop*.

Conflicted between its conditioning to seek out punishment, and obey the opposite command, it faulted for a moment.

Chayne repeated the command and it lowered its hand. He rubbed his face with both palms as if to wipe away the tiredness he felt. A thought came to mind and he placed his hands within its field of view. He made the hand sign for *return to where you sleep*.

The servant moved off and Chayne followed.

It went down two levels to the administration level and then to a flight of stairs to take it down again. Chayne had been below the Administration level only once before, on his arrival where he'd been placed in the dungeons. This time they descended only half the distance, placing the servant area as the floor between the Administration level and the dungeons.

The servant continued along a featureless corridor, passing through a door at the end.

As he entered, another servant, leaving, jumped back and made eye contact with Chayne, lowering its eyes and holding out its hand.

Chayne dismissed it and walked into the room beyond.

The room was huge and as unadorned as the corridor he'd just left and filled with servants going about tasks. At least a hundred of them in their cream attire milled around numerous tables piled high with clothing. There was no conversation and their movements were so silent as to be inaudible over the ruffle of a hundred articles of clothing being folded and stacked.

The impact on him was profound. The servants didn't even communicate with each other when out of sight of the palace occupants. Did they live their entire lives like this?

Almost as one they looked up and saw him. The sound of one hundred servants stopping and holding out there hands was almost deafening in its silence.

He made the sign *dismissed,* a futile gesture as they had their eyes downcast again and couldn't see it. He noticed his guide was still walking and leaving by a nearby exit. He went after him and left the room and the servants to get on with their duties, hoping they wouldn't stand there forever waiting for further orders.

As he entered the next corridor it ejected a servant from a side room, carrying linen. Upon seeing a master it froze causing the tower of linen to topple. Ignoring it, Chayne followed on, progressing from one large room to another adding a temporary splash of colour to the otherwise pale cream decor and occupants of each. The servants moved smoothly out of the way, no longer being surprised. It seemed somehow word was spreading ahead there was a master on the level.

More rooms and connecting corridors went by until the servant stopped and waited. An elderly servant approached. He was far older than any of the palace servants Chayne had seen. Dressed too in servant robes, he stood out by fact of staring directly into Chayne's eyes. He gave the hand-sign for follow, and walked down another corridor.

Chayne was led into a room conspicuous by its small size. The old servant led him through the first chamber into a second. Two men and a woman were sitting on soft chairs and each gave him an uneasy glance, as if also concerned of the consequences of eye contact with a master.

The one who led him in waved his hand towards an unoccupied chair. Chayne sat on the edge only. He went to speak but another servant woman entered. She looked ten-years younger than the other three and identically dressed. She carried a mug and brought it over to him, looking him in the eyes and giving a radiant smile, full of comfort and trust.

'My name is Angealla of the Incra, welcome to our home.'

'Incra?'

'Those you call servants.'

'You have no fear of speaking to me?'

'Of course, we are subject to the same punishments as are all Incra.'

'Why then?'

'We are the Rin-Uri.'

Chayne tried to translate. The nearest in Mlendrian was, *The Keepers of the Nothing.*

'I've not heard of it.'

'No master has. It has been passed down through generations of Incra.' She held out the mug. 'Please,' she gestured he take it.

It was hot and he began shuffling his grip from one hand to another. She had displayed no such discomfort.

'So why do you risk punishment?' he repeated.

She moved to the other side of the room and sat with the others.

The old man who led him to the room spoke for the first time. 'We are invisible to the masters. Not physically you understand, we have no mystical powers, we live our entire lives below their levels, wherever we happen to be.'

'For what purpose?'

'We are the spiritual leaders of the Incra.'

'Surely with only sign language, a concept as subtle as religion must be beyond teaching.'

'They can speak, albeit limited. You would probably consider it like speaking with a child. Although do not be fooled, they're perfectly intelligent, they just lack education other than to perform their functions.'

'How many Rin-Uri are there in the Empire?'

'Only us.'

'But what of the rest, servants are spread throughout the continent within the Empire.

'We lead them all.'

'It cannot be so. The size of the Empire would dictate the necessity for you to be of greater number and more centralised. And yet you are here on the edge.'

'We have come for you.'

Chayne held his cup too long in one hand and passed it too quickly to the other, spilling some of the thick, green liquid. He noticed a moment in each of those before him to move and clean it up. The response to clean up after a master was clearly hard to keep in check after a lifetime of doing it. A servant came in from outside and mopped up the spill until the floor was again spotless and dry.

'Why me?'

'Because you say you are the Zil-Sat-Shra. Is this not so?'

Chayne looked back to all four of the Rin-Uri. 'I will be truthful with you.'

'That is something we have not come to expect from masters,' spoke the older woman for the first time, the words holding undisguised malice.

'I understand, but I am no master.'

'You look like one, dress like one, although you do lack the superior manner of one.'

'My name is Chayne, I am from Mlendria.' Seeing no comprehension in the faces staring back, he added, 'Outside of the Empire.'

'There is no *outside*, other than savages. You don't look like a savage.'

'It's true the Empire has overcome most of the land, but there is a pocket of another civilisation remaining. The last one.'

The looks returned were more mistrust than surprise.

'Can your people resist the Empire?'

'We do not have the numbers to succeed with such a hope, but there is a set of mountains between here and my people. It prevents the Empire from sweeping over our borders and overwhelming us as they have done with the others.'

'Why do you seek us out?' It was spoken by the eldest-looking of the two men. He looked at least ninety years old. Such an age was rare back home where surviving the seventies was seen as a gift.

'My people are about to be 'brought' into the Empire. They're free people and will resist, many will die. If the Incra were to stop serving the masters, it would halt it. Perhaps forever.'

'Even if it were true, to resist the masters would bring suffering and death to the Incra. We would sacrifice ourselves to save your people.'

'There is a way the masters would no longer have dominion over you.'

'How can such a thing be possible?'

'Because without the servants obeying orders, everything will stop.'

'The masters would replace us with servants from the city. It would take time and cause disruption for the palace, but things would return to normal and we would be made an example to others.'

'I wasn't thinking of just the Palace.' Chayne met the eyes of each Rin-Uri in turn.

'He is thinking of the entire city,' Angealla said, returning Chayne's stare with a steady gaze of her own.

'You will sacrifice an entire city of our people!' It was the eldest one again.

'No, such a thing is beyond my comprehension. I am suggesting the evacuation of all servants away from Straslin, out of reach of the masters.'

The youngest one dropped his gaze to the floor. 'I foolishly allowed my hopes to be raised at your claim to the Zil-Sat-Shra, but you're nothing more than a deluded madman.'

'Perhaps not, Kirain,' Angealla said.

'What chance is there we could succeed with such an action!'

'What did you expect, our saviour would wave his hand and we'd be free?'

'Of course not, but is it any more believable we could leave the city with forty-thousand servants. You think they would not be noticed leaving their posts? It would be clear to the masters long before we reached the outskirts of the city. They would send the army. We have neither weapons, nor ability to use them. And if by some miracle we escaped them, where would we go, what would we eat or drink? Without water, the desert would consume us in days?

Angealla looked back to Chayne for answers.

'If I solve these problems, would you lead your people to freedom?'

'Can you guarantee their safety?' Angealla said.

'I cannot see how it could be avoided that some, perhaps many, will be lost. Will they be willing to make the sacrifice for freedom from the masters and their torture?

'No, they would not!' Kirain shouted.

'You do not speak for the Incra, Kirain,' said the second woman, until now unspoken. The words were said quietly. The effect on the others was pronounced. Even Kirain noticeably cooled.

'Sorry, Meleer, I did not mean to imply such–'

'You did not imply, Kirain,' interrupted the woman. 'Your reaction was without thought and born of fear for our people.

It was understandable, but we must consider this longer than just decisions based on immediate emotions.'

Kirain lowered his head again. 'Yes, Meleer, but our people will lose their lives.'

'Our people have no lives, Kirain, they only have duties.'

She returned her attention to Chayne. 'How do you propose to execute this task, for I too *feel* as Kirain?'

'I have a plan forming, but other things must first be in place. Within the next two weeks you must be ready to order your people to leave their posts.'

'And go where!' It was Kirain again, his temper returning at the lack of information.

'Lake Senca.'

'And what is at this, Lake Senca?' Meleer said.

'No more than that, a lake on the northern tip of the desert. There is plenty of fresh water, and food there. I have seen it in pictures from tomes in the main library.'

Kirain's eyes went wide. 'And what if these pictures were from long ago and the lake is now dry?'

'It's a large lake fed from the mountains, unlikely to have gone,' Chayne replied.

Meleer spoke before Kirain's temper flared again. 'We must charge ourselves with finding out the heart of our people in this.'

'But they would surly wish not to remain as they are,' Chayne said.

'These are not people simply taught to do tasks by their peers. They are a people woven from an early age into the fabric of the workings of the Empire. They also work as a whole to sustain themselves. Taking the Empire away within which they carry out their daily routines, would render them almost useless to help each other. If they found themselves one day without walls and roof, they would be confused, perhaps some would suffer madness.

A quiet fell over the room as each contemplated the vision.

'How will I know your decision?' Chayne said.

'A servant will deliver our answer.'

Chayne bowed his head. 'I would like to return now.'

The Rin-Uri bowed, except for Kirain who was looking away, angered.

Chapter 41 – Realisation

Chayne followed a servant back from the servant level. He re-emerged in gardens he'd not seen before. There was a wide road running through the middle leading to a breathtaking crystal archway set into the city building. He realised he was, for the first time, outside of the city walls and this was probably the main entrance. The sun shone down and hit the crystal arch producing a prism of multicolour on the palace walls and grounds around it.

While it was spectacular, it was trumped in magnificence by an inset revolving crystal doorway, twenty-feet high. People were pouring in on the right side and others exiting on the left. The crystal archway refracted light into the moving door creating a blaze of dancing colours at it turned – a fitting piece for the palace's entrance.

He stared, torn in admiration between the crassness and yet grand inventiveness of the Empire's artisans. As he watched so it began to give the impression of a magical portal transporting people to and from somewhere far away.

Time slowed and his mind reeled as a realisation dawned.

He knew what Tristaric was going to do.

Turning to the nearest available servant he snapped his fingers, frowning he'd again used the degrading form of command. He signed to be taken to the magii sector and added the sign for speed. The servant obeyed and led though the almost blinding light of the doorway. A long glittering hallway stretched beyond the door, it was several minutes before they reached the end. The servant continued to weave through the palace until Chayne recognised an area. He dismissed it and hurried to the medicinii, knocking into another servant carrying a tray of items, scattering them to the floor. Servants left recesses to clear the mess while the one knocked into held out its hand. Chayne waved it away and headed into the medicinii. He found Stalizar in one of the surgery rooms, and rapped on the glass to get his attention, beckoning to him urgently. The mage-surgeon looked irritated at the interruption and said something to the student with him before coming to the door, poking his large head around.

'This is delicate work; gaining my attention in such a way could have proven dangerous to the patient.'

'I know how Tristaric's going to avoid recasting the Rite to Rakasti.'

'Wait there,' Stalizar replied, and went back into the room. He spoke to the student at some length and returned.

'I don't have long.'

They entered Stalizar's private room and closed the door. Chayne went to speak, but Stalizar put up his hand. He then placed his other hand on his tiny manasphere in his robe and faced in different directions, concentrating. The air then shimmered around them making the room look blurry.

'Ok, it's safe.'

'He's going to create a portal through the mountain.'

Stalizar shook his head, his look of having his time being wasted. 'Portals are only useable over short distances. For centuries they have been researching the possibility of creating a portal network across the Empire to connect the major cities. Beyond a distance of a few feet, portals become unstable and breakdown. I'm afraid you will have to keep looking for your answer.'

'What about the thrinium focussing rings I saw to shape and stabilise the portal and maintain its integrity?'

Stalizar shook his head again. 'That requires magiis to maintain the stabilising field for each ring. Trying to maintain it beyond even three rings would distort the field and go unstable. We've tried it, it doesn't reach more than a few yards. And he'd be hard pushed to coerce half-a-dozen master magii's into service anyway.'

Chayne took a blank parchment sitting on Stalizar's desk and began feverishly drawing on it. When completed he tapped his fingers on the diagram based on a row of rings extending beyond those he'd seen in Tristaric's experiment. 'How about twenty rings, with a hundred or more magii.'

Stalizar shook his head again. 'The man is a genius of mathematica, one of the reasons he got to be the Emperor's personal magii so young, but the formulae to achieve integration of the stabilising fields with each other for a portal over such distance would need to be refined to an impossible degree. Your knowledge is too limited to grasp the impracticality of what you're suggesting. Anyway, it would take absurd amounts of thrinium to create enough rings.'

'Tristaric is ruthless and looking for a way to regain favour with the Emperor and return to his court. He has been asking for many books from the mathematica section of the Great Library. He's already had six rings made to my knowledge, and I have witnessed the tunnel first hand working up to three, it extending almost sixty feet beyond.'

Stalizar took out the parchment Pelenno had stolen from Tristaric's lab and checked through it again. It could be interpreted in such a way.

'Twenty,' he repeated to himself, absently.

Chayne pulled out another parchment from his robe. 'I do not yet understand the mathematica well enough for an accurate calculation, but by my rough workings it could be the right number.' He laid out the parchment, showing the calculations.

Stalizar took it and looked over the young Mlendrian's work. 'You did this?'

'Yes, on my way here. Is it wrong?'

'No. The calculations are unrefined, but are in the right order of magnitude to make your suggestion possible.' Stalizar was bewildered at the speed of the Mlendrian's progress. He was learning in days what it took high gradia masters months to learn.

'What do you plan to do if you're right?'

'Replace one of the magiis and collapse the portal.'

Stalizar didn't bother arguing with the young Mlendrian, he'd already accomplished what Stalizar considered unachievable. 'An uncontrolled collapse would generate a mana whip I doubt even a master could shield against.'

'I know,' Chayne said. 'It'll wipe out the assembled army and magiis, including Tristaric.'

'You would be killing thousands of soldiers, and yourself.'

'It will save thousands more of my people.'

'You do know, if you thwart the Emperor's plans again, he'll send the entire Empire's forces against Mlendria and annihilate them just to placate his anger.'

'I'm going to distract the Emperor with something closer to home. No more I'll say, but if it works he'll be unable to attack Mlendria, perhaps forever.'

Stalizar felt a flicker of irrational fervour. It was just so easy to get caught up with this young man's assuredness. 'You think Tristaric has managed to persuade over one-hundred masters to risk their lives for his glory?'

'He has a powerful bargaining position. If he succeeds he believes he will be recalled to Ashnor and the Emperor's side.'

'And that would release the head position of the magii shodatt here in Straslin,' Stalizar completed, seeing the logic.

'Wouldn't it fit?' I would bet Tristaric offered each of them the position. By the time they find out they've been duped, he'll be far away in Ashnor, out of reach of retribution.'

Stalizar looked at the young Mlendrian. 'I remember the first time we met. I healed you from Lathashal's anger.'

Chayne gave a simple nod and smile.

'Do you remember what I said about politics?'

'You said I would need to master it as much as my magic.'

'It seems you are achieving it.'

'But what if I'm wrong?'

'About what?'

'Any of it.'

Stalizar raised an eyebrow. 'Then your people will be punished and put to death for the transgression, and you will be tortured over a very long time, probably by Tristaric in front of the Emperor and until he tires of it.'

'It's pretty much what I expected.'

'And that doesn't deter you?'

'My only concern is I'm making these decisions for all of Mlendria without consultation with them. Those that die, whether I succeed or fail, will be because of what I do.'

'I cannot help you there. I have never been a man to change the course of history.'

'There are times I wonder if I'm a deluded lunatic.'

'Well, for what it's worth, my opinion is you most certainly are.'

Chayne frowned. 'I'll need your help.'

'I know little of portal magic, and I have my days filled with setting up the field medicinii units for the invasion.'

'I'll handle the portal magic, but I'll need a way to replace one of Straslin's magiis.'

'How can I help with that?'

'I need help subduing Kinarch so you can keep him sedated in the medicinii until it's over.'

'We cannot tackle a battle magii in straight confrontation!'

'It's not without risk. I have planned this with as much care in the time available. And I don't intend to fully defeat him, only distract him while you render him unconscious. Can you gain access to his personal room without him knowing?'

'As the mage-surgeon to the city, all magiis provide a magical passkey through their defence enchantments in case of emergencies.'

'And then you can use your Shroud Invisibilitii to be in the room when I arrive without him knowing you are there.'

Stalizar began to pace up and down the room. 'You're talking of Kinarch, a battle magii only two gradia less than Lathashal.'

'Like I say, if things go to plan he won't be meeting me on fair terms.'

'What if he still wins and keeps you alive long enough to betray me?'

Chayne noticed how the man was shrinking in stature at the thought of running up against another master. He did the same when confronting Lathashal. The man wasn't a coward, he just wasn't a born hero either.

'There is a weakness in the masters, all but you that is. They are arrogant in the extreme. If you push them enough they become incautious and lose control. Back in Mlendria we call it "pulling someone's levers." At that moment you will step in.'

'Is there no other way?'

'None to be executed within the time we have.'

The mage-surgeon ran his large hands through his ample, black hair. It was glistening with the beginnings of sweat. He stopped pacing and stared at his feet for a moment. 'May the gods help me.'

'I promise you won't regret it,' Chayne said.

'An absurd assertion. Just don't underestimate him, he's a second gradia battle master magii and able to release tremendous energies.'

'That I can promise,' Chayne replied.

He left the room and headed for his lab. There was much to do. He turned a corner and bumped into a man dressed in an array of colours going the other way. The man kept his head low and apologised something under his breath waving his hand back as he moved away at some pace. Chayne rubbed one of his ribs where they collided and continued on. Arriving at the lab he went to withdraw his notes including Tristaric's stolen piece of parchment, to find it missing. He checked all of his pockets. He rummaged around in the first pocket again looking for a tear in the lining. Then he felt the bruised rib he received during the collision with the man in the corridor. It was in the same position as the pocket. Had they been taken?

He retraced his steps to the collision. There, on the floor, were the parchments. He picked them up, clutching them tight. The corridors were always kept immaculate by the servants who would pick it up the moment it fell and take it away to be disposed. There were three alcoves in sight, all empty. It was luck beyond belief.

He thrust the notes into the bottom of another pocket, and returned to his lab.

Faust watched the Mlendrian find the notes and disappear out of view before ordering the servants back to their alcoves.

His training kept him from being detected behind the wall while spying. The higher mage-surgeons could magically sense the process of thinking over short distances. The only defence was to go into a deep trance. Few perfected it.

However, the magii had been thorough in his efforts to prevent being overheard or even seen well enough for lip-reading. This wasn't the normal way of the man. Faust considered him a coward, someone who throughout his life had been a lapdog to those in authority. Suddenly being so covert meant the man was up to something to get him into a lot of trouble. And if he was in collusion with the Mlendrian then it meant against the Empire, and therefore the Emperor's plans.

So first the Mlendrian somehow turns the head of a skilled yhordi to the point of her giving up her life to help him, and now he has a hero of the Empire, renowned for his aversion to politics and deception, needing to make safe a clandestine meeting from spying.

With his copy of the Mlendrian's parchment consigned to memory, he screwed it into a ball and took a piece of wire from within a bottle of oil. The wire began to smoke on contact with the air and he wrapped it once around the bundle and let it drop to the floor. The wire burst into a fierce orange flame consuming the parchment until no sign of it remained.

Chapter 42 – Final Test

Tristaric stood exultant before his creation. The morning desert heat was already uncomfortable, but, for once, such banal distractions were pushed from his mind. Ten aligned thrinium rings stood before him, stretching out across the sand. This was the last test. If successful, the rings, and the concluding ten rings on route, would be delivered to their final location. Twenty rings in all and over a hundred master magii under his command. It had taken the Empire's entire reserves of the precious metal, plus all the master magiis from dozens of cities. It was to be the greatest spell ever cast in the Empire's history.

It's first and possibly only use, would be to defeat the Mlendrians. It was pleasantly ironic he'd manoeuvred one of their own to come up with a key element in the solution. The young heathen was even more gifted than himself. He was even considering taking him back to Ashnor. Such a mind under his control would bring him great power. Perhaps enough, one day, to be Emperor.

He cast such heady thoughts aside as the last of the thirty master magiis indicated they were ready for the test.

Tristaric raised a hand and the final ring began to turn. His final breakthrough solution was not of magical origin, but mechanical. The final thrinium ring was mounted on running wheels. It took a single additional master to spin it up to high speed. It created a drag on the mana as it passed through making it twist the mana lines. The whole thing then spun out into a spiralling tunnel holding its integrity far beyond a static stream. So far it had proven successful out to one-thousand paces without losing its stability. This test would take it to five-thousand. His calculations showed, if it remained stable at that distance, the addition of the remaining ten rings would provide the distance he needed to achieve his final goal. As the ring spun up it began to create a whining sound. It increased to quite some level as the ring reached the desired speed.

Satisfied everything was in place, he prepared to start. Failure this time wasn't excusable. It would be a long and painful execution.

He fed his mana stream into the first ring. It passed to the second and third, jumping each time to the next when the mana built up to the appropriate level. Soon, over half of the ten rings contained the growing tunnel cone as is expanded both in length and diameter. Tristaric's eyes widened as the mana reached the last ring. It jumped with a loud spark to its final point marking the start of the portal tunnel. He watched as the thing grew forward, gradually at first, then faster as he gained confidence and poured more and more mana into the first ring. The tunnel continued to extend with no sign of instability. Intoxicated with the sensation of the huge mana passing through him, he let out a laugh and opened up his body to pass as much mana as it would take. The mana poured in and the tunnel surged out. He closed his eyes, revelling in the sensation of the energies under his control.

He opened them again to see the tunnel stabilised at the desired distance for the test and continuing beyond. He toyed with the idea of taking it even further, but resisted the urge. Too much was at stake.

He stopped the mana flow. Such was the quantity of mana in the system, the tunnel collapsed with a snap, destabilising the final ring and rocking it from its running wheels. It broke free still spinning at speed. The final ring magii was crushed into the sand as several tons of thrinium rolled over him.

Tristaric marked a note in the margins of his calculations to reduce the mana flow gradually in future, unconcerned with the fate of the magii. There were replacements for such eventualities.

Barely visible in the bright sun and going unnoticed to the retreating magiis, a mist of darkness swirled around the toppled main thrinium ring as if trying to coalesce and take shape.

It faded and disappeared.

Chapter 43 – Camp Encounter

After three days of recovery and another four searching the area and tracking patrols, Falakar stopped and dropped down. They edged up a rock to look over. Down below in a clearing was a camp of Ashnorian soldiers. Dozens of tents erected in perfect rows. In the centre were two larger tents, one several times the size of the other. The smaller of the two was surrounded by many guards, while the larger one had white smoke rising from a metal chimney in its roof. At the back of the camp a stream of workers were treading a path up into the mountain.

They held there position for an hour and soaked up the details.

'What do you see?' Falakar asked.

Garamon knew he was being tested. 'The small tents are for the soldiers. The largest tent is for the servants. From the smoke I would say it's also where the food is cooked. Do you think they have mages?'

'Well, it isn't a large force by their standards, so I'm guessing they won't have many.'

'I don't know what's in the other large tent in the middle.'

'From the number of guards at the door and the constant flurry of soldiers in and out, I would say it's a command tent,' Falakar replied. 'We need to get hold of the orders in there.'

He indicated the back of the camp. 'That point has good cover. We can take out the rear patrol and make our way in through the cover of the tents.'

'What about the soldiers in each?'

'We need something to draw the soldiers away.' Falakar pointed down the mountain.

Garamon followed the Ranger's finger to a main trail leading up into the Ashnorian camp. Through gaps in the rocks Garamon could see Ajoah and forty rangers heading up the main trail to the Ashnorian camp.

'I spotted them about an hour ago. Ajoah is tracking something, and as we hadn't come from there I guessed he was following the tracks of an Ashnorian patrol.'

'You used him to find the camp.'

'There are more of them. They can cover more ground than we can.'

'Aren't you going to warn them?'

Falakar located the sun and removed something hand-sized, wrapped in soft cloth, from his pocket. Unravelling the cloth it revealed a polished copper plate. He angled it to catch the sun and reflected it down into the pack of approaching Rangers. The group stopped and moments later a confirming signal returned.

Garamon watched as Falakar made tiny movements of his hand to send his message through a series of flashes.

Flashes were returned.

This went on for some minutes. The Rangers disappear from view into the surrounding cover of rocks.

'They will take out the next patrol and attack the camp. 'We'll use them as our diversion.'

'They are too outnumbered.'

'I haven't told them the numbers,' Falakar said.

'They'll be killed,' Garamon said.

'They're Rangers,' Falakar replied, checking his route into the camp.

Garamon was becoming less surprised with the callousness of his mentor. Being involved with Falakar the Legend wasn't a task for the faint-hearted. He realised he too must be a consumable asset, expendable for the common good.

The Ashnorian patrol left the camp. As they walked into the trap, Ajoah attacked with half his men from one side. The surprised soldiers turned and engaged allowing the remaining Rangers to attack from behind. The clash of steel and shouts could be heard bouncing from the rocks. The battle was short and the surprise complete. Garamon was relieved to see no losses to Ajoah's men.

Falakar stepped back from the edge. 'Let's go.'

The camp was packed tight into the available space of rocks allowing them to get close enough for a short sprint to the nearest pair of guards on the perimeter. There were a few moments of each circuit where the pairs of guards were out of sight of the other.

A clash of steel and shouts went up on the far side of the camp. The guards turned in the direction of the noise. Falakar raced to the nearest pair of guards, with Garamon tucked in behind.

One of the guards turned and went to cry out. Falakar's arm flicked and his knife buried into his throat. The other guard spun around to take a dagger through the exposed area under his arm. Falakar held the struggling man's mouth until he was dead and pulled him to the edge of the tent. Garamon grabbed the other to do the same, thinking him also dead. The soldier coughed once, spraying blood onto Garamon. Falakar grabbed the soldiers head and twisted it to the sound of a snap. The soldier slumped and was pulled on top of the other. They pushed fresh snow over the blood stains and returned to the tent.

With a tiny slit made in the bottom of the fabric, Falakar viewed inside.

Garamon could hear noisy activity in the tent and guessed the soldiers were getting ready for combat with the incoming Rangers. He checked for the other patrol and saw the two guards returning. Reaching out a hand to attract Falakar's attention, it was grabbed and pulled. He ending up in the tent through a long cut in the canvas. Falakar's finger was placed over his lips.

They stood behind some kind of packing boxes obscuring their entry from the other occupants. Waiting until the noise left the tent they walked into the main area. Double bunks were equally spaced around the perimeter and next to each was a chest, identical and polished. The bunks were made without a crease in the covers, maintained by two servants standing to one side of the tent, unmoving. An odd-looking glass ball with a long upright neck kept the place warm. The bowl contained a yellow liquid soaking up a wick to a horizontal glass tube on top. Both ends of the tube produced a bright flame creating enough heat to warm the place.

Falakar moved across to the tent flap and looked out. 'The next layer of tents isn't far.' He readied his bow and notched up an arrow. 'If anyone gets in close, you must deal with them.'

'Yes, sir,' Garamon replied, feeling the sweat in his gloves.

The tents were separated by identical distances, set in an area cleared of snow, not a trace of it could be seen. Soldiers were jogging at a matching pace from the other tents in the direction of the fighting. When the tents had emptied, Falakar moved across the gap to the back of the next tent and indicated a cutting motion. Garamon understood and sliced a five foot tear with his axe, the blade parted the material without a sound.

As expected, boxes were stacked inside, indistinguishable from the previous tent.

It was already clear of soldiers and they crossed to the tent flap as before and Falakar repeated his check. He cursed. 'The command tent is ahead, still guarded on the outside.'

Garamon took a look. 'There are too many, we have to return.'

'We complete the mission,' Falakar said.

There were a dozen soldiers lined up around the tent. Even with Falakar's skills and the power of the axe, Garamon couldn't believe it possible to succeed. There would be no chance to keep the fight quiet, more soldiers would come. 'I'm ready,' he said, licking the dryness from his lips and taking up a stance to rush out.'

Falakar placed a staying hand on his shoulder. 'First we cause as much disorder as possible so one of us gets the plans in the confusion.' He tore some linen from a bed, wrapping it around the end of an arrow. 'Stand back.' He hit the glass fire bowl with the hilt of his hunting knife, creating a crack. The yellow liquid was thick and oozed out, pooling on the floor. He dipped the tip of his arrow into the goo until soaked through. 'Use a goblet and pour plenty of this onto the floor at the entrance. Don't get it near the flame.'

Garamon did as he was told as Falakar poured more over the rear boxes.

When they were done, a small hole in the side of the tent was opened facing away from the Major's tent guards. Falakar lit the arrow. Fierce flames burst out. He set the arrow and fired it out of the tent hole.

'I've set the other large tent on fire, it's drawing away the guards to help, but there is no telling what will be on the inside, so be ready.'

Garamon stepped out after the Ranger into the daylight. He'd never felt so afraid. The remaining tent guards had taken the bait and were running to check on the screams erupting from within the other large tent. Keeping close to Falakar he raced across the gap to the command tent, slicing his axe down. His fear made him slit a line from seven feet high to the ground and into the rock. There was a flash and deafening crack blowing the tent cut wide open. This time there were no boxes for protection from discovery. Ahead of them was a large central table with various parchments pinned to it. Two men looked up and one of them shouted a command. Four soldiers guarding the doorway on the inside drew swords and ran forward, while more entered from the outside. With all chance gone of getting the parchments, Falakar loosed an arrow off into the chest of the one that gave the command before turning and running.

Garamon followed and they jumped back out. A quick glance showed the fire had almost been put out, with an Ashnorian healing magii in green casting some spell to quench the flames. The distracted tent guards were coming back and spotted them.

The two sprinted to the previous tent.

'Jump!' shouted Falakar, reminding Garamon of the oil trap.

As they did, so they almost collided with a servant who was cleaning up the flammable spillage. Falakar barged the servant to the back of the tent, dipping his arrow into the liquid as he ran and touched it to the flaming tube. He spun and fired at the floor in the entrance just as the first soldier ran in and slipped on the yellow substance, landing and coating himself in the sticky liquid, tripping others as they came through. Falakar's flaming arrow hit the middle of the patch, exploding it into flame which became an impassable wall of screaming, burning men. One of them staggered blindly into the middle of the tent towards the glass bulb still half-filled with liquid. Falakar grabbed Garamon and pulled him to the ground behind the packing boxes where a servant was already repairing the slice in the rear of the tent. Falakar dragged him and the other servant to the ground just as a loud *whump* preceded an explosion of flames licking over the top of their cover.

Falakar didn't delay and sliced a new tear in the tent. They ran through leaving the tent ablaze. The soldiers not caught in the tent inferno were running around the outside. Two guards appeared from the doorway of the next tent ahead with weapons and shields ready. They advanced.

Falakar with bow in one hand, and still holding his knife from cutting the tent in the other, couldn't get an arrow off. Instead he slowed hard allowing his attacker's first swing to overreach. Feigning a low attack with his knife, pulling the soldier's shield low, he whipped his bow across the man's face spinning him from his feet.

Garamon had no such subtlety at his disposal. He launched his axe at the incoming sword of his opponent, shattering it to pieces and carrying on to smash into the soldier's helm. The metal of the helm parted and the axe buried halfway into the man's head. It made a sucking noise as he pulled it free.

They leapt into the final tent and raced for the back. There, the servants had just completed the repair as Garamon tore a new one next to it. The two men jumped through. The remaining pair of perimeter guards were ahead of them. There wasn't time to take them down and climb the rocks at the back with the bulk of the soldiers behind. The way remaining was the path the workers were using. Falakar angled towards it and both men sprinted. The two outer guards were closer to it and moved to block them.

Garamon knew they'd no time to engage.

'I'll deal with them,' he shouted.

Falakar slowed a little allowing the woodsman ahead. As they reached them Garamon swung at the nearest soldier's shield intending to blast him into the other as he'd done when cornered on the mountain. But the soldier was faster and struck Garamon's shoulder with a vicious hack. There was a judder and his arm felt momentarily crushed from the impact, but no wound. The sword had struck the flat of Falakar's blade laid on his shoulder and deflecting the blow. Then, in a single fluid move the Ranger pushed into the soldier, knocking him back causing him to raise his shield to get balance just enough for Falakar to slice into the guts of the man.

The second soldier's shield had taken a hit from the follow through of Garamon's miss and his shield spun away so fast it snapped the soldier's arm dropping him to the ground. They leapt over him.

Passing workers carrying various tools and materials, they sped up the trail with the pursuing soldiers, paces behind. The Rangers were better suited to the terrain and began leaving the Ashnorians behind. A patrol of more soldiers appeared ahead and Falakar pointed to a low outcrop of rocks and both leapt up. The rocks proved to be difficult for the soldiers in heavy armour to follow quickly and the two made their escape.

Running for some time, Falakar slowed and stopped in a small clearing.

'Are we safe?' Garamon said, breathing hard, more from the fear than the exertion.

'For now.'

Garamon threw his axe away. It slid across the ground and disappeared under the snow before he bent over and threw up.

'You okay?'

'That damned axe,' Garamon replied.

'It seemed to perform perfectly, and your courage when tackling those two last soldiers showed you to be worthy of such a weapon.'

'I nearly cut a man's head in two. Pulling my axe out, I could see his brain.'

'There is no glamour in this task ahead of you, or any of us. Few choose this role out of preference. I would be a farmer, woodsman or builder.'

'Then why do you do it!'

'Because I don't want somebody dying on my behalf.'

'They don't do it for *you*. And would it make so much difference if you didn't, you're one man.'

Falakar flinched a little at the brusque comment. 'To me it would, yes.'

'But you don't have to. You could have stopped and gone back and become a farmer.'

'Could you have turned back when going after your friend?'

'No, but killing people is terrible. It makes us no better than the Empire.'

'Not true. If they stopped, so would we. If we stopped, they would continue.'

Garamon considered the words and looked across at the mound of snow were his axe lay buried.

'It's your burden to wield,' Falakar continued. 'As it was your Grandfather's in the Melenite wars.'

'I don't want such a burden.'

'For that reason I'm glad it's you who wield it.'

'I can barely use the thing!'

'Yet, since leaving to save your friend you are still alive after several encounters with the enemy that should have left you dead.'

'So you think I owe it something?' Garamon answered, incredulously.

'In truth I have no idea what the weapon is, or why it responds with its power only for you. But I know such a weapon in the hands of the wrong kind could rally an army of terrible destruction. Or in the hands of the right person, unite one to defeat it.'

'Well, I'm not the one. I'm just a woodsman who got into something where he doesn't belong. You should be the one with it. Why doesn't it pick you?'

Falakar walked over to the mound and pushed his hand into it, pulling the axe out. He returned it to the woodsman. 'The barbarians named you Heart of Sun. I think that's as good an explanation as I can give. There is something about you, son of Renous, with or without this axe.' He held the axe out to be taken. 'If there is such a thing as destiny, then this is yours.'

'And if I refuse?'

'I don't think destinies work that way,' the Ranger replied, resting the axe against the rock.

Garamon ignored it and walked away, looking back down the path of their escape. 'What do we do about the orders you wanted?'

'We need them, but there's no chance of getting them now.'

There was a slap to the side of Falakar on the ground.

Both men spun on the sound. It was a tied bundle of parchments.

'It's not all of them, but I got what I could.'

Garamon's face lit up to see Jontal sitting on the rocks above them. Then his smile faded. 'Do you mean we risked our lives for nothing?'

Jontal shook his head. 'I was watching with interest from on high. When you two got into trouble the remainder of the camp that hadn't gone after Ajoah went after you. I borrowed a servant's uniform and walked straight down the middle. They do have a blind eye to them; we should use that trick more often.'

Falakar picked up the bundle, untying the cord. 'Have you taken a look?'

'There's an interesting map.'

Falakar flicked through the parchments dropping those containing only writing. The last one was a folded parchment. He opened it out to reveal a map as wide as his arms could span. Brushing the snow from a flat rock, he set the map out. It showed the surrounding area for some distance. 'Many of the symbols overlaying the map are similar to those on the maps provided by the Ashnorian magii. But this one stands out. It seems to have been hand-drawn. It's a circle located within the Mlendrian forest connected by dotted lines to another on the Ashnorian side, just within the mountain. What does it represent?'

Jontal didn't look up from some intricate work he was doing with a small bottle and some thread. 'I've no idea, but it looks uncannily like a path through the mountain to me.'

'A cave system or underground river we have not found?'

Jontal shrugged. 'It does come out on our side deep within Sheergreen Forest. There are plenty of unexplored areas within it. I guess it's possible there's an area containing an opening we've missed for all these years.'

'I must see it on the Ashnorian's side.'

'I've already taken a look. There's an army stretching out into the desert, queuing to enter a man-made entrance into the mountain. There are also lines of supply wagons.'

Falakar looked over the map again. 'If they are digging a hole through the mountain, they could walk straight into Mlendria without detection.'

'Wouldn't that take years?' Garamon said.

Falakar nodded his agreement. 'I need to know more. It's the place we go next.'

Jontal absently dug some ice from his boot treads, causing a mini landslide fluffy of snow from his rock. 'I just knew you were going to say that.'

'Feel free to go your own way,' Falakar said, folding up the map and leaving the written parchments behind.

Jontal jumped down. 'Actually, I'll tag along. Things tend to get interesting around you two. Besides, we don't want this axe ending up in the hands of the wrong sort.' He picked up the weapon and pitched it to Garamon.

Garamon plucked it out of the air with a single hand, as if it were born to him.

Jontal smiled.

'Oh, and I discovered something interesting on my trip. The bandits are gone.'

'Gone?' Falakar replied.

'As in, not there.'

'But there are hundreds in these mountains.'

'Not anymore. I checked every camp I know and not a single one remained.'

'Any sign of a fight?'

'None at all, it's as if they all decided to leave. Men, woman and children, even the livestock.'

'What in the gods is happening here,' Falakar muttered.

'Just to confuse things further, I went to the nearest symbol on that map, above the camp. It was my return from there that made me bump into you two. It contains a large number of Ashnorian workers building something.'

'What is it?' Falakar said.

'No idea, but it looks serious.'

'Which way?'

Jontal pointed back towards the Ashnorian camp. The other two head out and he scooped up the discarded parchments sliding them into his jerkin. The documents contained detailed information that could be useful for his survival, depending which direction the war took.

They crested a rise and the view opened out to show the edge of the Hammerheads not far south. Beyond it was Ashnoria, stretching, so it was said, to the very corners of the continent, leaving only Mlendria not under the Emperor's grasp.

A plateau of rock stretched out below to the edge of the mountain. The place had been cleared of snow and looked typical of a construction site with huge wooden beams perfectly stacked at regular intervals. At each stack an identical number of workers were preparing the wood, standing in symmetrical positions doing the same job in the same way. Guards were posted at equally spaced intervals around the workforce.

The object of the workers activity was a large structure rising up out of the mountain standing at the edge. They swarmed over it as one wooden beam after another was hoisted to be connected atop the others.

'It's already fifty feet tall,' Falakar judged. 'From the width at the base I'd say it's going to be three times that when finished.'

'It looks like a tower,' Garamon said. 'Why would you build something so high when you're already at the highest point? It can't make much difference to the view over Ashnoria.'

Falakar was lost in thought. 'Where did you say you encountered the burnt out Ranger post?'

'Less than an hour northwest of Dulmurn's cabin.'

'It has a view of the entire Tiburn valley.'

'Rarely, Brother, the mist clears perhaps twice a year to bring the town into view from there.'

'Perhaps magic isn't stopped by mist,' Falakar replied. 'Do you remember the tower the mage climbed when we attacked their outpost in the desert?'

Jontal remembered it well. They'd managed to enter Ashnoria via the desert, but had to attack a bunker. A mage tried to climb a tower to send a warning message. 'It's one of those mage communication towers?'

'Along with another, I'll wager, being built in the area of the burnt out station. It's why they needed to take control of that area too. Given enough height I would think you could see the top of this tower from another one placed there.'

'And from there to Tiburn,' Jontal said.

Garamon shuffled uncomfortably. 'That would connect Straslin direct to Tiburn.'

'It would seem to be the case,' Falakar said.

'But if the attack is months away, why are they risking the towers being discovered now? They must know we can defeat a few hundred soldiers and destroy the towers. And how does this fit in with the dotted lines on the map through the mountain?'

Falakar took out the map and had another look, but shook his head. 'I don't know,' he said wearily. 'It's getting late, let's get back to Dulmurn's.'

'To avoid patrols, some of the route back will be tricky for our young friend,' Jontal said.

'He'll do fine,' Falakar replied.

Chapter 44 – Trapping

The others had been gone for some time looking for the Ashnorian camp. The waiting was grating on Dulmurn's nerves wondering if at any time the door would be broken down and soldiers of the Empire would rush in and drag him to a torturer. He had to do something to take his mind from it.

Unlocking the extra locks from his door, he went to his shed and took as many spare traps as he could carry. Heading out to the entrance into the bowl, he began hiding traps along the edge of the pathway in the deep snow not trodden by the Rangers. A larger force, like an Empire scouting party would likely trample wider to the sides of the path.

It wasn't foolproof, but it did something to make him feel a little safer. If he heard traps trigger, or more likely, the yell of a man caught in one, it might give him a chance to climb out onto the top of his cabin and hide.

'So this is your little refuge.'

Dulmurn jumped at the voice, almost setting off the trap he was arming. It was the man who led the group that kidnapped him from his mansion and threw him in jail. He looked up the path in hope of seeing the Rangers returning.

'No, I'm afraid they won't be back for a while,' said Strack.

'What do you want?'

'We ransacked your mansion. Not a penny. Rich people never have all their fortunes in a bank or investments. There's always a stash of cash somewhere.'

'I don't have one of those,' Dulmurn had a trap in his hand. If he could set it fast enough, maybe he could catch Strack in it.

'Oh, I know you well-heeled dandies well enough, and now I've found your secret in the mountains, I think I'll find what I missed before.'

Dulmurn continued to back away. 'There's nothing here but traps and piles of firewood.'

'This will go easier if you tell me where it is, Trapper. I can make things quite unpleasant for you.'

Dulmurn pulled hard on the trap and set it, throwing it at Strack's feet before running for the cabin. Reaching the door he flung it open and raced through. Agony shot through his leg accompanied by a loud snap as one of his own traps clamped around his ankle.

The snow crunched behind him as Strack approached at walking pace.

'The irony isn't lost to you, I hope?'

Dulmurn tried to open the trap. Strack kicked him over, making the pain shoot through his leg as the teeth bit further into his flesh.

'You bastard, get this thing off me.'

Strack stood on the trap so it rotated around Dulmurn's ankle. The trapper screamed out. Strack punched him hard in the face to shut him up. 'Yell out again and I'll add a fractured jaw to your broken nose and ripped leg. Where's the money?'

Dulmurn put a hand up to his nose. There was a wide split and blood was seeping out. 'There's no money.'

'I can put you through a lot of pain, none of which bothers me at all.' He went to push his foot on the trap again.

'Stop!'

Strack waited.

'There,' Dulmurn said, pointing into the raised fire pit.

'In the fire?'

'One of the floor fire bricks is loose.'

Strack got a jug of water and doused the fire over the area indicated. Seeing a loose brick he used his knife to lever it out. A handle sat beneath it. It was stiff and he gave it a hard tug, releasing it causing him to fall backwards to the floor. As he did, so a section of the room's large rug lifted, creating a bump. He stabbed in his knife and cut away the fabric. Underneath was a trapdoor, ajar. He pulled it to reveal an ironbound chest.

'If I have to waste time smashing the lock, I'll be doing the same to your face.'

Dulmurn reached inside his tunic and pulled at the cord around his neck, looped through a key. He threw it over as Strack lifted the chest from the hole. The chest unlocked with a click and the lid opened to reveal high denomination notes stacked to the rim from the Bank of Mlendria.

He whistled. 'Now that's a payday.'

'I've given you what you want. Now let me go,' Dulmurn demanded.

Strack walked back to the trapper.

Chapter 45 – Joining Forces

Garamon was struggling to keep pace with Jontal leading. The bandit was even more adept at travelling across the slippery landscape than Falakar, leaping across snow-covered rocks, slipping and recovering. It all looked part of the mode of travel for him, always ready for it and using it at times to his advantage. Falakar was at the rear and Garamon felt the pressure of the man, pushing the pace. Some of the jumps they made were precarious with a fall meaning injury. Never did this seem to bother Jontal, almost as if he didn't feel danger, being so confident of his footing.

Then, up ahead, Garamon could see a wide gap. He couldn't believe Jontal sped up to a sprint and leapt high, executing a perfect head over heels somersault midway to land comfortably in control and sliding to a stop. He looked back, a wide grin on his face.

Garamon stopped at the edge. It was a long drop.

Jontal gave a wave.

His brother shook his head at the antics.

'I don't think I can make it,' Garamon said.

'It's just the fear of falling. You can clear it safely,' Falakar said. 'Here, I'll show you how to remove your fear.' Falakar walked back and Garamon followed.

'From here you cannot see the drop,' said the Ranger. 'Now focus on the far rock. Locate a place where you can put your first footing. Can you see it?'

'Yes.'

Now count down inside your head from ten. At each count, focus harder on the foothold. Do not think of anything else.

When you reach four, you sprint. Keep counting down and focusing on the foothold, more with each count as you run. Time your jump to coincide with the count of one, and land on the count of zero. Understood?'

'Yes, sir,' Garamon replied. Concentrating on the landing point he removed thoughts of the drop. As he reached four he sprinted. At the approach he snapped out of the moment, throwing himself to the floor feet first to find whatever purchase he could. He slid to a halt with his legs over the edge, dangling down the drop.

'He'll never get over it now,' Jontal called over.

Garamon picked himself up and flushed out the snow piled in his jerkin. He walked back to Falakar. 'I'm sorry, I thought I was going to jump until the last moment, then I panicked.'

'Give me your backpack and axe, and try again.'

'I don't think I can.'

'Jump it, or stay.'

'Yes, sir,' Garamon said.

He turned to the crevasse.

'Focus on the point again, and start your countdown.'

Garamon tried. He counted down to seven but his mind interrupted his concentration with flashes of his near fall. He started his countdown again.

'Run!' Falakar shouted.

Garamon jumped at the sudden shout so close. 'I had to restart, I'm not ready.'

'Run, now!' The Ranger took off for the gap. He jumped and threw both Garamon's axe and rucksack to Jontal in-flight, clearing the distance and landing on the other side.

Garamon heard a noise from behind and turned to see twenty Ashnorian soldiers coming up behind him. Before he'd time to think he was running at the gap and leapt.

Falakar and Jontal were ready to catch him if he was short. He landed on top of the rock, passing Falakar's landing, sliding until he overbalanced and came to a halt on his back.

Jontal chuckled to his brother. 'I was wrong.' He dropped the axe and backpack and half drew his sword as the first Ashnorian soldier took the jump. The weighty armour and heavy shield was too much and he slammed into the rock face scrambling for a hold. He slid down and fell away with a cry before the sound of him hitting the ground far below cut it off.

The other Ashnorians stopped and looked across the barrier.

'Elleks,' Jontal called out to them, which angered them.

'What does that mean?'

'Something you do with your hand,' Jontal replied.

Falakar raised a brow. 'Let's go before they find a way around.'

They arrived at Dulmurn's cabin as the sun was setting. Jontal lifted the latch and stepped through the door, to back out again with a sword resting on his chest, his hands raised.

Falakar pulled his sword free. There was a faint rustle from around the bowl and several Rangers rose up on the surrounding rocks, bows set and aimed at them.

Ajoah stepped out from the cabin holding the sword.

'By order of Major Stimm, you are all to return with me for judgement of your crimes.'

'On what charge?' Falakar said.

'For aiding the escape of a prisoner, disrupting a council meeting with force, causing shock, and injuring several councillors with splinters.'

'Only because he didn't want his brother to be caught in the cells when the attack came.' Garamon exclaimed.

Ajoah looked confused for a moment, then to Jontal, then Falakar, who had closed his eyes.

'I see the resemblance now. Not sure how I missed it before.'

Falakar looked around at the surrounding Rangers, he sheathed his sword. 'We need to talk,' he said, walking passed Ajoah into the cabin.

Garamon followed close behind. 'I'm sorry, Falakar. I should have thought.'

'It's done,' the Ranger replied.

Ajoah followed in last with his sword pointing at Jontal. 'The Ashnorians are looking for us and I need my men out there on guard. Can I trust you not to try anything?'

'You have my word,' Falakar said.

Ajoah gave a signal to his men before closing the door and sheathing his sword. He joined Falakar at the fire, warming his hands. 'I lost a lot of good men back at the Ashnorian camp. I hope it was worth it.'

Falakar handed over the Ashnorian map. 'We got this.'

'Looks like a plan of the area, marking our patrols.'

'We think the dotted line through the mountain is a path to our side.'

'How soon will they attack?'

'They're lined up at the foot of this mountain as we speak, an army many times anything we can put against them.'

Ajoah returned the map. 'We must warn Stimm.'

'Brinley's got to Stimm, he won't hear of an invasion. I need you to disobey the Major.'

Ajoah was relieved, 'I'm glad they were wrong about you, sir. What are your orders?'

'It will mean your court-martial, Captain.'

'I think they'll have more pressing matters to attend,' Ajoah replied.

Falakar sighed. Ajoah was his best student. That it had come to this, the discrediting of such a fine soldier. It should be Stimm up for court-martial.

'We're going to find out what they're doing in the mountain.'

'What of him?' Ajoah said, looking at Jontal. 'I cannot afford the men to look after him or be slowed by him being tied up.'

'They're both coming with us.'

'Very well,' Ajoah said. 'I suggest we head out when dark.'

'They may have battle magiis,' Jontal reminded.

Ajoah looked to Falakar.

'Their mages can see us in the dark,' Falakar explained.

Ajoah grimaced. 'We saw one of their mages. He waved a hand at my men from a distance and lighting leapt from his hand striking three of them dead.'

'They have limited power,' Jontal said. 'And if you can separate them from their staves or the ornate box they carry, they are useless.'

'That doesn't sound so easy.'

Jontal shrugged.

The door burst open and one of Ajoah's men entered.

'None of our outer scouts to the west have returned. We may have been found.'

Ajoah cursed. 'We can't get caught in this bowl. Call in the remaining scouts, we head south immediately.'

The man disappeared out again.

'Where's Dulmurn?' Garamon said. 'He didn't even want to leave the cabin to collect snow without us.'

Falakar shook his head. 'He'll have to take care of himself, we have no time to wait for him.'

Garamon followed the Ranger out. He didn't like the idea of leaving the trapper behind, or at least to say thank you and goodbye, but he knew the man was experienced in the mountains. He would have to hope to meet up again later.

As he walked passed the shed he didn't notice the lock was hanging open, something the trapper never did. Inside was a body buried under the new logs Garamon had stacked.

Ajoah waited until the others left before opening the door to the back storage room.

Strack stepped out.

'This wasn't the plan, Ranger.'

'Where is the trapper, Strack?'

The thug shrugged. He didn't care if Ajoah knew what he'd done, Brinley would provide immunity through Stimm, but with a fortune sitting in backpacks in the room behind, he didn't want unnecessary attention.

Ajoah guessed what happened to the trapper and looked Strack in the eyes, menacingly. 'Stay well away from me. If I see you again, I'll cut you down.'

'You won't see me again, Ranger.'

Ajoah left the cabin walking into the cold, feeling ashamed he'd allowed himself to be turned against Falakar. Snow started to fall, not making the coming night's journey any easier, and he pulled his hood up over his head.

As he neared the others at the exit to the bowl, a bright flash hit one of the lookouts on the ridge above to fall back into them, smoke rising from his chest. The nearest Ranger checked him and shook his head.

Garamon ran up to where the man had been standing and held out his axe. Ajoah called out to get back. Falakar had seen what the woodsman was doing, but ignored him and continued directing the escape of the others away from the mage. Ajoah stood confused.

There was another flash of lightning. It hit the axe and sparked over the blade and handle before dissipating. Garamon fell to his knees before shaking his head and getting back up.

'By the gods, that lad's got guts.' Another bolt flashed out. This time Garamon was knocked onto his back and slower to get up. Ajoah scooped up the fallen Ranger's bow and three arrows and leapt up the slope to join Garamon. Yet another flash struck the woodsman's axe. This time he wasn't getting up quick enough. Ajoah picked out the mage from the advancing soldiers by a strange blue bubble of light surrounding him. He aimed and fired an arrow to see it bounce away as it struck the blue light. However, it interrupted the magii from firing another bolt of the magic lightning and he fired the second arrow, notching up his last one.

Garamon staggered back to his feet, his axe no longer raised.

'The rest are clear, get going,' shouted Ajoah, firing the last arrow.

Garamon was too dazed to understand and Ajoah saw the magii about to launch another attack. Dropping the bow he dived at the woodsman, propelling them both over the edge to slide to the trail floor as another flash flew overhead.

A face full of cold snow brought Garamon back to his senses.

'Come on, we've got to run!' shouted Ajoah.

Garamon shook the last of the effects from his head. As they ran the view opened up briefly through the mounds and Ajoah could see the Ashnorians giving chase.

Ahead, the main group of Rangers were approaching a bend. A shout went up from the front runners and all stopped. Garamon and Ajoah reached them to see the trail ahead was a long narrow channel with high rock on both sides, packed with snow. At the bottom of the slope, still some way off, stood as many Ashnorians as were behind them, forming into a column to fit the channel and marching towards them.

Jontal swore. 'Hammer and anvil.'

'Which one are we?' Garamon said.

'The horseshoe,' Ajoah answered.

Falakar turned to four Rangers. 'Give me your swords. Use your bows to stop those behind us from rounding the corner.

Ajoah took Falakar's bow and joined the rearguard. 'Keep the mage under fire, it stops him using his lightning.'

The men took up positions.

Falakar rammed the first sword into the snow wall at waist height. 'Knock this in up to the hilt,' he ordered Garamon.

The woodsman reversed his axe and hit the sword, burying it as instructed in a single strike.

Falakar offered up the next one at head height, staggered from the first, creating steps. Garamon knocked it in also.

'Place these last two in the same way.'

Garamon stepped up onto the first sword, lining up the third as arrows were fired. There was a flash illuminating the white snow of the trail and one of the Rangers flew backwards. Garamon faltered and Falakar's bark jerked him back to his task. He hammered the third sword in, almost too far.

He stepped up again. The bowmen were now firing faster. Another flash and another Ranger fell, although this time the spell didn't kill him.

'That was a direct hit, the magii's mana is getting low,' Jontal called out.

'The others are getting close,' shouted a Ranger from the front.

Garamon struck in the last sword and climbed onto it. It was high enough and he pulled himself onto the ridge, met by Falakar close on his heels.

'The magii is weak. Do your best to distract him while the rest climb,' Falakar said.

Garamon made himself prominent and saw the magii who pointed his staff at him. A feeble bolt of lightning crackled out and struck the axe. Garamon felt a tingle through is arms.

Jontal arrived next at his side with bow drawn and both of the fallen Ranger's quivers. 'Time to put the wind up that bastard.'

He loosed arrow after arrow at the magii in quick secession as the Rangers climbed. Bouncing from his shield, one by one, they kept him from attacking. Then one struck it and the magic blinked out. The arrow was deflected but got through and glanced from the metal cap on the magii's forehead, who fell back.

'That'll do it,' Jontal smirked.

Four more Rangers made it up the makeshift ladder and took positions firing arrows down on the advancing soldiers. Both groups of Ashnorians raised their shields above them, locked without a hint of a gap between them preventing the deadly rain from getting through.

'Damn, these men are well drilled,' Ajoah said, ordering the Rangers to stop firing.

The first group of Ashnorians reached the corner as the final Ranger leapt onto the first makeshift step. In his rush he missed his footing on the second hilt and slipped back to the ground. He scrambled for the first foothold as twin swords were driven into his back. Ajoah turned away, unable to watch.

Falakar showed no such distress. 'It'll take them time to assemble here and follow us.'

Garamon looked to the Ranger. Men had given their lives for him and yet he showed no moment of remorse at their loss.

A red glow appeared beneath them. Without sound, the snow began melting and forming into an avenue of steps wide enough for the column.

'I thought you said the mage was out of magic,' Ajoah said.

Jontal shrugged at the eerie spectacle before him. 'I guess snow is easier to melt than making lightning.'

They sped off.

The soldiers ascended the stairway and assembled their structured column before resuming their marching pace.

Jontal ran up next to Falakar. 'If they ever discover the order to run, we're going to be in so much trouble.'

Another column of soldiers appeared ahead of them. Ajoah changed direction heading away.

'They're boxing us in towards the edge of the mountain.'

'Then we better get their first and find a way off this plateau.'

The terrain was flat from eons of erosion of soft rock on the exposed edge of the mountain range, with little to hinder their pursuers. Eventually, they reached the edge. Thousands of feet below was the Ashnorian desert.

Garamon could see the lights of Straslin far in the distance. Somewhere in the city was his friend, Chayne. What was happening to him since he stopped the magii? Was he still alive?

'It looks so peaceful,' Ajoah said. 'Hard to believe such evil created it.'

'They would not believe they are so,' Falakar replied, looking over the edge for some escape.

'How can they not? You say they subjugate a slave class to the point of treating them worse than pets, and torture anyone for the most simple of mistakes.'

'I do not justify their way, it's against everything I believe in. But to them it's just a way of life they were delivered into. They know no better and would think us equally mystifying.'

Far below in the shadow of the mountain a column of soldiers stretched out, lining up and entering at the point of the dotted markings on the map.

'So many,' Ajoah said.

'Take your men, and break through the pursuing line and draw them away from us, Captain. Find Lindeg in the Bay of Waves and tell him what's happening. Trust no one else.'

Ajoah looked to his mentor.

'Bother,' Jontal interrupted. 'What you're asking is suicide. There are twelve of them left against dozens and that mage. How do propose they achieve such a thing?'

'They are Rangers, and Ajoah has been personally trained by me.'

Jontal gripped his brother's arm. 'He won't stand a chance.'

Falakar shrugged off his brother's hand, and returned his gaze upon Ajoah. 'There can be no failure in your mission. Do whatever you must and use your men as necessary.'

Ajoah stood and gave salute. 'Understood, sir.'

Jontal had no love for the Rangers, but he'd come to like Ajoah. The man was a professional, but also had an element of compassion for his men, unlike Falakar.

A call went up from a scout. Garamon could see him signalling that the enemy was approaching from several directions.

Garamon shook Ajoah's hand. 'Good luck to you, I hope we meet again.'

'Luck is good,' Ajoah replied. 'What we all need is a miracle.' Assembling his remaining men, he gave the order. They formed up and head out, cutting towards a small channel in the rock to give them some cover from the approaching enemy.

'You know it will take weeks to get the full force of your army to these mountains,' Jontal said, curious about what his brother was currently doing.

Falakar knelt down, leaning close to toppling out over the edge. 'We have no idea how long it will take the Ashnorians to get through whatever opening they may have found. Even if they've found some kind of natural path, it's a lot of men to march through tight caverns, and still they have to navigate days of dense forest.' He began to sniff the air.

The heads of Ashnorian soldiers appeared over the edge of the plateau.

'Not all are being drawn away, we don't have long.'

Falakar held a hand out to his brother. 'I need to see further out.'

Jontal joined hands with the Ranger as he leaned over the edge. 'Hurry, we're standing out like dogs on a pony.'

Falakar pulled himself back and removed his rope, spooling it over the edge. 'Here, tie this to your belt,' he said to Garamon. 'Both of you hold it, I have an idea.'

'Was that a clap of ominous thunder?' Jontal said with sarcasm.

Falakar wrapped the rope around him to spool it out over his shoulder. Garamon had seen the Rangers do it before, it allowed for a controlled decent without burning the hands.

'When I call up; Jontal, you come next.'

'Err, I'll only have him to support me.'

'You're the lightest,' Falakar replied.

Jontal looked to Garamon, who swallowed hard. 'I won't let you fall.'

Jontal cast his eyes to the sky for a moment. Just then a bright flash occurred like lightning coming from over the ridge in the direction of Ajoah.

'You wish more time to discuss this, Brother?' Falakar said.

The Ashnorian soldiers heading their way were going to be on them soon.

'At least the magii had gone after Ajoah.'

Digging their feet into the hard snow, Garamon and Jontal braced as Falakar stepped out over the edge. He quickly disappeared from view and soon the rope went slack as he called up.

Jontal slipped the rope around him and stepped to the edge. Taking a last look at Garamon, he took a long leap out over the edge. He fell some way before he pulled on the rope to slow him and bring him back to the rock face. The stop was quicker than he intended and it jolted the rope tight for a moment before it began slipping down in small jerks. It was clear the woodsman was slipping towards the edge. There was nothing he could do, the rock face was smooth and there was no sign of Falakar. Then the rope went slack and he fell as a pair of feet appeared over the edge above, followed by Garamon, falling.

Hands grabbed Jontal's waist and pulled him in onto a ledge with enough force to send him spinning inwards away from the edge. There was a yell of help as the woodsman passed them seconds later, but Falakar made no attempt to reach out for him.

'Oh gods, no!' shouted Jontal, scrambling forward.

There was a snap as the rope attached to Garamon's belt reached its full extent. Falakar had already secured his end around a rock on the ledge.

'Here, help me pull him up,' Falakar said, unconcerned.

'This was your plan all along?'

Falakar gripped the rope and began pulling. 'If I'd told you both, you wouldn't have done it.'

Garamon was pulled up onto the ledge and he dragged himself into a deep recess out of sight from above as the sounds of marching feet approached. Words were spoken in their language before the group marched off.

Garamon threw up. 'Have they gone?'

Jontal begrudgingly appreciated the shrewd deception, despite his brother's callous manner in executing it. 'They think we've fallen to our deaths.'

'I doubt even a magii could detect three bodies thousands of feet below,' Falakar explained.

'I'm beginning to understand how you've survived for so long.'

Garamon caught an unpleasant smell beyond that of his vomit, and wondered if his fear had made him do something worse.

Jontal smelt it too. 'I know that odour.'

'These mountains are riddled with tunnels and caverns,' Falakar said. 'I'm guessing it's what the Ashnorians are exploiting to get through the mountain. A variety of bat lives within them, spending the day in the dark, and hunting the crags outside at night. I was searching for the smell of their droppings over the edge, indicating one of their egresses. This was the first location coinciding with a ledge I could see from above. It leads in there.' He pointed to a fissure in the shadow of the mountain.

'One mother of a chance,' Jontal said.

'Sometimes it's all you have,' Falakar replied. He helped Garamon to his feet. 'Are you recovered enough to travel?'

Despite quivering legs, Garamon got to his feet. He knew the question was rhetorical, the Ranger would leave him behind to complete his mission. 'Yes, but I've had enough falling from cliffs for a while.'

Chapter 46 – Breakthrough

It was the last choke point. Two outcrops of rock separated by ten paces. ThreeSwords stood with the front line of plainsmen. When they broke this time there was nothing to stop the sea of Ashnorian warriors reaching his settlement. He'd only experienced tribal skirmishes between clans before. It amounted to no more than fifty men on each side. Now he stood with two-dozen plainsmen against over a thousand enemy. They had to hold the line until the Ritual of Giving. Too long.

The sky showed first signs night was fading and already they were preparing to attack.

Grostro walked up. 'It will take the intervention of the gods themselves for us to hold this time. How long do we have before we can yield?'

ThreeSwords didn't need to reply. His look answered for him.

'What do you intend to do?'

'Fight, kill and die.'

'Then I believe it is time I stopped watching and felt again the parting of flesh under my blade.'

'It will not be enough.'

'You underestimate me, Blackskin.'

'You're one man, the line will break and your men will run.'

'I will stay behind the line with my guard and join where it fails. My men will not turn while I'm standing.'

ThreeSwords hoped he was right. He scanned the rocks for inspiration that would give Kinfular some daring plan assured to fail, then to pull it off and win the day. None came.

A shouted command deep within the Ashnorian ranks split the morning silence. The wave of Ashnorian soldiers formed up. The ground was again uphill for the attackers and would be a disadvantage. A second call went up from behind the ranks and the advance began.

ThreeSwords could never remember the Ashnorians changing tactics. With such numbers it would be a simple task to charge the line. Instead they stuck to the single-minded tactic of wearing the enemy down until they were dead.

It wasn't going to take long.

ThreeSwords' first opponent was young, looking nervous and unsure. He brought the tips of his two swords together to form a wedge and forced them through the man's defence to bury them both into his chest. The young soldier blinked in surprise. ThreeSwords kicked him back into the line and darted forward to thrust his swords into the exposed flanks of the Ashnorian soldiers either side. Both soldiers fell away as ThreeSwords leapt back from a thrust from the next man in front.

The fighting continued at the constant pace set by the Ashnorians. Methodical and exacting, each soldier attacked in the same way. Some were more skilled than others, and some were stronger and some possessed better reflexes. The main advantage they had was numbers. While the defenders tired, the inexhaustible supply of fresh soldiers kept coming on, stepping over the dead of those fallen before them.

A call went up from the far left of the line. The Ashnorians had broken through.

ThreeSwords crossed his swords to catch the current incoming attack and pushed the soldier back. 'Close here!' The barbarians on either side moved to seal the gap.

At the breach, a stretch five men wide was open. The Ashnorians in the gap stayed their ground not taking advantage. ThreeSwords didn't have time to consider why as a battle cry went up from Grostro flanked by his guard, charging the gap. Even though the Ashnorians hadn't advanced into the breach, Grostro swept in with his guard. They smashed into the middle of the rupture slaughtering the front line of Ashnorians. With years of plains fighting the Chieftain had no doubts as to his own ability or those either side of him. He waded into the next line using his heavy broadsword and helm to stop and deflect the initial blows, reaching three deep before engaging. He smashed the first soldier from his feet with a blow.

His skilled guard either side protected his flanks while the plainsmen behind reorganised. He pulled back returning to his role of breach closer.

ThreeSwords stepped back into position and increased his tally of dead Ashnorians.

The fighting continued for only minutes before the shout went up again. ThreeSwords trusted to the Plainsmen Chieftain to close the gap and held his position.

Again the breach was closed.

The calls came faster as the barbarian numbers dropped until the inevitable happened. While Grostro engaged to stop one breach, the call went up for a second.

'The line is too thin, Blackskin. We need to run or die here!'

'ThreeSwords gave the command, and as one, the barbarians pushed out with their shields to force back the attackers, then jumped back to escape. Some were too injured to do so and faced their final moments delaying the attackers for as long as possible before dying under a hail of sword blows.

The rout was on, but again the Ashnorians formed up and pursued at a rapid march. With only a handful of plainsmen remaining and wider ground from here on, it was certain defeat to come. The Ashnorians were going to arrive too soon and Kinfular's plan would count for nothing.

They stayed ahead of the mass of advancing soldiers. The final corner approached. Beyond was a straight march to his adopted home of the Riaan. He decided he would use it to mask a final surprise attack into the Ashnorian line. It would do little more than create a moment of chaos in their ranks.

Grostro was ahead. As he reached the corner, he and his men crouched down in a battle stance looking at something out of sight of the Heslarian. He guessed one of the Ashnorian groups that split off earlier must have gotten around behind them. It meant the Riaan settlement had already been attacked.

His heart sank at the carnage that must have occurred.

He readied himself for his final act, to charge and enact his retribution.

He turned the corner.

At the top of the trail stood Sholster; his left leg in a splint, standing like a god come to earth, his face stern as if it could turn back the Empire alone. Aside him stood thirty Riaan warriors. On the high ridges either side of the pass stood Shinlay and twenty other women archers. There was no sign of Kinfular.

He sped past the plainsmen to join the new line, and without a word, settled in beside the giant warrior.

'I have been sent to help delay a few Ashnorian scum, not a handful our plains cousins,' said the big barbarian.

'They are with us,' ThreeSwords explained.

'Well keep them out of my way, or they'll be stains on the rocks.'

ThreeSwords nodded and pointed were Grostro should join the line. 'We must hold until the Ritual of Giving.'

'Is that all?' Sholster barked. 'I should send the rest of you back.'

'ThreeSwords was pleased to again hear the battle banter from the self-assured warrior.

The Ashnorians broke the last corner in a measured turn keeping the column in formation.

As they came on, the true extent of the force became apparent. Even with the front of the column within bow range, the back of it showed no sign of appearing around the corner.

'By Chinad's beer-swollen liver, does this line stretch all the way back to Ashnoria!' Sholster bellowed.

'They heard you were with us,' shouted down Shinlay.

'Then their mothers will hear the cries of their folly all the way to that rat-infested pit.' Sholster slapped his thrinium club against his door-sized hollowed-out half-trunk for a wooden shield. He set himself as the invaders reached the last twenty paces. 'Brains for dinner tonight lads!'

As one, the line of Riaan defenders ran forward.

The battle line crashed together to the sound of Sholster's shield smashing three Ashnorians from their feet into the men behind spreading them like skittles. 'That's it, fly away you chicken carcasses!' He then swept his club out creating a sickening wet crunch as he connected with the nearest Ashnorian whose helmet and head caved under the impact. His body smashed into the soldiers to the side, unbalancing three of them. All died within moments as the Riaan warriors took advantage of their open defences.

The fight raged, and at first it seemed as though the Ashnorian line was being pushed back as Sholster drove repeatedly his one-man spearhead into the Ashnorian line. But it was clear only he could withstand the onslaught and he moved back step-by-step to the Riaan and Plainsmen warriors.

Arrows streamed down from high on the sides, but the enemy would far exceed the quivers.

The Commander lost all patience; they couldn't push through due to a single massive barbarian. Yelling in frustration he swiped a backhand across the nearest of his sub-commanders, knocking him to the floor. He stormed off to find the contemptible magii, finding him in one of the mobile support tents. The magii was raiding the rations of the men now fighting.

Jewell turned and saw him. He thought his life was about to end and reached out for his manasphere.

'Do not fear me yet, magii. I shall give you one command. If you can carry it out I shall overlook all that has transpired on this assignment. If not, you should use that thing to end your life quickly, for I will not provide you such luxury.

Jewell swallowed hard. 'What do you want me to do?'

'There is a new heathen who fights next to the black one. He stands head and shoulders above all around him and he holds the heathens together. If he falls, so will their line. Kill him.'

Jewell had managed to recharge his manasphere a little overnight. It could release enough mana to carry out the Commander's wishes but would leave him cold without his warming field. It seemed preferable to what the Commander had in store for him if he failed.

He followed on.

'Around the corner,' the Commander snarled.

Jewell worked his way through until he picked out the man the Commander was taking about. He was truly a giant amongst men. This was a problem. Jewell had no intention of standing in range of those archers, and at this range his spell would be weakened. Then he smiled as he saw his chance, the barbarian was holding a solid metal club. From here the light even made it look like thrinium, which was absurd.

Electrocution was one of his favourite attack spells. He envied the masters who could conjure a full lightning stroke to kill a man instantly. He would have to resort to a thin arc of lightning connecting him with the target who would suffer great pain until the spell was released. It would have to be maintained long enough for the victim's heart to fail. The fact the giant held a metal club was all the better as it would conduct the energy straight down his arms to his chest.

He placed his manasphere into its locked position and calmed himself before placing his fingers upon the surface. It grabbed at his consciousness and he held it firm. Watching the club intently he pushed out one finger, ready. It would produce the thinnest arc and take longer to kill, but it would have the range required. It would also hurt like the hells as his finger would have to take the sustained release of magic alone.

Shinlay looked down across the mass of Ashnorian soldiers below. Her gaze fell upon a small circle opening up far back in the ranks. In it stood two men. Her eyes went wide as she saw a robed figure stretching out a finger towards the middle of the Riaan line. Sholster!

She screamed out a warning, but the distance and clamour of battle prevented any chance of it being heard. She notched an arrow. It was a distant shot, even for her. A breeze coming down from the mountain made matters worse.

A thin stream of blue lightning left the magii's finger, connecting with the end of Sholster's club. The man stopped and stood shaking before collapsing. She aimed and fired. The man with the magii slapped him on the back, seemingly congratulating him and knocking him forward. He followed on to catch him, replacing the magii's position. The arrow plunged in the man's shoulder.

The magii realised what had happened as she notched up another arrow and fired again. The arrow stuck home. But no, it bounced away harmlessly. The magii searched for her and raised a finger. She dived away to the cover of the rocks as a weak tendril of lightning flew overhead.

Jewell cursed as he saw the woman duck away just in time. He turned to the Commander. The arrow was deep into his shoulder in the direction of his heart. Jewell felt for a pulse as the nearest sub-commander arrived, raising his shield to cover any further arrow attack.

It was Kadjat, a brash young man filled with radical ideas, placed under the Commander to learn patience in battle.

'He's alive, but the arrow is close to his heart. Removing it could be fatal.'

'Repair it,' Kadjat ordered.

'It's not easy,' Jewell lied. He wasn't an accomplished mage-surgeon, but all field magii's had elementary training in the other disciplines. He could see inside the Commander's body and knew the arrow was pushing on a major artery, cutting off the flow causing the Commander to lose consciousness. He could ease the arrow out and repair the damage enough for the Commander to survive.

Pretending to concentrate, his hands moved quickly over the Commander as if in desperation to save the man. Then he focused on the artery under pressure and split it. Blood poured out into the surrounding tissue.

'It's hopeless, I'm sorry.'

Kadjat stood up, excitement building in his eyes. 'I shall take command. We shall wash over these heathens like a sea of blades. Come with me, magii.' He pushed his way through the men ahead of him.

'Shielding!' he shouted. The men around him raised their shields protecting him from the archers. As he reached the twentieth line of soldiers from the head of the column, he yelled out. 'Form a wedge, like this!' he bellowed, holding out his arms at full length touching at the fingers.

Arrows bounced from the shields around him. One got through to glance from his helm. He pulled free his sword and cut the head clean from the shoulders of the bearer whose shield failed to protect him. He returned his sword to its scabbard as another man replaced the fallen.

The wedge formed up ahead of him. It wasn't a practiced manoeuvre and they struggled with it. Kadjat marched through to the back of the wedge.

'Now run at them. Do not stop. Force them apart into two sides.'

The men responded to the order and the wedge of armoured human flesh drove forward.

Grostro called out across to ThreeSwords. 'Times up. These Yellowskins have come to their senses.'

Sholster was alive but dazed and being taken back to the settlement. Without his help in the middle the wedge crashed into the thin line of defenders, forcing them apart. ThreeSwords pulled back and called the retreat.

Kadjat hollered out at the success of his tactic, ordering his men to break formation and chase the heathens down. The huge pack of men stirred into movement from the novel command and soon hundreds of remaining Ashnorians were free-running. Some of them started shouting and a disordered battle cry began to ring out as more men took up the call. Soon the sound was deafening.

Kadjat revelled in the moment. Victory would be his and upon return he would be promoted to Commander. He watched as the faster heathens increased the gap from his men. It didn't matter now. They would catch them eventually, and when they did he knew the tactic to defeat them.

At the end of the long stretch of trail, it levelled onto a vast open area. His fleeing quarry was nowhere to be seen. His men had stopped, waiting further orders.

Hundreds of small tents made from animal skins stretched out in an uncoordinated mess before him. He was left in no doubt it was the heathen's settlement. Above it was a sizeable outcrop of rock protecting over half the camp from the elements.

He walked into the settlement with his men. It was wide and open. A perfect killing ground for him. Nothing could stop him now.

Chapter 47 – Open Betrayal

Calinsk Ducilly completed his Administrator duties for the day. Another eighty torture orders authorised, each one more difficult to sign than the previous. More of the Empire's subjects sentenced in the name of Yan production to extend the corrupt lives of the Elite at the expense of the majority.

He was glad the invasion of the North was now only a week away. It would provide a huge influx of new subjects into the Empire, requiring many new Administrators. It would take the pressure from him to supply so many to the chambers, some of whom were sentenced to high levels of correction for the merest infringements.

He snapped his fingers, making a sign in the air. A servant approached and poured a transparent blue liquid into a crystal goblet on the desk. He snapped his fingers irritably and repeated the sign. Another measure was added to the first. He downed it, the strength of it biting the back of his throat. He repeated the sign again, but before the servant finished pouring, he snatched the bottle impatiently and ordered the servant away.

Pouring several measures in one go, he downed half of it before slumping back in his chair, letting the drink wash through his veins releasing some of the pain from his soul.

He noticed the servant he'd dismissed was still standing in front of him. He should have marked it for punishment, but the drink was taking effect and he'd had enough issuing torture for the day. He waved it away again.

It didn't move.

Irate it had ignored him, he made the sign for punishment, waiting for the thing to hold out its hand. He was then aware of being looked upon. He glanced up to see it looking into his eyes. Such an insult was intolerable and punishable by death through correction. He got to his feet, staggering a little holding onto the desk. He made the sign again for the servant to hold out its hand.

It shook its head.

His eyes felt as though they were going to burst from his skull. Never had such a display of disorder been recorded within the Empire. He went to call out for the guard when the white clothing on the thing shimmered and dissolved into a plain blue robe.

'You are a difficult man to track down.'

Calinsk knew the face, but didn't show it. His anger began to tinge with fear. 'Who in the hells are you? How dare you intrude upon an Administrator in such a repellent disguise. I'll be making a formal complaint to the magii shodatt.'

'I'm not here with any shodatt, as you are well aware.'

'I have no idea what you're talking about, now get out before I call the guard.'

'Do not be afraid, I wasn't followed, and no one knows I am here.'

Calinsk dropped his pretence. Perhaps it would be the only way to get rid of his volatile visitor. 'You do not understand, there are–' He stopped as if not wanting to speak allowed the next word.

'I'm aware of the yhordi and how they operate,' Chayne replied. I have access to their secret and know they are not monitoring us.'

Calinsk looked startled.

'I have been busy, Administrator. How are the Lan-Chi?'

Calinsk raised a finger to his lips. 'Shssssh, do not speak that word in my presence.' His eyes darted around the room as if expecting someone to jump out of the shadows and arrest him. 'How did you discover it was me?'

'When enlisting my support you spoke to me behind bright lights to prevent me seeing your face, leaving me with the sound of your voice to remember. The authority you carry permeates your tone giving it a certain edge, easily recognisable. I heard it again during my interrogation by the Iicators, the same voice as when I first arrived here. You were in a large room surrounded by clerks and handing out punishments. I was terrified, and even though you managed only a single word before I passed out, the word was lodged into my head to play over and over in my dreams for some time.'

Calinsk vaguely remembered the incident from months ago.

Chayne pulled out a chair and sat down.

Calinsk blanched at the move. 'We have servants to do such a thing.' As he sat down a servant pushed his chair in.'

'You once asked me to risk my life for you,' Chayne began.

'To help you save your people, yes.'

'You risked much, contacting and enlisting an outsider like me. You must have had great motivation to take such a chance.'

'Perhaps.'

'Well, I delivered what you wanted, and you must have gained something valuable from it. Now I want you to do something for me.'

Calinsk took a measured sip of his drink, this time letting the flavours and strength have the greatest effect before sliding down his throat. 'I think you overestimate your strength in this relationship. I have fifty operatives threaded throughout the palace, and can contact other Lan-Chi leaders across the North who command thousands. You are nothing more than a minor resource to me.'

Chayne stood up and made a gesture in the air Calinsk didn't recognise.

'Command your servants.'

Calinsk paused for a moment at the request, but indulged. He snapped his fingers and gestured to pour some more of his drink.

No servant moved.

He repeated the order, snapping as loud as he could.

Again, no response.

He jumped to his feet and went over to one of them, gesturing straight into its face. It remained still. He went to the next, and the next, with the same results. Such a thing was beyond his comprehension. The things had been around since his earliest childhood memories. They obeyed without question or suffered terrible consequences. He stepped back, fearful.

'As you can see, Administrator, I command a far more potent force.'

'You cannot do this,' Calinsk said. 'This is an abomination.' He suddenly changed. 'I must stop you.' He went to call out for the guard and froze in position, paralysed.

Chayne walked up to him, his fingertips resting on a small orb held in a pouch attached into his belt. 'I have not been idle since Lathashal's death. Your magic comes easily to me, and I have discovered a secret unknown even to him allowing me to learn at an accelerated rate. Combined with Lathashal's notes, my progress is not to be underestimated. My entire people are at risk of slavery and worse. I have already placed myself once in what I thought would be certain death to prevent it. Do not miscalculate how far I will go to complete my task. Now I will give you the same ultimatum you gave me months ago in that dark room under those lights. Agree to help me, or you will not leave this room alive.'

Calinsk felt the constraint lift from his body. He thought to call out, but couldn't deny the power the Mlendrian now commanded in such a short time. Just what was he capable of?

'What is it you want?'

'At the appropriate time I need you to divert the remaining garrison in the city to the East.'

Calinsk looked puzzled. 'I cannot achieve such a thing.'

'You have agents within the army who will seed reports of a Mlendrian invasion from the West, making it large enough to leave the city commanders in no doubt of a complete commitment of the city's forces.'

'Even if such a thing were possible, it would be no more than hours before the commands were exposed as false. It would be tracked back to my operatives. Under torture it would lead back to me, and I, under the same, would tell of the other leaders in the Lan-Chi. It could wipe us out across the Empire.'

'I have a way out, for you and your operatives.' Chayne said.

'Out? There is nowhere in the Empire we wouldn't be found in days.'

'The Empire, yes.'

Calinsk's mouth dropped. 'You mean for me to leave the Empire?'

'During the diversion and subsequent confusion, the Lan-Chi will leave the city to the West.'

'I assume you have worked out where we will hide a hundred men in open desert to prevent capture?'

'There will be no pursuit,' Chayne replied.

'Gods man, and how do you intend to achieve that, or does the Emperor himself now bow to your bidding?'

'Your diversion will not be the only source of confusion, nor will you be alone in your escape. I need you to lead others.'

'Even if I could coordinate all of my men to do this, it will take extraordinary action to achieve. Perhaps I could rely on my men to do it, but how can I trust these others to response to my command?'

Chayne waved his hand. All servants in the room stood forward three paces. 'Trust me, Administrator. They are used to taking orders.'

Ducilly backed away. 'Them!'

'Not just these. The whole city.'

Ducilly stared. 'You're insane! The city would collapse, it would be chaos. People would have no food, water.'

'The people will no doubt be evacuated to the South to the nearest city. Such a sudden influx will cause disarray there, helping to delay any response from the nearest army.'

'This is lunacy, Zanthak has an army heading to the mountains. He will turn them back and hunt us down.'

The door handle to the room turned.

Chayne invoked his illusion back into a servant.

A guard entered, looking at the strange scene before him before standing to attention. 'Excuse me, Administrator, is everything in order? I heard shouting.'

Chayne prepared himself. He didn't want to harm Ducilly or the guard, but if it came to them or his people, he was prepared to do whatever was necessary to silence them. He wondered how he managed to change his ideals so much, and why now he was ready to carry out such an act.

Ducilly faltered, staring at Chayne as if fighting some internal battle. He waved a hand at the guard. The guard left and closed the door.

'Does this mean you're with me?'

'Tell me how you'll deal with the General's army.'

'Tristaric is under pressure to begin taking Mlendria. He is going to use some experimental magic. It's dangerous and will require all master magiis in this and many other northern cities. The result will allow Zanthak's army to take my people by surprise. But the spell is unstable and I intend to disrupt it, trapping the soldiers. The resulting explosion will wipe out both Tristaric and the magiis.'

Calinsk was dumbfounded at the scale of the attack the Mlendrian was planning. 'How do you intend to escape it?'

'Nothing in the area will survive when the tunnel magic is destabilised.'

Calinsk shook his head in disbelief at the fanatic. 'Are all Mlendrians born with this death wish, or are you an anomaly?'

Chayne didn't reply.

Calinsk walked back to his desk. He played with the glass for a few moments before pushing it away. 'Where do you have in mind for thousands of servants and my men to go?'

'There is a lake west of here called Li-Senca?'

'But that's on the far side of the desert.'

'Three days hard walk,' Chayne confirmed.

'My men can make it, but these…things. They're not used to such conditions.'

'That is not so,' came a voice from one of the servants stepping forward.

Ducilly's reaction was of a baby deer cornered by jackals. 'Kill it, kill it!' he said, trembling and pushing himself back around his desk. He was shaking his head as if trying to dislodge a nightmare.

Chayne walked forward. 'This is Angealla. She is one of the spiritual leaders of the Incra – the servants. She will not harm you.'

'What is it doing?' Ducilly began shaking violently.

'*She* wants to make a pact with you.'

'They cannot talk,' Ducilly began repeating over and over.

'Administrator!' Chayne said, trying to break the man from his growing hysteria.

Ducilly became aware of him again.

'The Rin-Uri have lived amongst the servants since the beginning. They are seen as their spiritual guardians and will be followed without question.'

'You don't understand, I cannot speak to *them*.' Ducilly only managed to get the final word out through a strangled tone.

Another servant walked forward and pulled the hood back from its head. 'I will liaise with them, Administrator.'

Ducilly's face went from fear to outrage. It was Pelenno. '*You* are involved in this?'

'I believe in the Zil-Sat-Shra,' Pelenno replied.

'The Zil-Sat-Shra is an absurd myth, you imbecile. You plot to stop the invasion and bring the wrath of the Emperor upon us for *him!*'

'He has told me of the Mlendrians and how they live. I wish to live as they do,' Pelenno said.

'Then I shall be happy to arrange your escape to the North where you can live your misguided dream.'

'But the Empire will soon overrun these people. It will be a short-lived dream,' Pelenno replied.

Ducilly looked ready to erupt at the betrayal of this young recruit. 'You have destroyed everything the Lan-Chi has strived for.'

Many of us have become disillusioned with the leadership and aims of the Lan-Chi, sir.'

'Many of you, what are you talking about?'

Pelenno raised his hand and half of the remaining servants in the room removed their robes to reveal ordinary clothing beneath. 'These are some who are with me, sir. There are many more.'

Ducilly looked around the room at the young faces. He knew them, but hadn't recognised any of them until now as they had been servants and not worthy of his gaze. 'How can you wear the clothing of these…*things*? It's disgusting. I would order you to the dungeons if it wasn't that you would disobey me.'

'Then what will you do?' Chayne said.

Ducilly slumped into this chair. 'I will organise your diversion. In exchange you will promise to take *all* Lan-Chi dissidents from my ranks and leave the city.'

Chayne turned to Pelenno who looked to the others. They nodded an accepted of the terms.

Chapter 48 – Demonic Challenge

Chayne sat staring at the cabinet of long drawers. Everything was now set. He hoped he'd done enough to align Pelenno with the Rin-Uri so they would act on the young man's instructions in his place.

All that remained was for him to replace the master magii, Kinarch. To do that he needed a more powerful manasphere than his gradia five. He didn't have time to see if he could strike up the same level of trust with another manasphere's demon as he had with Zystal. No, the only chance was to break the demon in direct confrontation so it wouldn't try to dominate when it detected him using it.

Pulling out a long drawer of a cabinet, he exposed three gradia six orbs and two gradia sevens. It was part of Lathashal's stock to teach students. Most drawers contained orbs below or equal to his gradia five containing Zystal. Some though, were more powerful. Each step in gradia represented a significant leap in contained demon.

Up to gradia six, orbs were boxed, but the two sevens were each set within a short staff no longer than Chayne's forearm. The smaller manaspheres were secured at the top by thrinium wire that twirled down the staves to a pair of thrinium plates halfway down. A magii would hold the plates to make contact with the orb.

Each staff was secured within the drawer with a tight leather harness. It then dawned on Chayne what would happen if two manaspheres touched? Would the demons fight it out, and if there was enough mana in the loosing demon's sphere, would its essence be pulled into the stronger one for that demon to escape? He made a note to look into Lathashal's diaries on the subject later.

He unstrapped the first staff, taking care not to touch the thrinium plates. The sphere was two gradia above his own containing Zystal, and this was the first time he would attempt to control a higher demon. He rotated the staff taking in the details. There were two bulges in the wood, one just below the thrinium plates and the other ten inches above. Chayne thought about the construction. He'd seen other magii use them. They would hold the staff above the plates until ready to use, the upper bulge preventing the staff sliding through the hands and accidentally connecting with the sphere at the top. Then, when needing to engage the staff's power, just a flick of the wrist slid the staff upwards to catch the hand on the lower bulge in perfect position over the plates.

He wondered what the demon was like in such an orb. He only experienced two manaspheres above his own. One was a gradia nine used by Lathashal to punish him, and he survived it by intervention of the master magii. The other was the one Lathashal attempted to sacrifice him. The demon within was of immense power. How such a one could be controlled was beyond Chayne's imagining, and yet somehow Lathashal had.

He looked at the small orb at the top of the staff. Inside would be a demon stronger than Zystal and would not be friendly as Zystal had become. He knew the moment he made contact it would be a battle of wills.

He sank into a meditation, and instead of using the staff's thrinium plates, touched his fingertips on the orb itself. There was a mental snap. It was strong and he strained to maintain the flow of mana through his body into the orb as the demon strived for domination. He managed to get control and the demon settled down. Then, confident he'd the better of the demon, closed his other hand over his own manasphere containing Zystal. He then slid his fingers out over the staff orb and touched his palm to it. The additional contact gave the expected result and he wasted no time resisting, he dived into the orb to seek out the demon.

He went deep, far deeper than in Zystal's orb.

'Demon, come to me!' he called out. The pull on his mind was huge. Sweeping away thoughts of failure he kept diving.

'Demon, I am your master, you will obey me!'

A dot of red light appeared in the distance. He accelerated towards it. It grew in size until he could see it was the demon's portal expanding. In the light of the portal, he caught sight of the demon. It wasn't humanoid as he'd expected. It had an array of eyes around the top of a body as tall as a human, but with no discernible neck or head. Six tentacles dangled below it. It's most prominent feature was its lipless mouth containing a row of tall pointed teeth. Either side of the mouth were two muscular protrusions ending in claws angled back into the monster. Once caught in them there seemed little chance of escape.

As he got close he threw out a ball of light to surround it. It writhed without sound for a moment before it leapt. It moved faster than Zystal and almost managed to reach him before he could will the thing to stop. It hung in the space before him, its arms trying to reach him, its array of needle-sharp teeth snapping. He pushed harder with his will and the creature floated back.

Becoming incensed at the action, it went mad, flailing.

The portal was widening. Even using every ounce of his mental strength against the thing, it still pulled mana through his physical body to grow the portal. He redirected a moment of concentration to stop the portal, but snapped back his full attention as the creature got a bit closer.

The thing was strong, but not enough to approach him and grow the portal at the same time. However, once the portal was established, it would be able to exert all its power and defeat him. It wasn't going to take long.

He strained against the influence of the thing, powerless to stop the portal from completing. It snapped into its final position and the image beyond became clear, as if the demon's world was a dozen paces away. The full will of the creature bore down on him. The gap between them began to close. It stretched out its claws.

'Zystal, help now!'

Chayne's body in the physical world convulsed as Zystal in the orb in his other hand pulled at the mana within the staff orb. The creature was aware of the presence of another demon as Chayne hoped. He remembered Lathashal's powerful demon connected to Zystal through some energy link. He had no idea how the link was made, but hoped placing his hands upon two orbs would use his body as the conduit. Demons appeared to have an innate hatred for one another and would battle it out above all else.

He watched as the demon's portal began to falter as Zystal stole away the mana. How his body was fairing in the physical world he didn't know, but he had to see this through now, he wouldn't get a second chance. The stronger demon countered Zystal's influence, but that weakened it enough for Chayne to do his part. He focused on the portal and it began to close. The creature spasmed in what looked like fury and went to attack Chayne again. Chayne refocused all his will on resisting the creature again, but now Zystal's mana-drain took hold and the portal continued to close. The demon before him flipped its attention back and forth between the two, but could not tackle the combined power of the human and the lesser demon. The portal continued to shrink until it was the size of a clenched fist, before flashing out and disappearing.

The creature went berserk, throwing itself at Chayne. Chayne slammed the creature with as much of his will as possible. The creature resisted the pressure and came back.

Chayne was losing, but kept every ounce of focus he could on the thing. It reached out a single arm towards his shoulder. He focused upon it, but couldn't hold back the creature overall and stop the single thrust. It came closer and reached his robe. The material parted and Chayne felt the pinprick of a talon as it broke the skin. He wanted to flee, but knew the creature would then have no resistance and would impale him in an instant.

The talon pushed into him. He cried out in pain, his strength about to fail. He closed his eyes against the horror that was to come.

The pain stopped.

He opened his eyes to see the creature floating before him, shrivelled up in a ball, its tentacles wrapped around itself. Its body shook and quivered. Its will must have failed just before his. Now it cowered, in apparent terror of the human before it. A single word hissed from its lips, almost unintelligible.

'*Master.*'

Not staying a moment longer, Chayne accelerated up out of the orb.

Returned to his body, agony struck him. He was drenched in sweat and both hands were charred.

The demon was beaten by the narrowest margin, but now it would remember him, and while still resisting him at first, would give way without risking a fight.

He headed off to the medicinii to be healed, and to confirm Stalizar was ready to play his part. If so, all was set for the attack on Kinarch in the next few days, so he could take his place.

Chapter 49 – Mating Ritual

Chantel led the way into the male smooth-demon's room. It was a young one, no wrinkles and his muscles were tight. His aura was of deep purple tinged with yellow, indicating a mix of sexual excitement and fear. Her own kind would never have such a mix of emotions. The males took females they could dominate, fear was the last thing on their minds.

His hand was shaking as he closed the door. Turning back to her he looked uncertain. 'This is my first time, you know.'

'Mine too,' she said, flashing a smile.

'Really!' He looked relieved and the yellow faded a little.

She moved over to the bed and lay out as she'd seen the female do before. He just stood there, his aura growing in yellow again.

'Would you like to remove my coverings?'

He was uncertain so she sat up and slipped a finger under a strap, pushing it from her shoulder. His eyes went wide, yellow and purple auras pulsed stronger together. Raising the finger as she remembered, she beckoned him over. He swallowed hard and walked towards her.

'You're such funny creatures,' she said, finding his hesitancy to lead strangely arousing. He was close enough now for her to reach out and she took his hand and slipped it under the other strap and pushed. The strap fell away and the top half of her dress fell to her waist. His eyes almost popped from his head as he looked over her naked upper body.

She pulled him closer and he toppled onto the bed.

'Close your eyes.'

He did so and she extended a single talon. It sliced through her dress down one side and then his upper and lower clothing. She pulled at them letting them fall to the floor. His heart was beating so hard she wondered if it was normal for smooth demons. She parted her legs and pushed him into her. He gave a cry and the yellow of his aura disappeared replaced with solid purple.

They began mating and she felt something strange within her. It was like no other feeling she had felt before. The more they mated the more it grew. He was becoming frantic now, but lacked the sheer force of her own demonkind that would have caused her pain. The feeling in her grew and grew until it felt like she was going to explode from inside. She closed her eyes and let it happen. The feeling took over her body and mind and she felt the most exhilarating ecstasy she could ever have imagined. It continued a while longer before fading and leaving her panting heavily. She sensed the smooth demon was no longer moving and a smell encroached on her senses. It became the overpowering scent of blood.

Full control returned and she opened her eyes. The smooth demon was still lying on top of her, its body broken and skin shredded; layers of flesh were peeled back. It was dead, the look still imprinted on its face from its final moments, was one of horror. She then saw her hands and arms were no longer transformed into human, and she'd returned to her demonic shape. They were cover in blood with human flesh hanging in threads from her talons. It must have happened during the moment when she lost control.

She pushed the thing from her and got up from the bed. There was blood splattered across the walls and ceiling in thick lines, and it had soaked into the white material they laid on. Her moment of ecstasy was his moment of terror and death. She then realised, if she'd lured Chaynie to mate, this would have happened to him. It was something she would never be able to do with him. She did want to feel that feeling though, it was too good not to experience again. If she couldn't get it from her on kind because they were too brutal, she needed to find a smooth demon strong enough to survive her.

She would return to Chaynie for now, she liked him and trusted him not to harm her. Eventually, she would have to find another.

Opening the door a small amount, she changed into cat form and pushed her way out.

Chapter 50 – Eye and Tooth of a God

They were halfway across the settlement with many tents cut down. Kadjat gave the order to halt. There was no sign of the heathens.

'Where are you hiding?' he said to himself. 'Tear them all down. Find them!' he ordered.

A fine glittering mist streamed up into the sky from the cliff at the back of the settlement. The backlight from the sun still to crest the edge created glittering rainbows that came and went as if in a dance whose melody was out of hearing.

One of his men called out, pointing to something.

Kadjat followed the line to the far end of the settlement still in the shadow of the cliff. There, dressed in mottled grey robes were a dozen men, kneeling facing the cliff with their backs to him, their foreheads touching the ground. They seemed oblivious to the peril behind them. Some kind of heathen sacrifice to appease him? Maybe they thought he was a god.

A figure rose behind them wearing a blood-red stained loin cloth. The rest of his bare skin and hair were stained with the same colour. He was built for war and radiated confidence in the face of a thousand invading warriors spread out across his home. He raised a thin rapier sword in the air and pointed it at Kadjat, spreading it out to encompass his men. He then flicked a small buckler on his other arm in a motion Kadjat took to mean for him and his men to leave.

Kadjat smiled, and began to walk forward.

The twelve grey-robed men stood and turned. As one they removed their hoods to reveal blackened faces. On each forehead was painted a large white eye.

Kadjat was amused by the bizarre spectacle. Then raised his sword in the air and dropped it sharply to point in the direction of the painted barbarian. His men charged. He didn't bother to have them form up, he knew how to take these heathens down now. It was against military protocol, but right now he didn't care for formality, his men were released from the restriction of empyrean tactics. They seemed to like it.

A line of red-painted warriors rose up either side of the first. They moved forward to stand ahead of the black-robed figures. There were less than fifty of them against almost a thousand armoured Ashnorian soldiers. Not rocks to limit their numbers this time. On open ground they had no chance. This would be over quickly.

He was so caught up in the fervour of his men, he almost drew his sword and joined them. He felt alive for the first time in his life. He took a moment to take in the scenery so unlike the cities and deserts he was accustomed. It held an inspiring brutality. That these people chose to live in such an uncivilised environment was becoming less of a surprise to him. The area was walled on all sides by a set of high cliff faces. The only feature of prominence was the vast pointed rock sticking out from the northern face over the settlement. There was a deep crack around the end, and in particular he could see a wide fissure down the right side. It didn't look to him a safe place to create a home, but then the cultures outside of the Empire were primitive with little understanding of such things.

They was a clash of steel as his men engage. The almost-naked red warriors fought with an unencumbered agility and speed of movement undoing his disciplined soldiers. He'd been overconfident and was losing men fast. Returning to his training, he gave the order to form up. His captains organised the men into a thirty-wide column, thirty rows deep. Their shields came together making a perfect line of red, silver and gold livery of the Empire.

The heathens cut down the remaining scattered front men before reforming into their own single line. It looked as though they hadn't taken a single loss.

Out from the line stood forth the first red-painted warrior. Kadjat was again singled out for a stare, the warrior levelling his sword at him, repeating the wave of his shield, as if pushing them away. This time he added one more gesture, bringing his sword hand to his chest and stabbing his sword at Kadjat. The meaning was clear enough.

Kadjat went to give the order to advance when the air filled with the sound of rhythmic singing coming from the grey-robed figures under the rock face. As it commenced, so the line of red warriors banged their weapons against their shields and set for the charge. The sound was unnerving, the whole scene so alien, the crisp, cold air, the crunch of the strange white covering on the ground under his feet. Perhaps this wasn't the place for him after all. It was time to be rid of these people, this place, and commit it to history forgotten, like so many the Empire snuffed out over the centuries. He raised his sword and gave the order to advance.

The column moved forward.

The barbarians began to back off, still facing their attackers.

Kadjat was pleased to see the heathens at last understood their peril.

The sound of the singing grew louder and more urgent, rising even above the sound of the column's marching feet.

The heathens kept their distance.

Then the singing exploded into a high note, the sound echoing around the cliff faces. The robed figures stood and raised their hands high, facing the far cliff in shadow. Kadjat looked up at the top and could see the glittering mist, brighter than before as the sun was about to rise over the peak. He then looked down at the heathens again. They'd stopped backing away.

Kadjat was at a loss for the purpose of the strange ritual. Some kind of heathen magic?

The ridge mist continued to brighten as the sun reached the edge. Then the robed figures turned and faced their attackers. Throwing back their robes to display their bare bodies revealed a round yellow eye painted on their chests radiating lines of white outwards. They brought their hands down in unison in a rush and pointed at Kadjat's men. The singing abruptly stopped and changed into a screaming call. The red-painted barbarians charged.

Kadjat called for his men to lock shields.

The sun broke the ridge top and shone through the glittering mist which amplified the intensity of the normally yellowish morning light into millions of tiny brilliant crystals of light. Against the previous shadow of the cliff the brightness was blinding. It was like the eye of a god beaming his radiance down upon them.

Kadjat couldn't see anything ahead and looked away. He could hear the sound of fighting as the barbarians timed their attack with the effect.

Kinfular led the charge into the ranks of the Ashnorians. Blinded by the Eye of Rolk, the soldiers held up their shields to protect their eyes. Easy prey to the prepared barbarians. They ducked under the shields to move through the front line, taking down the first three rows of one-hundred men in moments. With the sound of men dying, the next rows dropped their shields back into position with eyes squinting against the glare, able to do no more than wave their swords aimlessly to protect themselves from the approaching death. Without sight, their defence was all but useless as the barbarians cut through them also. With water streaming into eyes and no clear view of the coming death, the front lines panicked. They turned and ran into those behind. Kinfular and his men sliced into one exposed back after another.

Kadjat could hear his men falling row by row. If he didn't do something fast he would lose hundreds. He ordered his men to fall back. Not a command trained for. They hesitated before he screamed out the command and they began to back up. A sound came from his left and he looked through blurred watering eyes to see another wall of red-warriors charging his left flank. He couldn't make out numbers, but the effect on his panicked men was immediate. They stampeded in the direction remaining – towards the huge rock overhang. He ran with his men, hearing the cries of those closest to the heathens, dying as they attempted to escape.

As they approached the outcrop so arrows began to rain down. There were too few from too great a height to hit many of them, but it drove them under the outcrop for protection.

Kadjat gave his orders and was pleased to see the remaining sub-commanders creating a new column out of the chaos. This time they were facing toward both groups of barbarians with the sun to the right. The barbarians had played a clever trick. It was a courageous and inventive tactic Kadjat would have been proud. Perhaps it was going to be a shame to eradicate this race, but now they'd dealt there blow. Maybe it would have finished another mountain tribe, but an attack from the Empire held too many men to be defeated with such a tactic. He still commanded over five hundred men, and the new wave of heathens turned out to be only twenty-five strong. Now, protected from the archers above, and rock to his back, he held a strong position.

The barbarians stopped pursuing and formed a single line outside of the arrow-killing field beyond the rock. The dark-robed figures stepped through and lined up in front of them.

They began waving their arms into the air above him and his men.

There was a muffled thud above them, followed by a flurry of small rocks cascading around the edges of the overhang.

Kadjat chuckled. 'Perhaps they think they can bring the rock down upon us,' he mocked. 'If they want us, they will have to come in and get us.'

There was subdued support for the new Commander. He hadn't endeared himself to them with his choices so far.

Another thump sounded and larger rocks fell this time, some large enough to injure.

He looked back to the robed figures and wondered what they expected to achieve with such an act. Then he noticed something he'd missed before. The second group of red-warriors was a rag-tag mix of elderly men, boys and women. From their age and physical condition they were no warriors.

Kadjat then realised what had happened. These heathens were not the dumb brutes the Empire led him to believe. In the panic of the rout and the blinding sun, the second group only had to appear as painted warriors. They were used to ensure the invaders were corralled into this position.

There was another muffled thud, the largest this time, followed by the heaviest group of rocks yet to fall. Kadjat felt assured the overhang would hold. He doubted even the Empire's magic was capable of bringing it down.

Then he remembered the huge fissure.

All heard an enormous crack overhead and looked up. A black line appeared in the shadow underneath the rock at one edge. Some of the men became agitated. He knew how they felt. Realising their peril, some went to escape, but larger pieces of rock fell, changing their minds. There was another crack and the black line increased in length. Kadjat gave the order to form up and attack the section of fake red heathen warriors, before it was too late. As they did, so the false red warriors withdrew and the real warriors spread out to defend the whole line.

Another thump from above was followed by an extension in the crack and another rain of rocks around the edge. The soldiers began to advance with the shields raised. As they left the safety of the overhang so the barrage of arrows resumed to compliment the curtain of falling rocks. Their shields took much of the hits from both, even so, the losses prevented them from forming a complete line and the red heathens took advantage as they engaged the front. Then it was Kadjat's turn to walk the gauntlet through the falling rocks and arrows. The man in front of him took a hit from a larger rock and was crushed to the floor. Kadjat stepped around him and escaped the deadly attacks. Half of his men were already free of the danger. He then heard the loudest sound he could ever remember. Buckling away from the ear-splitting noise, he almost stumbled to the ground.

Fighting stopped as all looked to the overhang. It moved a fraction.

Thoughts turned to escape from the coming devastation. The wailing of the men still under the rock turned to cries as they dropped shields and weapons and ran for the nearest point out from under the rock. Kadjat saw the magii rise up from his position and fly over their heads to be pulled back down into the midst of the nearest soldiers trying to catch a lift to safety. Sparks exploded and men were thrown back from him. He again took to the air and made it to the edge, dodging rocks as they fell. Just on the edge of freedom, a small one knocked the manasphere box from his grasp. His flying ceased and he crashed to the ground. Arrows followed, peppering his body.

Then, with the power only a mountain could contain, the monumental volume of the end-half of the overhang began to slide. It broke into pieces and fell. Many soldiers were still underneath. The ground shook like an earthquake as the force of the slide hit the ground, crushing them and bringing everyone else to their knees. A blast of rocks exploded out from the impact followed by a windstorm of suffocating dust stealing away the air.

Chapter 51 – Doctor's Appointment

Stalizar checked again the mana level in his pocket manasphere. Normally used in emergencies to start hearts or seal a wound, it contained only a small amount of mana. Now it was to be used for a different reason, and one which the surgeon wasn't happy about. From the moment he'd agreed to play his part in replacing Kinarch with the Mlendrian, he regretted it. His hand shook as he placed his fingertips onto the tiny orb in his robes. They bounced off of its surface through his shaking as he tried to settle them upon it. He pushed a little harder until the pressure of contact overcame the trembling.

Closing his eyes, he shook his head. What was he thinking to accept this deed? If this was how he felt now, what was it going to be like at the time, faced with an enraged battle magii? He would have a merest moment to act to close off the artery. What if his fingers slipped on the manasphere and broke contact for just the briefest time? Kinarch would recover and slaughter both of them.

He wiped the sweat from his hand onto his robe. It quickly returned.

Sitting down he went to click his fingers to have a servant provide him a calming herbal tea before he left. They slid across each other and no sound was made. Instead he knocked twice on the table to get their attention and then made the hand signal. A servant left its alcove and went about its task.

'I watched you for a decade when you were the Emperor's personal physician…'

Stalizar was startled at the voice, he'd been alone. Looking around, a stranger walked across the room and settled into the chair opposite him. The direction from which he came had no entrance and so the surgeon knew this was a yhordi.

'…and yet in all that time I never saw you so disturbed.'

Stalizar couldn't remember seeing the man before, further confirming his status.

'What does the yhordi want with me? Stalizar barely avoided stammering, his fear building further at the thought of discovery in his part in the plot against Kinarch, and therefore indirectly the Emperor. He could feel his body heat building and already a bead of sweat was running down his temples.

'You never were one for subterfuge. A man of your skill could have gone so far in the Empire. Now you're nothing more than the head of a palace medicinii on its outskirts, as far away as you can get from the seat of power.'

Stalizar went to reply. The words got stuck as the tension closed up his throat.

'I could force you to talk of course through the application of pain, but I have a lot of respect for you and it wouldn't be a comfortable choice for me.'

The servant arrived and placed two cups of the herbal tea on the table before them.

Faust leaned forward. 'I hope you don't mind, I ordered one for myself.' He placed two drops into Stalizar's cup without being seen as he passed it to the man.

Stalizar took the cup in a shaking hand and had a sip. The hot liquid almost burned his mouth and he ignored the discomfort as the drink went down his throat. Within seconds his body began to react and he felt calmer. He took another longer drink and his fear disappeared. It wasn't supposed to work that fast. He felt relaxed and at ease. He then looked at the drink and back to the yhordi.

Faust smiled slightly. 'Don't worry, it's just a relaxant.'

Stalizar flicked a glance to his staff nearby.

Faust sipped his own tea and placed it back down. 'The compound slows your reactions. You'll never reach it in time.'

Stalizar turned his hand, flexing his fingers. They weren't responding as normal.

'I'm investigating Lathashal's assassination, something about as far from your ambition as I could imagine. I can find nothing tangible connecting you to his murder, but I've done this long enough to know when people are just too close to be coincidence.'

Stalizar stretched his eyes wide trying to gain some control over his features. His was feeling quite drunk. 'I don't know what you mean,' he slurred.

Faust raised one of Stalizar's eyelids with his thumb. 'I gave you a little extra to compensate for your size. It's having far too much effect. I'm guessing you've never been one to hold your drink.'

'Can't heal when drunk.' Stalizar stifled a laugh, finding the idea funny. 'Could lance a boil and end up popping an artery instead.' He went to take another sip and Faust removed the drink.

'Had something to do?' Stalizar continued, swaying, looking up at the ceiling as if finding something curious there.

'Ah!' he blurted, caught by Faust preventing him from tipping from his chair. 'Savin' the Mleembriam from ffffiiiite with Kimaaaarch. He'll be killed to death now, you know.' The surgeon slid from the chair to land with a thump on the floor, unconscious.

Faust's directive from the Emperor was to return everyone involved in Lathashal's death. He wasn't certain how serious a part the mage-surgeon played in it, but there was no time left to find out. He injected him with a long-term sedative and gave instructions to the servants to transport him to Ashnor.

With the man having been so afraid to be trembling and sweating, his part in saving Chayne must be imminent. It needed to be somewhere private, probably Kinarch's quarters. A directory of magii within the city would be kept in Lathashal's old lab.

He exited the room through the secret door and disappeared into the dullness of the yhordi corridors beyond, moving as fast as he could over the trap-laden passageways.

Chapter 52 – Kinarch

The door opened to Kinarch's suite of rooms and Chayne signed to the servant for an audience with the master. He entered while the servant went to inform his master.

The first room was dark, unlike any Chayne had come across before. It wasn't just that the lighting was kept to a level so it was hard to see; the decor was dark greys and black. It made the servants seem like drifting spirits. Indications were all around that the magii was about to embark on his journey to the mountains. Two trunks were stacked by the door beside a line of servants ready to leave.

He looked around for the presence of Stalizar. The man was invisible as expected and taking no chances to reveal himself.

An explosion of yelling came from the room into which the servant had gone followed by a bang against the door. The door was then snatched opened to reveal a stocky figure in the same black colourings as the décor. The servant could be seen on the floor behind.

'If this isn't a convenient time, I could return,' Chayne offered.

Even in the gloom he could see the magii's eyes burning with anger. 'I'm leaving the city for some time. I don't have time for house calls.' The voice was gravelly and not easy to understand, as if the man suffered some damage to his throat. As a magii could have had it repaired, Chayne guessed he kept it to support his persona, as it helped laden the threat behind the statement. This magii displayed no style or subtlety, as Tristaric or even Lathashal.

'I have come to ask for your help in understanding a problem I'm having with my manasphere.'

'Get out, you imbecile. I'm late and I do not teach neophytes,' Kinarch snarled. He went to turn away.

'With Master Lathashal gone and the Master Tristaric occupied on some powerful experiment, I have no sufficient gradia of magii to help other than you.'

'It's your *Master* that sets the task distracting me from my own research. His name is not welcome here.'

'Even so, I need help.'

Kinarch spun around. 'Gods boy, didn't you hear me. Get out!' As he tried to shout his voice broke and turned into a strangled squeak.

'There is something wrong with my manasphere, Master. I cannot work on my duties without it,' Chayne repeated, calmly.

Kinarch flared at being ignored and threw the staff he held in a stabbing movement. Chayne was ready and gripped the plates of his new staff from within his robes. The pressure of the repulsion bolt hit his new shield spell learnt from Lathashal's notebooks. It knocked him back only a pace or two.

Kinarch's eyes went wide. 'You dare to enter my chambers, inflame my wrath, and then resist my punishment?'

Chayne resumed his previous position. 'If you have not the knowledge to help, perhaps I should seek out another.'

'Why are you not afraid of me?' He stepped forward, slowly and walked a close circle around Chayne. 'What secret has Tristaric taught you?'

Chayne held his position and didn't move. 'Like I said, Master, there is something wrong with my manasphere. It's gradia five and yet even I can place my palm upon it and extract far more mana than normal.'

'Preposterous.'

'I am aware this should not happen, Master.' Chayne unlocked his manasphere box and raised the orb to the locked position. He placed a hand flat upon the orb with no effect.

Kinarch was now curious. 'Manasphere's only become inert after consuming a magii who was too weak to contain its power. He waved Chayne's hand away and placed his own palm on the orb. On cue, Zystal pulled mana hard through the magii into the emptied sphere.

Chayne knew Kinarch would be too strong for the little demon and it would be only moments before he would remove his hand. It was time for him to take his gamble. He snapped the lid down on Kinarch's hand and head-butted the magii in the face, using the distraction to kick his staff across the room. The magii roared and released the small supply of mana Zystal had stored through him.

Chayne was ready and deflected the spell again using his own staff, but underestimated how fast the master magii could store mana and the power of the spell thrown at him. It launched him back into the wall behind banging his head, and loosing grip of his staff. It clattered away.

Kinarch's hand began to burn as he allowed a sudden influx of mana to flow into the orb for the killing blow. Zystal enacted the next gamble and fled to Lluuelliun.

Kinarch felt a loss of connection and the mana storing stopped. He fired the little mana he managed to gain. The feeble bolt struck Chayne without his shield. Not enough to kill, it still threw him hard back into the wall again. Kinarch cursed and threw the box to the ground.

Chayne staggered to his feet and both men went for their staves. As he reached his, it moved away. He looked up to see Kinarch in the gloom, already holding his.

'Now!' Chayne shouted out to Stalizar.

Kinarch stood puzzled at the command. Nothing happened.

Chayne, realising something was wrong with Stalizar, made a desperate dive to grab his staff. It lifted and moved across the room to land behind Kinarch.

The battle magii levelled his staff and mana began to spark on its surface. Chayne braced himself for death.

Out of the dimness, hands appeared, wrapping around the arms, body and head of Kinarch. The effect on Kinarch was beyond repugnance. The man wasn't able to process the horror of servant fingers gently clawing at him. The man lost control of his stomach and threw up. He fell to the floor, shaking violently, looking like a frightened child without its mother. The man was paralysed with revulsion.

Chayne crawled across the floor to his manasphere. Placing his hand flat upon it he called to Zystal and the demon returned. He pulled as much mana from around him he could in the seconds he had. It was then a simple matter of tighten the major artery in the man's neck until he fell unconscious.

Chayne fell back to the floor. Pain wracked his body and his back felt like it had been beaten.

He looked up at the servants who stood still, uncertain of what to do next. He wanted to thank them, but no hand-sign existed for such a thing.

'Stalizar, are you here? I understand if you could not engage in the end, I forgive you, but I need you now.'

He looked around for the magii to materialise as he'd done once before after Lathashal's death, but there was no appearance this time.

He pushed himself up into a sitting position, pain shot through his body. Nothing seemed broken although he couldn't be sure of other internal damage. It certainly hurt.

Limping across the room he picked up his staff and produced light. Without the concealing effect of the low-light the place revealed a dull and soulless character. Dark grey and black fabrics hung from the ceiling, overlapping to cover all wall space. It was depressing and unpleasant.

Inspecting his manasphere box, not a scratch could be seen on the thrinium reinforced wooded container.

Moving into the connecting room, it was filled with the usual benches of strange looking items. Each bench had an open manasphere box on it.

He didn't know how long he had before the magii would wake, and found his notebook on the main bench. As hoped, the last entries were filled with the workings to do with his task set out by Tristaric and the portal. Pulling out from his robe his own material, a combination of the snatched piece of parchment by Pelenno, Stalizar's translations and his own notes, he rolled them all up and thrust them back into one of his deep robe pockets. It was the sum total of understanding he had on the portal tunnel Tristaric was to create. He would have to read them on the journey to the mountains, finding quiet places to use Zystal to take him to Lluuelliun to give him more time. He hoped it was enough to create a spell duplicating the appearance of the real spell Kinarch was to cast. This was his final gamble, and it meant combining everything he'd learnt from Lathashal's diaries so far. Most of it had little testing and practice. If any part of his plan failed, then all was lost.

Everything was in place and he moved back to the main room. Exchanging robes with the magii, he then tied the man's hands and feet.

But where was Stalizar? He had to arrive soon. The alternative was to kill the magii in cold blood, and he knew he couldn't do it, even with what was at stake. He had to take the chance to leave him and hope the mage-surgeon would get here in time.

He looked around the room. He should have been pleased to see the last of the palace, but with so much knowledge still to learn it was a compelling reason to survive and return.

He wondered about Fireball. The cat had been missing ever since that woman tried to seduce him. He hoped she hadn't stolen Fireball in retribution for his rejection. Garamon had brought it so far, now all for nothing as he couldn't take it with him.

'I hope they look after you.'

He pulled the hood up over his head to mast his face and left the room, heading for the assembly point with the other magiis.

Chapter 53 – The Chase

The spy hole revealed the room beyond to be empty. Faust pushed the finger-code into the wall lock, the secret door swung toward him and he entered the room. It was dark and he made a short number of clicks with his fingers. No servants responded to his command for light. It had never happened before. He took out a stick and bent it in half. There was a snap and bright light, tinged in green, poured out from it to fill the room. The place was empty of servants.

Spotting the open door to the magii's main room he went through to find Kinarch gagged and bound laying on the floor, stirring from unconsciousness. No servants were here either.

Removing the gag, Kinarch spat it out as soon as it had loosened.

'Untie me and get me my staff!'

Faust sat back. 'What happened here?'

Kinarch looked as if he was going to explode with fury. 'Untie me!' he said, his voice braking under the strain of the words.

'Answer my question, first.'

'I am Kinarch, master battle magii. You are in my quarters; now untie me unless you wish to spend the rest of your life as an experiment.'

Faust lifted his foot and kicked out into the magii's face, creating a resounding smack. 'I know you encountered the Zintar, and somehow he managed to subdue you.'

At the mention of the attack, the magii looked around, fearful. Seeing no servants he looked relieved.

Faust knew something odd had happened here, and the absence of servants was making even him uneasy.

'Th-th-they attacked,' Kinarch blurted. The man suddenly seemed weak and vulnerable, Faust would even judge terrified.

'Who attacked?'

'The servants, man! They touched me. They have gone mad.' Faust believed it, the words were spoken with such disgust.

'Where is the Zintar?'

'I don't know. He attacked me and they helped him.' His eyes snapped to Faust. 'How can they do that? He never even gave them a command. They just attacked. I had him, was about to kill him for his impertinence and they grabbed me. Pulled at my robe!' He looked down. 'Where is it?'

Faust pieced it together. Stalizar and the Mlendrian had plotted to disabled the master magii just before he was to join the host of magiis heading for the mountains. The Mlendrian was going to take his place and somehow try to stop Tristaric.

Faust would have considered the idea absurd but for the defeating of Lathashal and now Kinarch. Combined with his ability to place a palm on a manasphere, this Mlendrian was a dangerous and resourceful anomaly amongst the Mlendrians.

But last time, he'd been part of a larger team of Mlendrians who then escaped, so it was reasonable to assume they'd been contacted again to help him at the mountain. It meant all of the remaining culprits involved in Lathashal's death could be together there. He would round them up and return them to the Emperor on mass, neat and tidy.

His puzzle now was how a Mlendrian had coerced the servants. Then a thought struck him. An outlawed legend existed within Ashnoria of a Zil-Shat-Shra, a prophet who would deliver the servants from their bondage. It was considered an inane myth by the Elite. However, he knew differently. The stories were based on a fact only he knew. It would explain how the man had achieved so much in so little time and had such influence. The timing was a little early, though. Almost a generation.

Was it really *him*?

He removed a desiccant ampoule from his black syringe pack and fitted it.

'What's that?' Kinarch said.

'Something to remove your torment.'

'Will it last?'

'Permanently,' Faust answered, injecting the liquid.

The substance did its work and he swept up the powdered remains of the magii, placing them in a jar and putting it with the many others in the magii's lab.

Satisfied he'd cleaned the two rooms of evidence, he set off for the mountains.

Chapter 54 – Breakout

Ajoah hunkered down with the handful of his men remaining. There had been a path allowing them to lead the majority of the Ashnorians away from Falakar. He hoped it was enough and the Ranger escaped. His next problem was saving himself and his men. They were cut off with the Ashnorians closing in.

They were tucked in under a rock, out of sight and from the chill breeze. Soon the sun would set, handing the advantage to the mage who they said could see in the dark.

A faint but unmistakable sound of the rhythmic chink of armoured men marching encroached his hearing. He looked over the rock to see a column heading their way. A strange light shone ahead of them, travelling over the route he and his men had taken.

To get out from their current hiding place meant passing in front of them. There was no chance they wouldn't be seen, and every second they came closer.

'We cannot stay here,' Liegord said. It was Ajoah's next in command, a competent Ranger and a good man.

Ajoah readied the men and they leapt out over the concealing rocks. A call went up from the Ashnorian column. Ajoah sprinted for the safety of the rocks on the far side of the trail. Already, tiny lightning streaks were sparking, illuminating the mage who was holding out his staff.

'Down!' shouted Ajoah.

As one the men dived for the snow.

The air above them flashed as fingers of lightning few over. This wasn't directed as before at just one man, but spread out as if hoping to hit many.

The men were up and running again.

Jontal made it to the protecting rock when another warning shout went out. The men still exposed dived again for the snow. The area illuminated and this time a single bright flash struck the last in line of Ajoah's men in the leg. The Ranger fell, still alive, he drew his bow notching up an arrow, sending it low, skimming just above the ground into the advancing column. It slid under the shields and one of the soldiers fell with an arrow in his ankle. Another single thread of lightning flashed out of the ranks and struck the Ranger dead. It had given the remainder of the men time to reach the cover.

They ran into a long narrow pass providing them cover from the mage. Another column of Ashnorian soldiers turned into the far end of the pass, blocking escape. It was a trap. He came to a halt, looking for any way out up the steep rocks.

Liegord pulled his sword free and stabbed it into the side of the pass as Falakar had done before. 'We'll protect you as you climb.'

Ajoah went to object, but Liegord repeated Falakar's orders. '*There can be no failure in your mission, even if it means only one of you get through.*'

'You follow as soon as I'm up,' Ajoah ordered, leaping up onto the first sword.

Liegord ordered the Rangers for their swords. Ajoah took the next one and forced it into the packed snow a long footstep above the last. The ping of bows sounded out from his men.

'Keep firing at the mage, don't give him a chance to attack,' shouted Liegord.

'They're just bouncing off him, sir,' said one of the archers.

'We've seen one get through, keep firing!'

Ajoah pushed each sword in, climbing fast. He pulled himself up onto the last and still couldn't reach the top. Withdrawing his own sword he pushed it in too. It still wasn't going to be enough.

'Here!' Liegord shouted from below.

Jontal looked down to see the first sword being thrown up to him.

'No, no, you cannot climb without it.'

Liegord looked both ways and drew his own bow.

The Ashnorians were almost upon them and the archers were on their final arrows.

He saluted Ajoah. 'Good luck, sir. It's been a pleasure under your command.' He faced the Ashnorians.

'Liegord!' Ajoah yelled. He wanted to jump down and stay with his men to the last.

Out of arrows, and without swords, the Rangers drew knives and squared up back to back.

Sparks began building around the mage's staff again. He was looking straight at Ajoah. If it hit, everything his men were doing would be in vain. Ramming in the last sword, he leapt onto it taking a straight leap to the top of the climb and rolling away from the edge. Lightning flashed passed.

Anger flooded over him as he heard the cries of his men below. He drew his bow and kept back from the edge so as not to be seen, making his way to be behind the mage. Looking over the edge he saw his men fighting their last stand. They battled like champions taking down a dozen Ashnorians. But there could be only one outcome. He witnessed the first of his men fall and soon the man next to him went down too. Liegord and his last man stood back to back, surrounded.

Ajoah notched an arrow and pulled back on the string, his target standing out by the glow of his staff. The shot left as Liegord took a sword in the chest and went down. The arrow flew true and didn't encounter any resistance as it reached the mage. The powerful shot plunged into this back and stuck out of the front. Too late, the soldiers raised their shields in the direction of the attack. The mage slumped to the ground, no chance of surviving.

Ajoah steeled himself. With so many Ashnorians below, it gave him hope they didn't have enough remaining in the area to cover every way out. And without the mage they had no way to track him at night.

He made his best guess for escape and set off.

Chapter 55 – Aftershock

Kinfular awoke. The air was filled with choking dust reducing all vision to no more than arm's length. Pain made itself aware one side of his head and he raised his hand to a mix of blood and dust. The memory of the Ashnorian attack and the dropping of Rolk's Tooth came back. He got to his feet amidst the sound of moaning all around, indistinct shapes were staggering in the cloud of dust.

'Hlenshar?' called out a voice nearby. It was Dearen, one of his new personal guards.

'Here.'

A shape appeared out of the orange gloom, relief showing on the dust-caked face. 'We must finish them off,' he said, choking through the dust clogging his throat.

'No,' Kinfular replied. They are beaten. Gather their weapons, and kill those who will not survive their injuries. Then form a wall around them as best you can and allow none to escape.

The warrior looked surprised at the order.

'Do as I say.'

The warrior acknowledged and disappeared into the fog.

Kinfular began to help those around him. He turned over one of his men lying face down next to a fist-sized rock. It was Hreel, son of Bedsall. His forehead was caved in. Rolk chose to take him instead of the one next to him who caused this destruction. The way of his god was perplexing.

He left the man and wandered in the direction of the Ashnorians. It wasn't long before he came to the first body in metal armour. His back looked broken, although there was no obvious rock to have caused it. He continued on.

He came across enemy soldiers alive and standing. None were holding weapons and they just looked at him as he passed by, their faces showing no interest in further conflict.

The dust thinned and visibility improved. A group of Ashnorians were trying to roll a heavy rock from one of their own. He added his own strength to the effort. Combined they pushed the rock away. The man was dead, his chest crushed. One of the Ashnorian soldiers brushed dust from the man's shoulder guard revealing metal symbols fixed to the armour. The soldier then turned the dead man's face towards them. Kinfular recognised him.

'Kadjat,' the soldier said.

The word meant nothing to Kinfular.

As the dust settled, he took in the full extent of the power his god unleashed. The Riaan had lived for many generations under the huge overhang, being told by the Shaman it had been a sign from Rolk. It was called Rolk's Tooth and as long as the Riaan worshipped him he would protect them under it. Now his people had called upon him to attack the Ashnorians and save them. Kinfular had ordered Sholster and as many men as he could spare up onto the cliff to push boulders down upon the tooth. Many years of earth shaking had cracked the tooth and the Shaman said only the power of Rolk prevented it from falling. If it was Rolk's will to destroy these Ashnorian's then the tooth would fall.

So Kinfular steered the army of warriors under the tooth.

And it was Rolk's will.

Now most were buried forever beneath it. The price had been high. Many Riaan were killed and injured, and the settlement destroyed. Nothing remained recognisable of their ancestral home.

With Dearen disarming the Ashnorians, Kinfular walked back to the Shaman. They were still in a crouching position and paying tribute to the display of power by their mountain deity. Three of them were lying flat, unmoving, the thick layer of settled dust soaking up any blood that may have given away fatal injuries.

'I hope Rolk will forgive us,' he said.

The elder of the robed figures stood and faced him. 'You have called upon our god twice this day to save our people. Rolk granted you his power for both, Kinfular of the Riaan. You are in his favour, as we are in your debt. Be in no doubt as to his blessing in this.'

'But I have sacrificed many of our people and destroyed our home.'

'Rolk is the God of the Mountain, he will create a new home for us and lead us there.' The elder returned to his rumination with the other surviving shaman.

Kinfular bowed his head in deference to the old man and went to seek out one who he hoped survived. He looked for a concentration of men not Ashnorian and soon found him. As he approached so the Plainsmen's Chieftain raised a hand to acknowledge him. Kinfular notice the other arm was shieldless and hung loose at his side. 'Your god is strong,' said Grostro.

'I am glad to see you have survived,' Kinfular replied. 'You are as tough as the mountains themselves. Rolk must like you.'

'I have my own God to answer to, Peaksman.'

Kinfular acknowledged the comment with a nod. 'What happened to your arm?'

Grostro pulled his drooping arm up with his good one, displaying a piece of bone sticking out through the skin. 'One of your God's rocks I think. Perhaps he doesn't like me so much.' Even with such an injury the Plainsman showed no sign of the pain he was in. 'What now?'

'I must help lead my people to find a new home,' Kinfular replied. 'Then I shall assemble as many as possible and head back to the Mlendrians. This was only a finger poked at us by the Yellowskins in retribution for something we did.'

'This wasn't all of their warriors!'

'I've been told they have many times the number we faced.'

Grostro looked troubled. 'Can these Mlendrians defeat them?'

'I don't know. They are fine warriors, and many, but they were afraid of an attack.'

'Will more be sent to attack us?'

'The Yellowskins are an arrogant race, and perhaps for good reason. When their men do not return, we can expect a far greater number to avenge them.'

'Then we shall unite the mountain and plains tribes and join the Mlendrians.'

Kinfular shook his head. 'The mountain tribes have fought with one another for as long as the Elders can remember.'

Grostro was helped to his feet by his men and rested on his huge sword. 'When I was young, I dreamed of conquering the Plains. Such are the thoughts of a Chieftain's son. When my father died I was twenty years, but in that time had watched how the tribes of the plains battled each other with none gaining advantage. I realised, just two tribes working as one could defeat a single tribe. It took some time, but through a bond of marriage I made a pact with another tribe. We then hunted down and attacked the weakest tribe. Easily defeated, they surrendered before many of their warriors were slain. We added them to our army and went for the next weakest who also fell to us. This continued until we conquered all but a few tribes. I then challenged the original chieftain for sole leadership of what had become the largest tribe on the plains.'

'You defeated him?'

'No, he turned out to be as strong as he was ugly and took control. But his leadership was too weak to hold so many together and old feuds began within the tribe. In the end he was slain and I took over. I devised the Rod of Leadership, and claimed it was given to me by the gods. The shaman saw the chance for peace within the tribe and made it a spiritual icon. Whoever held it was the chosen leader.'

'It will take more than a stick to conquer the mountain tribes.'

'You are thinking only of conquest, as my predecessors did, Peaksman.'

Kinfular thought back to the chieftain's story. 'You suggest an alliance?'

Grostro nodded.

'They will take much convincing.'

Grostro stepped up to Kinfular and held out his arm in friendship. 'Then let ours be the first alliance, Kinfular of the Riaan.'

Kinfular looked into the smiling eyes before him and saw no deception. He accepted the gesture and clasped the man's forearm in his. 'I'll put it to Utal.'

Grostro left to seek out the remainder of his men.

A recognisable dust-free figure was making his way through the destruction. Behind him were two dozen men and someone his heart betrayed he was especially glad to see. Sholster and Shinlay had arrived back from the top of the ridge.

On seeing Kinfular still alive, Shinlay ran into his arms, no words spoken.

'They are defeated?' Sholster said. The boulders he'd rolled tested the man to produce an uncharacteristic look of weariness Kinfular never remembered seeing on him before.

'The plan worked.'

Sholster beamed.

Kinfular looked to his concubine. 'I am glad to see you have made it also.'

'It was close, we timed our jump clear just before the tooth crumbled beneath us,' Shinlay replied.

Sholster's smile broadened as ThreeSwords, limping and covered in scratches, blood streaked through the caked dust on his body, walked out of the gloom.

Kinfular felt Shinlay's heart beat a little faster.

'How do you fair, Darkface,' Sholster called.

'I do not know how I still live,' replied the Heslarian. 'Rocks were falling all around.'

'Splendid! It means Rolk has an even more spectacular ending for you, my friend.'

ThreeSwords gave a look indicating his opinion of such a thought. 'Then I hope you'll be right there beside me.'

Sholster burst out a laugh. 'If any god dares take me in battle he'll find a sharp poke in the eye. I'll be leaving this world in the arms of a buxom woman in front of a roaring fire with many sons singing my arrival into the heavens!'

ThreeSwords knew it was as much to be certain, as it was for himself one day to die standing alone in combat. Even so, he admitted the vision of the god-poker rested well with him.

'We have destroyed our home,' Shinlay said.

'We'll build another,' Kinfular replied.

'You think Rolk left us food?' said Sholster.

They all looked at him with the same expression.

'What?' he answered their disapproving looks. 'The battle is over, we have won. It's time for celebration and eating.'

'Many of our people are trapped. When all are free, you can eat,' Kinfular said.

Sholster, lost in the fervour of victory, played his gaze over the scene, taking it in for the first time. Without another word he headed into the thinning dust cloud and began removing rocks from fallen Riaan.

'Where is Baltrac?' Shinlay asked.

'The man was a coward,' Kinfular replied. 'When he heard of the Ashnorian army coming he took off like a Penjar with his bodyguard. I expect he's still running.'

'Do you think the Yellowskins will return?' Shinlay said.

'I will not wait for them to come. We'll find a new safe place for the Riaan, hidden deep in the mountains. When the elders are happy they can survive the summer, we'll help the Mlendrians fight these Ashnorians.'

Chapter 56 – Insurrection

Ment woke up in billet five of Tiburn's barracks. He'd rolled onto the lump in his mattress again. Shuffling his body it contorted enough to avoid the obstruction. It was supposed to be Grapple's turn in the bottom, but the young recruit had settled in before Ment got back from the mess and couldn't wake him. 'You owe me two nights,' he mumbled. 'Grapps, you hear? Two nights you owe me.' He punched the underside of the bunk above. The bunk lifted indicating Grapple wasn't there. 'Hah! Never could hold your beer, man. Now a piss has lost you a good night's sleep.'

He climbed out and staggered a step, catching himself on the bed. 'Has the time come already I cannot hold me drink?' He climbed into the bunk above. Pulling the covers over him he went to settle in and realised the bed was cold. Grapple was gone a lot longer than to relieve himself.

A shiver ran up Ment's spine, but it wasn't the cold bed. Something he thought he saw but ignored in his middle-of-the-night stupor made him sit up. Many of the bunks in the room were empty.

He slid back to the floor. 'Some kind of prank. Can't a man get some piece?'

He opened his bed locker to get some clothes and found his sword and knife was missing. Control of a weapon was the personal responsibility of each Ranger, once signed out of the armoury. Taking another man's weapon earned you five lashes.

'Damned odd.'

The lower bunk on the next bed was empty and he stepped onto it to get to Bullard who was sleeping. It took several shakes before the man woke. He turned over to complain and caught Ment's finger across his lips.

'Something's weird.'

Bullard shook his head as if trying to dislodge the fog of sleep. 'How much did I drink tonight?'

'Same here. I think we've been drugged.'

Bullard climbed down and went for his sword to find it missing.

'Mine's gone too,' Ment said.

Bullard looked more serious now and crouched down.

'The others?'

'Looks to be around a third of us have gone. From what I can see, it's all those recent enrolments.'

Bullard slid his hand around to the back behind his uniform in his locker. Removing a loose plank from the back he recovered a knife.'

'God's man, you'd be flayed all morning if they found you had it.'

'Family heirloom,' Bullard replied.

'Got any more?'

'Nope.'

'You lead then.'

Bullard screwed up his face. 'Thanks.'

They moved along the bunks and began waking the rest of the men, one by one. All the men woke in the same dazed condition.

They collected around the one man with a weapon, like it made him in charge.

Ment returned from the Captain's quarters at the end of the bunk room. 'Gone.'

'Do you think it's an unscheduled drill?' It was Bronk, a nervous sort from one of Tiburn's many surrounding farms. Forced into the army by the need to earn money for his family when the farm took a turn for the worse, he barely had the nerve to be a Ranger. They accepted him because he was a dead shot with his own bow he'd brought with him. It was the reason he slept with it and now held it in his hand.

Bullard wiped a hand over his bristly face. 'I hope so, Bronni. Until we know otherwise, we gotta find out about the other cabins and get our hands on some weapons. Quin, Drake and Piket, take five men apiece and see if the rest are the same. Avoid contact with who may have done this. If they can drug, disarm and remove so many of us, then they're serious.'

'We'll use the fire hatch,' Ment said.

They exited the billet through the trap door leading underneath. All barracks buildings we're on stilts to stop the wood floors rotting. It was a tight squeeze even when crawling.

The three bunk-search parties dispersed and Bullard led Ment and the remainder to the edge of the underside of the cabin. Looking out he saw the barracks ground was empty. No guards, not even on the Major's cabin.

The weapons store was centrally placed equal distance from each of the bunk rooms, which meant a thirty-yard dash across open ground. It was dark but the combination of a clear starry sky and the occasional flickering lantern around the camp made for enough light to show them up.

'Where are they?' Bullard said, fear growing in his voice.

Ment tapped him on the shoulder and pointed to the mess hall. Three men were walking out. Two of them Bullard recognised as Captains. The other was the fat trader, Brinley.

'Damned if this is an unscheduled drill. And those Captains seem too pally with him. And where's Stimm?'

A sound came from behind as somebody was coming through the men. Elbowing his way forward on his stomach, a welcome faced appeared.

'Captain Griggs, sir.' Bullard gave a limited salute in the restricted position.

'What do you know?' Griggs said.

'A third of the men in our billet are gone, along with all weapons. The rest of us seem to have been drugged, sir.'

'It's the same in mine. What of your Captain?'

Bullard pointed in the direction of the mess hall.

Griggs could see the two other Captains, including Bullard's. 'So the sweating bastard's made his move.'

'You knew of this?' Bullard said.

'Captain Shanks and I had suspicions about the guy, but nothing this bold. For now, trust only the two of us for orders until we know better.'

'Yes, sir,' Bullard replied.

'I see you have an illegal blade.'

Bullard wasn't sure what to reply. It didn't feel the right time to be disciplined. 'It's my lucky blade, sir; kept in the family for generations.'

'Fine initiative, I'm giving you a field commission to corporal,' Griggs said, pulling free a non-Ranger-issue knife of his own. 'We need proper weapons if we're going to take back the barracks. Take two men and get to Major Stimm. I need to know if he's with us or one of them.'

'What do we do if he's with them?'

'Cut his throat at the earliest opportunity.'

Bullard bulked at the blunt command.

'Corporal, this is bigger than some bandit heist. Somebody is trying to neutralise the barracks, which could mean a takeover of Tiburn and a foothold on the edge of the Mlendria.'

'Couldn't it just be a bandit raid on our weapons?' The voice came from the back and sounded like Bronk.

'Too ambitious for them,' Griggs replied. 'Make no mistake, we and whoever we can muster from the other billets, are all that stand before a possible hostile takeover of the area.' Griggs looked back to Bullard. 'So if Stimm, or anyone else is in on it, you take the bastards out and move on.'

'Bullard nodded.'

'Good hunting, Corporal. I hope your knife is as good as its reputation.'

Bullard crawled out and headed off with Ment and the other men under his first command. Skirting around behind and between the deserted barracks they made it to a point for a final dash across to the Major's cabin.

Giving the signal to keep low he led them out across the gap. Halfway, two men appeared from the shadows of the back of Stimm's cabin. Bullard stopped and lay down, listening to his men doing the same. The two ahead of them had weapons and looked to be keeping the perimeter guard. Neither were barracks regulars and one was eating a chicken drumstick, indicating he'd just come from the mess. It was enough to confirm to Bullard they were hostiles.

They were walking straight for them. There was no chance they wouldn't see him and his men. Bullard gripped his knife. He didn't know how much surprise he was going to get, but the chances of taking both men down, and without a sound, were nil.

With a dozen paces remaining he bunched his muscles.

An arrow flew out of the night and plunged into one of them, dropping him dead to the ground. The other guard was caught in a moment of surprise as a second arrow followed before he'd time to call out. It caught him in the thigh and he also went down. Bullard leapt forward and jumped on the man, grabbing him over the mouth before plunging his blade into his neck. Ment and the other privates were on the fallen men with seconds, removing weapons and dragging them back out of view behind the Major's cabin.

Bullard looked for the source of his saviour and saw Bronk sheltering behind a billet, bow in hand giving the thumbs up.

Bullard returned the gesture.

With the dead guards pushed under the cabin out of sight, Bullard led his men to a rear window. Making more noise than he wanted, he prised it open with his knife. Slipping the knife between his teeth, he pulled himself up and into the blackness of the cabin. As he stood to help the others he felt the tip of a sword push against his back. Somebody whispered into his ear. 'Help the others. And do not speak a word that I'm here.'

With the other two men inside, a small flame flared to reveal the room. Stimm was holding a match, his sword resting on Bullard. The man was calm, his expression one of curiosity. It was three against one, but all knew the Major was a fine swordsman and would take at least two of them down.

'This better be some kind of insane freshman dare,' Stimm said, moving the fluttering match towards a lantern.

'Please don't do that,' Bullard said, indicating the lantern.

Stimm stopped, the urgency in the man's voice telling him this was more than a prank. 'Talk fast.'

'I've been ordered by Captain Griggs to get to you, sir.'

The flame reached Stimm's fingers and he shook it out. The room was plunged into darkness for moment before another was lit to reveal nobody had moved. He withdrew the sword from Bullard.

'What's going on?'

'Captain Griggs thinks trader Brinley is trying to neutralise the barracks.'

Stimm looked bemused. 'On what evidence?'

'Two thirds of the barracks has been drugged and disarmed. The others are in the mess. The Captain recognised Brinley outside with Captains Teal and Ferrolax.'

Stimm brought his nose to Bullard's mouth and smelt the man's breathe. 'Maricula. Its affects are diluted by alcohol. Whoever gave it to you hadn't banked on Crencher's birthday celebration. Where is Captain Griggs, now?'

'He's waking as many as he can to attempt a raid on the weapons store.'

Stimm shook out the match, His voice cold and determined. 'Come with me.'

Stimm led them to the front room of his hut and checked out of the window. A couple of hundred men were assembling in the main courtyard. Their swords were drawn and they were breaking off into groups of twenty heading towards the billets. He estimated it would take five minutes to kill the remaining soldiers per billet before moving onto the next. It didn't give him long.

Three men headed his way.

'They're coming. What are Captain Griggs orders?'

'To cut the bastards down, sir. Including you, if you were with them.'

'Well, now they surrender or die.'

'Yes, sir. I only have a knife, though.'

Stimm moved through the dark and unlocked a display case. 'Here, take this. It's ceremonial, given to me when I reached Major. The edge is dull and I have no shield, so use it with both hands and aim to bludgeon. In this light just bring it down on their heads, they won't see it coming. Let them into the room before attacking.'

Stimm moved to the door of his cabin and quietly unlocked it, then waited behind it.

Footsteps assembled outside. The handle turned and the door opened. The men walked in. As they reached the centre of the room Stimm pushed the door closed with his foot. The sound alerted the intruders and they turned. Bullard, seeing his chance, stood and brought his sword down onto the nearest man's head from behind, cracking his skull and dropping him dead to the floor. His other two men rose up and swung their swords at one of the other intruders. In the dark the man had no chance to deflect both, and he went down, a deep cut in his side to be finished off with a sword in the chest.

The remaining one had an opening and plunged his sword into a stomach. He pulled his sword free to jump back and face them.

Stimm approached. 'Tell me what's going on and I'll let you live.'

'I'll tell you nothing, your barracks is ours.'

The man's head jerked to one side as a large ceremonial sword stuck it. Bullard stepped out of the shadows and brought his sword down on the exposed neck. It snapped and the soldier's head moved into a strange angle. He too, fell to the floor.

'Surrender or die. Major's orders.'

'A little more time to surrender for the next one, perhaps,' Stimm said.

'Sorry, sir.'

'Tilly is still alive,' Ment said, kneeling by the solder who took the sword in the stomach.

'Stay with him and try to stop the bleeding. He's going to be in a lot of pain, so keep him quiet and keep pressure on the wound.' Stimm ordered. 'Lock and bar this door behind me. Once they realise I'm out you shouldn't be bothered again.'

'Send them to the hells, sir.'

Stimm slipped into the shadows, the sound of fighting was coming from several billets, along with the sound of the dying. They were killing the unarmed Rangers in their beds. He made out Griggs and a few other men making their way to the weapons store. He headed off to join them.

Griggs led his team to the weapon store. In the dark they passed as rogue Rangers and they reached the hut without interception. Two guards were stationed outside.

Without proper weapons against armoured men they would suffer too many losses. Just then he saw Stimm walk around the other corner. The man seemed comfortable with the situation. Griggs had his answer about the allegiance of the man. He watched as his Commander approached the guards. He was delivering three swords. He must have killed Bullard and the others. Griggs berated himself for not sending more.

'I have swords missed from the search. Put them in with the rest.'

The men looked uncertain and ready to draw on him.

Stimm kept walking, showing no signs or alarm.

'We were told you weren't with us.'

Stimm walked up the steps and held out the swords to the other one. 'Brinley convinced me otherwise,' he said with a smile and rubbing his fingers together indicating money.

The man relaxed and chuckled. 'Yeah, he has a way of doing that.' He turned to unlock the store while the other one took the swords.

Stimm pulled his knife and stuck the man through the back into his heart. The other reacted, fumbling to use one of the three weapons he held. Stimm slashed across his throat, preventing him from calling out before pushing him away to fall down the steps.

'Griggs, get your men over here.'

Griggs came running with his men. 'Thank the gods you're with us, sir.'

'Get weapons and armour to the billets and arm as many men as possible. Get them to surprise these murderers when they enter, and cut them down. With luck we'll kill half of them before they get a chance to raise the alarm and regroup. Move fast, Captain, our men are dying.'

'Yes, sir,' Griggs replied, eagerly.

Stimm looked out across the barracks watching the murder gangs leave their initial billets and head to the next set. Two of the billets flickered through the windows from fires.

The screaming of the dying was beginning to waken adjacent billets and men were running out to see what was happening. In nightclothes and without weapons, they were hacked down in seconds by the approaching mobs.

Stimm watched the slaughter. How could this have happened under his nose? To be so played by a trader and his thugs. But now wasn't the time for self-pity. He had been a fool on a grand scale and now not only his career but his men were being destroyed. He couldn't work out the trader's motivation for the attack though. Tiburn was his base of operations, his lucrative trading would stop.

Griggs returned with thirty men and began to take more weapons and armour to the next billet.

A sudden explosion from one of the furthest billets sent splintered wood from its roof far into the air. An illegal hooch still, Stimm guessed. Flames roared up after and began to illuminate the barracks.

'We're going to be seen, sir,' Griggs said.

'I'll distract them, Captain. Continue with your orders.'

Stimm made his way across to the mess hall, avoiding the two perimeter guards. Pulling himself up onto the rear porch he entered the unlit kitchen and making his way to the door to the main mess hall. A gap gave him a view only a few feet wide down the middle of the hall. He could make out Captains Teal and Ferrolax at the far door. The trader was not in view.

Removing his hipflask of the finest brandy supplied as a gift by the trader, he pulled off the cap. 'It's going to leave a sour taste in my mouth now anyway.' He poured the liquid into the kitchen's fat barrel and struck a flint. The liquid ignited and soon the fat started to spit. He checked the door to the mess to see Teal walking his way with hand on sword hilt.

The door opened and Teal saw the fire and shouted out the alarm, running in to put it out. Stimm's sword went into the man's side. 'The penalty for treason is death, Captain.'

Stimm was now visible to the men in the mess and they drew swords. The fat in the barrel was now burning furiously, the flames reaching the ceiling. Taking Teal's sword, he ran around to the back of the barrel and slid both blades underneath heaving upwards. The barrel fell forward spewing out the now liquid fat and creating a river of flame filling the kitchen ahead of him.

The soldiers in the mess leapt back. The doorway was now impassable and they headed for the front. Through the raging fire Stimm saw Brinley looking back. The trader was furious and shouting something unheard over the crackling of the fat.

Stimm ran for the back and leapt out over the rear balustrade heading for the weapons store. There was no sign of Griggs nor his men as he approached and he kept running passed the store and towards the billets Griggs had been releasing, hoping the man was in one of them and hadn't been captured. Griggs then appeared in a doorway and saw the situation. He shouted orders into the room and Rangers began to pour out.

'Change of plan, Captain,' Stimm shouted as he approached. 'Get all the men out, we're going to have to take the barracks back in open combat.'

Stimm turned and faced down those chasing him. The rogues stopped their advance, outnumbered by the men joining the Commander. He replaced his sword.

'The takeover has failed. Lay down your arms and I'll spare you a hanging, you'll spend the rest of your lives in a cell. If not, you can take a chance to escape and remain on the run with sizeable bounties over your heads waiting for a sword in the guts or the executioner.'

The two growing groups of soldiers began to face off in the centre of the barracks. It was clear to the renegades they were going to be outnumbered three to one. Even so, Stimm judged many of his men to have been murdered in their bunks. The thought turned his stomach.

He watched as Brinley walked forward, leaving a few men in front to avoid an arrow. He was still twenty paces away across the space between the two groups. Stimm considered making a dash for him, but the distance was too great before the coward would fall back into the ranks.

'I expected to see your lumbering carcass heading in the opposite direction,' Stimm called out. 'Justice is going to be swift for you.'

The trader took out a cigar and lit it, blowing a puff out into the still air. 'On the contrary, Major. It is you who should be running. You have betrayed your men, barracks and your oath.'

'I played no role in this rebellion, and you know it. I may have taken a few bribes to raise your profits, but I would do nothing to risk this town. You murdered my men in their sleep.'

'They're soldiers, Major; dying is what they're paid for.'

'Not in their beds, drugged!'

Brinley took another puff of his cigar and shrugged his indifference.

Griggs walked forward to stand by Stimm. 'The men and I don't want to see these vermin live. We're right behind you if you give the order, sir.'

'Thank you, Captain. I've lost enough men tonight through my stupidity, I don't want to lose more if I can avoid it.'

'As the trader said, sir, we're soldiers. Dying is what we do, and we're ready to join these murdering bastards in the hells.'

Stimm raised his voice across the gap again. 'Feelings are running high this side. It seems the thought of you living while so many friends are dead doesn't sit well. I'm inclined to agree.'

The sound of several hundred men readying swords behind him sang out its cold slithering chime.

Someone then approached from behind the trader and whispered in his ear. A broad smile broke out on the trader's face. 'Then I guess you must do what you must do.'

The man's coolness gave Stimm pause. Such men were cowards at best and Brinley was in no shape to fight.

However, it was a pleasant vision seeing the fat man with a sword in his guts. He began the advance. Still the trader didn't move, although a slight waver in his smile told Stimm perhaps the man had been calling his bluff.

As they reached halfway, Brinley's smile faded and he backed into the line of his men who weren't too happy about it. Confidence was faltering as the Ranger's approached.

Stimm could sense something wasn't right, the trader wasn't moving fast enough?

As he continued so a sound began to be heard over the flames of the burning mess hall. It was faint at first, creating an eerie echo throughout the barracks as it bounced off the many wooden structures. Stimm raised his hand and his men stopped their advance. The sound grew and soon a rhythmic beat began to form.

'It's coming from the mountain trail, I think, sir,' Griggs said.

'Get a man on a billet and report.'

Griggs turned and gave the order. A young Ranger ran to a billet and climbed to the roof. He stood and almost fell back as he looked out.

'What do you see?' shouted Griggs.

'Soldiers, sir, marching this way.' The young man's voice was filled with fear.

'How many?' prompted Griggs.

'I...I don't know, sir.'

'What do you mean man, you don't know?'

'I cannot see the back of the column.'

Griggs sheathed his sword and followed the path of the young Ranger onto the roof. He stood next to him and looked out. 'Dear mothers of the gods.'

Stimm called out for a report. Griggs simply pointed in a direction over the heads of Brinley and his men.

Stimm could now see the column. The men behind him shuffled and took steps back. He searched for the trader. The man's eyes were burning with victory. 'Gods man, what have you done…'

Heavily-armoured soldiers, twenty abreast and stretching back over a hundred lines approached the barracks. Behind them were an assortment of wagons and other contraptions Stimm was left only imagining their purpose.

'What are they, sir?' came a voice from one of the men behind.

Stimm noted the question wasn't *who*, but *what*. He understood, the soldiers in shining livery marched in such perfect time and movement it didn't seem they could be human. The weird metal devices being pulled at the rear shining in the fire of the exploded billet added to the ominous and surreal vision.

'It's the Empire, son. They've finally come for us.'

Fear flared across the men.

Stimm watched as the front of the Ashnorian column approached the perimeter fence. Two robed figures walked to the front and pointed to the wire. A section wide enough for the column smouldered before bursting into flames. Moments later the metal melted and fell to the ground. The robed figures withdrew and the column continued unheeded into the barracks heading towards Brinley.

The sound of their perfect marching was loud now as their boots hit the hard-packed mountain soil.

'What do we do,' shouted Griggs from on top the billet.'

A streak of lightning flashed out from behind the front ranks of the Ashnorian line blasting the young Ranger next to

Griggs from his feet and over the edge. Griggs dived for the edge as a second bolt flashed just over his head. He dropped over the edge to land hard on the ground safe from another attack. The young Ranger lay dead, smoke rising from a blackened hole in his chest.

Another bolt shot out and struck a Ranger in the front line close to Stimm throwing him back into the men behind. The line broke and the Rangers ran. Stimm stood a moment longer, catching the trader meeting an Ashnorian civilian not in armour. The Ashnorian bowed.

Griggs returned to his side. 'Sir, get out of here.'

Stimm didn't take his eyes from the trader. 'Get the men to the town. Wake everyone and start the evacuation to Hunter's Hold. Get all those who are of age, including Ranger veterans, to start building barricades. They need to be high enough to hide us so the mage's cannot target us with their lightning. Use everything and anything. Make a killing zone in the main street and hide archers on the upper levels in the buildings on either side. And see if Thrane can be ready to answer with some magic of his own. Somehow we'll have to hold the Ashnorians off long enough for the town to escape.'

Griggs acknowledged the order and left. Stimm sheathed his sword and walked towards the line of Brinley's men. With the death of so many men on his hands, and a hanging, he decided his time had come, and if he took a bolt in place of one of his men in retreat, so much the better. He reached within ten paces of the line and stopped, surprised still to be standing.

The men in front of him parted and Brinley pushed through.

'Commander.'

Stimm saw the gloating look. He wanted more than anything to cut him down. 'You have betrayed an entire civilisation. How can you live with yourself?'

'Oh, I shall be living very well. The Empire has riches and style of living beyond anything you could imagine. I am to be given a place in their Elite, surrounded by silver, gold and jewels, the rarest foods and wines, and clothes made from the finest silks and linen. I'll have a dozen personal slaves, and beautiful woman who will satisfy my *every* desire in a life extended a hundred years.'

An order was shouted and the Ashnorian column marched up to a halt just behind Brinley's men.

'Well, I think it's time for me to leave,' Brinley said. He turned and walked back through his men to stand to the side of the Ashnorian column.

'I'll find you, Brinley,' Stimm yelled.' I don't care how long it takes, I'll find you and gut you, you murderous pig.'

'Major, Major,' Brinley shouted back. 'So much hostility against a man who's about to give you the best advice you'll ever receive.'

'What advice could there be I would want from you?'

Brinley began to laugh. 'To run.' He waved his hand at the Ashnorian he'd spoken to earlier and an order was given in Ashnorian. The column drew swords and marched forward. Stimm watched as Brinley's men began to shuffle, looking uncertain about what was happening. As the Ashnorian column reached them the line of silver and golden shields were raised and swords thrust forward. Brinley's rogue Rangers began to die. The rest started yelling and running. Lightning flew out again, striking more down.

Stimm ran too. He could hear the column of soldiers continuing to march. Lightning flashed again and again and the sounds of men dying were behind him. One for the faster ones caught up as Stimm felt the heat and brilliant light of a bolt streak passed him and deprive the man of his escape in the last moment of hope. The proximity of the blast toppled Stimm to the ground. Without rising, he pulled himself elbow over elbow to safety behind the billet. He got to his feet and risked a peek around the corner. He saw Brinley laughing uncontrollably, looking at him with raised hands, applauding and bowing a salute to his getaway.

Stimm drew his head back out of sight. 'I'll get you, Trader. I'll have that laughing head from your shoulders and feed it to your damned Elite.'

Chapter 57 – The Mouth of the Lion

Their soft footfalls echoed from the natural rock walls illuminated by Falakar's tiny lamp and Garamon's glowstone. It was enough for gaining a footing and avoiding drops, but didn't cast far into the distance, so they were often stopped by a sheer wall of rock and forced to move along it to find an opening.

Garamon envied the ability of the other two men to move with such confidence over the mix of jagged and smooth surfaces. A single slip could result in injury, which down here could be a serious problem. At least they were no longer pursued by Ashnorians. Falakar's gamble at the rock face worked, for none had followed them over the edge of the cliff.

'How do you decide which way to go? There have been other paths we could have taken.' Garamon said.

The Ranger stopped. 'From which direction is the air flowing?' he asked.

Garamon licked his finger and held it up. 'None, the air is still.'

'Lick your lips and open your mouth. The air will evaporate the moisture. Your lips are many times more sensitive than the skin of your fingers.'

Garamon did. After a few moments he felt a tiny tingle across his lips. 'That way,' he answered, surprised.

'Is there a smell?'

Garamon sniffed. 'Just the smell you say is from bats.'

'That's no use. Is it sweet, pungent, like wood, grass, pine?' Falakar prompted.

Garamon sniffed again. 'It's not sweet. Perhaps like the smell in an ironsmith when the metal burns.'

'Good,' Falakar replied. 'Track it to its source.'

Garamon took the lead walking in the direction he sensed the air flow to be coming. It was slow work as he stopped often to keep a bearing on the breeze, but eventually he came to a small opening in the floor.

'Stick your head in there and take a breath,' Falakar said.

Garamon did and recoiled from the smell.

'Is that it?'

Garamon nodded.

Falakar unravelled his rope, tying one end around a rock.

'Wait here. If I call for you, come down after me.' He jumped out backwards into the middle of the opening and disappeared.

After a while, Garamon heard a curse come up out of the fissure. 'I need more rope.'

Garamon tied one end of his rope around the top of Falakar's, and allowed it to slide down. There was a sound of it hitting the Ranger below, followed by another curse. Garamon grimaced at his error. Jontal shook his head with a grin at the woodsman.

The instruction to climb down arrived. It had a distant echo. Garamon set the rope around him as trained and jumped out like Falakar into the blackness and dropped a few feet. He detected no rock around him and hung there swinging for a few moments before letting the rope play out through his gloves. After a while he came to the knot Falakar tied. Garamon couldn't imagine how such a thing was achieved while dangling from the first rope. With some effort he got passed it and continued down. The scene was as black as a moonless midnight with Falakar's lantern giving the only clue to the landing point.

'Be careful, it's slippery.'

Falakar's hands steadied him. The rock was uneven and greasy.

Jontal arrived soon after. 'Which way now?'

'The Ashnorian entrance is likely the largest,' Falakar answered. 'So we follow the strongest air flow.'

The ground soon lost its slipperiness and before long the sound of running water began to grow. Falakar led them until the echoes around them changed, indicating they'd entered a large cavern. The air was colder, damp and the sound of hundreds of water droplets could be heard hitting a body of water ahead. In their lights they could just see the edge of the water a few feet ahead.

'Time to swim?' Jontal said, tapping his boots in the water.

Falakar took out a ration of dried meat and threw it a few feet into the lake. Nothing happened immediately, then ripples could be seen heading their way. They turned into more ripples, until it seemed like a giant arrow was being formed in the water aiming at the floating morsel. As the head of the arrow met the food so the water churned. It became a frenzy of broiling small fish, each the size of a man's fist. The ration disappeared.

'Pirains,' Jontal said, grimacing. 'I've had a fear of those since a child. They can strip a man's flesh to the bone in just minutes.

'The air flow is coming from over the water. The opening must be beyond it,' Falakar said.

Jontal took out his bow and poured half of the liquid from a small stoppered jar onto an arrow tip. Notching up the arrow, he touched the tip to Falakar's lantern and fired it high ahead of them. The arrow burst into a brilliant orange flame leaving a smoking trail behind, illuminating a lake filled with spires of black rock rising from it, some halfway to the ceiling.

'There,' said the bandit, pointing off to the right.

There was a dark hole in the cavern wall off to the side. Falakar took a small jar of his own, dipping his finger into the pot and removed a bead of translucent paste.

'Smear some of this around your ankles.'

'What's it for?' Garamon said.

'Fish dislike it.'

'I hope they know that,' Jontal said.

'We'll climb across those rocks and try to stay out of the water.'

'And if we can't?'

'They're attracted to disturbances. The water droplets should mask our movements, if we move carefully.

With the salve applied, Falakar led the way.

Access to the first rock was a few feet into the water and the three men entered the shallows making as few ripples as possible. Garamon felt the water rise to his ankles and water seep into his boots. He kept looking for fish, but his glowstone couldn't penetrate the surface rippled by their footsteps.

The depth increased a few more inches before Falakar reached the first rock. It was taller than his head and taped steeply. The surface was covered in cracks and made for easy purchase.

They climbed, taking care to leave the water with minimal disruption, and edged around to the other side. The next rock was close enough to step onto, smaller but nevertheless good to get a firm footing without slipping into the water.

They continued, stepping and jumping from pointed rock to rock, looking as though they were going to get across without having to resort to getting back into the water. Then their luck ran out. The rocks sank away. The distance to the far side was now only yards. Falakar pushed his foot into the water. His leg sank up to his knee before it found a footing. He lowered his other leg and began walking out across the gap. The ground rose and fell and he was having trouble balancing. He dropped lower and was up to his waist. With his hands held out, he kept wading across, the water swirling gently in his wake. At one point he almost tipped sideways and waited until he'd regained his balance. Continuing, he rose out safe on the other side.

He beckoned Garamon next.

Jontal stepped forward. 'If I don't go now, I'm not going to be able.' Without waiting for argument, he stepped out into the water. His urgency to complete the crossing kept him from stopping and steadying as Falakar did. He made it across without pause, kneeling down and breathing heavily.

Seeing the bandit in distress didn't help Garamon, and he slid his foot in until it met the first solid surface beneath the cold water. The rocks beneath were pointed and uneven and it took him a moment to find a position between two points allowing his weight to be transferred before stepping in with the other leg. He waded out as Falakar had done. Each step took him far longer than the bandit, as he tried to find a flat surface. More often than not, his choice was to squash his foot between two rocks and pull his other leg forward. It was a precarious manoeuvre and his balance wasn't good. Nevertheless he made it to the point where Falakar sunk to his waist.

'That's where I almost fell. There are three pointed rocks. You must find the first and balance on it with one leg while dragging the other through the water to find the next. Hold your axe out in front of you to stabilise yourself. The second one is higher than the first and the last is deeper than both.'

Garamon stepped to the first position and his foot sunk onto a narrow point. His landing wasn't perfect and he starting tipping to the right. He wasted no time and pushed off hard to correct the imbalance. His rapid movement churned the water and splashed. He looked to the Ranger as he moved forward.

'Do not stop, and clear your mind. There is only one outcome. You will make it across.'

Garamon's momentum carried him forward and he took the next step. It was flat, as if the spike had broken away. It was higher and he pushed up, managing to get both feet down. He gave a yelp.

'Something bit me!'

'Stay focussed and make the next step. Remember, it's lower.'

His foot dropped, missing the peak and sliding down the side, stopping between it and another rock. He stepped forward with his other leg and went to remove the first. It didn't come free. He yanked at it several times.

'My foot's stuck!'

There was another bite at his leg and he gave out another yelp.

'Do you think it drew blood? Falakar said urgently.

'I think so. Falakar, get me out of here.'

Falakar put down the lantern and stepped into the water, grabbing the middle of the woodsman's axe. 'Pull yourself out.'

Garamon tried. 'It won't come free.'

There was another bite at his leg and then another, both more painful than the previous.

'Falakar, they are biting me, more of them.'

The water splashed out in the lake. In the light of the lantern it churned and a mass of tiny ripples appeared, moving to form an arrow pointing at Garamon.

'Help me!' Garamon shouted, pulling on his stuck foot.

'Stop fighting, your foot is getting further wedged in. On the count of three, we both pull hard.'

Garamon nodded quickly, and the Ranger counted.

They both pulled.

'It moved, but I'm still stuck!' A mass of writhing fish were now heading his way.

Jontal fired an arrow into the fish, slicing several. The response was as explosion of scales, fins and teeth as hundreds of them, drawn by the blood of the injured, ripped into them. It lasted only moments.

'I have two arrows left,' Jontal said, notching up the next one and firing.

Falakar jerked the axe to get the attention of Garamon who was transfixed by the flesh-eating frenzy and counted again. Garamon pulled with everything he had.

'It won't budge!' he yelled. He eyes were filling with tears at the thought of his pending horrific death.

The third arrow fired.

'You have one chance remaining, then I must leave you.'

Garamon nodded as the last arrow did its work. The count completed once more and he pushed again with his free foot and pulled the other.

His foot moved.

'It's coming!'

The fish swam in.

A yank from Falakar and the foot released letting Falakar fall backwards into the shallow water. Garamon, scrambled up the incline as the Ranger was dragged out on his back by his brother.

The leading fish were pushed from the masses behind up into the shallows, flapping about. Garamon and Falakar kicked them away as Jontal struck several hanging from both of the other men's boots and leggings, flicking them into the water. The water writhed in renewed turmoil as the hacked fish were devoured.

Garamon lay back, panting. His attention was drawn to a single fish still flapping around on the rock nearby. He was surprised to see how small it was, although its body was built for one thing, to power the vicious teeth in a mouth little more than a hole in the front of the thing. It was snapping, making a clicking sound. He dropped the side of his axe onto it, which surprisingly, squashed it far less than he expected.

As quickly as they'd come, the concentration of fish dissipated bringing calm back to the water as if nothing had happened. The three men gathered themselves. Without saying a word about what might have happened, they continued on.

The exit from the lake cavern fed into a tunnel. It was wide enough for them to walk side-by-side.

'This is smoother than any mining shaft I've known,' Jontal said.

'It's a lava tunnel,' Falakar replied. 'At some time in the past, these mountains must have been volcanic.'

'To erupt anytime soon?' Jontal said, edgily, not calmed from the fish encounter.

Falakar shrugged.

'Great,' the bandit replied.

Garamon caught an uncharacteristic smirk from the Ranger as he turned his head away from his brother.

They passed other tunnels connected with the one they were in, and each time Falakar chose one leading in the direction of the entrance the Ashnorians were using. After some time he held up his hand and stopped, listening.

'Put away the stone,' he said, dousing his own lantern.

Garamon did. The darkness was completed. 'I cannot see where I'm going.'

He heard the Ranger set off, walking a little noisier than normal. No doubt for his benefit.

'Close your eyes,' Jontal said. 'It will help you connect with your surroundings.'

Garamon thought it an odd instruction, but found it did heighten his other senses when he wasn't straining to see what couldn't be seen.

As they walked, a strange noise began to impose on their hearing. It was a like the turning of a miller's grinder, only purer and a single higher note. The sound grew louder as they continued and he bumped into Falakar who had stopped. He opened his eyes. There was a dim light along the tunnel with a hue like the blue of his glowstone mixed with red.

The tunnel turned sharply ahead. The strange light was brightest there and Falakar got down on his stomach and crawled to the corner. Taking out his copper signalling plate, he angled it to catch a reflection from beyond. He put it away and nudged his he out, beckoning the others.

Garamon glimpsed around the corner. Their passageway opened out high above the floor to a wide cavern that could have swallowed his parents' farm several times. It was filled with the blue-red light coming from a swirling tunnel of colour starting in the middle and running down the centre to the rear rock face. Small groups of magii were casting magic along its length. At the start stood a single magii, it wasn't clear what he was doing. The tunnel of light increased in size from the single person, passing through rings, each larger than the previous one. The whole thing finished in a huge spinning ring at the back wall of the cave.

Two long columns of soldiers marched into the magic tunnel, one on each side, through some kind of archway made in the tunnel walls.

'What is that?'

'What does it look like to you?' Falakar said.

'Like a magic tunnel through the mountain,' Jontal replied.

Falakar nodded.

'But why, what's in the mountain they want?' Garamon said.

'This is where the dotted lines were on the Ashnorian map.'

Garamon's eyes went wide. 'It's a tunnel to the other side!'

'We have to find a way to stop it,' Falakar said.

'There are thousands of soldiers, Fal, and it looks like over a hundred of their magiis; impossible even for you to consider attacking. The best we can do is–'

'We'll wait until the last of the soldiers have entered the mountain.'

Even in the dim light from the cavern, Jontal knew the determined look on his brother's face.

'It looks as if the single magii is pouring magic in the start of the tunnel,' Falakar continued. 'Perhaps if we stop him it will stop the tunnel.'

'We might destroy their entire army,' Garamon said, eagerly.

Jontal pushed his voice from a whisper to a hiss. 'You cannot be serious, there are three of us. Even with the main army in the mountain we have to get beyond at least fifty guards on this side, and then stop a magii, who, from his position out there, I'd say is one of their most powerful.'

'There is a pillar of rock halfway. We could get there in its shadow.'

'It's too risky.'

'Perhaps forcing the single magii to engage us will stop him casting?' Garamon said, getting caught up in any possibility of saving his family.

'You have no idea what you're talking about,' Jontal said, hotly. 'We know nothing of what's going on down there. And what if we did succeed? What happens to us, surrounded by guards and a hundred magii? What's your plan for getting out?'

Falakar didn't answer.

'Oh, great,' Jontal said. 'We die in glorious honour.'

'And save Mlendria.'

'Yes, and they will no doubt sing songs for generations in your memory. The mighty Falakar, Ghost Ranger, saviour of Mlendria. It would suit you, wouldn't it? Well, I'll tell you what'll happen. We'll die in this ridiculous attempt to stop the magii, who will kill us with a flick of his wrist, even if we get passed the guard. Even then, if by some unbelievable luck, we succeed in briefly stopping him and disrupting the spell, which may or may not destroy the army, we'll be dead within seconds of achieving it.'

Falakar jabbed a hand out and grabbed his younger brother's tunic pulling him close to his face. 'Then run away into some hole to come out when things are safe, or do your deals with the enemy and line your pockets. Sell out your people to torture and misery. The fact is the world isn't fair, and sometimes true men have to step up and do what they must for the good of others, even if it means giving their lives in the attempt.'

Jontal went to pull away, but Falakar held tight, waiting for an answer.

Jontal glared back into the accusing eyes. 'Then this is where we split, Brother. I thought there was a chance we could at least live with each other's differences, but living no longer seems to be in your future.'

He pulled away and broke free.

'Can I expect you to at least give us our chance, and not call the guard to gain favour with the new order?'

Garamon thought Jontal was going to draw his knife, such was the anger in his face at the insult. The man held his gaze a few moments before walking away into the dark the way they'd come.

Jontal stayed in the shadows until his brother led the woodsman on the suicide mission.

Falakar's last words struck deep. It stirred enough anger to have him believe he was happy for him to die in his plan for immortalisation. It vindicated the bandit's ideals, and that he was finally proven right. He wasn't so happy about the woodsman. He was young and idealistic. He doubted the lad wanted to die, and was going along due to the exaggerated belief of success Falakar created in those around him. People did that for Falakar, such was the man's reputation. Many had died in the man's quest for his so-called justice, while he survived. Well, this time he wouldn't, the odds were impossible.

He started strumming his fingers.

Why did he have to say those things? Of all the words he'd said over the years, the accusation he'd sell out his people to torture and misery was most hurtful. In part because Jontal wasn't sure that it might be true.

He watched from a distance as the two blackened their faces and wrapped cloth around all reflective surfaces before disappearing over the edge to climb down to the cavern floor. He went to the edge and peered over for one last view of his brother.

The two reached the ground and began making for the pillar. It did indeed cast a suitable shadow for them, but all the trouble started after that.

Despite its evil intent, the spectacle of the multi-hued magic running through ever-increasing circles of metal was a sight he would never forget.

He watched the last of the soldiers enter the mountain. 'I'll tell your story to the bards, Brother.'

He turned to leave when something caught his eye, half-tucked into the shadows below. It was huge. He'd seen something similar before. The fact it was here, and from its design, meant it could only have one purpose.

Chapter 58 – Open Defiance

'What happened, Corporal?'

The patrol snapped to attention and saluted their sergeant. They looked fearful, even the corporal.

'It ignored us and ran, sir.'

The sergeant took out his red bound torture book and began making an entry. 'You are demoted to Private and will report to the chambers for correction for false reporting.'

He turned to one of the Privates. 'Tell me what happened?'

The Private didn't want to speak, but not doing so was also was punishable by correction. 'We found it outside of the palace. We challenged it for orders and it…ran, sir.'

The Sergeant looked to the next soldier.

'Is this true?'

The next soldier unwillingly nodded his head.

Walking up to the bars of the wagon, the Sergeant snapped his fingers at the servant within. It didn't react. He repeated the action a few more times before stepping away, almost as if afraid of some terrible infection. He tore out the charge sheet, screwed it up and placed it into his pocket.

'You think it insane, sir?' It was spoken out of turn by one of the other Privates. The vague quiver in his voice gave away his hope his superior would confirm his suspicion.

The other soldiers looked anxious for judgement.

The Sergeant was hearing of similar reports across the city. Such occurrences had to be kept from the population before panic spread.

'Keep it away from the others and have it corrected to death. You will never speak of this to anyone, under punishment of execution.'

Chapter 59 – All in Place

The previous day, Chayne had watched beyond awe as Tristaric poured mana into the start of the portal tunnel. A line of manaspheres were held within a feeder mechanism. As he exhausted one orb of mana so he would push a lever and it would be discarded to be replaced with the next. The tunnel spread from one thrinium ring to the next, larger one, and then the next, until it reached the final ring. At fifty-paces wide the last ring represented a colossal amount of thrinium. Covered in intricate engravings to improve the flow of mana into the correct patterns, it was testimony to the Empire's growing mechanical dominance as much as magical. The whole thing was set into the ground and rose up almost to touch the cave ceiling.

The ring was spun up to high speed from a union of magic and metal mechanisms. The magic from the previous ring fed into it, twisting and being sent forth into the solid rock face. But instead of being absorbed by the rock, it somehow twisted reality and opened a tunnel through it, the magic extending out as far as he could see. Strange black shapes flickered around the thrinium rings, swirling in and out the mix. He had no idea of their purpose. Twin archways of rune-covered thrinium were built into each side of the magic, allowing two columns of soldiers to march through and join up inside, then to march into the mountain as one.

He'd lost count the number of men, wagons and equipment it had swallowed. His rough estimation brought the portal out on the Mlendrian side in the deep forest, away from Ranger patrols and going unnoticed as they assembled. An attack would then ensue with complete surprise. It was an inconceivably bold move by Tristaric, and indicated the risks the man was willing to take to support his ambition to succeed. It was beyond anything Chayne could have imagined.

Only half of the magii were engaged at once, allowing time for them to rest. Tristaric had stayed in place for the duration. Soon it would be time for Kinarch's group to be called for the final stretch. It meant the last of the army would soon be entering the mountain. How many troops had got through to the other side, he'd no way of knowing. He could only hope the destruction of the tunnel would cause an explosion at both ends, removing as many of them as possible from the invasion.

His willingness to kill so many wasn't something he could have conceived before. Lathashal ended up killing his own parents, and while such a thing was far from his own feelings now, the magii hadn't had such feelings in the beginning either. Would such a heartless state happen to him eventually? The final hour of his life would end the speculation. For that, at least, he was glad.

A call went out for the next rotation, and an administrative figure stood holding out a parchment ticking off names as magii lined up and moved passed him. Chayne fell into line keeping his hood up to maintain his disguise. It came to his turn and he placed his hand on his utility staff within the folds of his robe. The man attempted to see under his hood and Chayne dropped his head and enacted his spell to speak in a gravelly tone.

'Makarec.' Lack of practice affected his attempt to modify his young voice and broke out as a half-squeak.

He felt the clerk's hand on his shoulder to stop him.

Concentrating harder, he shrugged off the hand and repeated himself. *'Makarec!'* This time his voice came out loud and ragged. The clerk jumped and scratched a mark on the parchment.

He moved on.

His station was at the fourth ring. As he arrived so the first of the three magii attending the ring released his spell while the other two maintained the magic. His manasphere was removed from the stand and a fresh one replaced. The first relieving magii in Chayne's group took up the position and began casting from it. This was repeated for the second magii.

Chayne moved into position after the last magii had stepped away. He knew he couldn't yet control a demon within a gradia ten sphere and hovered his fingertips close enough to fool the other two magii without touching it. Even a brush with it would mean disaster uncovering his deception.

He placed the fingers of his other hand on his gradia seven staff hidden in his robes and began projected his illusion of the mana feed. It shimmered a little at the start, drawing some attention and he adjusted its colour and texture. It seemed to satisfy those around. The finishing group departed leaving him and the other two magii alone.

It took more than two hours before the last line of the army column entered the mountain. Wasting no time, he began building the power behind his destabilising spell.

Chapter 60 – The Machine

Garamon jumped the last few feet to the cave floor. They were exposed to small groups of guards patrolling the perimeter of the magic tunnel. Only the shadow of the pillar and the strange flickering light of the magic kept them from discovery. It played tricks with the eyes creating dancing shadows making it difficult to discern objects from their background.

Reaching the pillar, Garamon pushed his back against it, his heart racing. They were close enough now to hear the chinking of the guards armour over the hum of the large ring.

'What do we do now?'

'We need a distraction,' Falakar replied pensively, looking around the cavern. 'A big one.'

A sound shrieked behind them, like a thousand pigs being slaughtered. No obvious source could be seen before it halted. Falakar risked a peek around the rock to view the soldiers. They were all looking in the direction of the sound.

'Magical alarm?' Garamon said.

'They look as uncertain as us.'

The screeching began again. This time, something lurched from the shadows near where they'd climbed down. A huge machine appeared out of the dark. Its speed wasn't much more than walking pace, but its direction was clear. It was heading straight for them.

The noise of the thing operating merged in discord with the whirl of the massive ring at the back of the cave. Lumbering towards them a shout went out from the nearest patrols and they formed up into a column and headed towards it. It looked as though they were going to escort it. Falakar pushed out his hand to flatten Garamon against the rock as the patrol came into view and marched passed them.

The thing lurched again and changed direction towards the advancing patrol.

Falakar crouched.

'This has to be our chance.'

Garamon swallowed hard. It was going to be the last minutes of his life. A brief thought flickered in his mind that he wanted to stay and leave the Ranger to do the job alone. Thoughts of his family came back to him and how they would never see him again. He knew his father would understand and would be proud of him, but his sister and mother couldn't. He hoped, somehow, if they succeeded, their story would get back to Tiburn and be told. He wondered if his Grandfather was looking down at this moment. The thought gave him courage.

Falakar checked out around the spire and tapped Garamon on the arm before running in the direction of the target magii.

As Garamon moved out, the enormity of the task ahead spread out before him. At this closer range the light of the swirling magic lit them up as they dashed across the rocky floor. The nearest patrols were now behind them, still bearing down on the strange device, although more were coming from further around the tunnel to cover those displaced. They were spotted and a patrol increased its pace to intercept. At the Ashnorian's marching pace Garamon knew it would be close if they were to reach the magii before the men.

Then something became apparent as they ran closer. A shimmering field, twice their height, and enclosing the inner tunnel magic and the magii, stretched between pillars of the near-indestructible Ashnorian metal. It started from the back wall, circling around the front and back again to completely enclose the tunnel of magic and the magii. Magiis stood halfway between each of the pairs of poles, firing a beam of magic into it. They were also on the inside.

'Falakar, it's their shield magic. We cannot get through.'

Either the Ranger didn't hear him, or chose to ignore the warning as he ran up to the shield and threw himself at it. It rippled outwards as he bounced off with equal force, landing hard onto the rock. Shaking the impact away he got back to his feet.

'Use the axe, get through it!'

The nearest patrol was getting close as they marched around the shield perimeter. Garamon hit it with his axe. The axe flared blue and passed through the shield, but Garamon was repelled. The axe came back out with him still holding it and he stumbled to the floor much as Falakar had just done.

'What now,' he cried.

Falakar was looking around with no answers.

There came a screeching sound behind them. They turned to see the strange device coming up behind them. It was surrounded by guards trying to climb it, but slipping back down metal ladders on both sides. It kept coming right at them. They had nowhere to run.

'It cannot end like this!' the Ranger yelled.

The machine stopped a dozen paces from them and a head popped out from the top of a tangle of pipes and struts, twenty feet above them.

It was Jontal.

The bandit cupped his hands to his mouth and called out to them. 'Climb up the front.'

They ran and took a running jump onto two massive metal pinecone shapes at the front. The cones were huge, each the size of a barn door. Each was cover in lines of metal strips Garamon recognised as similar to those used on hand-held quarry drills in Mlendria, only these were hundreds of times larger. They made for easy hand and footholds to the top where they found a small cabin area filled with levers, and

Jontal standing in front of the largest cluster of them. 'I found a drum of oil up here and poured it down both ladders. It seems to be keeping them back for now.'

Falakar looked over one side and saw the oil was thinning and the soldiers were getting a footing.

'They're starting to climb now,' Falakar shouted to Garamon, pointing to the other side for him to cover.

Garamon took up position discovering the Ashnorians had made a better job his side and the first was about to rise level with the cabin area. Getting used to the power of the axe he poked the soldier in the face with its butt and the man went flying out from the ladder to land far below onto the hard rock.

Jontal pushed at the levers, the screeching sound returned and the machine lurched forward, but each time it would come to a halt again. Heads of Ashnorian soldiers appeared on the pinecone shapes.

'Hold them off,' Jontal shouted, pointing forward. 'There's a lever I need to find.'

Falakar, still having a few moments before the soldiers managed to beat the oil defence on his side, leapt up between the struts in front of Jontal. There was no way to defend the cabin from three sides with two defenders.

The next soldier reached the top on Garamon's side. Seeing the way his predecessor was dispatched he grabbed the top rung of the ladder with one hand and swung his sword at Garamon. Garamon replied with a defensive swipe, fracturing the man's sword, sending him back to dangle by one hand. The soldier kicked out instinctively to get a footing, dislodging the next man down.

Oil dripped from the gloved hand no longer holding the rail into the eyes of the man below. The soldiers were covered in it. Garamon had an idea. As the next soldier came up level, he struck the rail hard at an angle. Sparks and tiny balls of molten metal shot out. The oil on the soldier's gloves, face and front of his armour caught alight and began to flare. The soldier screamed and Garamon did an overhead swing driving the man downwards through those below him. As he passed each one so they also started to burn.

Each began the urgent need of putting out the flames. Some fell, dislodging those below them. It became an avalanche of burning men. As the first one hit the ground and the pooled oil, it burst into a flame creating a cloud of black smoke. Men were screaming as they burned.

Garamon wasted no time and raced to the other side of the cabin. Falakar was still fighting above Jontal as the first soldier was just arriving at the top of the other ladder. Garamon wasn't going to make it and threw his axe end over end. It struck the top rung between the soldier's feet, severing it in two and jamming there. A single spark flew up to lodge in the soldier's leg armour who looked down to see it hadn't caught and grinned seeing Garamon now with no weapon. Just as he was about to jump down Jontal pulled on a combination of levers that lurched the machine forward once more. The soldier slipped on the oily rung and held out both arms to catch himself. Garamon saw his chance and leapt up and head-butted the solider in the stomach with enough force to send him back into the man behind, although not enough to dislodge them. Dropping his hands to his axe, it slid free. The soldier, recovering his footing, froze. Garamon slid the axe along the rail creating a spray of sparks into the soldier. This time there was no chance and the man caught fire. Garamon swung his axe and the soldier tried to get away and fell. Soon the ladder was aflame with burning men as before.

He jumped up to help Falakar as more patrols added to the frontal assault. The Ranger was darting from side to side, just coping with defending the wide platform. Garamon took up his position on one side to help. The front of the machine wasn't designed for fighting, and with it lurching from Jontal's efforts, Garamon struggled to maintain a good footing. His first attacker came at him, below his position and stabbed out at his foot. Garamon jumped, but the machine lurched forward at that moment and he landed awkwardly, falling back into the cabin. His attacker climbed into the gap left by the woodsman, exposing Falakar's flank. As Garamon fell he landed onto a red lever away from the main set Jontal was using. It snapped down and there was a grinding sound from the front of the machine. Screams rang out in front of Falakar and were abruptly cut off. The Ranger was forced to kneel behind his small shield, as blood, bone and metal fragments fired up at him.

Jontal got to his feet and looked out between Falakar's legs. 'That's the one!' he yelled in triumph.

Garamon's attacker was the last one standing. Protected from the missiles by his larger shield he lunged at Falakar's exposed side.

Jontal grabbed his brother's tunic and kicked out at a lever. The machine stopped driving on one side, turning the whole thing hard right and propelling the soldier and Falakar outward. Jontal held firm to Falakar, while the Ashnorian fell forward. The sound of his short scream told Garamon he was finished. He looked out next to Falakar to see the horror he'd unleashed by releasing the red lever. The two cone-shaped devices were spinning, creating a massive grinder. Anything caught in between them was crushed and ripped into small chunks.

The device lurched into a straight line again as Jontal pulled the kicked lever back into position.

'Aim for one of the shield poles,' Falakar called down.

'I can't see a thing from down here,' Jontal exclaimed.

'Ten degrees left!' Falakar ordered.

'Hang on,' Jontal shouted, 'I've only seen these things being controlled by their engineers a couple of times.'

They held tight as Jontal pulled a lever back. The machine pitched left and he pushed the lever forward again. Falakar held up a thumb.

It wasn't a centred strike but the two cones were large enough to overcome the inaccuracy. The shield either side of the thrinium pole had little effect stopping the massive machine's two cone points. The spirals of destruction rammed into the pole bringing the machine to a halt, its wheels spinning round and tearing away the rocks beneath. The thing juddered as it attempted to get grip, but the thrinium pole held firm. He pointed to more approaching soldiers.

'More power!' Falakar yelled.

'You think so!' Jontal yelled back and grabbed at a random lever. The rotating cones began to tilt downwards. As they touched the ground, it exploded outward firing blocks of rock into more approaching soldiers. It kept drilling down and the machine began to move forward as it tipped into the hole of its own making. The thrinium pole started to wobble as its foundations were torn away.

'Keep going!' bellowed Falakar over the deafening clamour.

The destruction continued until the rock gave up its hold and the pole was ripped out and swallowed by the spinning cones. The shields either side of the pole flashed and blinked out. The magiis creating them screamed and burst into blue flame before turning to chard twigs. There was a terrible screaming of metal as the thrinium pole and metal cones fought for supremacy. The cones began to wobble then the thrinium pole was spat out at speed, scything through an approaching patrol. The cones were now off-centre and the machine went mad. It upended and began to cut into the rock straight down. Garamon held on to a support bar as the machine jerked uncontrollably. He could see the other two men doing the same. Then a huge lurch pulled his grip free and he was thrown out. To his surprise the fall was short as the machine was now up to its cones in depth. He landed with a thump against the rock and rolled away. Looking around for the others, the machine gave another groan and shuddered, the ground shook and there was a crack from beneath it. The thing heaved, suddenly dropped a few feet and stopped. There was another crack. Then a hole opened and the thing fell. Garamon scrabbled to the edge to see the machine falling far into a black chasm. It disappeared from view.

He looked around frantically for Jontal or Falakar, but there was no sign of them still with him. They hadn't been thrown from the machine.

Tears formed as a maelstrom of conflicting emotions burst within him. His friends where gone. The futility of his existence amongst the plans of evil men exploded in his soul. All around was destruction. Behind him were burning fires and dozens of enemy lay about unmoving, all illuminated in the strange dancing light of the magic tunnel. He heard approaching soldiers and remembered his mission.

His friends were not going to die in vain.

Grabbing his axe he turned on them. It flared as if echoing the intensity of its wielder. As they reached him he lashed out. The impact was terrible. Three shields shattered and the soldiers were blasted back, knocking down a dozen more. In a berserk rage he struck out into any soldier nearby, smashing them from their feet or cutting them in half. Moments later he stood in the middle of a semi-circle of men. He glared at them and yelled his defiance. Despite their training, drilled into them since birth, never to disobey an order or run from battle for fear of horrific torture; something more primordial took over. They back away.

With the path clear, Garamon turned and fixed his eyes and his hatred on the magii. His blood fury coursed through his veins and he yelled his first battle cry, 'Grandfather!' and raced towards his target.

Tristaric watched the commotion unfold. It was beyond his comprehension, the incompetence of others. He had to admit he hadn't counted on the mining machine being used to breach the shield wall. It was a nice touch, but only a single attacker now remained.

He set up a brief sustaining flux to maintain the flow from the manasphere into the portal before pulling out his utility staff and firing a spread of lightning bolts into the guards who let the attacker through. He then flicked another bolt at the trespasser closing in and went to turn back to his work. He was surprised when the spell hit the axe blade and spilt into two, forcing the wielder to slow but otherwise continue.

'So the heathens are smarter than we thought.'

He saw the dislodged thrinium pole and stretched out his will. It lifted and raced across the ground towards the intruder. He allowed himself a moment of pleasure and powered all his force into the strike.

Chapter 61 – Disturbance

Chayne completed building up the power of the disruption spell. It was time to destroy the portal tunnel magic and be responsible for hundreds of thousands of deaths. He dropped his illusion getting the attention of the other two magii feeding the ring. The air around him shimmered as he enacted his new double-polarised shield spell learned from Lathashal's diaries.

'What are you doing, Makarec? You'll destabilise the portal.'

Chayne didn't know the magii. He lifted his head to expose his face under his hood.

The magii looked confused. 'Who are you?'

'I am Chayne. I am a Mlendrian. And I am here to save my people.' He turned to the portal and raised his hand to release the destabilising magic. Masked from Tristaric by the walls of the tunnel magic, the spell built up into a swirling confusion of red, purple and blue-coloured mana forming into a ball in front of him. It thrashed as if angry to be contained. He pulled his hand back ready to throw it into Tristaric's masterpiece.

The ground shook, almost making him lose the containment of the spell. A screeching sound cut in, even over the droning of the final ring. A huge machine was smashing into one of the thrinium shield poles on the other side of the tunnel. The tunnel magic was blurring most of the detail, but from its design it looked to be for excavating or drilling. It was going berserk and tearing downwards into the rock. Fires were burning behind it. It was clearly having some catastrophic failure. The thrinium pole gave up its defiance and was ripped out from the ground. The shield walls on either side of the pole blinked out, the magiis maintaining the two sections of shielding vanished in a blaze of flame.

Perhaps the machine would do his task for him and crash into one of the thrinium rings. His hopes faded as the ground cracked and the thing fell into some hole he couldn't see from his position. Refocussing, he was ready again to cast his spell.

There was a flash of lightning from Tristaric's direction and Chayne flinched thinking it was directed at him. His eyes strained through the shimmering tunnel magic to see someone running at Tristaric. For a moment the tunnel magic swirled to give a momentary better view. What he saw filled him with fear, joy and confusion. It was Garamon.

His disruption spell raged in front of him. If he didn't release it now, it would go unstable and shatter, freeing a blast of energy into him. But if he completed the spell it would destroy the tunnel and kill his friend.

He watched the discarded thrinium pole rise up and be thrown across the ground by Tristaric's magic.

Tristaric saw the heathen catch sight of the pole at the last moment and swing his axe. The tip of the thrinium bar separated, trailing molten white-hot droplets of the metal in its wake. The defender kept his footing as the rest of the pole fell to the ground with a clang.

Tristaric looked on amazed. 'And the blade cuts through four-inch diameter thrinium as well? I see some long nights ahead studying that piece.' He raised his staff again and outstretched his hand. A deep red mist consolidated in the palm of his hand into a blur of sparkling energy. 'No chance for you this time, Heathen.'

He released it.

Garamon held his axe ahead and continued forward. As the spell approached it rose up above him and spread out dropping around him like a red mist. The axe flared as he swung it around inside the mist, but it only dissipated what it touched. He felt his skin tightening on contact with the mist and he began to slow. It continued to restrict him until he stopped, frozen in place with the axe glowing resisting the touch of the mist.

He could see the magii raising his hand. The axe was no longer in the right position to defend from the strike to come.

Then a glowing white haze flew past the magii from behind. It reached Garamon and exploded into a sudden gust of wind blowing the red mist away. He felt movement begin to return to his body.

Tristaric's eyes went wide. He invoked a shield and turned on the one who dared to interfere with his attack. One of his magii stood in the distance, hood covering his face.

'You will suffer a lifetime in the chambers for this!' Tristaric swore, raising his staff.

The other magii pulled back his hood.

Garamon stared in disbelieve. 'Chayne!'

Tristaric gave a sigh. 'It would be interesting to know how as a novice you learned to dispel Makrid's Paralysing Mist, but there are more demanding affairs to attend. First of which is to remove your troublesome carcass from existence.'

He levelled his staff and a yellow flash flew at Chayne. It deflected away.

Tristaric closed his eyes for a moment, trying to swallow his humiliation. 'You are a mystery, Heathen. In just months you learn to cast spells far beyond any novice, and now you deflect even *my* attacks. I'm guessing it's something you have found in Lathashal's lab, but whatever you've discovered it won't be enough to resist me for long.

Garamon pushed against the stiffness in his body as if he was wading through water. The magic was fading and he was already at walking pace.

Tristaric sensed it. 'Just a moment,' he said to Chayne, calmly. He waved his staff at the portal and renewed the sustaining spell feeding it from the manasphere. He then drifted from the ground to float out of reach of the approaching woodsman.

Turning his attention back to Chayne, he threw a larger bolt at him. This was deflected as the first, but Chayne flinched at the effort and it forced him back a little. Chayne fired his strongest bolt and watched it bounce away from the master magii. Tristaric created a crackling ball of shifting colours. He and the ball advanced in the air together.

'Now, this won't hurt at all.' He poked a finger at Chayne. The ball began firing magical bolts of a multi-coloured mana.

Chayne felt no impact from them, but his shield was being drained by them. Tristaric was playing with him. The shield began to flicker.

Tristaric floated closer.

'You can take two more, I think.'

Chayne angled all the remaining shield magic to the side facing Tristaric and ran for the nearest group of magiis feeding a ring. Two more bolts hit his shield and it gave out as he reached them and dived behind the cover of the first as an electric-blue bolt hit the magii instead, killing him. The other two magii looked alarmed; it took at least two magii to keep the ring fed.

Chayne landed hard, and rolled, standing behind them.

Tristaric faltered, he couldn't risk hitting another magii.

Chayne had to make the man fire. He began to laugh at him. He watched as Tristaric's eyebrow began to twitch. He continued but the man remained in control. He noticed him look back to the start of the tunnel. The sustaining magic would soon need replenishing.

Chayne needed to goad the man to fire. Then it came to him, he knew what he had to do. He smiled at the floating magii, and in perfect Ashnorian, spoke a single word.

'Heathen.'

Tristaric's body trembled. The man's face looked as if his head was going to burst from his neck.

Chayne angled himself to stand aligned behind the remaining two ring magiis.

Tristaric built up a bolt of lightning so great it sparked out around his staff for several feet. He raised his arm and took aim. Chayne dropped both hands onto his orb with Zystal and powered everything he could into Lathashal's secondary layer of shielding.

The bolt released with a brightness illuminating the whole cavern as if daylight. It slammed into the first magii, blasting a hole through him and absorbing most of the spell, then clipping the second, spinning him around. The remainder of the bolt hit Chayne, dissipating his shield in a single spell and causing him to fly backwards landing with his head inches from the tunnel magic.

The sustaining beam from the clipped magii swung around with him, breaking from its target ring to strafe across the magii on the other side, causing him to lose his concentration and break his spell. The portal tunnel flickered around the ring and the effect began to spread along the tunnel to the next ring.

'No!' Tristaric yelled, breaking off his attack and flying back to the start of the tunnel. The disturbance spread and Chayne watched as the magii began to pour huge amounts of mana into the start of the tunnel spell to stabilise it. Regardless, the disruption reached the next ring, bolts of jagged energy spreading out from it striking the air and magii alike. The magii were not killed, but the effect was to break their flow of mana into the effected ring. As the last magii at each ring was interrupted so the ring flared for a few moments before going dead.

The tunnel magic beyond the ring reacted by snapping to the next ring in line causing a pulse of explosive energy outwards sweeping into the nearby magii and blasting them from their feet. The effect repeated and spread to the next ring with an even greater detonation of magic. With four more to go before it reached the main ring, it was clear to Chayne the explosion from it would devastate the cavern. He turned to see Tristaric frantically pouring fresh magic from both the manasphere and his staff together, renewing the failing tunnel magic. Chayne lifted his staff and built up his strongest repulsing bolt. He wanted to ensure the master magii would be disconnected from his orb, and not be consumed by it as Lathashal had.

He released the magic with a single word.

'Mlendria.'

The bolt shot forth and slammed into Tristaric's defensive shield. The shield flickered but held. Tristaric didn't appear to even notice the attack. Chayne had nothing stronger to challenge him.

Garamon couldn't reach the floating magii and considered throwing his axe. Instead he saw his chance and leapt forward, bringing his axe down upon the first manasphere. As the opposing magics came together, Garamon and the orb were launched from their positions in opposite directions. A shockwave of magic travelled down the portal tunnel and up the mana streaming to Tristaric. He resisted it and became locked into a battle to prevent it reaching him.

A shudder shook the floor. Rocks and dust fell from the walls and ceiling of the cavern. Garamon looked back to see the destabilised tunnel magic had reached the last ring. Some of the magiis gave up and began taking flight, heading for the cavern exit. The ring became unsteady in its runners, energy pouring out into the rock around. There was a stronger tremor and a whole section in one corner of the cavern collapsed.

A scream came from the floating magii. Garamon looked up to see his staff smoking and then burst into flame. The magii held it a moment longer before the thing cracked and shattered, dropping a tiny manasphere to the ground. The stream of magic from the tunnel's main orb struck him and held him in place above ground.

Garamon backed away as the magii began to glow within himself. Tristaric screamed out as the glow intensified to a shining white light.

'Run!' It was Chayne shouting in the distance.

Garamon turned and ran. The light within Tristaric became bright enough to cast a shadow ahead. Then it gave a final blinding burst. Garamon felt the explosion slam into his back, tumbling him over and over across the rock floor. When he stopped he looked back to see the mana flow ceased and the magii gone.

He saw Chayne. He couldn't hear him over the clamour all around, but the two mouthed words and urgency were clear enough. *Get out.* Just then a huge tremor dislodged several pieces of the cavern roof, one of them across the start of the portal tunnel between him and Chayne. There was no way he could get to him now. Believing the rock fall to have missed him, he turned for the entrance to meet him there. Magii were flying overhead joining the other escapees on foot heading for the entrance.

Another tremor, the largest yet, struck the cavern bringing down vast sheets of rock and burying rings and magii alike. Garamon looked on in horror as the ceiling over the entrance gave way, robbing his escape.

Then the humming from the last ring stopped. It had broken free of its fixings and was floating in the air. The magic around it had died down as if spent of its energy. A gentle glow remained. It then began to grow. It increased in intensity until Garamon had to cover his eyes. It lasted a few seconds longer before it too blinked out. Then, from the centre of the ring, a ball of swirling fiery energy began to expand outward at running pace. It ran over the ring which flared and burst into white hot flame.

The diameter of the magic increased and grew in pace as it moved outwards. It expanded out to touch walls, floor and ceiling, causing smoke to rise from the rock itself. It then reached an injured magii who hadn't fled. It swept over him and he burst into flames and shrivelled, not even having the time to cry out. Another soon followed. A shield popped into existence around a third as the wall of energy swept over him too. His shield lasted but a moment before collapsing and he also became engulfed in flame.

The horror of the deaths broke the bizarre beauty of the magic, and the remaining magii and soldiers scattered. With no way out and magic shields ineffective the magii took off for the furthest corners of the cavern.

Garamon looked for Chayne on the far side of the obscuring rubble. The destructive magic was approaching his last position. Anguish grabbed him. All the other magii had fallen to the magic. What chance would his friend have?

He backed away as the magic approached. It swept out, igniting everything at the first touch. He looked around, hopeless for an escape. He caught sight of the hole the digging machine had fallen into and ran over to it. It was deep and disappeared into utter blackness. The machine was nowhere to be seen.

'Which is the better way to die?'

He looked up at the approaching wall and watched as a terrified magii was running just ahead of it. 'Help me!' he screamed. Then the wall rolled over him. Garamon averted his eyes as the man flared. He took another look down the hole, and then back at the approaching wall.

There was a crack from above and the section of ceiling over him shook as if about to fall.

He closed his eyes for the end, and jumped.

Faust raced across the cavern. He watched the Mlendrian jump into the hole made by the excavating machine. He had seconds to do the same or perish in the fire wall. He snatched something up from the ground just as the ceiling gave way above the hole. Letting his instincts take over he ran and dived, making a clean entry into the opening. The heat of the fire wall almost burned his back as it passed over the hole. It was prevented from pursuing him as the cavern ceiling dropped behind him, closing the access. He fell some distance before hitting water hard, disappearing under and swimming away to avoid falling debris.

It wasn't long before he reached rocks and pulled himself from the water. He could hear more than one voice still out in the lake. It was unlikely in the dark they could have recognised him as anything other than falling rock.

He took a moment to get his bearings. The cave complex was well known to him. There was only one way out and he headed towards it. It was going to take him and the surviving Mlendrians deeper into the mountain to a place he didn't want them to find, but then they weren't going to live long to tell of it, once delivered into the hands of the Emperor.

Chapter 62 – The Barricade

Fennock sat behind the barricade in Tiburn. He pulled his cloak around him, closing the gaps in his over garment to keep what little heat he'd left within his clothing and armour. 'Do you think they will break through?'

Harlow blew into his hands and held them as close as he dare to the makeshift brazier. 'You saw how many there were, son.'

'I don't want to be tortured to death,' Fennock said, almost with a whimper in his voice.

Harlow had few words for the new soldier. The Ashnorians were going to come and smash through the barricade with ease and then slaughter the defenders with little more difficulty.

'Now, now, lad, you're a Ranger now. We've defended this town and the whole of Mlendria for a hundred years from all attackers.'

'You were in the Melenite wars?'

'I hope I don't look *that* old,' Fennock derided. 'But my father was. Terrible times. They were a strong enemy, but we held them, although the cost was great.'

'You were in the service a long time?'

Harlow could hear the true purpose behind the question.

'Yes, son. Long enough to know what I'm talking about. And yes, I've survived many battles. Thirty years as a soldier and ten as a Captain.'

'You were a Captain?'

Harlow smiled and nodded. The freshman was gaining confidence by the moment at the thought of fighting next to an established veteran.

He shuffled a little closer. 'I like your medals. I hope to have some one day.'

Harlow unpinned a medal of bravery and pinned it to Fennock's chest. 'It looks good on you.'

Fennock rubbed his thumb over it. 'I cannot accept this.'

'Take it, you'll have earned it when this is over.'

Fennock sat back and clutched his hand over the thing. 'Thank you.'

He sat quiet for a while before talking again.

'Are you glad you're fighting again?'

Harlow couldn't hold in a laugh at the comment and received a rebuke from a Captain behind. He lowered his voice again.

'Retirement was initially dull, I'll admit. But soon the idea of waking up each morning, knowing time is my own, began to take effect and I started to think of hobbies and things I always wanted to do.

'What did you do?'

'I set up a hardware store.'

The look on Fennock's face told of a certain loss of awe in his new idol.

'Hey, so I like working with tools.'

'Oh, I didn't mean to offend. It's fine work.'

'Yeah, well, if you need a hammer, there's no place to find one finer. I take pride in my work, son.'

Fennock dropped his head and the conversation went quiet again.

Feeling he'd been too harsh on a young man unlikely to see old age, Harlow put on a false smile and gave him a hearty thump on the side.

Fennock looked up.

'Whatever comes down the street, lad, you just stick by old Harlow and we'll down a merry number of those Yellowskins.'

The mood of the young Ranger stayed sombre as he nodded his agreement.

'Form up!' came a command from behind, and Rangers stood and faced up the street, readying weapons.

'Harlow?' Fennock said, standing as the others, pulling his sword free and holding up his shield in shaking hands, his voice wavering as it did before.

'Yes, lad?'

'I don't want to die.'

'Do you want to run?'

The reply was delayed for a few moments.

'No, sir, I cannot run.'

Harlow smiled again as he looked through a gap in the barricade into the perfect column of glittering soldiers approaching. He picked the one he judged would be opposite him when the line struck, noting the gaps in his armour. 'I knew you deserved that medal.'

'I'm afraid.'

'As am I, and every man in this line.'

'Do you think?'

'I know it, now stop talking and pick out your man.'

Fennock found a hole and did as he was told. He gasped at what he saw. 'The gods help us.' He stopped peering through, his hands shaking more than before.

'They're just men. Live or die, you take down as many of those bastards as you can, and let them know the price to attack our land and our people.'

Fennock nodded.

'Harlow?'

The veteran sighed, the Ashnorians were almost on them and he needed to concentrate. 'Yes, lad?'

'I'll run your hardware store should you fall and I live.'

Harlow felt a lump in his throat.

'Stop talking such melancholy, it makes a warrior soft.'

As the line approached, archers appeared at the upper windows of every house either side of the column. Stimm gave the order and the archers fired.

Dozens of Ashnorians fell. A cheer went up from the defenders.

An order was shouted out in a language unknown and the attackers raised their large oblong shields to form a roof of metal.

Stimm gave his second order, a hundred archers behind the barricade fired over into the now exposed front of the column. Most the first line of attackers went down.

Fennock laughed aloud as he peered through his spy hole. 'We can win!'

Confusion reigned for a moment as the column was attacked from both above and the front. Then fingers of fire leapt from the back of the column to strike into the upper windows of the houses. There was an explosion in each room as the upper floors of the houses burst into flame. The men within began yelling, and many became human fireballs as they leapt from the upper floors to die where they fell to the ground below, steam rising from the snow.

The street was soon ablaze. Cries of hope turned to despair as the defenders behind the barricade saw their shops and homes burning.

With the attacks from above thwarted, the Ashnorians returned their shields to the front. The advance began again.

The column walked up to the barricade and began hacking at the pile of wagons, tables and assorted wooden and metal items. The swords of the invaders weren't the best weapon to tear down a barricade, but they were many and persistent.

A section fell away. Stimm gave the order and a volley of arrows converged on the gap. The Ashnorian soldiers formed a barrier with their shields and didn't move through, taking no casualties. More sections began to fall with the same defensive tactic. Stimm realised they were going to bring the whole barricade down enough to walk up and over as a column. Defended by their well-formed shield wall they'd rendered the tactic of the barricade useless.

The final section gave way and the order went up from the Ashnorian commanders. The whole column advanced together, half-stumbling as they crossed the broken debris.

As they reached the top so Stimm gave his next command and the Rangers leapt up to engage the attackers as they reached the mid-point of the broken barricade.

Harlow stepped up onto a broken cupboard and it gave way under his weight trapping his leg. He felt Fennock's hand under his arm and was pulled clear of his trap.

'Thanks, lad, you saved my life already.'

Fennock didn't have time to reply as his first real combat was upon him. Harlow had a couple more moments before his opponent would be in range and he watched as the young Ranger put his training into action. Deflecting the first cut to his side with his shield he thrust out below the Ashnorian's shield aiming for a leg. The Ashnorian side-stepped to avoid the strike and slipped on the unstable broken barricade and fell. Fennock saw the opening and plunged his sword into prone soldier's neck.

'A Ranger indeed,' Harlow said to himself. Then his time came to engage and he stood back and let the Ashnorian come to him. He waited until the soldier placed his weight on the same cupboard he'd fallen through moments before. The result was as planned and the soldier fell forward. Harlow chopped his sword across the Ashnorian's arm, cutting through to the bone and severing the muscle. He kicked out at the soldier, forcing him back into the one behind. They both fell from the rubble into the men behind. More stepped over them.

The battle raged on, the Rangers fighting ferociously to defend their hometown. The line had fallen on either side and Harlow knew how this was going to end. He'd watched Fennock fall, fighting without fear, taken down a good tally of three of the enemy before falling to a thrust into his chest. Harlow knew it was now his turn. The Ashnorian before him was in his prime and full of energy. The first downward slash numbed Harlow's shield arm and knocked him back from his footing. He stumbled onto his back and raised his sword in anticipation of the next slash. Instead it was a low lunge and he only managed to deflect it with the edge of his shield. He stabbed out a feeble response, not connecting. The next defence wasn't so lucky. His last thought was of his hardware store.

Stimm watched the battle. He may have attained his position of Barracks Commander illegally, but no one questioned his tactical prowess. He surveyed the small battlefield ahead of him and watched as the Rangers were reduced to nothing more than a double line. The weak an inexperienced were gone and the strongest fighters remained. They were doing the right thing and allowing the Ashnorians to come at them with each attack, then giving ground a single step to allow the attack to miss before stepping back in and cutting through the defence of the Ashnorian before them. It steadily lost ground, but it was a strong tactic for which the Rangers were well trained. They were making Mlendria proud, but it would not create victory. Three quarters of the Ashnorians remained.

Knowing there was nothing more he could do, he gave the order and his men broke and ran. They leapt across an oil-filled ditch stretching across the street. Stimm, prepared for the mages, signalled to the two fire bearers on either side of the street. They plunged their touches into the ditch and flames raced out to meet in the middle. The scorching barrier roared high preventing any chance of the attacking mages targeting the retreating men.

Once they were away, Stimm gave the signal to Thrane. The mage walked to the middle and stood alone facing the flames. Wisps of blue mist coalesced into a ball before him as he built up his spell. He waited until the signal was given, indicating the Ashnorian line was close to the flames. Raising his hands, wind began to rush around him, whipping up dust, his robe and hair. He then threw his hands forward releasing the spell. A rush of wind flew out from him into the flames catching and blowing them horizontal at the front of the column. Oil from the ditch flicked out and was sent spraying over the soldiers. They burst into flame many rows deep. The wind continued for a few moments longer before dying down. Thrane turned and ran for cover with Stimm as lightning bolts shot blindly through the concealment of the flames.

'Nice work.'

The street was alight, the first buildings to be caught by the Ashnorian mage-fire were now roaring into the sky with each adjacent building catching. Soon the whole of Main Street would be ablaze spreading out to take the majority of the town.

Thrane looked on. 'A day I hoped never to see.'

'The garrison will handle this lot,' Stimm replied.

A lightning bolt cracked into the wood next to them, splintering the planks. Stimm blanched at the near miss and pulled the mage back out of view. 'I don't think their magiis like competition.'

'Agreed,' Thrane replied. 'Let's get to the rendezvous.'

There was no pursuit as they made their way through the town's alleyways, and soon they left the safety of the buildings to cross the outlying farms. Reaching the treeline of the forest, they stopped to catch their breath.

'Half the town is ablaze already,' Thrane said, ripping away his robe to the knees which was hindering his running.

'It's mostly wood,' Stimm replied.

Thrane uncharacteristically spat. 'Bastards.' He noticed Stimm was looking confused.

'What's up with you?'

Stimm wiped the sweat from his face, smearing a line of black soot down one cheek. 'All of history tells of them invading across entire borders stretching out as far as the eye can see.'

'History exaggerates.'

'But they could have attacked down the main trade route straight into Tiburn with a column five times the width. Why take a small number on a minor trial to come out behind the barracks. And why not send them all at once? Tactically, it makes no sense. It's almost as if it's a diversion, but there's no other way across the Hammerheads.'

'They've never fought anyone so advanced as us. They think a few of their magiis, added to some soldiers, will break through and cause panic.'

Stimm knew there had to be more to it.

They resumed a fast-march, heading to the nearest garrison at Hunter's Hold, leaving their town blazing behind. After a while, Stimm was supporting Thrane as he hobbled, wincing with every step.

'Too much time sitting around in your mansion, mage. Your feet must be softer than a dintoose's backside.'

'You're compassion overwhelms me, Major.'

'Can't you fly us there or something? I heard the Empire's mages buzz around like flies.'

'It's like *bees*, Major, and the gods restricted such ability to birds and insects. Stories of the Empire's mages are also greatly exaggerated.'

'Is that just spell-envy, perhaps?' Stimm mocked.

Thrane gave the man a sideways glance. The Soldier's dry wit could cut a little too deep at times.

Stimm stopped at a signpost and pushed his shoulder against it, moving it a quarter turn pointing away from the nearest population centre.

'Well that should turn back the invasion,' Thrane said.

'You'll be surprised how many tricks like this buy precious time.'

'Aye, well, time isn't what we need right now as much as a well-equipped barracks not infiltrated by the enemy.' Thrane saw Stimm take the comment harder than expected. It was meant as a joke but clearly the man felt guilt for all the destruction. He smiled at him. 'Come on, let's go find a nice big Garrison,' he encouraged.

Stimm tucked his shoulder under the mage's arm again and they continued on their way.

It took until dawn was showing its first signs, before lights from the garrison came into view. Its defences were made up of tall vertical timbers secured together with iron. The main gate was large enough to allow a column of men, which was fine for the operations of the Rangers, but inadequate for the mass entry of refugees from Tiburn. The road was swollen with families, rich businessmen, councillors and farmers. All reduced to equals in the rout.

'If they come after us now, it'll be a slaughter,' Thrane said.

'They don't kill their enemy. Just enslave them,' Stimm corrected, sullenly.

Just then a bright flash lit up the sky in the direction of the Hammerheads. The two men turned to see more flashes, far to the east of Tiburn. Blue-white, tinged with red and mauve, it illuminated the entire peaks nearby before fading out and stopping. Moments later the sound of thunder rolled down the valley.

'It's deep in Sheergreen forest,' Stimm said. 'I've never seen lightning like it.'

'It wasn't lightning,' Thrane replied. 'The colours…it was some form of magic.'

'What magic could light up an entire mountain?'

'None that all the mages in Mlendria could produce, combined,' replied the mage, his voice betraying his deep unease.

'Perhaps they *can* fly?' Stimm said.

Thrane nodded.

Chapter 63 – General Trouble

Zanthak picked himself from the forest floor. His men were scattered all around, along with supply wagons and servants. Even one of the engineering shodatt's tree-felling machines was on its side. The industrious little workers were already devising some pulley system to right it.

He looked back to the mountain. Something had gone wrong with the tunnel magic, separating them from the rest of the army. His quick assessment told him only half of his army had gotten through, and thousands of those were injured. It still left almost half-a-million fighting soldiers. In his hands it was more than enough to defeat the Mlendrians.

One of his aids stepped forward, holding his head and blinking the afterglow of the bright flash from his eyes.

'General, I think many of the men are still to come through.'

'Consider them lost,' Zanthak replied. 'I'm not waiting to give the Mlendrian's time to assemble their army.'

'What of the injured who cannot fight, sir?'

The general paused for a moment as if perhaps caring what happened to them. 'Finish them off.'

The aid nodded and left the General alone.

Zanthak helped a few soldiers to their feet before wandering out into a clearing made by the machines before the tunnel exploded. He looked back down the wide path created by the engineers' creations. Their usefulness was at last showing through. If it hadn't been for the tree-fellers clearing a path at a marching pace, most of the army would have perished close to the mountain when the explosion happened.

He watched as the stocky little workers set about their task. They were far more reliable than magiis. He looked back across the now-closed rock face, blasted clean of vegetation and snow. The back of the column nearest to the mountain had disappeared. Not even a smoking boot.

'When I return, magii, I'll have you strung up by your damned manaballs for this.'

There was a sound of crying metal as the overturned machine was brought into balance before tipping the rest of the way and landing with a crunch. The engineers then swarmed over the thing, checking and repairing.

Chapter 64 – Decree Absolute

Estatoulie gazed over the bloody symmetrical carvings in the young man's flesh. It was one of his finest pieces for months and almost complete. And while the engineer's pods were more efficient at the process of creating Yan under torture, he still preferred to provide some from his own efforts on the altar in front of his court.

An aid approached and stopped at the bottom of the altar.

'Yes, what is it?' Estatoulie said, angered his work was interrupted.

The aid held out a parchment. A magii pointed a finger and the parchment lifted from his hand to land in Estatoulie's.

Silence fell over the throne hall, not giving away any of its three-hundred occupants as their Monarch read.

Estatoulie completed the message and let it fall to the floor. 'They have failed me – again?' His tone was too calm.

The aid began to shake. 'There was an explosion, Emperor. The mountain entrance collapsed. All the army had entered.'

'How many made it to the other side?'

'We have no way of knowing. No one on this side survived.'

'Then why have you disturbed me with half a report?' The voice remained sterile.

'No more information is coming out of Straslin, Emperor. Our magiis say they have lost communication with the city.'

'Lost communication with an entire city?'

'Yes, Emperor. They are trying now to recouple.'

Estatoulie went quiet. He pulled the knife from the victim on the table, slowly enough to make a sucking sound on its way out.

'Come here.'

The young aid complied, climbing the altar steps to stand three feet from his monarch, the nearest allowed by decree.

Estatoulie flushed. *'Come here.'*

The young aid edged his way closer, trapped between two immutable laws. He stopped inches from his Emperor.

Estatoulie rested the knife with a small hook on its tip, under the aid's chin.

The aid's legs were twitching with the adrenalin to escape.

Estatoulie savoured the moment, feeling the aid's dilemma. To run would be to suffer unspeakable torture. He heard a whimper from the altar behind him, reminding him of unfinished business. He pushed the knife slowly upwards. The aid screamed for a moment as the blade worked its way through the flesh and went deeper, skewering his tongue.

'You will not speak of this again.'

The blade was then turned a quarter turn and pulled back out, dragging the tongue down with it through the bottom of the mouth.

The aid cried out a toneless rasp as the knife was pulled free, leaving the tongue protruding through the new hole.

'Stitch him up as he is. And cut off his fingers, I don't want him writing either.'

The aid flew back from the magii's repulsing spell, to fall at the bottom of the steps.

Estatoulie turned back to his masterpiece on the altar. Hours of work and now the moment had been ruined.

He shrieked out, plunging the knife into the man's chest over and over, ruining the art and yelling out his frustration.

He finished, panting hard. 'Get me Rakshawl and Aarople.'

Several aids bowed and hastily left the room.

Estatoulie snapped his fingers at the magii and flicked a finger at his blood-soaked clothing. The magii held out his hand. A red mist began to coalesce from the blood stains in the monarch's clothing and made its way to the magii. A ball of blood formed ahead of him the size of a man's fist. The magii closed his hand over the grisly sphere and it flashed leaving only a trace of smoke.

Estatoulie's robes were left spotless.

A soldier entered the room. His size, beyond any of the many guards in the room, portrayed him as a champion among ordinary men. Scars that could have been removed by mage-surgeons, crisscrossed his face and arms. His dented heavier and unpolished armour made him stand out against the shining metals of the guards. The rhythmic chink of his footsteps echoed around the hall.

He stopped short of the Emperor.

Without looking at the man, Estatoulie gazed ahead as if seeing into the future.

'Lathashal, Tristaric and Zanthak have failed me. Mlendria has stood against me for a second time. Descend upon Straslin with every soldier in the Empire. Arrest every citizen, including your soldiers stationed there. Then move on Mlendria, with or without magiis, and capture the entire population and feed them to Straslin's chambers. No man, woman or child is to remain. No animal is to be left un-slaughtered, no building left standing. Grind their existence into dust. Then burn and poison the land, from the mountains to the sea. Nothing must grow there for a thousand years.'

'What of your personal defence?'

'Nothing can get through the tower's shield. But leave my battalion, if you must,' Estatoulie replied, distantly.'

Rakshawl acknowledged the order and left the room, passing the hunched form of Aarople waiting at the bottom of the altar stairs. He was the only other member of the royal court not to be garishly dressed. As the head of the newly-formed engineering shodatt, he was seen by all but the Emperor as the runt of the Empire's leadership. His oil-stained tan leather clothing and array of odd tools hanging from his belt, and various tubes around his neck, made him stand out as uniquely amongst the court as Rakshawl.

Aarople nodded a smile at the Commander-in-chief of the Empire's vast armies as he passed. It wasn't reciprocated.

He climbed the stairs to the Emperor and bowed.

'Your Majesty, it is my pleasure to serve.'

Estatoulie turned his still-bloodied blade over in his hands, fascinated by the macabre patterns the remnants of exhumed organs and skin tissue formed. 'I want Straslin turned into fifty-thousand chambers within the year. Rakshawl will be delivering the race of heathens of Mlendria for correction to death. I want the chambers running day and night until every last drop of elixir is extracted and they're dead.'

Aarople had many reasons for such a task to be impossible, but would never disobey his Emperor. 'I will need many thousands of new engineers and materials to build and run the chambers, Majesty.'

'Straslin and its population are condemned. Use the citizens for labour, dismantle every building for resources.'

'Yes, Emperor.'

A minor wave of Estatoulie's hand indicated the master engineer was dismissed.

Xrearna slid back into the ranks of courtiers. If Tristaric was dead, her benefactor would consider her life forfeit also. She had to find a way to disappear from his reach. It meant finding a powerful new ally quickly. There would be a heavy price to pay, but it wasn't her first time.

Chapter 65 – Death of a City

Calinsk looked out over his beloved city from his office in the palace. Fires were burning and the sound of fighting could be heard to the West. People were running blindly in the streets, their orchestrated existence of an empyrean citizen gone as quickly as the servants drifting from their alcoves into nowhere.

The city was confused at first, but soon anger flared. Then the anger turned to fear and the fear twisted into panic.

The Lan-Chi had achieved their diversion and many paid the price with their lives, holding up the army from discovering the exodus of the servants into the desert to the West. They fought well and the sacrifice spread the city's garrison thin, who were also trying to contain the chaos and rioting.

'Just an illusion of perfection,' he said to himself.

He watched a woman run down the street, screaming hysterically, being caught and held down by two soldiers.

'Only ever hours from anarchy.'

He read the note again from his Lan-Chi scouts, spying the mountain from a distance. They reported the army invading Mlendria, along with hundreds of battle magiis, had been caught in some magical disaster and the mountain had fallen upon them, Tristaric included. A second missive reported contact was also lost with the army sent into the barbarian territory.

It seemed impossible.

He clicked his fingers to have the curtain closed.

No servant came.

He walked to the side of the window and pulled a cord he'd seen a servant do before. The curtains slid to a close at the centre.

Sitting back at his desk, he picked up the magii communication that was in reply to his emergency message to the capital. It was the last message received before all communication stopped. The Emperor was sending the entire army, three million strong, with a thousand battle magiis to raze the city back to the desert. No trace was to be left of its existence and all record of it and its occupants were to be erased from the Empire. He and the other administrators were to sort every citizen into forced labour camps for the task of rebuilding the city into a mass of correction chambers – including themselves.

The army would then march on Mlendria.

A fleeting thought crossed his mind about running. He laughed at the absurdity. Death was preferable to living with the knowledge the Empire was only ever moments from what was outside now. He knew the burden of such realisation would drive him mad.

He pulled out a drawer and piled all the blank red-bordered torture orders onto his desk. He knew the name of every individual under his jurisdiction in the East side of the city. He began filling out the orders, one by one.

Chapter 66 – Lost

Chayne opened his eyes. It was dark and the air was freezing, as though outside.

Confused, he recalled his last moments when the wave of magic approached, the portal magiis before him bursting into blue flame. Each of them had used a shield to protect them too, but in their case the portal magic had rolled over them and been too strong for them. They'd delved too deep into their manaspheres to maintain their shield domes and the demons had taken control, pulling enough mana in to gain escape to their own world. At least the magiis had been disintegrated from the heat before being taken by their demons.

He knew his befriending of the demon within his own manasphere had stopped the creature from fleeing and kept it absorbing the magic as it swept over him. Even so, the magic wave had contained incredible levels of energy, overwhelming him.

But where was he now, and how did he get here?

He spread his fingers across his manasphere and summoned illumination. There was an explosion of multi-coloured light throwing him to the floor, his arm left throbbing with pain. The normally impervious wooden box of his manasphere was smouldering. The colours around him dissipated into strange swirls jumping and twisting. In their sporadic glow he saw he was no longer in the cave, but on a flat landscape. The swirls faded leaving him again in the dark.

Remembering his experience when Tristaric attempted to kill him in the portal test room, and Zystal had become 'drunk' on the mana absorbed into the manasphere. He entered the orb again to check on the demon. The mana inside was far thicker than before.

Diving to the usual depth where he found the demon, he called out. There was no response. He attempted to detect it and caught the merest feeling in one direction and moved that way. The creature came into view with the mist providing only a few feet of vision. It was gently spinning, its eyes tucked up into its head and its tongue lolling out of its mouth, dripping saliva. Chayne felt for a pulse not even knowing if demons had such a thing. It was strong and rapid. Poking him gently in the stomach the demon drifted slowly to a halt a few feet away, almost to be lost in the fog.

Unable to wake him, he returned from the manasphere and felt the biting cold. He thought to create a heat layer to warm himself, but the experience with the light spell made him wary. Would it end up incinerating him instead?

Wrapping his robes tight around him his concern was most for his opened sandals and the potential for frostbite to his toes. He needed to find shelter.

Allowing his eyes to adjust to the dark after the brightness within the orb, he still couldn't see far and the ground was smooth in all directions, like the surface from cooled lava. Checking the sky, the stars were in constellations he'd never seen before.

He spotted an indistinct glow far away on the horizon. Within it was a tiny point sticking up. With no better indicating of a way to go, he headed towards it.

Legends Awakening

Book Three

We hope you enjoyed the second book in
The Walkers of Legend series.

Information on other books in the series can be
found on the official website:

www.thewalkersoflegend.co.uk

And social media:

Facebook: TheWalkersOfLegend

Twitter: WalkersOfLegend

www.ingramcontent.com/pod-product-compliance
Lightning Source LLC
Chambersburg PA
CBHW071147250626
47159CB00001B/16